The Knife's Edge

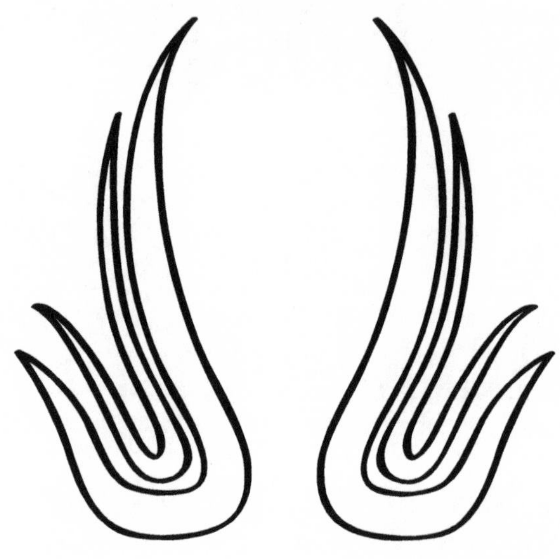

THE KNIFE'S EDGE

Book One of The Ronin Saga

Robin —
Enjoy!
To a new world...

Matthew Wolf

ISBN-13: 978-0-9891483-2-0

Map Art– Flavio Bolla
Cover Art – Noah Bradley
Book Design – Emilie Christensen
Author Photo – James Mendoza

To my devoted editor, friend, and all around rock—my mom.

The Abyss
FARHAVEN
Death's Gates
Burai Mountai
The White Plains
DE'GRAEL
Sobeku Plains
The Green Valley
Moonshire
Koru
The Silvas River
Burmen's Bank
Lakewoo
THE LO

DAERVAL
Rimdel
Merkal Desert
The Gold Road
EASTERN KINGDOMS
The Crags
The Wastelands

Contents

THE THREE RULES

One

Only nine of the twelve kingdoms will be chosen and deemed "The Great Kingdoms", those who bear the eternal elements as their sigil: wind, sun, leaf, fire, moon, water, stone, flesh and metal.

Two

The warriors known as the Ronin, with nine magical swords, will be bound to the kingdoms—each matched to their elemental power in turn: Baro for steel, the ambassador of Kingdom of Steel, Seth for fire, Hiron for water, Aundevoriä for stone, Aurelious for flesh, Dared for moon, Maris for leaf, Omni for sun, and lastly, their leader, Kail for wind. They will be the peacemakers of the land, the arbitrators of justice.

Three

A prophecy will be forever engraved upon the walls of each Great Kingdom, words to spell the future of the world.

The Tale of the Ronin

"Gold is god and greed is good." – Unknown, saying of the Old Age.

Long ago, the world was chaos. Twelve kingdoms fought for wealth and power, creating an age of darkness and death. Kings were killed in the dead of night, citizens thieved from their homes by nameless beasts. Ceaselessly, rain soaked the lands as the heavens cracked open, shedding tears of sorrow for the never-ending death and misery. But even the heavens were helpless against the twelve kingdoms' insatiable greed that tainted the land to its very marrow.

Then one day, as the stories say, there came a robed figure. Tales differ, some offering that he walked upon the water with nine men at his side, others that the robed figure descended from the clouds in motes of shimmering light, while fewer still believe he simply walked across the desert, a man born of a different land. But all agree, the nine were at his side, men who would become known by one name above all others: The Ronin.

The robed figure came with a contract. The war would end and the lands would know peace, but in exchange the robed figure demanded The Three Rules.

Above all, however, every man and woman was sworn to peace, for if any ruler grew greedy once more, the nine Ronin would unite, and with the might of a thousand storms siege the unruly kingdom and install a new monarch to ensure peace. So it was, that for a thousand years peace was known. Crops bloomed and the people breathed the sweet air without the stench of blood, felt sunlight upon their skin, and laughed freely once more. All was good… but nothing can stay good for forever. One day, a seed of evil erupted as a blade of light was thieved, and war once again took hold of the prosperous lands, turning them upon one another. The age known as the Lieon, or the great war. At the heart of it all, the Ronin were blamed.

From here it must be mentioned that only whispers of truth remain: It was said that Kail, their leader, turned mad, wandering the land and killing all until he disappeared into the forest; while the rest of the Ronin joined the side of darkness. Upon wraith-like steeds with monstrous creatures born from nightmares at their side, they sieged the armies of good. In an act of desperation and salvation, the evil was finally thwarted, but not defeated. The darkness fell back into the lands to brew, waiting to return one day…

As time turns, and the lands began to grow again from the rubble like seedlings sprouting through ash, tales floated upon the winds. Bards and minstrels spun accounts of the war and the evil sworn to return…

An evil known as the Ronin.

*****

> Nine men whose names were once spun like gold on the tongue of every bard are now spat and hissed from both old and young. Once heroes, they have become fearful rumors whispered in the soulless night.
>
> I fear I am the last one who still remembers the truth of what happened. Even those of my code grow weary of my stories. Am I mad as they say? No. It is the world that is mad. And with my death, their sacrifice will be lost to the sands of time. Yet the legendary Ronin will ride again. And I dread the day. For when mist and myths take form, the world will know fear…
>
> - Algari Stormshield's last entry
> Book of the Devari, 189 A.L.

The Return

Kirin ran. Using the tooth of the battlement as a stepping-stone, he launched himself at Ren. Blade arcing, he landed in Water Upon the Rocks, an attack from above. Steel clanged as metal sparked, and his muscles strained against his master's parry.

Ren's thin lips curved into a smile, making his peppered beard rustle. "Keep that up and you'll have my title before long."

Eyeing him through the mesh of their swords, Kirin smirked. "It's all yours."

Immediately, he realized his mistake, but it was too late. His pressure waned as his concentration slipped. Ren's heavy biceps flexed. Kirin was blown back as if by a gust of wind, feet scraping along the gray stone. He threw a leather boot to the ground in a Low Moon stance, his knees bent and back straight. At the same time, he tossed a hand to the rampart's wall. His palms scraped the stone merlons and he skidded to a halt. He looked up. Ren's sword hurtled towards his face. Pressing against the ground, he vaulted backwards, diving beneath the blade's tip. Landing on the balls of his feet, he peered through his brown hair.

Ren rose to his full, impressive height. Despite the chill in the air, the man was bare-chested, wearing only a pair of frayed brown pants with leather strings. His frame was tanned dark from the unforgiving sun. A long scar ran diagonally across his chest. A few more white lines marred his shoulders and arms. There was not a scrap of fat on him. Lit by the dawning sun, Ren stood in High Moon. His back leg was heavily bent, holding the majority of his weight, while his front foot rested lightly upon the ground. It was a stance most could learn, but few could ever master.

Kirin rose. “You tricked me.”

Ren broke High Moon. Sword tip to the stone, he leaned on his pommel, lounging. He was beginning to lose his hair, pate wearing thin, but what was left was plaited back into a komai tail, a black and gray braid of traditional Devari code, but far longer in accordance to his rank. “Don’t listen to me then, or, better yet, don’t talk back. Besides, you should know my tools by now—tools which a blademaster should always have at his disposal.”

He scoffed. “Tools? They are clearly tricks and you know it.” His palms stung and he saw peeled callouses, raw and pink, like a shaved beet. “And why do I always seem to get hurt around you?”

Ren shrugged innocently. “Not sure, I don’t get hurt.”

There was a subtle shift in the air, and Kirin focused, becoming acutely aware of his surroundings. Sharpening his senses at will was a skill of the Devari harnessed over years of intense training. Ramparts, crenulated towers, and scaled rooftops surrounded him. What he felt was the guard changing as hundreds of fresh bodies were beginning their first patrol of the day.

He embraced the leaf, using his Ki. Suddenly, his veins chilled. He stood inside a soldier’s cold limbs, felt his stiff joints, and heavy lids from recently shed dreams. The man excused another tired soul to the hard sacks of the barracks. With a breath, Kirin retreated from the guard’s body, flowing back into his own.

What I wouldn’t do for a soft pillow. He envied them, for a Devari never slept more than several hours. But deep down, he did not envy their softness, or at least, he would not trade for it. Brushing the dirt from his black tunic and brown pants, he regained his feet and raised his sword. But Ren was looking away, gazing over the bailey’s walls. Something weighed heavily on his master’s features. There were shadows in the man’s eyes. “Is it true?” he asked.

“Rumors are rumors, Kirin. Besides, you should not concern yourself with prophecy. As Devari, we are above such things.”

"You're avoiding the question. I want to know, is it true they are back?"

"Say their name lad. Only a fool fears a name."

"I can't…"

"Then I'll say it for you."

"Don't—"

"Ronin," Ren said, interrupting him.

Kirin's breath caught. He looked behind. The rampart was empty and he breathed a sigh. Though he knew the guards would not disturb Devari training and they were safe from prying ears, to speak their name aloud was a crime punishable by death.

"It's only you and me up here, Kirin. And as for your question, I've outlasted a hundred false returns, each one more absurd than the last. Though a false return is nothing to smile about. Each causes its share of pandemonium. I've seen hangings, riots, even full-scale wars at the hands of a false return." The man was holding something back.

"But I'm not asking about rumors. Though I have heard them all… whispers that the elvin prophet is on her deathbed, that the Patriarch is to decree this coming as a True Return, that Taer and Maldon are shutting their doors to outsiders completely."

"Taerians have always been a foolish, superstitious lot, and Maldians follow on their heels like a trotting dog," Ren said contemptuously, "and I don't know what you've been hearing, but the Patriarch has uttered no such thing."

He continued undaunted, "All of Farhaven's magical creatures are fleeing to their sanctuaries. The whole Citadel is in an uproar. Things I'd have to be blind to miss. I'm not asking if something is happening, Ren. I know something is happening. I'm asking what you think."

Ren turned, looking away. He was silent so long Kirin didn't think he was going to answer. At last, he spoke, "This time, something seems different. I feel there is a deadly sliver of truth within the rumors. After two-thousand years, I fear the Return has come."

The Return… The phrase alone was even more terrifying than Ren's fear. But the feeling of dread in the Citadel of late had been palpable, nothing short of the Return seemed likely. "The Gates separate Farhaven from Daerval and the enemy has never crossed the Gates, right Ren?"

"Farhaven is safe, lad," Ren said. "Don't you worry."

Kirin looked out over the Citadel's curtain wall in thought. He saw the courtyards with sculpted shrubbery. The baileys were filled with winding stone paths, training dummies, and rows of haystacks. The morning bell tolled, announcing Neophytes to their daily duties. Out over the Citadel, its field of towers, and heavily fortified keeps was a magnificent city; and where the sun beat back the mist, it revealed pockets of the land below.

He saw dirt streets. From this height the people looked like colored ants. To Kirin, the city was an awning that covered the land, reaching into the dunes of the Reliahs Desert. It was the great desert city of Farbs, Kingdom of Fire. It was truly breathtaking. Often he wished he could leave the walls and walk among the people. But such a thing was not possible for a Devari.

"Wake up!" Ren bellowed, and he was glad to see the years had shed from Ren's face. His master's stance switched from High Moon to Low Moon, one leg sweeping back. Kirin saw his opening, but kept his face blank. "So are you going to sight-see, or for once are you going to actually hit…"

He didn't let Ren finish and charged with a fierce cry, sword raised for Heron in the Reeds. Ren smiled as if he were waiting for it, blade flickering into Full Moon, covering his head. In the last moment, Kirin gathered his meager power. Using the element of moon, he summoned a blanket of darkness and flung it before him like a black shield. It was a weak and dismal spell, but it was enough. His cry pitched and he dove through the shield. Ren's sword appeared from nowhere, but he rolled beneath the man's blade. As he landed, he twisted. Fisher in the Shallows. He lashed at Ren's legs, ready to retract the blow in victory. Ren had lost. Elation lanced through him. Abruptly, his master smirked and his hand smacked a hidden block of stone.

A sphere of dark purple appeared from thin air, hovering between them. The liquid darkness swiftly expanded. It touched his outstretched arm and he recoiled, but it was no use. His muscles twitched as if suffocated in stone, and the darkness swiftly slid over him like a second skin.

The world turned black as night.

Kirin was weightless and falling.

The Seven Trials

Vera inhaled the incense that burned in the brightly lit room. On any other day she would complain about its putrid sting as she walked past the Oval Hall, watching as people flocked towards the great chamber.

Today, however, the incense smelled sweet.

Her face glistened with sweat. Seven women surrounded her. Each stood on one of the seven points of the Star of Magha, set in the white marble floor with gold veins. Each point stood for one of the elements of the Great Kingdoms. She stood on the red flame of the Citadel.

All the elements were present, but one. The forbidden element of wind.

The women surrounding her breathed heavily, wearing looks of loathing. They fear what they don't understand. She took in their stares and noted their different strengths. Merian stood on the emblem of flesh, Sara, water, Tamiko, earth, Resa, sun, Eliwyn, fire, and the others she did not know. The only thing they shared was that they were years older than her, and nearly all of them despised her.

With a portion of the spark, Vera twisted a strand of water with a thicker thread of light. Any trace of dampness was sucked from her dress, like poison drawn from a wound as gray wool was simultaneously straightened and smoothed. Immediately, pain jolted her as if a small firework erupted within her brain. She gasped and fell to her knees. Looking up, she saw Merian had snapped the link tight.

The link was a connection of visible gold between her and the others, like a wagon-wheel's spokes, stemming from Merian. For that mere moment, the link between all eight women glowed brightly. The other women gave Merian curious, if not entirely disapproving looks. All except one. Eliywn looked at Vera with sympathy. It was well known that the use of pain outside each individual Trial was strictly prohibited.

"Do not use the spark during the Trials for anything but the Trials themselves," Merian snapped. "At least not until we are done with you." The woman's lips pursed, as if she were thinking up something truly cruel to say. "And I would save your energy if I were you. You will need every morsel you can conjure in the next Trial, or you will fail miserably."

Vera brushed her fall of auburn hair behind her ears and rose to her full height. There was a fire in Merian she had not seen until now, and she nearly applauded the woman for showing her backbone at last. Then she eyed Merian's red robes. The robes of a Reaver. She looked around the room at each woman. Each bore the robes of a full Reaver, a title she craved to hold more than air.

"Neophyte Vera, you have completed the Sixth Trial. The final Seventh Trial will begin now," Merian quoted line for line.

With the veil of obedience, Vera smiled. "As you wish, Reaver Merian." Each woman looked like coiled desrah snakes ready to strike. She grinned, inviting it, and together, the women attacked.

Spokes of light flew forth, striking from all sides. She threw up her hands, erecting a shield of light. The spokes of light moved through her shield like water, racing towards her. Too strong. Seven Reavers could not be bested by any but an Arbiter in a match of raw power. The Seventh Trial was not one of strength, but a test of spirit. It was not meant to be won. But she was not done.

Vera summoned a shield of darkness and it launched from her fingertips, spreading in the air. Her gaze narrowed like an arrow's sight on Merian whose eyes blazed with hatred. She unleashed her bottled power with a scream, uncaging the tendrils of living darkness, but in the last minute wove threads of moon to disguise the power's dark form. The light and darkness collided with a powerful crash and an earth-shaking clap rattled the room. The bars evaporated like mist. But in the moment before their collapse, the darkness funneled up the spoke of light and sunk its teeth into the wielder of the link.

The thunderclap of air blew the women back.

Slowly, the women rose to their feet. A foul smell like burnt hair hung in the air, but no others seemed to notice. At her feet, Vera saw fragments of colored glass from the windows high above, and shreds of priceless tapestries depicting grand scenes of the Lieon, the Great War.

Resa, a bull-like woman, spoke, "Never has the test of light been

countered with a shield of moon. Moon is the weaker of the two elements, but somehow it worked. Truly remarkable and worth the coming ceremony. You are now the youngest to pass the Seven Trials in history. Congratulations, Reaver Vera."

"Congratulations," the other six said, their voices a single hum from the Link.

"Merian, sound the chime," Resa ordered. "It is complete, the Citadel must know. The ceremonies must commence." She hadn't noticed. Neither had the others. There was a stark silence. Vera smirked, reveling in their confusion. The seven women's eyes widened in sudden recognition, their feelings connected through the link. As one they looked to Merian.

The woman knelt, her wide-eyes brimming in horror. "My power is gone!" the woman shrieked, and gave a bloody cry.

"Merian!" The women swarmed around her, dropping the golden glow of the link.

Resa touched the sister's forehead and recoiled with a gasp. "I cannot heal her. It is far beyond my skill." She grabbed Tamiko. "Take her to an Arbiter and quickly. Perhaps they can grab the spark before it recedes too far."

"She… it's gone? But how?" Tamiko stuttered.

Vera smiled at the woman's shock. Like a wide-eyed doll. She always thought Tamiko's hair and face too done up to be attractive, though most of the men of the Citadel didn't seem to mind.

"Stop asking questions and go!" Resa yelled. Tamiko bolted to get help and Resa turned. The woman's eyed blazed. Come to me, Vera beckoned. Resa rose, moving towards her. Her heavy steps reminded Vera of a cerabul before the charge, or one of the Devari guards stalking postures, which made her think of Kirin. Behind the woman Vera saw others. Curious and fearful Neophytes flowed into the room, faces pale from the sound of Merian's chilling scream. Eliywn rushed to Vera's side. Resa approached and Eliywn straightened to her fullest height, which was a hand or two shorter than Vera.

Before Resa could speak Eliywn proclaimed in a rush, "She did nothing against the law of the Citadel, and she obviously didn't mean—"

"Leave," Resa seethed.

Eliywn bristled as if slapped, and she looked ready to respond. The girl knows not when to quit. Ignoring Resa's direct order would meet with serious punishment, for Reaver of three stripes vastly outranked Eliywn's one. She touched her friend's arm. Eliywn frowned, but understood, and grudgingly took her leave.

"What was that?" Resa whispered, breathing fire. The woman's body practically shook with desire to hurt Vera, likely not even with the spark, but with pure, animal-like rage. She would… thought Vera calmly.

"What was what?"

The spacious hall filled with Neophytes and Reavers, rushing to see the cause of the uproar and whispers spread like fire.

"Heresy," Resa sputtered. "Merian might die, if she doesn't, the spark inside her is shriveled and likely the spark is gone from her forever! You desiccated her!"

The word gave Vera chills. Desiccating meant being deprived and cut from the spark, like a still beating heart carved from one's chest. For a Reaver, it was a word far worse than any curse.

Vera returned the woman's wrathful glare with a small smile. Words would clearly not affect some women, she knew, no matter how profound. Resa snatched Vera's robes. "If I ever, ever see anything like that again, Citadel law or not, I will personally pluck your haughty eyes from your head, without the spark."

I was right. Vera dipped her head, casting her eyes downward. "Apologies, Reaver Resa. My power went beyond me," she lied. "I will learn to control it." That much was truth.

Resa's meaty fist rose, ready to strike. At last, with an unattractive snarl, she turned and stalked out of the chambers, following the two women who held the muttering, half-conscious Merian on a cloth stretcher.

And for a brief moment, she felt a note of pity. No one should suffer that fate… She would take a thousand deaths before she would take a life without the spark. Ignoring the eyes of others, Vera pushed her way through the whispering crowds of Neophytes, heading to her quarters.

The Neophyte Palace

The corridor shook with the peal of tower bells, announcing the completion of the Seven Trials. Vera ground her teeth in irritation and turned the corner swiftly, running headlong into a figure. She rubbed her arm, looking up to see the worried frown of Enise, a bookish Neophyte.

"I'm so sorry, are you all right?" Enise asked.

The girl looked every bit like a startled bird—sharp nose, spiky fray of white hair like plumage, which was even more frayed and bristly than normal, and bright, wide eyes. Enise was one of the few who didn't loathe Vera. She wondered if the girl had never heard the rumors. Either way, she liked Enise.

"I'm fine Enise. It was my fault."

"No no, it's mine, I know I shouldn't read and walk, Ali—err, Reaver Aliye always yells at me for it." Enise fell to her knees, gathering up the fallen volumes.

Vera knelt at her side and helped, noticing the faded gold titles. The Last Reliquaries of Tremwar. Accounts of the Final Battles of the Kimon. Tales of the Great Schism. The Battle of Gal, Letters of a General. The Kyomen Wars, and a dictionary on Yorin, the old tongue. "Quite the collection. Brushing up on your history?"

Enise blushed nervously. "Just a little reading. Ethelwin—I

mean, Reaver Ethelwin lectured briefly on the betrayal and how they destroyed the world. She explained their heresy, but even as a girl I knew of their betrayal. Yet even back then I felt something was missing, but it was smaller, like an itch I couldn't scratch. Then yesterday, during Ethelwin's speech, I felt the itch grow. And I knew something was truly wrong with the stories."

"You're talking about the Ronin," Vera said.

Enise's gaze flickered to either end of the hall. "Vera! You can't say that name."

"I've gotten in enough trouble today, what else can they do?"

"They'll hang you. You know that."

"No one will hear," she said. "Have you found anything yet?"

The girl sighed. "Not yet. Just the same history we all know. It's strange, but it seems as if even these old things are missing pieces." Enise shook her head as if coming to her senses. "I really shouldn't be talking of this. Wait, why were you in such a hurry?"

"Didn't you hear?" Vera glanced upward.

"You passed!" Enise exclaimed. "Congratulations! When are the ceremonies? Are you going to—"

Vera wasn't listening as two Devari passed, moving with deadly grace. Where many men dared to eye her slender form and perfect curves, the Devari's attention never wavered, eyes on their destination. She looked back. Enise was still talking. "Enise," she interrupted, "if you see Kirin, can you tell him I'm looking for him? I'll be in my room if he asks." She thrust the books into the girl's arms and left her kneeling wide-eyed.

She moved through the halls until she reached the grand antechamber of the Neophyte Palace. Hundreds of Neophytes swarmed the broad floor, rushing to chores or lectures. In the center of the room was a grand staircase, each step large enough for a small house to sit comfortably upon.

Feeling too exposed, Vera took the staircase swiftly. Above was a dome with a series of large windows. Between each window were huge portraits of the Arbiters. Only five Arbiters had ever been born, and each lived for thousands of years. It was said their lifespan was due to the power of the spark they held, for the weakest Arbiter was stronger than a hundred Reavers working together with a link. The thought of such power made her knees weak and she glanced to the painting of the man in grand flowing robes of gold and white. The Patriarch. He was the oldest and strongest of all the Arbiters and Guardian of the Citadel. There had only ever been one Arbiter to hold the mantle of Patriarch in all time. The man was a legend.

Suddenly she spotted a familiar face. Evalyn, tall, buxom, and never two steps away from her pet Rosalyn. She hated Evalyn. The girl was admittedly beautiful, and powerful too, but she viewed others like pieces in a game of Cyn, sacrificing Followers to get to the Mark. Not to mention, Evalyn had an obvious taste for Kirin, which put a sour taste in Vera's mouth. So she was glad to see Evalyn turn the corner towards the courtyards.

Reaching the top of the stairs, she took a crowded hallway when a presence ripped her breath from her lungs. At the end of the hall, a tall man walked briskly towards her. All others in the crowded corridor seemed to disappear. Despite his simple brown robes and gray cape with a flaring collar, he filled the corridor with his presence. His eyes fell on her. Despite all her confidence and power, in that moment, Vera felt like a shriveled weed beneath his foot.

Arbiter Ezrah.

What is he doing down here? Arbiters kept to themselves, rarely seen beyond the restricted upper halls of the Citadel where great magic resided.

Ezrah passed, lips moving soundlessly. Something touched her. Vera felt a chill as if dunked in ice water. Suddenly, the tolling of bells was absent. There was only silence and Ezrah's quiet mumbling. A spell… she realized. Ezrah quickly passed, taking the bubble of silence with him as he turned the corner. She took a breath and the others in the hall came back into her awareness. Neophytes and Reavers whispered in fear and awe at having seen an Arbiter.

She left them, knowing what awaited her.

Today, Vera would unlock the sword's true power. Today, she would surpass the limits of a mere Reaver.

A Night to Remember

Still moving, Kirin hit the ground. Instinctively, he tucked and rolled on the hard dirt. He came to a stop and his stomach churned, the world spinning.

The ramparts were gone, as if evaporated. The stone was now replaced with hard earth, and he felt bits of gravel between his nails. On his left, a stone's throw away, a group of girls in gray dresses sat on a grassy knoll shaded by old silveroot trees. The trees' glossy bark glistened like a fish's scaled belly. They listened attentively to an older woman in scarlet robes, who wove luminescent green strands of nature between her hands like a seamstress—as she did, a silveroot's nearest branch miraculously lengthened, bending to touch her outstretched palm. Elsewhere, groups of women roved the grounds, conversing lightly, ignoring his sudden appearance in the middle of the courtyard. To his left, near a stack of barrels, a pair of older Neophytes trained, tossing a large flame steadily between the two.

He recognized it as one of the four courtyards of the Neophyte Palace, where female Neophytes trained. The Palace itself loomed nearby.

"I didn't know there was a transporter there," he told Ren who stood calmly in the center of the courtyard.

Ren shrugged. "I had to do something. That was quite the move.

I doubt I would have evaded it. You moved like the wind."

"Not fast enough, but I guess I'll accept the fact that you had to cheat."

Ren gave a burly chuckle. "Speaking of moving like the wind, for a moment there, I thought you weren't moving, but shifting. While the transporters were developed by a hundred Reavers using the Link, it is nothing compared to the Ronin's abilities. The Ronin could teleport at will, and not just to one designated area like a transporter, but anywhere. They called it shifting. Quite the ability."

Kirin scratched his head. "That'd make sense if I could harness the spark more than a trickle, Ren. A rock has as much natural ability as I do."

"No. A rock can probably harness more of the spark than you."

"Thanks."

"… but you, Kirin, have raw ability."

"With the sword, maybe," he replied. The man said nothing. "I've been tested, Ren. Dozens of times, remember?"

Ren shrugged. "The tests have been wrong before."

He narrowed his eyes when he heard a voice call out his name. From the grand arched entry that led into the Palace, Enise, his young friend with a startled fray of white-blond hair, charged down the wide steps.

Enise approached. "Kirin—"

He steadied the girl with a hand. "It's all right, slow down. What are you doing here? Is something wrong?"

"You haven't heard?"

"Heard what?"

"Listen!" Enise put a hand to her ear.

The sounds of the bells hit him like a hammer's blow. "She passed!" He grabbed Enise's hands and danced in a circle, sending her into a fit of laughter. "I can't believe it," he said. "The youngest Reaver in all of history." And he felt as if those bells chimed for both of them, for he never thought he would live to see this day.

Looking back, he vividly remembered passing through the giant black gates of the Citadel as an orphan. Tired, hungry and on the verge of death, he had entered a world he had always feared. A place rumored to be full of the most powerful wielders of the spark, behind cloud-scraping black walls. He could still remember the feel of his pounding heart as he took in the Citadel. It gleamed like a vast gem of obsidian, the red-robed men and women demanding respect just short of kings. Since then, he had been tested in every way to get to where he stood now, and those chiming bells were a testament to their triumph.

"She wants to see you," Enise said.

He turned to Ren. "Master, I know I'm training, but…"

The man laughed and waved him away. "I'm done with you for now. The girl is waiting. Go to the Oval Hall and celebrate, and tell her congratulations from me."

"She's not in the Oval Hall," Enise said. "She left."

"Wait, she's not staying for the ceremonies?" He knew Vera wasn't one for fanfare, but this was the Trials! She had been dreaming of this moment since they were big enough to don the smallest of gray robes. "Why?"

Enise shrugged. "All I know is she was headed for her rooms in a hurry."

"Then to her rooms I go. Rekdala Forhas," he spoke solemnly.

"Till honor and death my friend," Ren mirrored.

"Will I see you at the Patriarch's meeting?"

Ren rubbed his jaw. "You will. He wants me there, as well as the Commander of the Citadel Guard, and all other Captains, though I'm not sure why." He shook the oddity off. "Until tonight then."

"Until then." Kirin ran out of the courtyard and vaulted up the stairs. Halfway up the marble steps, he brushed the shoulder of a girl fast approaching from the other way, and a flush of fear flashed through him. He nearly stumbled with the sudden disturbance to his Ki. A dark feeling pressed against his heart as the midday torches along the walls sputtered. He looked back, but the girl had disappeared.

Ahead, something was coming.

* * *

The Palace was vaulted and filled with skylights that let in shafts of morning light. Women walked quietly among hundreds of shallow pools, weaving through a sea of ivory pillars. Hundreds knelt in prayer.

Kirin turned the corner and a woman stood before him. He was two-hands taller than her, but somehow he felt the shorter of the two. Evalyn's chest heaved from running. He admitted it was not an unattractive sight in the least. She was well built, with slender shoulders, a slim waist, and a pretty face. The problem was she knew it all too well.

"Hello to you too, Kirin," she said with an arrogant twist to her lips.

"Morning," he said, and turned to the girl tucked behind the woman, "Morning Rosyaln." Rosyaln was pretty and smart. Sadly, she was Evalyn's shadow. Rosyaln smiled in return. Evalyn looked behind, and the girl's smile became a frown. Kirin sighed. "I don't have time for you this morning, Evalyn. I'd love to stay and chat, but if you'll excuse me I was just on my way…"

"To see Vera," Evayln interjected. "I heard there was an accident, do you know what happened?"

"An accident?"

"That's what I heard. I do hope she is all right," Evalyn said then lowered her voice to a whisper, "I even heard that someone was desiccated in the process…"

A flush of fear shot through him. "Was it Vera?" Kirin strode forward and gripped Evalyn's arm.

The girl looked taken aback, her bravado gone. "I'm—I'm not certain. I only heard someone was," she said, and then winced. "Kirin, you're hurting me." He let go and moved around her, sprinting through the halls. He prayed it wasn't Vera. What would Vera do? She always said she couldn't live without her power… He knew it wasn't an idle threat. Reaching her room, his senses flared. He touched the door's warm handle. It sent a tremor up his arm. Then, as quickly as it came it was gone. Without a second thought, he opened it.

He froze.

Black tentacles hung in the air.

Then he saw her.

Vera knelt in the center of the room, hunched as if hurt. From her back, the darkness expanded, unfurling like black wings. Kirin's grip tightened on the door's handle and he moved to free her when his Ki shouted in warning. As the dark feelers slithered over the walls, one of the black tentacles touched a nearby dresser and it snapped like dry tinder.

Kirin's mind reeled. Suddenly, a frigid numbness shot through his body. He looked to his feet. An inky darkness pooled around his boots. His limbs refused to move as the darkness crawled over him. He pulled, but the darkness only slithered faster. It clawed higher, touching his thigh, reaching out like liquid hands. He opened his mind, picturing the leaf, and as he had been trained, he threw his rising fear into the floating leaf. He took a slow, heavy step. One leg at a time, he pushed forward as the dark hands crawled higher, until he reached Vera.

Her skin was pale. Green and blue veins spidered across her features. More veins pulsed in her slender neck like thick, tangled roots. She's still alive. He held onto the thought like a drowning man. Quelling his terror, he grabbed Vera. Then he saw it. A blade protruded from her back, buried to its hilt within her stomach. His fingers clenched on her robes, and he gagged as warm blood poured over his hands. He touched the sword and pain shot through his arm, bursting inside his skull. His vision went black. But he held on, pulling the sword from her gut. Vera let out a gurgled cough. At the same time, he felt the darkness reach his torso. His vision cleared and he saw the dark tentacles now engulfed the room.

Voices sounded and the door blew open. Five men entered. Two wore shining plate—palace guards—and the other three wore dark brown leather and black mail. Devari, his brothers. Then he saw Ren. The man stood in the doorway, eyes wide, and sword raised. He realized every blade was directed at him. Glancing to the sword in his own hand, covered in Vera's blood, he put the two together. "It wasn't me!" He looked to his master. "Ren, you have to believe me!"

In the air, the tendrils wavered like a black snake waiting to strike.

"I believe you, Kirin, now put down your sword and drop the girl."

"Ren, please, she's dying, you have to help!" he pleaded, raising the frail body in his arms. In his hand, the sword seethed, as if eating at the light in the already dark room.

Ren's expression narrowed. "We will, but first you must drop the sword! Don't you see? Whatever is attached to you and killing Vera stems from that blade. Drop it and we will save Vera." But something felt off to Kirin. The words and the world around seemed fuzzy, as if he was seeing it all through another's eyes, and in his gut, something burned like a fire.

He looked down as Vera's breathing slowed and then stopped. "No..." Something came over him. It flowed from the sword and into him, dark and powerful, plying him with promises. A dark mantle fell upon him, and when he looked up, rage consumed his vision. "Why didn't you help her?" The sword tightened in his grip, and he felt the dark tentacles. He rose to his full height, holding Vera in one arm. The black tendrils that filled the room now sprouted from his back like dark wings.

Upon the ground, the darkness slithered. It neared a guard's boot. Kirin tried to open his mouth, to yell in warning, but nothing came out. The guard shrieked and fell to his knees. The other palace guard watched, torn between his friend's cries and the sword directed at him. His wild eyes settled on Kirin. The man charged with a fierce cry. The darkness was faster. The dark wings from his back lunged like lightning, perforating the man's head with a fist-sized hole. Then it lifted the guard from the ground like a sack of flour, and flung him to the wall with a sickening thud.

Ren stepped forward, ignoring the pooling darkness. Kirin flinched, something begged the man to stop, to go no further, but his voice was robbed from his throat. "Stop this madness, Kirin!" Ren called. "I know you're in there!"

Kirin railed, hearing the man's voice. Ren took another step, and the dark feelers lifted, coiling. Ren raised his sword and Kirin cried out, but his voice was swallowed—it was no use.

He was lost.

* * *

The other palace guard let loose a chilling cry behind Ren.

Ren pivoted. A dark pool had gathered at the man's feet, crawling over his legs and torso, dragging him down. Forgha grabbed the man's outstretched arm, the only thing not seething in liquid darkness. Ren watched, but knew already. The darkness had the man. The guard's grip tightened, screaming for Forgha to hold on, and Ren watched as Forgha strained, groaning as his muscles bunched and knotted, but soon the crawling darkness spread over the arm. Forgha snapped his hand away and just in time, as the darkness encased the guard's head, snuffing his cries. A deathly quiet returned to the room once more. Ren gave a shiver as he turned his attention to the threat before them.

He spoke softly, "This thing, whatever it is, cannot be fought." Ren saw no other way, and he could barely say the words. "We must kill the source."

"How do we get to it?" Mearus asked, sizing the creature that was Kirin.

"You two must distract it. Do not endanger yourselves—merely pull its attention. I will get inside."

"I'll go left," Forgha stated.

Mearus nodded, grip tightening on his curved sword.

"Get to the farthest sides of the room," Ren instructed, "it will buy you time. Go. Now!"

At his command, the two men moved like stalking wolves, strafing to Kirin's flanks, all the while watching the living, moving feelers that were suspended in the air, crawling over the stone and consuming the room.

Abruptly, the heavy glass window behind Kirin burst. Instantly, the wing-like feelers on Kirin's right burst forward with astonishing speed, diving for Mearus. The man dodged, rolling to the left, and the arms smashed through a pile of furniture, raising a shower of splinters. At the same time, more tentacles shot towards Forgha's head. He lashed at the darkened limb, cutting it in two. The two halves fell and Ren watched as they writhed upon the ground. Confidence stirred in him.

But then Forgha, all muscle and sinew, let loose a chilling scream. The man's dark brown eyes bulged inside his skull. Ren watched horrified as the dark liquid poured down the man's sword, burning like acid, flowing over his muscled arms and turning them to mutilated stumps. Another feeler shot out, ending Forgha's bloody screams.

Mearus unleashed a fierce cry, diving towards Forgha.

Ren cried out, "Mearus! No!" But it was too late. He cringed as two more feelers bolted towards the man, cutting off his leg above the knee while the other punched a hole through his chest. The man gurgled blood, his eyes turning to Ren in disbelief as he fell to the ground.

Ren looked up, grip tightening on the haft of his sword. "Kirin..." he seethed, eyeing the boy he once knew. "I know this isn't you.

Wake up damn it!" This isn't you, he repeated the words, wanting to believe them. In the heat of battle, Ren held a tight rein, his emotions locked behind a steel door, but now he felt it all spiraling beyond his control. His arm shook, sword rattling, though not in fear. He knew what he needed to do. If he could avoid the lightning quick feelers he could do it. He just needed to get in range…

He dashed forward. The feelers shot out, even quicker than before. He dove to the right. The dark limb crashed into the stone, sending powder and stone shards into the air. Ren let out a furious cry, dodging left and right. Two more liquid feelers skinned his torso and arm. Kirin lifted his arms, dropping Vera, and the nightmarish limbs moved quicker, attacking from every angle. Ren's cry pitched, giving into his rage, weaving beneath the limbs. He dove into a swift roll. When he looked up he was inside, only an arm's length away. He lunged forward, and grasped the boy's arms in one mighty grip. He pressed his sword to Kirin's throat.

"Kirin! Wake up, damn it! I know you're in there! Don't make me…" He pressed the blade tighter in the final moment, blood peeling beneath the razor-sharp edge. His muscled arm was ready to cut, to finish it as he knew he should.

The boy's green eyes stared into him, glazed. And Ren realized the boy was gone. Ren took a breath and uttered a final prayer when Kirin's head shook, just a little. Ren opened his mouth and gasped. He looked down. A dark, liquid feeler protruded from his stomach. Ren sputtered, trying to form words but dark, frothy blood came out. He tried to swallow it back, but it was no use as more flowed forth.

Falling, he knew. He knew it as soon as his sword didn't cut.

"Kirin…" he sputtered and the darkness consumed him.

* * *

Kirin distantly saw Ren fall. All of it came rushing back, as if he were waking from a dark slumber. He saw the room, bathed in blood. It dripped from the ceiling, coating the stone walls and shattered furniture. His mind railed in confusion.

The darkness retreated back into the sword, pulling itself from the four corners of the room and sucking into the blade. The sword glowed for a moment, brighter than a star, then its sheen returned to normal. In the hallway, alarms sounded, echoing throughout the

Neophyte Palace.

At his feet, Vera's corpse lay, blood pooling. Slowly, he backed out of the room. Outside, with the sword in his bloodstained grip, he ran, fleeing to the only safe place he knew.

An Arbiter's Gift

Kirin reached the uppermost halls of the Citadel. He had trusted his Ki, as it guided him down corridors restricted to all but the highest-ranking Reavers. Always he heard the guards' footfalls sounding through the Citadel like a broken dam. Twice he felt the presence of Devari. Luckily, they weren't as strong and he sensed them first, instead of the other way around.

At last, he stood before the oak door. He threw it open. The room was shaped in a curve, fitting to the tower's shape. Inside, he saw gold stands, opulent carpets, Saerian vases, windows with a view of the city, but all of it was a blur in his vision. He rushed towards Ezrah who stood behind his wooden desk.

Kirin opened his mouth, but nothing came out.

Ezrah saw his gore-covered hands and moved with unexpected swiftness. A power surrounded the Arbiter like a nimbus, and the flush of white filled the room making the tapestries flutter and knocking stacks of papers off the table. Ezrah touched his temple. Images poured through him in a flash—scenes of everything that had happened until now. At last, his vision raced to this moment, to where he stood. He gasped and pulled away.

"Light and flesh..." Ezrah cursed, and grasped his shoulders. "You... you have to leave, my boy, at once." He whisked towards his desk, and more papers and tomes showered to the floor as he flung them aside in search.

Kirin opened his mouth, his breath returned in a rush, but he could barely inhale before the next exhale fell.

"You're going to faint, you must slow your breathing," Ezrah instructed as he opened and slammed drawers with the flick of his finger.

"I—I can't," he gasped. His grandfather returned and put another finger to the side of his head. His breathing slowed, but his mind didn't—it reeled in fear, anger, denial, confusion, and a thousand other emotions. Yet one thing was clear, and it overrode all else. "I killed them all… I killed Ren," he whispered in horror, eyeing the blood on his hands and arms. Vera's blood.

"You did not kill them, Kirin. It did." Ezrah pointed to the sword. Kirin dropped the blade as if it burned. The blade clattered on the stone floor. "This you must trust, it was not your fault. Always remember that."

"How could I possibly forget what I've done?"

"Soon you will not remember this, but you deserve to know what has begun this night. Many years ago, when I was still but a Neophyte, I stumbled across a book of prophecy. I later discovered, to my horror, that what I held was the prophecy that foretold of the true Return that would tear the world asunder."

A cold seeped beneath Kirin's skin. The true Return was a story that scared children to bed, and made old men curse and spit. It was the nightmare all the world feared.

"I kept the prophecy secret. And day and night, I worked to decipher what I could in the effort that the Return would never come to pass." Ezrah cursed. "Now I see I was a fool to think I could alter the prophecy, and a blind one to miss that the most important piece was right beneath my nose."

Kirin shook his head. "What does the true Return have to do with me?"

"You are at the center of it. There is a power inside you, one that is both terrible and great beyond imagination. That you hold the sword without pain is evidence that you are the destined wielder the prophecy speaks of."

"What does the prophecy say?"

Ezrah hesitated.

He gripped his grandfather's arm. "Tell me."

"The prophecy states that if you do not learn to control the sword and your power, your fate will be one of sorrow and death. You will wield a power more dreadful than a hundred Returns, ultimately bringing the world to its knees."

Kirin backed away. "You're wrong…"

"It is not your fault, for the sword holds a terrible darkness," Ezrah said, eyeing the blade, "A darkness borne of its previous owner."

"Vera?" he said in disbelief.

"No. The sword is called Morrowil. It was once held by Kail, the leader of the Ronin."

"You mean the betrayer of men…"

"Some call him that. Regardless, whether by your own design, the sword's, or another's, it is your destiny to become the harbinger of chaos."

Kirin forced his racing thoughts to slow. He shook his head. "Damn the prophecy! Whatever it says, that's not me! I will fight it!"

Ezrah's reply was quiet and cold, "Just as you fought what you did to Ren and the others?"

He swallowed, looking away. "Is… is there no hope?"

He felt a strong hand upon his shoulder. "You have me. And there is one chance, but it is not without peril." Kirin looked up. "I uncovered a slim passage of prophecy. Where countless paths lead to ruin, there is one that treads death and chaos, but leads to salvation. It is a prophecy called the Knife's Edge."

"What am I to do?"

"You must flee," Ezrah said and hastened towards a dresser made of polished silveroot. He murmured something, and then plunged his hands into the bookshelves. As if there were no books, the man's hand extended, flowing beyond. Ezrah's face contorted until a look of satisfaction settled and he pulled his hand back from the magical bookcase.

Kirin watched as Ezrah returned and in the palm of his hand sat a pendant with the symbols of the Great Kingdoms. "This is what you will need. It is very rare. Under its protection you can cross the Gates, then from there, you will find safety in Daerval, in the land of the Lost Woods. The path is far from certain and there are many pitfalls along the way, but this is our only hope." Ezrah smiled, his deep-set lines becoming, for the first time, warm. "Take it," he said and tightened Kirin's hand into a fist around the pendant

Kirin gripped the pendant, looking around the room. The candle flickered on the desk, and the fire crackled in the corner. The scene was too serene, too starkly quiet to match the chaos that roiled in his mind. Were it any other day, he would be fireside, huddled over a bowl of soup after a long morning of mental or physical training, close to his brothers, the other Devari in their warm, lively halls. "I will do whatever it takes," he said.

"There is one last thing. You must take that as well." Ezrah motioned to the sword on the ground.

"No, I…" Suddenly the visions returned and he fell to his knees. He saw their faces. Forgha, Maerus, and Ren, and he whispered in horror, "I killed everyone."

"It's all right, my boy, but you must be quiet." Kirin heard the rattle of boots in the halls and he forced himself to silence, but he couldn't stop the visions. He heard his grandfather's soothing voice, "I can make it stop. I promise, but there will be a price."

He gripped his grandfather's robed sleeve. "Anything," he pleaded.

"I will cleanse you of what you have seen, for your sake, and for the sake of the prophecy," Ezrah replied. "However, it will only be temporary. One day, you will remember who you are, and where you came from. But for now, you must leave all that behind."

"Who am I to be then?"

"At your core, you will always be Kirin. We never lose ourselves, even if we forget our names, or our ways."

Kirin tried to slow things down, and make sense of his tangled thoughts. Though he desired more than anything to forget his visions, the horrible image of Vera impaled on the sword, the look of betrayal and horror on Ren's face, he could not imagine the thought of losing everything he knew. All my memories gone. The thought was somehow more terrifying than death.

Ezrah looked to the door again as boot strikes sounded, and the alarm echoed through the thick door. "There is no more time. They will be here soon."

Kirin's mind was already made up. "I will do what I must."

"So be it." Ezrah's robed arm extended as he touched the side of Kirin's head. "This is going to be painful, I apologize in advance."

"I'm ready." As he spoke, pain spiraled through him, coursing through his body and making his back bend until he thought his spine would snap. He threw open his mouth in a howl and a barrier of silence stuffed the cry back down. He shut his eyes and let the pain fill him, embracing the leaf, but even the leaf shattered, lost in a whirlpool of mind-numbing pain. Slowly the world returned and he opened his eyes.

"It is done," Ezrah whispered.

"What do you mean?" he asked. "I'm still me. I still remember everything."

"The spell will enact as soon as you leave the walls of the Citadel," the Arbiter replied.

"Then how will I know what to do, where to go if I lose my memory?"

"The spell will guide you. I have imparted all the knowledge you need to know to make it safely across the gates, and to find your destiny. Everything you know now will be temporarily held behind this barrier.

"Lastly, you must leave the name Kirin behind. There are those within these walls that seek the sword as well, and it's safe to assume they will soon know of the events that transpired here. Take the name Gray," Ezrah said with a smile. "It was what I wanted your mother to name you, if I had my choice." He turned as boots thundered just outside the door. "Now we must get you out of here."

As he spoke, a hard knock rattled the door to his chambers. They both turned to the noise, like thieves caught in the act. Ezrah snatched Kirin's cuff. "No one must know you were here, quick!" Kirin grabbed the sword as the Arbiter dragged him across the room to the other end. Ezrah pulled back another bookshelf, letting tomes shower to the ground.

The knock came again, even louder than before.

"Who is it? Who dares bother me in my studies?" Ezrah called, his voice now booming. The voice of an Arbiter.

"It is me," came the reply, equally, if not more powerful.

Kirin froze. Ezrah did the same. Who could command his grandfather? Whose voice was that?

Ezrah nearly stuttered. He turned, reaching behind the bookcase, tugging it further away from the wall. He moved behind it, pulling Kirin with him. "One moment," he replied, "You caught me in my studies. I didn't know there was anything of grave importance happening today." The bookcase still hid them from the sight of the entryway.

"Open the door," came the brisk command, even more menacing.

Instead, Ezrah touched a stone in the wall and it slid out as if well-slicked, and instantly Kirin recognized it. A transporter, he realized, hidden by the bookcase. Ezrah embraced him. "Good luck." The knocks thundered even louder, "Remember, the power of the Arbiter flows in your veins, listen to it well, for it is not the power of strength, but the power of truth. I will be with you every step in my own way."

Kirin summoned a smile, his heart pounding fearfully in his chest.

Suddenly, the crack of bursting timber echoed throughout the room. Ezrah smacked the wall, and a dark purple light surrounded Kirin, holding him like a casing of stone once more, and the world went black. The last image he saw was his grandfather's smile and the white hem of the Patriarch's robes, turning the corner of the bookcase.

* * *

The blanket of purple evaporated. Kirin opened his eyes, and saw he was standing in the cold shade of a narrow alley. Beyond, he glimpsed the busy streets of Farbs.

"The Patriarch? his voice echoed in the silent alley. He knew he didn't have much time—the death of the leader of the Devari would not stay contained in the Citadel. It wouldn't be long before the whole city was alerted, and the streets would be swarming with Citadel and elite Farbian guards.

I'll have minutes, maybe more, before the alarm is sounded, Kirin calculated, and even if I get passed the guards, those giant doors will be locked, ruling out any chance of my escape…

The alley was empty save for the tan walls, and clotheslines hanging high above. Nearby, in the damp sand, lay the pendant. He grabbed it and rose, moving to leave when he felt something. He looked back. There, in the shade of the alley, lay the sword. Kirin wished he could toss the cursed blade in the darkest well and not think of it again. Instead, he reluctantly strapped the blade to his back, sheathing it where he once put his trusted sword, and with a deep breath he stepped into the desert street.

Before he knew it, his feet moved as if of their own will, guiding him through the streets, and press of bodies. Fear pounded in his veins as sounds crashed in his ears, and a thousand bright sights paraded before his eyes.

At one point, his feet stopped in the crush of people. His mind railed, heart thumping against his ribcage. What's going on? A voice yelled in fear, blood pumping in his ears, and a cogent thought shot through like an arrow. It's happening. Is this what it feels like to go insane? But then it was gone. As he moved through the streets a voice grazed his consciousness, screaming to wake, but always it left and he kept moving.

People crashed into him, bustling, moving, the indistinct blur of pockmarked streets rutted from daily wear, the shouts of loudmouthed hawkers, of watchful guards standing in the crossroads and flanking bridges—he avoided their gaze especially, pulling his wool hood forward, but then he heard the blood, pounding in his ears. His feet flew even faster, as he pushed and shoved his way through the crowd.

Above, the sun turned a dark, ripe orange. He was losing time and something deep, something primal told him he had to move faster or all was lost. He had to make it. Then finally, at long last, the crowds thinned and he saw it—the tip of the tall, bronze colored gates. Abruptly and violently it sounded, cascading over the buildings and echoing through the streets, deep and ominous—the intoning of a bell. The alarm had been sounded.

Kirin, lost in a fog, didn't know what it meant exactly, but something inside him tensed. All around him, others stiffened. Their eyes panned up as they listened. Far ahead, at the gates, there was commotion. He ran.

He neared and watched as guards flocked to the doors, blocking the giant, arched entry that led out of the desert city. He watched, confused. Something inside him fell, disheartened, but still his feet told him he had to continue. And so he did, not sure what he was doing. As he approached the giant outer gates, his steps slowed as he remembered something dangerous. A dying part of him yelled at him to flee and run from this place. You bear the mark! Kirin looked down to his arm, and peeled back his sleeve to see a strange black insignia. He couldn't understand it. All the lines of it made sense to him, but the whole of it was strangely unreadable. He fearfully eyed the row of armored men, their halberds crossed, sharp edges catching the light of the setting sun. They will not let you pass! They will kill you if you try! Still, Kirin's pause lasted only a moment and his feet moved again, slowly forward. He tried to stop them, but to no avail. His eyes flickered to each of the tall sentries garbed in plated metal and black cloth. They stood before the immense open doors like a wall of muscle, and metal. He swallowed. For a moment, their eyes locked onto him. He stood frozen, surely caught, and then, just like that, they passed, brushing over him to watch the milling crowds beyond. It was as if he was never there, no more than a wisp of desert sand, visible, and then gone the next moment.

He took another step. Still, the guard's eyes never shifted. He ducked beneath the crossed halberds of two tall guards, crossing the threshold of the gates and something deep hit him. He turned and looked at the city for a moment, but that tie fled too and he turned away once more. Kirin continued. He felt something in the pit of his stomach, as if he was losing something important and long held with each step.

With the next step, he forgot his name, but even that worry and strangeness passed away like a desert breeze, as if it was just a trifling memory. As he walked, the young man watched the giant sand and stone archway overhead, and then before he knew it, he was beyond, and looking into the blustery, cold winds of the Reliahs Desert. Behind him, there was a thud as the huge gates slammed shut.

As if standing in another's feet, the young man took one step and then another into the harsh desert, protecting his face from the fierce sand flurries, with the cloth of his tattered cloak. Moving, always moving, into the south and to another world, to the world of Daerval.

Awakening

Gray awoke with a strange, but familiar sensation.

It was like many mornings, but this time he felt the pressure of eyes on him so heavy it ripped him awake, tearing him from a pleasant dream. Normally the sensation was reassuring like being tucked inside a blanket, almost as if he were being watched over. But today the blanket no longer felt sheltering, but suffocating. He tried to shift his mind from it.

He looked around the dawn-lit chamber, reassuring himself with the familiar image. His room was small and simply furnished. Each piece of furniture was a rich brown, burnished from time and carved from Silveroots, the long-standing monarchs of the Lost Woods. His bed was tucked against the wall farthest from the door. Beside his bed was a small stand, his creation. A heavy bookcase lined the wall opposite. It was filled with tomes of Mura's, most of which Gray had already read. His favorite book sat on his bedside stand, the pages heavily worn. He glanced to its leather cover, eyeing the gold lettering: Tales of the Ronin.

He sat up, letting the covers tumble, and then groaned in pain, noticing the welts on his body like purple snakes—outlines from Mura's training staff. Suddenly, the door to his room burst open.

Mura stood in the doorway, garbed in forest hues, with soft leather boots suitable for stealth. A grimace lined his weathered face. "Still in bed?" In his right hand, Mura gripped a polished quarterstaff.

"Still? What are you talking about? The sun's barely up."

Mura grunted. "Barely and is are not barely different."

"What? I don't even think you know what that means," Gray grumbled. "You should know better. Wine ought to be drunk at night Mura."

"It means if you don't get out of bed now, I'm going to take that bed out from beneath you, and your feistiness with it." Mura thumped his staff on the floor for emphasis.

"All right, hold on," he slowly pushed back the covers and—

In his periphery, he saw Mura heft his staff. Not good. He scrambled out of bed landing in a crouch balanced on the balls of his feet. His blood pumped and his covers were haphazardly draped across his half-naked body.

"I see you can move when you need to."

"Now that you got me up, mind helping me out? Toss me those," he said, pointing to the pair of britches next to Mura who glanced down, grimace deepening, then wordlessly used his staff and tossed the pants.

Gray snagged them from the air, and sat back on the bed slipping them on. Soft and worn, though fitted enough for hunting or stealth, his pants were one of the few articles that remained from his past, along with his much-treasured worn gray cloak. It hung from a hook upon the wall. He eyed its emblem of twin-crossed swords and wondered again, guessing at their significance. He often conjured stories about the mysterious insignia, imagining faraway lands.

The thought reminded him of the other item of his past. He pointedly avoided looking to the cubbyhole behind the bookcase, not wanting to attract Mura's keen eye. He had not touched the blade for two years, but he still felt it. Its casing of cloth did nothing to dampen the fear that turned his stomach when thinking about it. It pulled at him, even now, like a moth to a flame.

"More training today?" he questioned.

Mura grumbled. "I'm not sure how to answer you when you ask foolish questions. Of course we train today. Now finish dressing," then the hermit paused, revealing a devious smile. "Oh, and bring your sword. I want to see it now."

The door shut behind him.

For two years, the man had known all along. Gray dove towards the bookcase and hauled it away from the wall. There sat an unassuming bundle of white cloth. It was more than twice the length of his forearm. He carefully examined the bundle's surface. There it was. A single strand of his brown hair rested on the white fabric. It was just as he'd left it long ago, as if not a day had gone by.

"Tricky old man," he muttered, running a hand through his hair. Grabbing the bundle, he unwrapped the sword. The bright steel glinted, dangerous and beautiful. Dried blood, a blackish red, caked its keen edge—just as the day he found it. Its silver hue glowed beneath the blood

His grip tightened, loathing the blade. With water from the washbasin, he scrubbed the blade with his bare hands, turning the bowl a dark scarlet, then inspected it under the light of the window. It gleamed as if brand new. He quickly wrapped the sword, running out of the hut.

An early morning fog was fading, unveiling the clearing. The hut sat in the center of a glade, surrounded by the dense Lost Woods. Mura stood near an old stump used for chopping firewood, where a stubborn piece of oak sat which Gray had been unable to hew.

Wordlessly, he handed the blade to Mura. The hermit assessed the blade, scrutinizing it with a careful eye. If Mura knew the origin of the blade, he might uncover more of his past. "Does it look familiar?" he asked.

Mura's peppered hair swayed. "I'm afraid not. Where'd you get it, boy?"

Such a simple question, but when Gray reached into his mind to answer, he saw nothing of his past. As if it was shut behind a door that he didn't have the key to. "I don't know," he replied.

Running a finger along the blade's edge, Mura shrugged. "Your past is your own, lad. I've never asked, and I never will."

Gray gripped the hermit's arm, stopping him before he continued, "I wish I knew. I have nothing to hide from you, but I simply can't remember. My last memory is holding the blade when I entered the woods. Other than that…"

Mura rubbed his jaw. "Sometimes things are forgotten for a reason. Now put your sword away. We won't need it today."

"I doubt it's much good anyway," Gray agreed.

Mura twisted and the blade arced faster than light. It cleaved the stubborn hunk of firewood, slicing like molten iron through paper. The two halves tumbled to the forest floor. "It can cut well enough, but this is a weapon of death, and it has seen much blood. I'm afraid it would not suit for our practice today."

Gray tried to hide his surprise. "Then we'll train with staffs?"

Mura winked, handing back his sword, disappearing into the hut. He came back with two strange looking blades, constructed from light wood. Mura handed him a blade. "Today I want to test your skill and limits with a sword. These are made of yen boughs, so they should only smart a bit. It won't do to be slicing each other to ribbons just yet." Mura turned, walking away.

"Wait, where are you going?" he asked. "Aren't we sparring here?"

Mura looked back with a wink. "I have something else in mind. Today, we'll train like never before."

Kail's Tree

Kail was a statue of calm, sitting cross-legged beneath the shelter of a yen tree. The blades of grass leaned away from the wanderer, but the shadows drew nearer.

A tiny speck shot into the night sky like an arrow. It slowed to a stop, as if stuck in the starry web, and then suddenly it burst into golden rain. A chorus of good cheer erupted. Eyes closed, he listened to the sound of laughter as if hearing it for the first time. How long has it been since I've felt the warmth of an inn, the taste of wine, or even shared the company of another? Ages, he knew. The chill darkness was his only comfort now.

Shunning the thoughts, he closed his eyes and sought relentlessly. Not with his eyes, but with an entirely different sense. Outside his mind, the shadows from the ground and tree inched closer. The black tendrils reached for his limbs.

As he had done many times, he stalked closer to the nexus within his mind. Others had reached for the flow before and been less than lucky—grasping the power too quickly could incinerate one's body, like a burning ember to dry tinder. Once he embraced the nexus, he was gone.

His vision flew forward, over the green fields. He raced toward the Eastern Kingdoms. The grass turned to sandy plains, and then to the rocky Crags. It was an impenetrable terrain of rock and towering boulders. In its center was a deep chasm called The Rift where it was said the world split thousands of years ago, before even Kail was alive, and now tiny Crag beasts dwelled. Somewhere in that land, the ancient Kingdom of Stone, Dun Varis, still existed. Kail had heard the rumors. A whole city and its people, resurrected from the ashes of the Lieon, but even his eye could not attest to the truth of it.

To the north, the land was just as pitiless. The rocky Crags became the white plains of the Merkal Desert. There, the cruel sun took out its aggression on the sunbaked people, the foul-mouthed traders of the east. Still, there was nothing. No sign of what he sought and time was wearing thin, for he could only hold the vision for so long. Where are you?

Back under the tree where his body sat unaware, the groping shadows turned black as fetid oil. They encircled him.

Within his mind, Kail pushed forward, flying north. His vision swooped down into a wide basin. There sat the jewel of the Eastern Kingdoms, Rimdel. A trader's paradise. It was a capital with no central rule, inhabited by only thieves, ruffians, and traders as hard as stone. But where once was a sprawling city, teeming with life, now sat a ruined and ashy pit that sprawled for miles. Far and wide, the land was dyed a soul-sucking black. The Eastern Kingdoms are done. Still it was not what he was looking for. Time was closing around him like a noose.

Back beneath the yen tree, his nails sunk into his palms, creating a thin stream of blood. The oozing black crept up his clothes, sucking in the moon's sickly yellow glow as it moved. It inched higher up his thick neck, like liquid crawlers, approaching his mouth. It left behind a trail of blood and red bruises. It reached his closed mouth and found his flaring nostrils. Slowly, it seeped inside, stealing his breath. The bulk of the shadow struck, constricting around his torso like a monstrous snake with the power to shatter bones. At the same time, the shadows inside expanded, pressing fine poisonous fangs into the soft skin of his throat.

However, he was far away, unaware that his body was dying. He traveled even faster. The world was a blur beneath him. His head swam, and he felt his mind ripping into two parts from the heat of the power. Finally, he smelled it. Their scent was on the wind—ancient yet new. He followed it and snowy plains coated with blood filled his vision. His eyes caught a trailing fleet of hulking beasts and at their head nine men upon tall deathless steeds. His eyes fell upon one of the dark figures with a huge spike upon his shoulder. The figure twisted, as if looking straight into Kail's soul. Despite the distance, for a fleeting moment, he saw a flash of red. Then, like a cudgel to the side of his head, the vision shattered.

He sucked in the black liquid as his vision broke and he rushed back to his body like a tempest. His eyes bulged as the last drops of air were expelled from his lungs. With the darkness crushing him from every angle, he slowly rose, and shut his eyes. A maelstrom of wind pulsed out from his center, streaming out of every pore. He crushed the heavy black shadows like the sun's light on the last vestiges of night.

His shoulders rolled in a stretch. Even while holding my power they came. Which means they are either getting braver, or more desperate. He hoped it was the latter, but knew better. Wind flurries died at his feet and in the moon's pallid light, he watched the last of the black liquid slink along his hand. He brushed it off without looking. Then, with a touch of his power, he ignited it. The darkness cracked and hissed like water upon hot coals, and then disappeared as if it were never there.

He looked north and east. A cold settled over him that was not from the chill night. He had found them. And they were coming. He felt an all-too familiar regret, eyeing Lakewood.

At his back, he felt the presence of a shrouded forest—the ancient woods whose canopy was too thick for even his vision to penetrate. Kail's scarlet eyes hardened. His gray cloak emblazoned with crossed swords wavered in the wind. He knew what he had to do. At last he turned, and stalked into the night. Into the Lost Woods. What the boy carries must not fall into their hands, he vowed. He had worked too hard to prevent that—even become the traitor to keep the blade upon its destined path.

And if he failed, Kail knew, Daerval would be the first to fall before the entire world crumbled.

A Hymn to an Ancient Forest

Gray watched the hidden pockets of darkness.

The Lost Woods possessed a haunting beauty. As he followed the hermit, he admired the mammoth tree trunks and knotted branches that twisted up to form a canopy. He inhaled the musky smell of decaying wood.

Before him, Mura hummed a pleasant melody,

Oh', Ancient trees and forest sullen,
Those who do not, will not, see.

Yet, dull wits, will not hinder thee!
As I bask beneath the great yen trees.

Oh, I have seen battles great!
Fate that has seen the end of love,

But truth have I seen, so great.
And hate, that blinds
Of all great minds,
Since sadness follows me.

Late has come my death,
But I have seen Kailith topple kings,
And Omni battle giants,
When Seth screams defiant.

Ancient trees and forest sullen
Those who do not, will not, see.

So who am I, to sing of sorrow?
When there is always 'morrow.

After a while, the canopy thinned and the trees turned to saplings. The terrain rose steadily. Gray saw teeth marks gnawed into the base of one of the aspens, a beaver's missive, and suspected Mura must have been leading him to a body of water.

His mind strayed as they walked, thinking of his favorite stories, fantasizing about the legends and their heroic deeds.

"Mura, I've never heard that song before. How do you know it?"

"Are you curious about the song, or about Kail?" Gray missed a step. "I saw your face when I sang his name, you'd be hard pressed to hide a look like that."

He rubbed a hand through his hair. "Kail and the song then. Both."

Mura waved a hand dismissively. "Ah, the song is just something I picked up in my travels, either in the taverns of Lakewood, or the eastern trading provinces. As for Kail… seeing as you've read most of the tales, I suppose you want to know more than the average stories tell."

"I do."

Mura thumped his staff and gave a wink. "Lucky you, for I always find the stories of Kail the most interesting as well! So, how about the rumored legends of how he can never die? Or the tale of the fabled Vaults in the Hall of Wind, where they say he stashed the most precious of weapons. A weapon crafted by the gods."

"What about the other Ronin? Together they could take him right?"

"Well, each of the Ronin had powers beyond any mortal. They were capable of vanquishing whole legions. Baro the Bull, slayer of giants, led the vanguard. Maris, the Trickster, had a tongue that was quick and sharp, and only his sword was quicker. Hiron, the Shadow, the voice of wisdom moved like water. Dared, the King-Slayer, never spoke, though always dealt the final blow. Aurelious, the Confessor, guided by truth, always took the final verdict. Aundevoriä, the Protector, viewed life tantamount to all else. And finally, Omni, the Deceiver, who was Kail's right-hand and dealt death like the seven winds." He paused for emphasis. "It was said the last thing his enemies saw was always and inevitably his frozen-blue eyes beneath his shrouded mask. All of them powerful, all of them legends. But Kail was the strongest of all.

"They say his attacks could never be seen, even by the Ronin, that his blade was so quick it had never been seen out of its sheath. That he moved faster than light itself!" Mura exclaimed. With each word Gray's pulse beat faster, and with the last words Mura suddenly pivoted, his staff flashed, racing towards him.

Gray tensed, backpedaling, though raising his yen sword in the last moment and the two collided.

"Ha! Guess I'm not as fast as the fabled Kail, or perhaps you are," Mura said with a wink.

Gray shook his head with an exasperated laugh. "You really are unpredictable sometimes."

"Only sometimes?" asked the hermit, sounding disappointed, and flashed another wink, before turning and heading back down the trail, whistling as if nothing had happened. Gray's blood cooled, but the stories still swirled in his head until the hermit announced at last, "We're here."

A Sight to Behold

The sound of raging water filled Gray's ears. Beyond a stand of trees he saw glimpses of rushing water. Mura quickly turned and headed towards it, and Gray dashed to catch up. He wound through the last few trees, ducked beneath a low branch and as he left the shelter of the woods, his right foot stepped out. But there was no ground to catch it. His step extended out over an abrupt ledge that spiraled down to a misty pool far below. He threw his weight backwards, groping when a strong arm clasped his own.

"Fool boy, always needing help," Mura muttered as he pulled him back from the dangerous precipice.

"You could have told me," Gray said, his heart still thumped inside his chest, one hand planted on the firm forest floor

Mura snorted. "Well I didn't think you would go charging out of the woods like a blind boar! Besides I didn't want to ruin the surprise."

It was Gray's turn to grumble as he pushed himself up, standing far back from the shelf. He brushed himself off, and for the first time, he was truly at a loss for words. The scene was suffused in light. The slim trail led to the side and onto a large rock outcropping that jutted out over the deadly drop. Far below the haze he saw a gleaming pool. His eyes followed the path upwards to the largest waterfall he had ever imagined. It flowed over a cliff arcing gently downward and then cascaded over the natural bridge, crashing against it, continuing its great descent. Furry moss covered the stones at the top of the falls, like teeth from which the mouth of the waterfall's torrent spewed.

"What do you think?" Mura's gruff voice was muffled by the roar of the falls.

"It's beautiful."

Mura laughed. "You do have such a way with words, my lad. The hermit looked at him, curiously. "Have you ever seen a waterfall?"

He shook his head. "I don't think so." He tried to dig through his memories, but like every other time, he ran into a barrier and frustration filled him. "What is this place called?"

"Maiden's Mane. It's one of four known as the Great Falls. Now are you ready to begin?"

"We're sparring here?"

The hermit backed up onto the rock bridge. "Come and see for yourself, it's as sturdy as can be."

Gray waved his hands. "Oh, no. You won't get me out there."

"Well I can't spar with myself. Come now."

"What is wrong with this nice patch of solid earth?" Gray stomped on the ground. "Why make things difficult? I'll slip and break my neck, if I don't plummet to my death first." Mura only stared at him. Gray sighed. "Is it safe?"

"If you'd look, the rock is covered in rough lichen that's as good a footing as any."

"Why though? It seems an unnecessary risk."

"I have my reasons. Do you think every fight is fought on fair and even soil, with no obstacles and no distractions?"

"Well, no, but how often will I need the skills to fight over a waterfall?"

"Look beyond your own two feet, boy. I've taught you better than that. You should know at least one reason."

"Surroundings?"

Mura grunted. "Go on."

"I guess if I can learn to fight here, I can fight anywhere."

"Aye, lad, once you put that head of yours to work, you really aren't the hay-in-the-hair-bumpkin you pretend to be. But why just fighting?"

"What do you mean?"

"It goes beyond battle, lad. In any situation there are any number of distractions. That is how a man gets a dagger in his back, a lighter coin purse, or any other misfortune. A man who does not know his surroundings is a man half blind to the world around him. You must always be aware. Understand?" Gray nodded. "Good, now come."

Walking out upon the furred rock, he put a hand down, to feel the lichen surface. The gray-green mat was coarse and grainy.

"You're afraid of heights?"

He didn't look up.

"All the more reason," Mura replied. "I can teach you to conquer your fears, but I would rather you confront them. A man who knows his fears lives longer than a man without."

With a heavy breath, Gray strode forward and raised his yen sword before him. A fine rain fell upon his face. "I'm ready." He tried not to look in his periphery, tried not to imagine the sickening drop and his body smashing upon the sharp rocks.

"Good," Mura said and ran a finger along the line of his jaw as he appraised Gray's stance. "But a sword is much different than a staff. You must learn to hold yourself properly before anything else."

Mura instructed him in a patient tone and Gray listened. He wondered if he had used a blade before, for holding the yen sword in his fists felt right, like a forgotten dream. His feet shifted in anticipation. Water thundered, and tension built.

Renmai

Wind whipped his cloak alive, and strands of hair lashed his face. Kail stared over the cliff's edge. He watched the two men.

They stood twenty paces apart. The boy practically trembled with excitement. As his fingers flitted at his side, the cloaked man froze, marveling at the odd and familiar gesture. The boy moved, and took a stance. The difference in his posture was far too subtle for anyone else to recognize or understand.

"Sa Hira…" Kail whispered. A smirk creased his lips when the old man spoke. Kail extended his hand, curling his fingers into a cup. He focused on the hermit's mouth. With a scooping gesture, as if carving out a handful of air, he caught the breath before the hermit's lips and grappled it towards him. Words took shape as if whispered in his ear.

"No, my boy. Standing as surely as a wolf in the brush is just lounging. A Renmai Stance. I never thought I would see it."

"So he's more than just a hermit," Kail mused. Suddenly, a call echoed through the woods, barely audible. It was far too muted for the two below, especially under the water's roar, but he heard. His eyes shifted and muscles tightened like steel ropes. A hand was on his plain leather scabbard. They're close.

Kail knelt. With one hand he stripped away layers of moss at his feet, and put his palm to the ground. The dirt was soft and wet. He waited until the cry resounded again, and this time, he chased it, smacking his palm to the ground. Upon impact, his senses rushed into the ground and he was toppling over the ledge, tumbling down the face of the falls, flowing with the racing torrent. He escaped the sucking rush of water and flew into the woods. He wove through the trees with his second sight. Shadows rushed towards him, while others shrieked, shirking away as if his presence was poison.

The cry ricocheted and he followed it. But the sound was dying quickly. He could almost see it like a thin wisp in the air, receding into the woods. Kail flew faster, pushing harder to catch it. Finally, the sound stopped. He was still charging forward, rushing to catch it when he saw the trap. He knew he was caught, unable to slow his headlong dash, and a huge blade from around the last tree rushed towards his face. Its gleaming edge pierced the tip of his ethereal form. There was nothing he could do. Without a second thought, he severed the cord between his two selves.

He rushed back into his stationary body, eyes snapping wide as if ice water had drenched his skin. Immediately, he vomited to one side, and wiped his mouth with the back of his gloved hand. A mounting feeling of insanity, of his mind shredding into two parts, rose to the surface. Forcefully, he shoved it down. Snapping the thread between forms was dangerous, at best, and even he didn't know the full extent of it. He felt something, and glanced down at his muscled forearm to see a tremor ripple beneath his flesh.

Calmly, Kail stood. The boy will die first, he thought emotionless, withdrawing into himself as he turned. His cloak snapped and whipped with purpose.

A Rising Wind

The silence broke with the screech of a hawk.

Gray leapt and crashed against Mura's staff with a thwack. He inched closer to the hermit's face, seeing an opening. Suddenly, Mura's weight shifted. With an agile twist his sword sluiced off, and Mura's staff halted, parting his hair with the force of its descent. "If you want to ever master that sword of yours, you'll have to master your emotions."

Gray attacked again, trying everything he knew, seeking the hermit's openings. Mura's shoulder opened up. Gray twisted, striking horizontally, but pulling the strike in the last moment before Mura's parry. The yen tip dashed for the hermit's torso, but collided with the staff, sweeping his strike aside.

"Too predictable! You want my midsection? Then attack my head!" Mura yelled.

He raised his sword striking for Mura's head, repeatedly hammering all three angles. He gave the hermit no time to counterattack as he advanced, driving him back with each grueling step. The cascade grew louder, deafening in his ears as he rained blows upon the hermit. Mura slipped his staff to block his side once more, but Gray lunged inward, thrusting with a cry. He pulled the blow and swung upwards, aiming for the most unpredictable target he could imagine—his yen blade flashed fast as lightning, and he imagined himself a corded bundle of energy as it arced upwards scraping the hermit's leg until—thwack.

He landed heavily, mossy stone softening his fall. Only when he opened his eyes did he realize what happened. His chest throbbed. He looked up. The hermit's staff was extended rod-straight, still in the strike. Slowly, the hermit let the staff fall.

"A mind has many parts. Never focus to the exclusion of all else that you become blind. If you attack offensively, always expect an opening." Gray rubbed his chest, trying to catch his breath. "Are you all right?"

Gray was surprised at the compassion in the man's voice. He rose to his feet. "I am, but no matter what I do, I just can't hit you."

"You can, and you will. But remember," he advised, "a castle is meant to defend and attack."

"What's that supposed to mean?"

"If a castle only defends, what then? If it never attacks and its people only watch, and stand arrogantly behind its high walls?"

"It will fall."

Mura jabbed his temple with a thick finger. "Ah, now you're using your head! You see, even in defense there is offense, and the same is true of the reverse. Always imagine that if you fight with only one part of yourself, or only one way, you will always lose. The greatest fighters use all parts, like the High Generals of the Lieon."

"And yet they still lost," he replied.

"A valid point," Mura said, "Let it be said though, there was no real victory. But that's a history lesson for another time. Focus now. Mind, body, defense, offense, softness, hardness. All of these and more must be considered, and always in union." Gray attacked again. He swung from above then below, moving slowly at first, but building pace, flowing smoothly from striking to blocking. "Good!" Mura barked. "You're getting it!" he said, parrying a strike.

A smile grew on his face as he weaved the thrust into an undercut, and the ease of the movement sparked something. Fisher in the Shallows to Dipping Moon—a snaking thrust to an upward strike from which its power is derived from the bending, and swift upward lift of the legs, said a distant, familiar voice. He stumbled as the knowledge and images flooded his mind, and when he regained his senses he saw Mura's blow racing towards his head. Instinctively, Gray ducked and rolled beneath it, and the world came into spinning focus as he reached the ledge, the fall teetering in his vision, the spray and rocks beneath racing forward.

Mura grabbed Gray's shoulder and flung him back, and the together they landed heavily on the solid stone. "Let's not do that again," Mura said. "What just happened? Your past?"

"I'm not sure. I saw images of moves. I think… I'm starting to remember," he said, his fist clenching on the rough, green lichen.

"Good!" exclaimed Mura. "Then show me what you learned!"

The hermit jumped to his feet, lashing out, and Gray leapt over the staff and retaliated, giving into his mind and the sword. Mura retreated. Gray's Lopping the Branch grazed the hermit's brow. Stepping back, Mura breathed hard and Gray hid a smile. "Do you need a rest?" he yelled over the sound of the falls.

The hermit dove towards Gray. "Parry!" he shouted, striking down and Gray swung his sword to his shoulder, covering his flank. "Strike!" And he struck. He flowed through Mura's commands. "Parry, strike, evade!" And at the last strike, Gray blocked. Mura held the block for a moment, and then with a twist of his wrists, he flicked the blade like an adder's bite.

Gray rebounded, feet scraping along the mossy stone. There was no extra strength in Mura's block and yet, he was pushed backward by that simple added twist. "Teach me that," he said.

"Teach you what?"

"What you just did. What was that?"

Mura shrugged. "A little trick."

"That was more than a little trick," Gray replied. "You gained power from nothing."

"Not nothing," the hermit said, "There is power to be found and added in every move, and not always in the might of ones arms, but often in the hidden movements. First you must loosen your whole body, it must be like a cord that snaps tight at the last moment. Imagine yourself like a bolt of lightning, quiet and deadly, and only upon impact do you shatter stone and splinter wood." Gray did as he instructed. With each strike he began to understand what Mura meant—the added flick became audible, adding a whoosh to the tip of his yen bundle.

"You've got it," he proclaimed with a broad sweep of his arms.

With a flash of his yen sword, Gray struck Mura's open flank, this time adding the snap to his sword. Mura threw up his staff and the two weapons collided. But with Gray's added power the hermit toppled backwards, falling into a nearby bush.

"Caught you behind your castle wall did I?" Gray asked as he extended a hand.

Mura wiped an astonished look from his face and grumbled, "Aye, aye, well done lad." He took his hand and rose, brushing dry twigs and leaves from his pants. "Seems you've learned enough for today, and besides, the weather appears to be taking a turn for the worse." He eyed the ominous black clouds that gathered in the distance.

Looking around at last, Gray observed that they had not only backed off the bridge during the fight, but also now stood in the glade before the falls. A stand of trees obscured the view. Glancing back to his companion, he noticed with frustration that only a trace of sweat dotted the hermit's forehead. Other than that, Mura was breathing no harder than if he had just come back from a walk in the woods. However, the smug smile was off his face, and he thought he could sleep easy at that sight. If I can sleep, as the bruises that covered his body coming into focus. He glanced to Mura who was now examining some strange looking blood-red mushrooms in the path.

"What is it?" Gray asked.

"I'm not sure," Mura said, scratching his head. "These shouldn't be here…" The curious red color of the mushrooms tugged at Gray's curiosity. He approached and a smell like rancid meat hit his nose and he cringed. Pinching his nose with one hand, he reached out with the other to check if they had gills when Mura yelled. "Don't touch them!" The authority of the order made his hand shoot back.

"Why?"

Mura walked over and knelt down beside him. He stared at the mushrooms and scrubbed a hand through his stubble. "I don't know, but something tells me to be cautious about them."

"Even more than usual?"

"Aye, I've lived here for years, but something feels different… A strange presence," the hermit muttered, and then stood. "Let's head back, lad. It'll be good to get out of this cursed wind," he grumbled to himself, walking back towards the house, muttering something about a pipe and a fire.

Gray gave one last look at the peculiar red mushrooms. At his side, his fingers burned as if he had touched the strange fungi. Oddly, even his wrist tingled and he pulled back his sleeve to reveal the sinuous tattoo upon his wrist. Turning, he hurried after Mura beneath the shrouded canopy, towards the darkening clouds.

The Harrowing Gale

Gray opened the door of the hut and was greeted by the aroma of stew. Throwing off his boots, he rushed to the fireplace. "When did you have time to make this? We've been out all day."

Settling into a chair, Mura picked up his favorite dagger and began to whittle. "You were asleep. It's been simmering all day, which might I add, is the only proper way to make stew."

The whole house smelled of spices, onions, and roast chicken. Warmth seeped back into his numb fingers. Outside, the wind howled, and the chimes that hung from the low eaves crashed. "The wind is really picking up."

Mura grunted. "Las Fael'wyn, the elves call it, or in the common tongue, 'the harrowing gale'." He continued his calm strokes, letting the shavings fall into a bowl on the floor.

"Fael'wyn…" Gray said to himself in thought, "Wait, isn't it 'wind'? I mean, doesn't it mean 'the harrowing wind'?"

Mura looked up in surprise. "How'd you know that?"

"Because you taught me…"

"Did I?" Mura asked. Gray couldn't tell if he was joking. "Well then, I'm a good teacher. Yes, I remember now. I told you about the basic structure of Elvish." He chuckled softly. "I might have skipped a few things for practical purposes, but, yes, that is what it means. Wyn is the Elvish word for 'wind'."

Gray repeated the term, wondering how many things the elves had named. Grabbing a spoon that hung from the brick fireplace, he stirred the stew. His mouth watered and he eyed a piece of golden brown meat. He snatched it, and then juggled his steaming prize before popping it into his mouth. It singed his tongue and he yelped.

Behind him, Mura chuckled. Gray turned with a glare. "Are you ever going to finish that thing?" he motioned to the piece of wood in the hermit's hands that vaguely resembled a pipe. Instead of saying anything, Mura calmly put down his tools and disappeared into his room.

Gray heard him rummaging, and then dragging what sounded like a large object across the wooden floor. With a grunt of success he came back out carrying a dark blue trunk with a tarnished lock and gilded with silver oak leaves. He set it down with a heavy thud.

Grabbing the stool from the table he placed it before Gray, and then sat back down. "Sit," he said. Gray had never seen the ornate chest before, and a thousand questions wrestled in his head. Shadows played on the chest, and the ornate silver looked out of place in the rustic cabin. From his vest pocket Mura extracted a key, and then inserted it into the lock. With a deft twist, and a scratching whine, it unlocked. Mura lifted the heavy lid. He hid the contents and drew out something. Then, he shut the lid with a bang, and relocked the chest.

In his hands lay a tome as fat as a brick. Gold and silver reinforced the thick spine. The hermit stroked the book's worn cover. "Ages has it been since I've held this."

"Where'd you get it?"

Mura words were quick, as if it was a well-worn memory much like the book. "I purchased it in the unlikeliest of shops, just shy of the port, in the city of Reym, when I was your age." He must have seen Gray's look of confusion. "Reym is a traveler's city. It's not far from the great Tir Re' Dol, used as a waypoint. Many interesting things can be found there if one knows where to look." Despite the hermit's earnest tone, something seemed absent from his story. The hermit continued, "There is something I want to show you." He peeled opened the book and Gray saw strange patterns upon the aged parchment.

Gray faintly recognized the symbols. "I've seen those before," he whispered, but as he tried to remember, he hit the same wall. Frustrated, he shook his head. "Go on," he said, and Mura continued.

"These symbols stand for each of the nine Great Kingdoms. Each representing an element of old," Mura said, pointing to each in turn. "Leaf for the Kingdom of Eldas, home of the Elves, the element of leaf; water for the ancient city of Seria within the Grand Falls, often called the city of tranquility; stone for the stronghold of Lander, whose walls were thicker than small cities, fortified within the rocky crags; moon for the city of Narim, coveted in the dark hills—half above, and half beneath the land, a vast, subterranean gem; sun for the shining keeps of Vaster, like alabaster jewels, always in the dawn's light; metal for the city of Yronia, backed against the deep mines, a land of steam and gleaming steel; fire for the dark Farbs whose incantations ignite the night sky; and at last, the Kingdom of Flesh for Covai, a city of men, women, and beast, the land of the Mortal Being, the largest spiritual sect of all the lands. Each are called the shining jewels, the Great Kingdoms of the Lieon."

Gray leaned forward to get a closer look.

"Of course," Mura said, sitting back. "However, there is one kingdom that is often forgotten." The hermit paused, his hand running over the coarse paper as he turned the page to reveal a symbol that made his pulse skip.

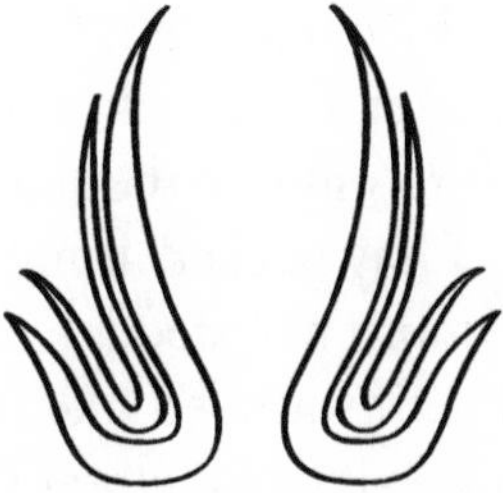

Mura spoke in a dark tone, "The symbol of wind. It stood for the ancient city of Morrow, upon the windy cliffs of Ren Nar that oversaw the world. It is the banished element."

Gray looked to the snaking pattern of wind, losing himself in its design. He wanted to trace his fingers over its familiar shape when Mura snapped the cover shut with a thud, shattering his trance.

The hermit stood. "I'm giving it to you," he said, hefting the book.

Eyeing the unreadable glyphs upon the cover he asked, “And how am I to read it? I don’t even know what language that is.”

“The language is called Yorin. I will teach it to you. For now, simply treat it well,” he said and then stretched. “The stew looks ready. Go ahead and serve it up. I’ll put this in your room with the rest of your books.”

Gray set out two wooden bowls along with a crusty loaf. Chewing on a small hunk of the bread, he hooked the teakettle over the fire’s flames, when there was a soft thunk from outside, barely loud enough to be heard over the wind. He cursed. Probably just another loose shingle from the roof, and I’ll be the one that will have to fix it. As he turned, a loud rasp made him freeze. He leaned forward, peering out the darkened window. Branches swished. Just the wind, he repeated when a movement caught his eye. “What kind of animal…?”

A shriek split the wind’s moan, and he backed away from the dark window.

“Douse the flame boy!” Mura kicked the kettle. The fire hissed and the room plunged into darkness.

He snatched the hermit’s sleeve. “What’s going on?”

Mura put his fingers to his lips. Pale moonlight lit the man’s features. In the silence, Gray heard it. Low grunts and snarls. “Go to the back door,” the hermit whispered. “Then when I tell you to—”

With a roar, the door burst. Gray was blown back. In a daze, he crawled behind a nearby chair when he saw the gleam of metal. Mura’s dagger. He gripped it, then tucked it in his leather belt.

Like an apparition, Mura slid into the shadow of the wall. Unease in the pit of his stomach, Gray peeked around the chair, peering at a cloud of dust where the door once stood.

Click… click… click… it sounded like nails rapping against the wood floor. Click… click… It came closer still.

Then, it stopped.

With his back pressed to the chair, Gray twisted to look for Mura and saw only shadows, when a clouded breath filled his vision. Silently, he scrambled away, moving to the other side of the chair. He looked back and saw his nightmares confirmed. A massive head swiveled to the sound—where Gray had been only moments before. The beast gave a violent, jagged snort. With a rasping breath that frosted in the air, the massive head slunk back. The room returned to a chilling silence.

Gray caught his breath as more shadows skulked across the window, their strange shapes reflecting on the wall. He eyed his open bedroom door. In a bent dash, he slipped from one dark shadow to the next.

A rough hand clasped over his mouth. “Stay quiet.”

He glanced over his shoulder and saw the hermit’s lined features. He nodded and silently, they made their way to the back hallway. Gray saw long scratches along the wall, and pockmarks in the wood floor like the rivets of a nail. He paused.

“I can’t leave it,” he whispered and Mura raised a thick brow.

“What are you talking about?” Mura reached out, but was too slow and Gray scrambled to his room. Inside, other than the broken window, the room seemed unscathed. Strange ruby light came through the window and lit his bed. There it was. He breathed a sigh of relief at the sight of his cloth wrapped sword. He grabbed the bundle, when the rapping sounded again.

Click… Click… Click…

Slipping through the window, he stayed low and kept to the shadows of the walls. Quickly, he made his way to the back of the house. The hermit was waiting for him. Gray released a breath he hadn’t known he had been holding.

Mura scowled. “You’ll explain that to me one day, and I’ll win that argument.” He gripped his shoulder. “Stay close to me, and don’t stop for anything.” And together they moved into the Lost Woods.

The Spire

Karil shoved another set of riding clothes into her pack and turned from her bed. Her room was still, but her heart was not. Even the serene night mocked her frantic mind.

From the window above her bed, azure scrolls lit her room. An ornately carved bookshelf sat in the room's corner. In the center, a wide-table, its stout legs made of silveroot, flowing as if alive with liquid silver. Elvin craftsmanship fit for a princess. A tranquil scene, but still her hand trembled, for beyond these walls lurked danger. Her gaze jumped to the plum-colored door made of heartwood. Heartwood was harder than most human metals—it would take a small army to break it down, but she knew that wouldn't save her. He will be here any minute, she prayed.

She looked down and saw the polished stone in her palm. The rock was carved with a pattern of a leaf, stunningly real, as if the leaf had shed its skin upon the emerald stone. It was a gift of her fathers, something she had long forgotten, and childhood memories flooded through her. Only things I can't live without, she repeated. She set it aside, placing it in a pile of books, jewelry, and precious things likely never to be seen again. Surely it's too small to matter, she thought and quickly tucked the smooth stone in her bag.

The hard rap of knuckles sounded on the door. Karil grabbed a fistful of her split- riding skirt. Three knocks. She remembered their code and rushed to the door, unlocking it. Rydel flowed inside like a tempest. He passed her wordlessly and strode to the window. His grand hando cloak of black and forest green fluttered as he moved. Karil knew the cloak silently demanded respect, for he was one of only ten elves who bore the same shroud. He took the room in two giant strides, throwing back the drapes.

Outside, lights from the kingdom glowed. Hues of amethyst and sapphire lit the forest. A vast canopy was obscured by mist and cloud. Far below, tiny white dots blushed where twisting paths wound throughout the forest. The whole kingdom appeared as if stars were flung amid the trees. Each tree was a towering guardian, their trunks the width of cities. Below, a staircase glimmered, as if made of shimmering glass. It encircled the main structure they were in, the massive Spire, twining all the way up the Great Tree.

"Is it time?" she asked, stepping forward. Her voice was strong. She was glad for that—the tears shed were all but a memory. Rydel was quiet. His slender elvin eyes, a piercing green, watched the staircase. His sharp ears pricked, as if hearing sounds her half-elf ears could not.

Karil joined his side. "What is it? What do you see?"

"I see them. They are coming." Rydel turned. He grabbed her shoulders. "We must leave, now."

"So soon," she said, "Somehow I thought there would be more time. Is everything ready?"

Rydel grabbed her pack. "The horses are waiting in the stables. All that is required now is to get to them, from there I have cleared a path out of the woods." She heard the unspoken message in his words. If we can make it there…

"How many?" she asked.

"A dozen in the halls, maybe more, and hundreds scattered around the grounds of the city." She saw his hesitancy, as if he was afraid to speak the rest, "What we feared has come to pass. Dryan is seizing upon the chaos of your father's murder. Elves are joining his side in droves. There will be hundreds, if not thousands looking for you soon. You are the only thing standing between Dryan and the throne now."

"And what of our supporters?"

"Most are dead or swayed to his side."

"Then Dryan has won," she whispered.

"No. Not yet. It will not be long before the entire kingdom is crawling, and then all hope of escaping will be lost. But there is still a chance if we leave now."

If all things good can go to ruin so quickly, what did it matter? Karil rested a hand upon the windowsill. "I can always trust you, can't I Rydel?"

Rydel answered without hesitation. "Forever, my queen." Karil tensed. The title was daunting, but somehow he made it sound true and good.

"Lead the way," she ordered and he nodded.

They left her quarters and swiftly navigated their way through the labyrinth of halls, taking the least used routes. Though they moved quickly, they were high in the Spire, where all the nobility resided. They turned a corner and saw shadows nearing. They threw themselves against the wall. The shadows revealed themselves as servants trailing robed nobles. Karil breathed a sigh. For a moment she considered gathering them as allies. Judging by their robes that were shades of green, they were of the House of Nava, a staunch supporter of her father. She shook her head. No one could be trusted.

As they ran, she caught glimpses through wide windows of bright lights like dashing sprites in the night. Rydel abruptly pressed her against the wall. Karil waited, listening, the elf's rock-like arm holding her in place. He pulled them back further, moving into a carved niche, tucked behind a standing vase of Merilian Silver. She looked but saw nothing. The halls were silent. Then, around the bend, something shifted. Karil's breath caught as a guard in black elvin plate-mail appeared, as if melting from the wall. He had been hiding in plain sight. His eyes skimmed just past their hidden nook. At last, he moved down the hall. Now she knew what pursued them.

The Terma.

As a girl, she had both looked up to and been afraid of these elite guards that protected her father. Even back then, she would cling to his leg when a Terma entered the room. Her father would simply stroke her hair as she trembled. The Terma lived and breathed their training, with the skill and agility of a hundred normal elves.

However, there was another rank, a secret echelon. The black-armored Terma were one rank below Rydel, and it was said that difference was the span of chasms. For there was no one higher than one of the Hidden, those who bore the hando cloak. But one against hundreds?

As they wove through the halls, she kept to Rydel's side, watching the dark corners. Four more times Rydel halted them. Each time a Terma slunk out of the shadows, always impossible to see until revealed.

At last, they reached the stables. Relief flooded her. She entered. The dawn light lit the rafters and stacks of hay.

Rydel returned, guiding their horses. She saw Rensha, her white mare, and was glad for the familiar face. She stroked the horse's muzzle and Rensha nickered. Rydel swiftly strapped down the saddlebags. She normally rode her cormac—faster and more intelligent creatures that were more attuned to the spark, but such a creature would be far too conspicuous beyond the gates and within Daerval, a land without magic.

Karil nimbly mounted Rensha. Rydel took to his large black warhorse and together they turned towards the wide archway when the ground rattled. Abruptly, the door behind burst open. Shards of wood rained down. Rensha spooked, bucking in terror and she fought to gain control of the frantic animal.

"Karil! Run!" Rydel shouted.

She slammed her heels into Rensha's flanks, bursting towards the open archway, but her charge was brought to a sudden halt as she was flung forward. When Karil gained her senses, she was on the ground. Twenty or so elves in black armor poured into the stables, surrounding them with silent, deadly ease. She saw the one that had flung her from her horse. He stood before her, tall and muscular. Where Rydel was broader of shoulder and arm, this elf was slender like a blade, with long straight blond hair that draped over his shoulders. He held Rensha's reins casually with one powerful arm as the creature bucked. His other hand gripped a long, curved dagger. Karil swallowed with a rush of comprehension.

"So then, Dryan has no intention of letting me live," she said. The blond elf grinned, showing uncharacteristically human-like emotion. Karil's blood ran cold. "I see. That's clever of him, crushing all opposition here in the quiet, where the chaos will flow over and wash away his questionable deeds."

The elf sneered as he approached. "Oh, you misunderstand. You're not a threat to an elf like Dryan. Nevertheless, dead is always simpler than alive. Rumors are easy enough to quell. You have been too outspoken for your own good."

Anger rose inside Karil. "You're more of a fool than I thought," she replied. "Dryan has no claim to the throne, and never will. Who would ever believe him?"

The elf laughed openly. "You don't get it, do you? They will believe what we want them to believe."

Karil took a calm breath. She summoned her ka. It was weaker than most elves because of her half-blood, but undetectable for that same reason. In the corner of her vision she saw Rydel. Surrounded by ten other elves, he looked like a cornered tiger. He flashed her a look. She nodded. With a fierce cry, she lashed out, pulling every shred of her power into one invisible cord. A root from a nearby tree plunged upward through the thick ground, sending a shower of dirt into the air. Startled, the elf bounded backwards. He cut at the tubers, but the roots were quicker. They shot out, snaring his legs. The elf was thrown to the ground. At the same time, Karil leapt to her feet and bounded into Rensha's saddle.

Behind, she heard the cry and clash of Rydel with the other elves, but she didn't spare the time to look, trusting her companion. She bolted for the open door, when Rensha bucked again as if colliding with a brick wall. She turned and saw the blond elf held the reins. His face twisted, muscles cording with strain. Three more guards were approaching fast behind her. In one swift movement, she unsheathed her slim dagger and slashed the elf's hand. He unleashed the reins with a cry and she broke free. Suddenly, Rydel was at her side, riding hard.

Twenty more elves alighted from thin air and she pulled her reins short. Too many, she thought.

A fierce battle cry rang through the clearing, and the Terma froze. Karil followed the sound, but saw nothing. When suddenly more elves burst from the woods. Her heart rose as she glimpsed their green armor. The two forces clashed and cries pierced the night. Green armor upon black, swords flickered like a blur. A Terma was thrown into Rensha's flank. The animal bucked wildly. She gripped the reins and clung to her mounts back. Through the haze of swords and tangle of Rensha's mane, she saw him once again.

The blonde Terma cut down a green armored shadow with menacing ease. The other elf fell to his knees clutching his chest, vainly trying to stop the flow of his gaping wound. The Terma lifted his sword to finish the job. Karil wasted no time. Holding Rensha's mane in one vise-like grip, she lunged for her dagger, hurling the blade. It flew over the crowds and sunk into his back, biting deep between his shoulder blades. She watched him fall and then unsheathed her sword and looked around, but in a matter of seconds, the fighting was over.

Bodies littered the ground, mostly the Terma. She turned to her defenders. Their breathing was heavy, faces ragged. They wore green cloth, loose and light with a few added pieces of leather armor, piecemealed together. It was the garb of the Lando, as they had started calling themselves. In the common tongue, it meant Liberators. Karil noticed the last subtle difference in their armor. Small trinkets the size of her finger were pinned to their breasts. She recognized them as the shattered pieces of her father's crown.

Rydel approached. "Are you all right?"

"Fine now."

Rydel looked to the elves, with a note of respect. "They saved us again. But the Terma are not done," he said. "You know as well as I, that was only the first. More will be coming, and soon."

She nodded. The elves now stood in a file, all facing her. As one they clapped a hand to their chest, and spoke in unison, "Tel Merahas." Then they took to one knee, their armor rustling in the quiet night.

Her heart welled with pride and sorrow. Every one of them had abandoned everything to protect her, to protect the side of light against the tide of darkness. Her people. Most of them were young, but their youthful faces were far different than two days ago. Whatever softness had once been there had been hammered out. She regretted it all, feeling somehow that it was her fault. Yet such were the times, her father would have said. She swallowed, choking back her emotions. "Twice you have protected me. Words can never express my gratitude for your brave acts, both two days ago, and tonight." She let the words hang in the air. She felt Rydel's presence and knew the gap for their escape was closing, but it was because of these elves she had survived. The elves waited for her command, and she felt the weight of all their fates. "Time is short. I would wish to say more, and though I do not want to I, we must leave now."

"Then we will accompany you," said one, immediately standing.

"We will have your side," said another, a slightly older guard with longer ears and deeper-set eyes, but with equal fervor.

She shook her head firmly. "You all must stay. With Rydel, I can make it past the border. I would ask one more thing of you, as your queen." The words tasted bitter on her tongue, a taste she would gladly spit out for another. Her first order as queen was to strip them of their pride, but she knew she must. "You must forsake your pledge to me until I return. Furthermore, for now, you must wear your normal armor."

They looked hurt and confused.

She pointed to the small trinkets. "I know what it represents to you. You fought with great pride that day, but the honor you hold is not in some trinket upon your breast. Just as the power my father wielded, and your love for him did not derive from the crown he bore. So please, spread the word: take up the normal armament of the guard, and assimilate back into the ranks." And live. She swallowed hard at the command. She knew she was doing it for them, but she also knew many of them might have chosen death, instead of losing their pride. And many of them had died. Yet she would not allow anymore, at least not because of her.

Karil felt Rydel, urging her to leave. She owed them one more thing… "Not far from now, where we stand, I will be back to take the throne, and on that day I will call for you to fight and take back what is rightfully ours." Pride returned to their faces.

"My queen," Rydel pressed. At the same time, Terma guards appeared like shadows from thin air, attacking from every angle, but the Lando charged.

"Sirvas!" they cried as one, cutting a path through the enemy. The dark armored Terma faltered, taken back by the sudden retaliation, but only for a moment, and the tide was quickly turning in favor of the dark elves.

A shout rose, "Run, my queen!"

One elf, the older of the bunch, gripped Rensha's reins in one hand. "Heed your own words. Live, my queen. One day we will see you again, and return the honor that has been stolen from you. I swear to you, we will not see your father, the true king, die in vain." He clasped a fist to heart and dove back into the fray. The Lando bellowed as they were sliced down, but still they fought.

"Karil!" Rydel shouted.

At last, guilt wrenching her, she turned, dashing through the opening they had created for her. Rensha's hooves pounded as she raced into the woods, away from her kingdom. Karil chased the image of Rydel's whipping cloak, heading towards Daerval, with the bloody cries of elves loud in her ears.

The Shadow's Hand

Gray's legs burned as he followed the hermit's cloak through the night. The tree limbs seemed to reach out, lashing at him as a roar cracked through the woods. The forest was a blur as he ran. He skidded to a halt, nearly crashing into Mura. They stood in a small clearing. To his left was a sheer cliff with a view of the vast canopy of the lower woods, far below.

He slumped against a tree, catching his breath. "What's happening? Those things were vergs weren't they?" He shivered at even saying the name. Vergs were monstrous creatures, myths rumored to have lived during the Lieon, but no more than that.

Mura didn't seem to be listening. He moved as if searching for something. "It was here! It has to be," he muttered. He set down a strange scimitar that Gray hadn't seen until now with brown sheath and obsidian-like handle. The hermit's hands grazed the trunk of a silveroot. He tore into the brush at the base of the tree, ripping away clumps of tanglevine. Gray watched in confusion as the hermit's fingers pried into the tree's base, pulling away a perfectly square hunk of wood from the trunk and unveiling a dark cubbyhole.

He stepped forward. "How did you know that was there?"

"Because I created it, a long time ago, and have kept it concealed for a much needed time." Reaching in, Mura extracted a brown bag.

"I will answer all, lad, but this is not the time. Now come forth."

Mura grabbed a handful of the forest floor, and then rubbed the soil between his palms. He then put a hand to Gray's head. The warmth of the man's palm against his temple was comforting. He opened his mouth when a bright light bloomed. It grew as Mura chanted in Elvish. A chill coursed through his body. "What did you do?" he asked. "That was…"

"Magic," said Mura. "It's not much, but it will hide your scent for five days, and buy you time to leave the woods."

"But where will I go?"

"North and stop for nothing. Follow the Silvas River. It will lead you out of the woods and to safety. Once out, get to the town of Lakewood, and I will find you there. I swear it. But you must go now." He picked up the bag and pressed it to Gray's chest. "Here, take this."

"What's this?"

"Some of the answers to your past," said the hermit, "Now, go! There isn't much time." The howls grew louder, emphasizing his words.

He unsheathed Morrowil from his back. "I won't let you fight them alone. I can help."

Abruptly, the woods darkened, and even the silver light from his sword dimmed.

"Go!" Mura shoved him, withdrawing his blade.

Gray startled at a sound like rushing air. A black mist appeared, and then vanished. "What is that?"

"A creature not from this world," Mura said.

Like dark lightning, the black mist leapt from one tree to another and a voice hissed from everywhere at once, "Handle them. Kill the boy and take the sssword."

A figure stepped out from the shadows, head scraping the belly of the bent boughs. Despite uneven shadows, Gray saw teeth like hand-length daggers jutting from a wide mouth.

"Run, boy! Now!"

Gray took a step backwards.

The verg gave a throaty laugh. "You should listen to your master," it said, guttural voice rasping like a saw, as if it were not meant for speech.

"Flee!" Mura yelled.

Something flashed within the dark slits of trees. The shadows materialized, leaping towards him. He dove to the ground, pitching beneath a set of glistening fangs. His sword tip caught the dirt and was ripped from his grip. He turned to see a large black wolf. It turned its massive head, eyeing him with burnished red eyes. Gray's heart hammered as he grasped for his sword. It was nowhere to be seen. He twisted, and in the pocket of his vision he glimpsed the blade. It was several feet behind him, teetering on the cliff's edge.

Slowly, he edged towards it. In the corner of his vision, Mura leapt over the verg's massive swipe, moving with incredible speed. As he looked back, the wolf lunged. Gray reached for his sword. As he gripped the handle, sharp teeth snatched his arm scraping against bare bone. He screamed in pain. Still, he gripped the sword and kicked at the beast, slamming his heel into its muzzle. The wolf didn't budge, its teeth like iron pincers. It snarled and shook, ripping at his flesh. Gray gasped, pain blotting his vision when he saw trunk-like legs pounding towards him.

"No!" Mura cried out.

The verg's huge hand seized Gray's arm and heaved him into the air. He cried out, stretched between the wolf's snarling jaws and the verg's brutish grip. Mura dove, lashing at the verg, lacerating its trunk-like legs with his sword. The verg gave a bestial roar. The earth shuddered as its fist cracked the ground and dirt flew. Gray's body whipped like a wet rag. Through his agony, he felt the wolf's teeth slip. He heard a loud pop and his vision clouded in pain, voice too hoarse to scream.

When his sight cleared, he saw Mura. The hermit was slumped against a cracked tree trunk. The verg eyed the hermit like a child playing with a broken doll. It turned its massive head. Gray closed his eyes, feigning unconsciousness. "The boy is ours," the verg rumbled.

Suddenly, something pressed against his back, digging into the root of his spine. His dagger.

"No, he belongs to her," a voice replied, darker but far less booming than the verg. "She is his keeper." Gray opened his eyes a fraction and saw the wolf. Its pale lips moved, snarling each word. The wolf speaks…

"She does not command us, beast," the verg growled. "We answer only to the Rehass. We are the Shadow's Hand. Flee to your mistress before I crush your bones where you stand."

The wolf's red eyes gleamed. "Perhaps I will bite off your flapping tongue and deliver that instead. Along with the boy's body," the wolf snapped, its snarl rising in intensity. "Give him to me."

"Never," the verg said, its deep growl shaking the ground. Gray's heart slammed inside his own chest. His left hand dangled, painstakingly he inched it closer to his concealed dagger.

"The boy's alive!" the wolf snarled and lunged for his leg.

Gray reached for his dagger, but the verg moved quicker. The beast swiped at the wolf, protecting its bounty. Struck by the mighty fist, the wolf yelped, skidding to the cliff's edge. At the same time, Gray unleashed a cry of rage. Ignoring the stunning pain, he grabbed his hidden dagger. He whipped it around and slammed it into the verg's fist, piercing its thick hide. The verg howled in rage, then flailed. But Gray held on. He sliced down, cutting bone and tendon. The beast roared. With its free hand, the verg gripped him around the waist, and threw him with a grunt.

Gray was ripped from the dagger and he catapulted through the air. He hit the ground, skidding towards the cliff like a pebble across water. His fingers clawed the ground, but it was useless. The last thing he saw was Mura's horrified face as he slipped over the edge and beyond, falling towards a sea of trees.

A Journey Forward

Blinding white flickered across the darkness.

Light… the notion skittered across a distant field of thoughts—each thought like a tiny flame dancing in the darkness of Gray's mind. He drifted back towards slumber and darkness when a voice sounded through the gloom. Wake up! He ignored it, but it spoke again, Sleep is for the weak and the dead.

Am I dead? he asked the voice.

Not yet. Now rise.

Gray let the distant light fill him and his eyes opened to the blinding brightness. Suddenly the fall and all else came back to him in a rush. He gasped as if water filled his lungs and he was drowning. Gradually, his breaths slowed.

With pebbled dirt beneath his cheek, the world appeared as if seen through thick glass. High above, he gazed upon a screen of branches. A canopy. His eyes adjusted to the bright light, and he saw broken branches and a hole in the awning. His mind reeled. How am I alive? He propped himself upon his elbow and his arm burst in a fountain of pain. A jagged gash ran down his left arm. He recalled the scene with the wolf. The wound was peeled back at the surface, looking like gnarled lip, and congealed blood covered the gaping cut. He winced. "I'll have to clean it soon," he voiced aloud, looking around for a stream or nearby brook.

Suddenly, he remembered his sword and fear ran through him. He turned and spotted it beside a nearby tree. Relief flooded him.

He rose to get the blade and throbbing pain wrenched his other shoulder. Gently, he rolled it, and sucked in a sharp breath. It felt detached. He looked around in uncertainty, when a memory flashed. Stumbling to his feet, he hobbled to a thick oak. A strange, familiar calm came over him. At the height of his exhale he rammed his shoulder into the tree's trunk. There was a loud pop and pain bloomed before his eyes, but when it cleared he could move his arm again. He smiled in relief, but knew the hermit had not taught him that.

"Mura," he whispered and memory of the hermit flooded through him. The last image he had was of Mura slumped against a tree.

He moved towards the cliff and placed his hands to the looming mountain of stone and dirt. Mura had told him to escape the woods and quickly. I will do as promised. I can pass through the woods easily enough following the Silvas River. Once he reached the trading city of Lakewood, he would find safety and wait for Mura. Five days before the spell wears off, he reminded himself. Five days until I see Mura again.

Snatching up his sword, he found a nearby stream and rinsed his wound. The clear, crystal water rinsed over the deep cut. As he ignored the pain, a leaf flashed in his mind's eye. He paused curiously when a fish darted among the rock bed, and his stomach growled. When the cut was clean, but in need of a bandage, he made his way back to the clearing, hunting for his bag, but after a while his spirits sank.

"It's gone…"

He leaned against a tree and looked up. There, dangling from a nearby bough, was his bag. A slim smile spread across his face. After nimbly climbing the tree and retrieving his pack, he pulled out the food and bandages. He wrapped his arm, the wound stinging as he tied the cloth snugly. That should do for now, he thought when he finished wrapping his arm, admiring his handiwork.

Famished, he set aside two red apples and a hunk of orange cheese wrapped in waxy cloth. He finished his meal quickly. With the tang of cheese still on his tongue, he wished for more, but already he knew he would have to ration it out if he were to survive. He began to rise when he caught a flash of silver.

Gray reached into his pack and withdrew his hand. A silver pendant glinted in his palm, and he remembered what Mura had said about the pack containing an object from his past. The pendant was divided in parts by lines, and in each part, was a symbol.

The eight symbols of the Great Kingdoms. The hair on his arms stood on end. "There is one missing," he said, remembering the emblem of wind that Mura had shown him in the cabin; and he realized the curious tome the hermit had bestowed upon him was now likely gone forever…

His grip tightened on the pendant and magically the two halves of the metal twisted as if on hinges, and then snapped whole once again. Now four of the symbols were on one side, and four were on the other. He twisted it once again. Now two showed. The pendant's surface glinted.

If the stories were right, the kingdoms held different strengths. Perhaps… He twisted it again, trying to order them from most powerful to least. Aside from wind, sun was the most powerful, so the stories said. Then leaf. Sun, leaf, fire, ice, stone, moon, metal, flesh. Twisting, Gray lost himself to the symbols, until the last one clicked in place. He gave a triumphant smile, revealing the eight symbols of the Great Kingdoms in order of power. Abruptly, all the symbols vanished in a wave of light.

In their place, was the emblem of wind.

The pendant grew hot and he threw it to the ground as a sudden light flared from the pendant, lighting the clearing in a flash of brilliant gold. He approached. It was warm now, no longer hot, and he twisted it once. The glow vanished and all the symbols returned to the way they were. All eight.

He shook his head and laughed aloud. He looked up, as if expecting someone to see what he had just done, but he was alone. The clearing was empty. A small breeze emphasized his solitude. Gray went to put the pendant back in the pack when his hand halted, and he slipped it around his neck, tucking it beneath his shirt.

He strapped his sword to his back then slung his pack over his shoulder, looking towards the early morning sun. With a last glance behind, he moved out of the clearing, into the forest, and onward.

Towards Lakewood, wondering what was around the next bend.

Legends

Vera left the camp and walked east.

Her boots crunched on the dry leaves, peeking out from her dark dress. A modest collar revealed faint green veins on her slender neck and chest. The dress was well fitted, flaunting her perfect curves. A strip cut from the side revealed glimpses of her pale, slender legs. It was something she wouldn't have worn in the Citadel, but she was altogether different now.

Above, the canopy was thick. It was part of the reason hiding from him had been easier, but it made it difficult to tell the time of day. Between the branches she caught hints of the brightening moon.

Her meeting with her companion should be now.

Not far behind, her niux made camp within a small clearing. The contrast between the inviting woods and her cruel, nightmarish beasts almost made her smile.

Two massive vergs, even larger than the rest, were constructing a crude fire, snapping huge limbs from nearby trees. Though fairly intelligent creatures, they looked almost awkward with the act. The beasts ate their meat raw and saw better than most creatures in the night. She had told them to build it without explanation, for she knew the shadows were not only their allies. While they hunted, he also hunted in the darkness. Meanwhile, the others, six saeroks, tall lanky beasts made of raw sinew and thin hair, and four other hulking vergs fought over the remains of their last kill, tearing and shredding into the disgusting carcass of a werebear. She put the noise and commotion of the camp out of her head, dismissing it, when the woods rustled. She stopped.

"You can come out now."

The biggest wolf she had ever seen stalked out of the shadows. It stopped in the middle of her path. "Mistress," it snarled, dark fur ruffling in the wind.

Sitting on its haunches the wolf stared her in the eyes, now of equal height. She knew that her attitude, and the lack of fear she emanated was part of her control over the beast. If she let it waver, she wondered if the creature would attack her, or if they had gone beyond that. So close, she sadistically imagined the creature lunging and she knew its speed. She imagined her neck caught in its vicious teeth, the press of its barbed teeth on her soft skin.

"You're late, my pet," she replied.

The wolf bowed its head lower.

She continued walking and the creature slipped in at her side like a shadow. "Speak, precious, what news of the boy?"

"The boy…" it growled.

"Yes?" she questioned, turning to look. Already, disappointment spiraled through her and it began the moment she sensed Drefah's presence. The boy was not here and neither was the sword, and that was all that mattered. All else was worthless news.

Suddenly the forest shifted, and a wind tore through the woods, wracking the trees and howling. If Vera had a pulse, it would have quickened. She sensed Drefah's fear as well, watching the hackles rise on its massive body. "What is that foul smell?" the wolf asked.

She eyed the woods calculatingly. "It's him."

"Who?"

The muscles in her jaw twitched. "Kail. The legend."

Drefah had no idea who she spoke of, but his snarl heightened. He took her words seriously, as he should. The frightening bay of wind grew louder. Though in reality, it wasn't the sound, but the feel of the wind. It felt powerful. More powerful than all of them. Her pet's snarl grated her nerves, and the mere thought of him vexed her.

Vera turned and saw the same fear echoing through the camp

behind her. Vergs stiffened and saeroks loped, climbing trees as they watched the woods in fright. It bothered her that she had weeded out every single coward from the bunch and still they trembled like barn mice at his presence. Granted, he had killed four of them already. Not to mention, their fear was instilled in their blood, something born in the Great War, but it still annoyed her, like a sharp splinter she couldn't pry from beneath her skin.

"Tell me how you lost the boy," she said.

"A Nameless and its niux, under orders of the Great One, tried to steal the boy. But in the process, the boy was flung over the side of a great cliff. The fall would have killed any human. I searched, but found nothing, not even a scrap of his scent." The wolf sounded especially irritated about the last part. Its large ears wilted as it spoke, as if it had failed her, and it had, though not entirely.

"It is not your fault, my pet," she said softly. It seemed appropriate, and her hand absently grazed its waist-height black fur. "They hid his smell with the spark. The old man did. It was nothing you could do." She scooped a handful of dirt and let it fall to the ground. Simple magic, she thought with a slim, but impressed smile. She looked up, glimpsing the bright moon through the canopy. "I underestimated them, this time. The one who cast the spell was not from this land. I should have anticipated that the prophecy did not reach the Great One's ears only. I had heard whisper of a prophet from Eldas, a human-blooded cur, but dismissed it as rumor. The man was likely sent as his guardian from beyond the black gates with the knowledge of the prophecy." She did not mention that she had heard that the prophet was the queen, and her death a timely, fortunate part of the Great One's ultimate plan. Sometimes she wondered if his plans were the result of coincidence or much more.

The wolf growled in affirmation. "It is as you say. The old man did not move like any human I have seen. He might be elf blood."

Vera shrugged. "Elves, humans, it does not matter. The man's power is minimal, but his knowledge is what I fear. We must assume now that he knows everything about the power of the sword and the boy."

"But, mistress, the boy is dead."

"No," she hissed. It was the first time emotion had entered her voice and the wolf flinched under her hand. "The boy is alive. He will not die until I twist the blade in him with my own hands." Her fingers clenched, grasping his fur. "I want to feel my dagger slide into his heart as I watch the life vanish from his eyes."

"Why do you hate him? He is a mere human," the wolf said.

She turned to the massive wolf, her violet eyes flashing dangerously. "I don't. He was everything in the world to me once."

"And now?"

"Now he simply stands between me and the sword," she stated matter-of-factly. "And the sword will be mine." Nothing would deprive her of that. Not a fall, or the Great One, not legends. Not even you Kirin. She turned with a wicked smile. "Do not fret, my pet. I know where he is heading, and the boy does not know the darkness of what he holds. We shall see him soon."

The wind howled, and this time she laughed, answering the legend's call, power filled her voice, overwhelming the sound of the wind.

Strange Paths

Gray watched the bright woods as if it were a cutpurse or murderer. In the distance, he heard the gurgle of the Silvas River, often called the Sil, reassuring him of his path. Something glinted ahead.

As he turned the bend, he saw a moss-covered stone spiraling heavenward. Could it be? He wondered, remembering the stories of the watchtowers of old.

Mura had told him of ancient towers that were placed all over Daerval in order to watch, night and day, for The Return. The idea of an ancient watchtower made his heart quicken. A time not long after the Ronin walked the earth, he thought. It was followed by the fearful question. And do they again?

Gray stone jutted from the earth, touching the forest's high canopy. Moss, roots, and tanglevines covered its surface.

He neared in wonder. Throwing off his pack, he grabbed hold of the nearest tanglevine, tearing it from the statue's face. He worked quickly and soon enough, he pried the last gnarled vine from the stone. He wiped his damp brow and took a step back.

Five spires shot from the ground. Each were approximately the same size, except for the fifth one, which was shorter and stouter. He made out the wrinkled grooves at the knuckles and the slender curvature of veins as thick as his own forearm.

"A hand the size of a giant," he whispered in astonishment.

His tired legs wobbled beneath him, and he decided this was as good a place as any to stop. After a quick lunch beneath the shade of the hand, he continued. He left the statue, eyeing the relic one last time as he turned the bend. Gray halted. Straight ahead, the woods forked into two paths. Nothing he remembered from Mura's tales mentioned the road splitting.

Reaching the split, he slowed. The familiar sound of the Sil was gone. Running back, he searched for the statue, but it was nowhere, as if the woods had shifted, and panic roiled through him.

He was lost.

Overhead, thunder cracked, promising a storm to shake the land.

* * *

Rain came in sheets, cleaving the canopy, and falling on Gray's makeshift shelter.

He had made camp beneath a marmon tree. Mura always called marmons the safe haven for the wayward traveler, for the hollow trunk and awning-like branches was a perfect shelter.

Cold and hungry, he pulled flint from his pack and sparked it against a stone, but with no luck. He eyed his sword at his side. The blade glinted through the cloth bundle. Curious, he grabbed it and struck the flint against the flat of the sword. Sparks flew, lighting the tinder. He laughed in success and saw the blade had not even a scratch.

Gnawing on a hunk of bread, Gray eyed the two trails, waiting to be chosen. He looked away, stoking the fire with a stick. He knew he should sleep, but he wasn't tired. Instead, the fire of purpose burned in his gut. At last, he walked into the downpour to stand before the two trails. One path was shrouded in cobwebs, the other paved with green moss.

"Often what is darkest is that which pretends to be light," he quoted, remembering the words from the one of the tales of the Ronin. Mura told him people from beyond the forest said the Lost Woods were alive; that it had a mind of its own. But the woods had never betrayed him before.

The pendant grew warm. He pulled it from his shirt and it glowed silver. Curious, he stepped forward, lighting both paths in a silver tint. Rain soaked his hair and skin. He closed his eyes and held the pendant before him, following a strange instinct.

When he opened his eyes the pendant's leather thong was parallel to the ground, as if pulled by a fierce wind towards the darker path. In wonder, he took a step toward the cobwebbed trail. The pendant pulsed as if in agreement. With a laugh of triumph, he snuffed his campfire, strapped on his sword and pack, and then plunged into the waiting trail.

Darkness enveloped him. What he could see, he almost wished he couldn't. Enormous webs hung from tree to tree, blending with the mist, from which spiders clung, each bigger than his fist. They scuttled as he passed, but he continued. At last, shreds of light pierced the darkness and he realized that night had turned to morning.

The day wore on, the light faded again. With the return of night, the spiders crawled from the trees, watching him with red eyes. Twice, a thick web blocked his path and he pulled his blade free, cutting it down. Once, a spider fell upon his shoulder and he knocked it free, running until his legs burned, but still he jumped when a branch brushed his shoulder. He distracted himself by cutting a notch on his leather belt, marking the passing days. Two days, he counted now, starting from the day he fell from the cliff. He had to keep track of time. Five days until the spell wears off, he reminded himself. Which means, I only have three more to make it out of the woods. He marched through mist, web, and vine. As he walked, his wound itched fiercely. He wanted to check it. It's healing, something told him, and he trusted it.

Gray moved as if he could see Lakewood around the bend. Only when his legs could move no more, he stopped; but only to kindle a quick fire for a few short hours of sleep. In the light of the small fire, he nibbled on a small hunk of cheese, or sliver of dried meat; but his rations dwindled quickly, and each time his gut felt more empty than last. Worst of all, he dreaded sleep and the inevitable nightmares.

Always his dreams involved Mura. Most times he was back in the clearing where he had left the hermit. Mura would cry out, and each time Gray would turn and flee. Other times, he would see the misshapen image of Mura's head on a pike, eyes glazed in horror. Being awake was not much better.

Several times, a strange mist rose from the soil. It was so thick he could barely breathe, and he would scramble off the trail into the underbrush. Sword clutched to his chest, he listened to animal-like howls and cries. At last, exhaustion overtook him, and he slept restlessly until the mist of morning announced the dawn.

Gray awoke from one of those mornings. It was a particularly frightening night with snarls that sounded in his ear. It was still raining and he felt as if his clothes were now permanently attached to his soaked skin. Still groggy, he glanced down. Barely an arms-length away, imprinted in the mud was a head-sized cloven hoof-print. He tensed, peering through the foliage. Overhead, thunder cracked. It shook the woods like the rumble of a giant. He glanced to his leather belt.

Five notches, he realized, today will make the sixth. He was out of time. A shiver traced his spine. What if I'm on the wrong path? What if I've wasted all this time? He hadn't heard a murmur of the Sil either, not once, and that was his only way out. He shook his head and cast the thoughts aside. No, he would trust the pendant.

More thunder roiled above, sounding closer. Gray looked up. Another storm was brewing, and something told him, this would be far worse than all the others. He unsheathed the sword from his back and rose, moving forward.

Into the thickening mist.

The Hawk

Karil rubbed her hands before the red flames. They made camp on the desert, just outside a ruined town. The nearby trees cast shadows on the flat land. She watched them out of the corner of her eye, reassuring herself that they were not creatures standing still in the night.

"Find anything?" she asked, noticing Rydel had slipped into the camp like a shadow and now stood beside a nearby tree. The elf threw a cloth bundle on the ground and she unfolded it.

Rydel held up a small root. "This'll be enough for me. The rest is yours."

She eyed several shriveled roots the color of dirt, and a green head of leaves. Grabbing a long root, she nibbled on it. It was bitter, nothing like she had ever tasted in Farhaven. She thought of the farms of Eldas. What she wouldn't give for a lignin fruit, head-sized melons that hung from small trees or the crisp tang of moonroots plucked on the twelfth night of every moon. She took another bite. At least it was edible. It had been two fortnights since they had left Eldas and her heart panged with thoughts of her home.

"What's bothering you?" Rydel asked.

"Nothing."

"It is a strange thing when you lie," he said. "It is truly not elvin."

She said nothing, staring into the flames as she ate.

"I understand your sorrow," he said softly.

"Do you? Or is caring for those you loved simply my human side as well?" She regretted the words immediately. It wasn't Rydel's fault. But sourness gnawed at her insides like a poison.

The elf looked pained. "I did not mean to offend. I loved your father, too."

She shook her head, feeling a fool, and touched his arm. "I know you did. Forgive me."

"By tomorrow, we will see Lakewood, and your uncle," he said, changing the subject.

The thought lifted her spirits. For a moment, she wondered how different Mura would appear after two years outside the realm of magic. It was said that ten years within Farhaven was the equivalent of one year within Daerval. "And even more pressing, we will finally see the boy of prophecy," she said. "My mother was right, as always. I was forced beyond the Gates. Now I must continue to follow her words. I must watch over the boy, and ensure his survival."

"And how will you do that?" Rydel asked. "We've seen the destruction the enemy has wrought. He may already be in danger."

Karil couldn't deny the truth of that. Upon their journey, they had come across barren towns, and ruined villages, each more horrifying than the last. Fear for the boy's safety wormed its way beneath her skin like a deep cold.

Suddenly there was a disturbance in her ka. Rydel turned, seeing it in the darkness before she could. The air distorted with the flutter of wings. Come, she beckoned in her thoughts.

From out of the darkness, a hawk appeared, landing upon her pack. It was a beautiful creature, even in the dim light, large with golden plumage, slightly ruffled by its sudden change in course. It eyed her regally.

"Sa mira, kin ha elvia su nivia," she whispered, enjoying the feel of her language as it flowed across her tongue. At her words, the bird leapt into the air and landed upon her arm. Its sharp claws gripped her harmlessly. She smiled and the hawk tilted its head, listening attentively. She touched the bird's side calmly, closing her eyes. Save the boy, she implored. Watch over him. But aloud she voiced, "Tervias su unvas. Remlar uvar hil."

The bird twisted its head, as if in acknowledgement and then flew off.

"At least now we will have eyes on him," she answered, watching the creature fly away until it was obscured by the dark night. Attuned to the spark, the creature knew her words. But it was still the bird's choice to follow her. The bird had answered simply. It would obey her command unto death.

"Get some rest, my queen," Rydel said.

"I will take first watch," she replied, eyeing the nearby trees again. When Rydel looked ready to argue, she raised a brow. "That's an order." The elf grumbled, and settled beneath his dark green blanket, asleep in moments, sleeping dreamlessly as full elves did. The notion of dreams gave Karil a shiver. Her watch was not wholly altruistic. She feared her dreams and would do anything to stave them off for as long as she could. She huddled closer to the red flames that warded off the cold night. With thoughts of the boy and her uncle, she looked south, praying to see Lakewood soon.

The Gathering Dark

Thick plumes of smoke obscured the red moon. The screams had finally settled.

Vera had traveled quickly to make it here. The message had been clear. Come or die. And she valued her life, greatly. It was perhaps the only thing she did value anymore.

She paused outside the inn, feeling the warm glow of the common room on her back. She looked down. The once-thick snow was now trampled flat by thousands of cloven hooves and stained crimson. Her fur-lined coat was covered in blood as well. She threw the coat to the snow, embracing the cold, and stepped to the side, out of the light.

Vergs and saeroks stalked past, joining the swelling army. Her cool glare panned up, and even she had trouble keeping her features smooth.

Wreathed in shadows, the nine sat on deathless steeds. Beasts that made Drefah look tame. Those dead eyes were rimmed in red that writhed with maggots, and hides as black as a moonless night. The beasts appeared as if crudely put together, patches of flesh missing from the animal's torsos, exposing their white ribs. Steam flared from their nostrils and their hooves beat against the ground with power.

The Kage.

"Is it done?" the leader asked, the closest of the nine. His voice was like a claw raking inside her ear.

"Yes," Vera answered. "All the inhabitants of Tir Re' Dol are dead, except for the one. I gave him the message and he will relay it. You can be sure of that." She couldn't help but smile. With the fear she had inspired in him, their pawn would ride until his eyes burned and the horse fell beneath him. "We left him a beast to ride, but it will take him some time until he alerts the rest of Daerval."

"Good," said the nightmare. "Then it is finished."

"However," she paused. The nightmare turned again, and she almost regretted her words. Still her driving need for knowledge overrode her better judgment. Her voice gained strength. "What's the point? Why warn the prey before the kill?"

A dark hood hid its features, but she felt as if the nightmare was smiling, as if it knew her hunger for knowledge. It squared to her. The jutting spike on its metal pauldron—differentiating it from the other eight of its kind—was the length of her whole arm. Its black cloak wavered as it took a step forward, red snow crunching beneath its plated boot. It took another, and still she remained motionless, until it stood towering head and shoulders over her. She looked into the nightmare's hood, but saw only darkness. Still she knew that arrogant smile was there.

"Do you fear me?" It asked calmly.

"Yes," she replied. Her voice was smoother than she anticipated, but the words stung. There was no use lying. She didn't know what the other eight Kage would do, and it was almost certain death, but she wouldn't let him lay a hand on her.

"Not nearly enough."

She swallowed. "You didn't answer my question."

It laughed, or what she hoped was laughter. "It will do them no good. It is the Great One's wish that they know their demise. A week is no matter. Besides, it will take us several days here. We have things to do still," it said, and she knew that smile turned wicked. "There are still several towns within the mountains to destroy before we finish the southern lands."

"But why? They will know of your arrival, and if they have any wits about them, they'll flee." She was careful of her tone, trying not to bite off each word. The fools. He'll slip right through their fingers.

"Fleeing serves no purpose without the key. And if they flee with it? Then they run right into our hands."

Vera released a hidden breath as it turned its back; at the same time, she glimpsed its true features and saw merciless scarlet eyes. She sunk to one knee, pressing a fist to the snow. Head bowed, she was glad they could not see her teeth grind in fury. "Am I done?" she asked.

The nightmare turned and its cloak, edged in blood, flung behind him.

"Burn it all, than you may take your leave."

She coiled with restrained lust. Her hands rose at her sides, a pale glow surrounding them and she shook with power. She threw them to the sky and the inn ignited, sending flares into the night air. She unleashed a fierce cry, and fire roared to life, consuming all it touched.

At her feet, a man held a small girl. She watched the two corpses burn. Holes were torn through their abdomens. Such a shame. The fool girl and her father would have lived, if only for a while longer, had they not run to her for help. The thought sparked an idea and she knew how to get Kirin. Oh, Kirin, your luck has run out. Soon you will be leaving the safety of the woods and I will be waiting. The sword and its power will be mine.

She walked through the huge gate, flames hot on her back. Ahead, her niux waited. To the east, she spotted the tail of the dark army, leaving the city as well, roving towards its next kill. Vera's boots left red prints in the fresh snow, as she approached her niux.

"We follow the Kagehass?" A verg rumbled, watching the dark caravan.

Drefah growled. Aside from her pet, none were allowed to speak. The huge leathery skinned creature knew it too. At any other time she would cut its tongue from its mouth, but instead she answered, "We do not." The beasts trundled. To disobey the Kage was a fate worse than death.

"Then where to, mistress?" A saerok rasped. It stood on the balls of its feet in the thick snow. Standing several feet taller than her, its patchy fur ruffled in the wind.

"We go south," she told her dark army, "towards Lakewood, and towards the sword."

A Fire Lit Within

Gray's pulse beat in time with the flickering flames. The fire raged before his closed lids, pushing back the shadows in the quiet glade.

Cross-legged on the ground, the leaf sat in his mind's eye, but it was not what he sought. A swirling ball of air flashed. He reached for it, but it retreated, racing away. This time he didn't let it go. Eyes clenched, he followed it, pushing into his consciousness. The ball of air was just beyond his reach. He reached out. Pain shot through his limbs as he ran into a wall. His concentration wavered, but he held on, bashing against the wall. At last, it shattered. His eyes opened, returning to the real world. His heart raced as he took in his surroundings.

Before him, the fire still burned. Shadows danced in the trees, as if waiting to move into his small camp. But everything seemed different. His world was crisper, sharper.

Slowly, he stood, confused but calm. He was soaked in sweat. It rolled down his limbs as he reached for his sword that stuck upright. He gripped the handle. It had never felt more right.

He inhaled deeply. With two breaths, he gained control of his breathing, something he had never done before, but somehow knew he could. Still, his heart beat wildly. There was nothing but his body and the sword.

Heron Rises on One Leg, a voice whispered, and the sword parried an unseen blow. Without slowing, he twisted the blade, disarming the shadow opponent, and striking. Crane's Beak. Before the strike was finished, his left leg circled, raising a fan of dirt as he swept the opponent's legs. Ten Moon. He switched his grip stabbing behind. His muscles flexed in the last moment, power resonating through the flashing blade as the sword snapped to a halt. Setting Sun. With a cry, he spun, pivoting in a full-circle and cutting down a charge of unseen foes. Still, he was moving. Wind Dances in the Reeds. With the momentum of the spin, he dove into a fluid roll, cutting left and right at the enemy's legs. Tempest's Fury. Gray unleashed a cry as he pounded his feet against the ground, and sprung backwards. He flipped, head over heels. His back arched as he landed on his feet, and drove the sword down with all his might, and slammed it into the ground.

His breath challenged the fire's crackle. Again, he stilled it in a matter of seconds. His limbs shook, but inside he was calm. He eyed his camp and saw his pack showered in dirt, and the ground torn up.

His hand trembled, but not in fear. "My memory is coming back."

Unwinding his bandaged arm, he saw only smooth skin. The wound had healed.

Cautiously, he reached into his mind. The swirling ball of air came forth and his world expanded. Suddenly, he smelled a rabbit as it raced down a game trail. No. He felt it. He reached out and his mind shifted.

He sniffed the air, wet nose twitching as he smelled for danger. Nothing. He continued, moving through the grass, searching for tender stalks. He hopped closer, nibbling at a leaf, eyes flitting all the while. Suddenly, he froze. His muscles stiffened, fur ruffling from a sudden wind. His heart hammered faster. DANGER. The sensation flooded him. He leapt, pounding through the brush. SAFETY. AHEAD. The words were short and simple. Feelings, not whole, concrete thoughts. His heart beat harder and he saw the tangle of brush, taking a final leap and—

Gray gasped loudly, breaking from his trance and staggering backwards. He reached for his sword, looking up and behind him. He clutched his racing heart. His heart. "What was that? It's as if I was dying…"

There was a fluttering sound and he turned. Perched upon a branch, was a hawk. Its head swiveled and he followed its gaze. Upon the stone, beside the fire, was the carcass of a rabbit and his hunger surged. "Is that for me?" the hawk tilted its head. "All I've had to eat is dried meat and cheese, you have no idea how hungry I am." A few minutes over the flame and… He reached out a hand and touched the rabbit's soft fur, when a flash of pain ran through him. He leapt back as if stung. His hand appeared unscathed, and yet it felt as if he had just put it to the flames.

"I had its sight, smell, and feelings ripped from me as you caught it," he said. "I must still feel its pain." He shook his head, turning. "It's all yours. I'm not as hungry as I thought. Go on." The hawk seemed to understand and swooped in, tearing up the small animal.

He turned his head, unable to watch, and then sat down on a nearby rock, staring into the flames. He wished Mura were here. He glanced sidelong at the hawk as it ate. "I suppose you don't know what's happening do you?" The hawk finished its meal and was now cleaning itself, watching him. He marveled, wondering why the bird still stayed. "Perhaps you're lost like me," he mused, and then paused. "You need a name. How about Maris? He's one of the Ronin. My favorite, aside from Kail of course. He was quick and sharp too, not to mention the most unpredictable of the bunch. Sounds like you, right?"

The bird ruffled its brown and gold-tinged feathers.

"No? Well, how about Motri? I had… something named that once when I was younger, I think," he said with a half-hearted smile. The bird squawked, louder this time and unexpectedly flew closer, alighting upon the pommel of his sword. Gray's smile deepened. He took it for agreement. "Good, then it's settled! Motri it is."

Motri squawked again. He laughed when suddenly the bird gave a fierce cry, and flapped its wings. "What is it?" Motri continued to flap his wings, and then took off in a flash of feathers. "What did I say?" he whispered, and then looked up and froze.

A figure stood in the darkness. In its hand a black blade gleamed.

Gray's own sword stood upright, paces in front of him. Two steps, he calculated, heart pounding. His vision flickered up to the figure. It hadn't moved. It looked like just another shadow, but it was surely there. I can reach it, he thought, eyes rooted on his sword. He looked straight into the dark outline and lunged. A flurry of wind rushed over him. The figure stood, an arm's length away, spanning the gap in the blink of an eye. The man towered, shrouded in a frayed cloak, face hidden by a dark cowl. Fear roiled through Gray.

"Let go," the man ordered in a deep rasp.

Gray shivered, but held onto the sword. "Who are you?"

"I won't ask again. Let go."

"No. Not until you tell me who you are." The man gripped his wrist. Gray pulled at the sword and a tremor of pain shot through him. He cried, falling to his knees. Something beckoned inside his mind. The swirling ball of air. He let it come. Tempest's Fury, it whispered, filling him with power and confidence. He rose.

"Stay down," the man seethed.

Gray's body was smashed to the earth by an invisible force, his breath forced from his lungs. He tried to rise, but his whole body felt coated in stone. He saw wisps of wind. They layered his body, flowing over his limbs. "What is this?" he cursed.

Calmly, the cloaked man reached for Gray's sword and gasped. The man's arm shook as he pulled the blade from the ground. "You're a child playing with something you don't understand. Something you can't even begin to understand." The man ran two fingers along the blade's surface. Gray watched in wonder as the sword changed. Darkness flowed over the blade. The cloaked man knelt before his face and the blade's point flashed before his eyes. "Master the sword. Do not let it master you."

"Who are you?" Gray whispered.

The man stood silently, and within his hood, Gray glimpsed a flicker of color. Scarlet red eyes. With a gust of wind, white clouds swirled and the man vanished, and Gray's bonds fell. Shaken, he rose to his feet and eyed the woods. He wiped his cheek, feeling a thin line of blood.

She's coming, the wind hissed. Gray twisted as leaves crunched in the near distance.

Kirin

"Kirin…" the whisper, sifted through the glade. Gray tried to track its origin. He glanced to the sword. It had returned to its normal silvery sheen. He snatched it, clutching it in both hands. There was a rustle and he twisted.

There, standing at the edge of the woods, was a woman.

She had a slender frame, and wore a black dress that more than hinted at her lean body. She stood coolly. His eyes panned up, taking in her raven black hair and then her face. She was beautiful.

"Hello, Kirin." Her voice was as familiar as a lover.

Gray shook his head and stepped back. "I'm sorry. Do I know you?" He gripped his sword tighter.

"You don't remember me?"

He searched her face. "I'm sorry," he admitted at last. "How do I know you?"

She stepped closer. Gray raised his sword and its sheen flared bright for a moment. "Really, Kirin? You would harm me? Have you changed that much?"

Danger, a voice warned. "Stay back," he said, more bluntly.

She bit her bottom lip. "I'm not armed. See for yourself." She turned full circle, showing off her perfect curves. The dress was even more form fitting in the back. "No? Fine then. You always were stubborn." Confidently, she reached down and pulled back her skirt to expose her thigh and its flawless pale skin, higher and higher.

"Enough!" he shouted at last, throwing out a hand, then more calmly, "Just… stay there."

She looked up, dropping the skirt. "I'm not armed, Kirin," she said. "And you should know I would never hurt you."

The simple name struck a chord. "Why do you keep calling me that? That's not my name."

"I see. What do you call yourself now then?"

"My name is Gray."

"Interesting." Again, she said the words as if he were playing a game. It was infuriating.

"And yours?" he asked.

"Vera," she replied. "As always."

He shrugged. "Sorry, it doesn't ring any bells. Your face is familiar, that much I'll admit."

"If my face is familiar, I'm curious why your eyes are spending so much time on the rest of me."

"What do you want?" he asked, changing the subject and raising his sword.

Vera took a step forward, slowly, assuredly, and then another. "To talk," she said. He followed the fluid sway of her hips. She took another step, and the tip of his sword pressed against her pale throat. A pinpoint of blood formed. He hesitated and Vera pressed the sword away. "See? That's not so bad."

"Who are you?"

"Who are you is the better question?" Vera said. "What happened to your memory?"

"I… I lost it."

"Curious… I wonder how… I suppose you don't remember that as well?"

He shook his head. "Only bits and pieces. It happened several years ago."

"I see," Vera said. "Well then, I'm a friend of yours from another life. We were very close in fact." Truth rang in her voice. She knew about him.

"How close?"

She smiled with a light in her eyes. "Very."

He swallowed. "You've still yet to prove anything. Do not think I'll trust you blindly. I've lost my memories, not my mind."

She laughed and it stirred his blood. "Kirin's fire still burns within you it seems." She approached and snatched his wrist, too fast for him to react. But he didn't retract. Instead, he watched as she twisted his hand in her cold fingers and pulled back his sleeve to expose his black marking. She grabbed her own sleeve and pulled it back. A black insignia was scrawled across her wrist. It was the same mark. "Do you trust me now?" she asked.

A vision filled his mind. A woman stood in a courtyard of green and he stood beside her while others trained. The woman turned to look at him. It was her. "I remember," he whispered and gripped her arm. "Why are you here? This place is not safe."

"That's sweet, Kirin, but I'm afraid you're the one in need of saving. Surely you know what tracks you." She scanned his little camp, his makeshift fire, its flames now sputtering, and his pack. "He was here, not long ago, wasn't he?" A sudden fire lit her voice, and the sputtering flames roared.

"Who?"

Vera turned on him, eyes venomous. "Don't play with me, Kirin." She snatched his shirt with surprising strength. The fire snapped and popped and her eyes burned, reflecting its intensity. "Tell me," she seethed, "he was here wasn't he?"

Gray pushed away. "He was, but he's gone now. Long gone."

"I'm sorry," she said breathless. "I shouldn't have done that. I…" she looked up and pain roiled in her eyes. Such pain… he wanted suddenly to hold her. He settled for taking her arm and helping her to sit on a nearby rock. Still, he kept his distance. "You see," she began, "He has taken much from me. From all of us, and though I know I cannot face him myself, I would give everything I have to see him pay for what he has done."

"What has he done? Who is he?" Gray questioned.

"Kail," she whispered. Gray's mouth went dry. "So you know who he is?"

"Yes."

"He has many names," she said, eyeing the woods. "The blightseeker, the cursed one, but of course most commonly… the wanderer, not to mention, the rightful bearer of Morrowil, the sword you now hold. Of course some say he lost his mind when a loved one died, or that his power grew too much to handle, or that the bloodshed of the Lieon took its toll. But the real truth is that the blade in your hand is the grand sword, an object of horrible power that tainted him. It is the reason he is now mad. That blade is the destroyer of men, and it will destroy you too."

Gray looked down at the blade, torn between sheathing it and keeping it close at hand. "You still haven't answered what you are doing here."

"It's a long story," she said.

"I have time."

She rose and circled him as she spoke. "Once I heard you'd left the Citadel and crossed Death's Gate I couldn't believe it. I was hurt, but I needed to know what happened. I talked to the guards at the gates and a few gave accounts of a man bearing your description, and carrying a strange sword. That very night, as I was walking back to the Citadel, an attempt was made on my life. I survived, but the next day I found that the guards I'd talked to had been killed." She breathed a heavy sigh. Gray felt her breath at the nape of his neck. "Naturally, I knew I needed to find out more about that sword. Researching in the old libraries was purely forbidden, but I had to know. And that's when I found out it was Kail's. He killed all those who saw the blade. He needs it to fulfill the Return and destroy the world as he tried to do long ago." She paused, her face a breath away from his. "Don't you see? As long as you hold that blade, you won't be safe. I... I don't want to even imagine what he would do to the bearer of his sword. I knew he would hunt you down, and that's why I had to find you first."

Gray nodded slowly, it all made sense. My past... he thought, pulse racing. Vera slowly ran a finger down his arm towards his sword. His eyes focused on her hand. But one thing didn't make sense. "He already did find me. You said he would kill me as soon as he saw me. He didn't."

"I was going to ask that myself. How did you survive?"

"He warned me and then left. There was nothing more to it. Your story doesn't add up, Vera."

Vera sighed as if he were daft. "Is that so? Well, I guess all men need to be told where to put their feet on occasion in order to stop them from tripping over themselves. Answer me this, when he came to you, did he grab the sword?"

"Yes," said Gray. "But he gave it back."

"And when he grabbed it, did it cause him pain?"

"It did," he answered slower, curious.

"You see? He cannot simply kill you and take the sword."

"What do you mean?"

"It is in the prophecy, Kirin," she said. "Once the sword chooses a new bearer, the old owner must wait for the sword to ascend, but once the sword turns, any can bind their soul to its purpose. Until that time, all but the true bearer will be pained by its touch," she explained. "In this phase, Kail cannot wield it. Instead, he waits for you to turn the blade before he can grasp it once again."

Suddenly something rustled in the brush. The woods abruptly darkened. The fire sputtered dying in a rush.

"They're coming," she said.

"Who's coming?"

"Those who follow Kail, the ones I came to protect you from. This is not something you can face alone," she said. "There are so many…"

"The town of Lakewood is not far," he said, "You should run now."

"You don't understand!"

"I'm not leaving you," he answered, when a sliver of darkness crept along the blade. Master the sword, the words echoed in his head.

"Damn you and your stubborn pride," she cursed. "You haven't changed at all. So be it. Together, then." Strange pink light filled her palms. She tilted back her head, as if letting the power consume her. Faint veins in her neck glowed green. She stood beside him, facing the woods. "Last chance," she offered.

"Like I said, I'm not going anywhere." Gray watched as a darkness slunk along the ground, nearing until it was almost upon them. It reached for his boot. He stepped back quickly, but before he could, the darkness shrieked. He looked to his sword in surprise. The darkness is afraid of the blade's light, he realized. The blade roared, as if in response, its silver luminescence pushing back the darkness. He looked at Vera. The darkness avoided her all together.

It moved away, crawling up the trees, and it turned the leaves to black ash with a sizzling hiss. Gray swallowed hard. Vera's eyes didn't even flicker.

Vergs stepped out of the woods, and saeroks stalked behind. Just like the stories, they were covered in sparse fur and loped on all fours. They rose onto two legs, standing twice as tall as him upon the balls of their clawed feet, as if mocking a human's posture. With mangy skin and blotchy patches of fur, they looked like misshapen wolves, while their faces bore a terrifying foxlike semblance. The saeroks crooked their heads as one, sharp snouts sniffing the cold air. Gray swallowed again as their lips parted, revealing rows of bristling teeth slavering with ravenous hunger. Thick-hided monstrous vergs, their steps rattling the earth, lurched out of the woods, a steady stream. They were completely surrounded. Abruptly, the vergs laughed. Saeroks echoed their nightmarish brethren, and the sound blended together in a blood-chilling chorus. Gray saw an opening, and charged with a cry. Words flared before his mind and power filled his limbs. Quenching the Fire.

He cut into a saerok, severing claws as it attempted to parry his mighty blow. The blade cut with liquid ease. The saerok cried out, and its jaws flared wide. A roar like fired sounded, and a seething ball of black hurtled over his shoulder. It smashed into the creature before him, tearing it apart.

Gray saw Vera in the corner of his vision as a verg swiped at him. Fear fueled his limbs, and he rolled between its legs hacking left and right. It howled in pain. A saerok appeared before him, lashing out. Its swipe caught his shoulder and he rolled aside. Gray lost himself in the movements. A voice whispered. Trimming the Stalks, meets Wind Dances in the Reeds, flowing into Tempest Fury. Vera fought by his side. Beasts fell before her fiery black bolts, even quicker than his sword. What was more, he could swear in his flickering glances that the beasts looked shocked as she cut them down—it seemed the only reason they weren't dead. Gray dove beneath a strike when a cry sounded beside him.

Vera.

She clutched her chest. The menacing dark power that surrounded her quickly dimmed. Saeroks and vergs descended upon her.

He shouted and ran towards her.

"No!" she cried, thrusting out a hand, "Run, Gray! Run you fool!"

The words sounded all too familiar. Gray stopped, paralyzed by the words. No! Not again! He dashed towards Vera, heedless of the corpses that littered the ground.

A saerok jumped before him, blocking his way, and he cut, but the beast grabbed for his sword in one powerful hand. Gray pulled with all his might, slicing its hand. The creature cried out, but two more saeroks joined it, falling in at its side. There are too many. It was the voice of a warrior who knew an unwinnable battle.

"Run," a saerok said mockingly as blood poured from its wound. Other saeroks and vergs were still coming out of the woods. They approached in a slow, ominous death-stalk. Gray cursed loudly, his mind filled with rage.

Finally he turned, and tore through the woods. He heard the breath of saeroks on his heels and the crash of brush behind him, and he ran faster. He dared not look back as he jumped over root and vine, tearing heedlessly through the shrouded forest.

At last, he glimpsed a light like a beacon through the trees.

Lakewood.

A Festival

The light of the town was lurid in Gray's vision as he ran, nearing the stone gate. Exhausted, he fell to his knees. "Someone help!" he bellowed and pounded on the gate.

He glanced over his shoulder, flinching, expecting to see beasts hurtling out of the night and across the stretch of earth—but there was nothing. The creatures that had been scraping on his heels were nowhere to be seen. He paused, as his breath came quick and hard. Suddenly, he heard sounds and lights danced, bobbing up and down upon the rampart. In the center of the door, a slot scraped open. A helmeted eye peered out. "Quick, I need help! Someone's hurt!" The slot slammed shut. His fists clenched and he shouted, "What's wrong with you? Why will you not help?"

Suddenly from behind, he heard the clop of hooves on the soft dirt. He twisted, half expecting to see the monsters. Instead, he saw an orange light in the darkness. He hid behind a nearby rock as the light approached, resolving itself into a cart. A skinny man, wearing the simple garb of a merchant sat in the driver's seat. Who else would attempt to enter at this time of night? Gray wondered. The cart full of hay rolled closer. The merchant stopped before the door. The slot slid open again.

"Who is it?" a voice called.

"It's me, open the door!" the merchant ordered.

"Show me the sign!"

The merchant grumbled and pulled back his sleeve, exposing his forearm, showing the guard something Gray couldn't see. This was his chance. Gray slid from his hiding place. He dashed towards the cart, staying low and quiet. The merchant's back was still turned and he dove into the mountain of hay, wriggling and burying himself deep. There was a scraping sound. The gate slid open. Through the hay and the wooden slats of the cart, he saw a soldier in leather and mail approach.

"Did you see a young man?" the guard questioned gruffly.

"Man? I saw no one," the merchant replied. "What are you talking about?"

Gray was right below the merchant's seat and could hear the man's wheezing breaths. Moist straw pricked his flesh all over, and sweat trickled down his brow as he waited for the two to speak again. What were they doing?

"I suppose I was mistaken," the guard said at last. "You see and hear strange things at this hour. The darkness plays tricks on you. What's your name, brother?"

"You may call me, Erebos," said the merchant.

"Was the road difficult?" the guard asked.

Erebos snorted. "I did not travel from the lands to the east, moving day and night to exchange pleasantries."

"Whatever you say," said the guard. "So it is time then?"

"Soon enough. We must prepare for their arrival. Are any suspicious?"

"None yet. However, there is a new presence in town giving orders."

"Who is it?" Erebos asked.

"I'm not sure. They arrived just recently. I heard it is a woman. The watch has been doubled already. It is only a matter of time until someone suspects. I'm not sure if I can wait any longer."

"Steel your nerves," the merchant commanded under his breath, "The reward is well worth the wait." A straw pricked Gray's ear, and another tickled his nose. The desire to itch made his skin crawl, and he struggled for a breath in the stale air.

"What's in the cart?" the guard asked abruptly, moving closer, so close Gray smelled the guard's breath that stank of ale. If he wanted, he could reach out and grab the man's sword from his sheath. The guard pushed at the straw with his gloved hand.

"No use looking back there, just hay," Erebos said. "I stole the cart on my way here, and killed the man who owned it. I saw no use emptying it. It proved useful and aroused less suspicion. Now if you don't mind, the last thing I want is to be sitting in the cold and jabbering with you. Direct me to the nearest hovel and I'll be on my way."

"The Golden Horn is our best inn," said the guard, "Talk to Mishif. He knows everyone and everything that goes on within Lakewood. He'll set you up. Till next I see you, brother."

Erebos grumbled something in reply, and Gray heard the horse nicker as the merchant flicked his reins. The cart rumbled through the gate, and he glimpsed the tall stone walls, and the cobblestone road.

As soon as he entered the town, and got a fair distance from the gates, he slipped out the back of the cart, and rolled to the street. He ducked into the shadows of a nearby roof and caught his breath, brushing hay from his clothes.

Beyond he heard sounds of laughter and cheer. He saw colorful displays of tents. Delicious smells hit his nose and made him groan. A festival? It's as good a place as any to look for Mura. He headed towards the lights as a round of explosions lit up the night sky.

Lakewood

Fireworks exploded in the night sky.

"Come join us, Darius!" a group of girls called in unison.

With a smile and a bow, Darius declined, for something more interesting caught his attention. A laugh rose above the others. Cari stood behind the counter of a nearby apple stand.

Darius dodged through the crowd, and with a nimble twist ended up right in front of the stand. He rested an elbow on the counter and added a wink.

"Happy harvest, Darius," she said shyly, but her light blue eyes were not shy.

"Evening, Cari." She looked sweet, but somehow different. Her heart-shaped face was framed by dark wavy hair. He liked how she wore it down and loose, unlike the others girls who pulled their hair back. He realized in that moment that she was no longer a girl.

"What can I get you?" she asked.

Darius looked back. He eyed her until she blushed, then he laughed and she did the same. Appearing out of nowhere, a batch of girls swarmed in from all sides. They tugged at Cari, giggling and coaxing her to join them.

Darius turned on his most charming smile. "Evening ladies."

"Darius," Vivian said as she arched an eyebrow. "What sort of trouble are you causing tonight? Come, Cari," she said, and before he knew it they had linked arms and were tugging her away.

He sighed, snatched an apple off the counter, and tossed a copper onto the empty stand. Turning, he moved into the crowd when he was hit hard. Knocked from his feet, he landed in the dirt.

Dazed, he shook his head as a hand extended before his face. He looked up into the face of a young man roughly his own age. His disheveled dark hair matched his brows, and his angular face was smudged with a thin layer of dirt and a weeks' worth of unshaven stubble—not much more than I can grow, Darius conceded in the back of his mind.

The man's deep-set, green eyes were the only clear feature. "Are you all right?"

Darius took the hand and stood. With his other hand, he deftly checked to make sure his bag of coins was still there. Cutpurses were rare in Lakewood, but they were not unknown.

"Quite all right," Darius replied, brushing himself off and taking another sidelong look at the young man. "You look a bit travel worn," he said, and thought it an understatement. He bowed. "Darius is my name. What's yours?"

"What does that matter?"

Darius shrugged. "I just want to know, that's all. Not many visitors to Lakewood. Don't get your hackles up."

The stranger looked embarrassed. "Gray," he said, shaking his hand.

"Good," said Darius, "Now that we have that settled, what brings you to town?"

"A friend. I'm looking for him." Gray ran a hand through his hair, as if nervous.

"Is he a newcomer?"

"Yes, I was told to talk with a man named Mishif? Can you direct me?"

"Bah," said Darius. "You don't need to talk to Mishif." He put a hand on his shoulder, drawing him in. He noticed Gray's tattered gray cloak and its insignia of two crossed swords. "First off, he'll talk your ear off, and go on about regulations so long that you'll realize you've spent a month standing in the same spot, and your friend has off and left town. And second, because I know everyone in Lakewood, including the newcomers."

Gray looked relieved. "That's excellent! So then, you know a man named Mura?"

"Hm," Darius paused, finger to his lips. "Nope."

"But you just said…"

"I never said I was good with names," Darius replied, raising his hands defensively. "But if you give me a description, I'd be glad to oblige."

Gray narrowed his gaze. "All right, he's probably a hand shorter than you."

"Good start," said Darius nodding.

"…And he dresses in gray and black, and he will likely be worn from travel. He will be unshaven, and he wears his gray hair pulled back loosely in a knot."

"And he looks like he can chew leather and clean his teeth with sharp steel?"

Gray's eyes brightened. "Yes!" he said and then paused. "Well, I suppose that sounds like him."

"Don't know him," said Darius as he cuffed Gray's arm. "Just sounded like a good description." Gray looked as if he were ready to hit Darius in the jaw. He laughed, shaking Gray's shoulder to ease the tension. "Hey, come on, relax."

"I don't need to relax, I need to find this man," he said and turned away, once more looking over the heads of the crowd. "It's important."

"Hey you, stop!" A voice cut through and Darius looked up as a guard's helmet bobbed over the heads of the crowd. The guard pressed his way through the throng of revelers, causing a commotion. He was heading straight for them.

Darius spoke quickly, watching the guard's approach over Gray's shoulder, "Sorry, my friend, but this is where we part. I wish you the best of luck in Lakewood and for the record, I meant no harm."

"What are you talking about? Where are you going?"

The guard broke through the last set of men and women. Darius twisted, his fingers dangling at his side anxiously. He looked for a way out but saw none. The guard was tall and would surely see his departure. Suddenly, there was a scuffle and a man tripped, falling into the guard's path and slowing his advance.

Now's my chance. He gave Gray's shoulder a parting grasp, and then slipped away, ducking through a gap in the crowds. Thanking Lokai for saving him yet again, he hurried away. But curious, he paused before he had gone too far, and looked back.

The guard grabbed Gray by the arm, and pointed angrily to his sword. Gray fought but the guard hauled him away. What? He wasn't after me, he was after him.

Who was his new friend?

The Courtyard

The guard pulled Gray to a halt.

They were on the keep upon the hill, and had taken a circuitous route through various courtyards and hallways to get here. Ahead, a series of stairs led to a training yard open to the bright night sky. It was filled with men and women in rings. In one, a man instructed while others sparred. On the far side of the yard, men faced stacks of hay with bow and arrow. Despite the time of night, the grounds were alive with energy, and shouts filled the air. A full moon and orange paper-lanterns lit the scene.

"She's waiting for you, over there," said the guard, pointing.

"Are you going to give me my sword back?" He eyed Morrowil, which the guard held in his wrapped bundle. Gray hoped he didn't touch it, remembering the pain it had caused others. The fool had no idea what he held.

"No. Swords are forbidden in Lakewood. It will be kept in the Tower until you leave our walls. Besides, you'll have no need for it. Lakewood is a safe town. We make sure troublemakers like you don't stay long."

"We'll see about that," Gray said. He turned as a female's voice, full of power and grace, cut through the din of battle. Now loose from the guard's grip, Gray debated running. But his curiosity was too great, and he followed the voice.

As he moved through the combatants, he noticed the skill of two men who clashed in the center of a circle. Too wide a stance, he remarked as the smaller of the two retreated under a flurry of blows. Gray saw the small man's face break out in sweat, furiously parrying. The tall man pressed the clear advantage, ready to win.

The small man will win, a voice said. He squinted, curious where the thought came from, but it was clear it was his own voice. At last the small man cried out, smoothly side stepping a thrust from the tall man and smashing down with his sword. He stopped a sliver away from the tall man's neck. His opponent wore a look of disbelief as a round of applause erupted from the circle. Gray smiled and continued, maneuvering his way through the combatants until he came to the stand of willowy yen trees from where the voice carried.

Guards conversed over long tables with scrolls spread across their surface, while couriers in black and red livery rushed to and fro. To their right, more men and women stood in congregation. They were dressed in fine silks of rich purples and blues.

Gray heard the woman's voice again.

"You will not see them because they do not want you to see them. Not until it is too late. Only then will they strike.

"This meeting was called for one purpose only—to discuss the future of this land, and the lives of your people. Why we are here is to piece together the truth from the rumors and decide on the path for survival." A round of unruly voices sounded from her last word. Her voice overrode it. Gray ducked and dodged to get closer. "It is now no longer a matter of fighting and winning, you must get that through your heads this instant, or fall to the coming darkness. To understand this you must understand the enemy. They are from an age where magic reigned supreme, a time with kingdoms and armies dwarfing everything you know. Even then, as you have heard from your stories, the great armies failed against them. They wield powers that you cannot begin to fathom. We have only one option, we must find safety. We must go north."

"Run? To where?" voices broke out.

"No! We must fight!"

"You speak only of rumors!"

The woman paused, as the quarreling of voices continued. Turning slightly, her eyes locked with Gray, and he froze. She said something he couldn't hear, and the others turned to one another, conversing heatedly as she left the circle. She approached, and Gray held his ground. She wore white silk from head to toe with a scarlet red cloak upon her shoulders—the cowl of which was pulled far forward. A tall, broad-shouldered man in green, cloaked and hooded as well, walked at her side. More like stalked, he corrected.

"So this is him," the tall man said as if it were a long awaited announcement. Beware this man, Gray's internal voice cautioned, eyeing the sword at the man's side. The woman watched him.

Gray's gaze shuffled between the two. Though he could not see their faces clearly from within their hoods, he felt their stares. They eyed him like a piece of steel before the forge. "Sorry, do I know you?" he asked.

As if waking from a spell, the woman laughed. "Forgive me," she said. "It is one thing to hear about you, and to know you exist, and another entirely to see you in person." She bowed. "My name is Karil, and this is Rydel," she said with a wave of a hand. "It is truly a pleasure to meet you. Mura has told me much about you."

He moved to grab her arm, but immediately thought better of it. "He's all right then?"

"Mura seems to think very highly of you. I am glad to see that his admiration is not one sided. And yes, he is alive and well," she answered, touching his hand kindly. Her touch was warm.

"Where is he? Can I see him?"

Karil smiled. "Of course. I only wanted to see you for myself first, and I am glad I did." Again, the woman made reference as if she knew him, as if he were a character from a story. She must have seen his curiosity, for she continued. "I apologize. Sometimes I have heard that it is truly elvin to talk in riddles, and Mura has a fondness for it as well. I am not an inhabitant of Lakewood. My home is Eldas, the home of the elves."

Gray was breathless. He looked around to see if any others heard, but it seemed talking with her had made a ring of space between them and the others. "An elf," he whispered. "I thought they, I mean you, were only stories."

"Come," Karil motioned him to follow, and Gray obeyed. She led him around the corner of the palace to a bench beneath a yen tree, hidden from the crowds. Before he could speak, Karil withdrew her scarlet hood, unveiling her features. Silver eyes. They held a startling luminescence. The rest of her was equally captivating. She had high cheekbones, a narrow chin, and a slender neck. Pointed ears stuck out from her straight, long white-blond hair.

He turned his eyes, and apologized.

"Do not apologize," she replied, "The sight of an elf is a strange thing to many, though in truth I am only half-elf, unlike Rydel." She motioned to Rydel who stood respectfully behind her. He pulled back his hood. Rydel had an angular nose, a strong jaw and longer pointed ears. He noticed the more human side of Karil in contrast.

"I was not surprised because you are an elf," he said at last, then amended, "Well, not entirely. I just never expected elves to be so beautiful." Karil's eyes fanned wide, and he could tell he caught her off guard. "Sorry," he said, "I realize how that sounded."

"Don't be. I was pleasantly surprised, that's all. And I wasn't sure if the comment was for Rydel either," she teased.

He laughed and glanced to Rydel. The elf said nothing. He could teach a rock how to show less emotion. "Why did you bring me here?"

"To see if the sight of an elf would trigger memories of your past, but it seems it does not."

"So Mura told you of that as well?"

"He did. What is more, no one besides you and Mura know that I am half-elf," she said, "People of this land are accustomed only to their stories. If any of those stories actually became true, I'm afraid of how they would react."

"You think if the people of this town saw an elf they would be… what, afraid? Don't you think they are wiser than that?" He wondered if he was overstepping his boundaries.

Karil did not seem provoked. "Fear born of of ignorance is a powerful thing, Gray, and something to be cautious of, but you are right—I simply worry that they would not understand, and they do not need another thing to cope with at this moment. Daerval is in enough turmoil as it stands."

Gray nodded. "I don't mean to be rude, but if you're done with me…"

Karil held a smile in her silver eyes. "You would like to see Mura," she stated, lifting her hood and hiding her features once more.

"Do you know where I can find him?"

"Ah, but you must be famished from your long journey. Are you hungry?"

Gray realized as his stomach growled, that he was starving. "Starving, now that you mention it."

"Then I'd venture my way to the Great Hall." She pointed up the hill. "That would be a good place to look, if I were you." Her silver eye winked within her hood. "And be at ease within these walls, Gray, I know your journey has been long and hard."

Bowing and thanking them both—even the quiet statue-like elf—Gray took his leave. Moving through the dark courtyard, his stomach churned, and fear and elation collided with one another after the many long days. He hadn't stopped worrying about the hermit, and to know he was alive and well and within reach made him overjoyed.

More people walked the paths of the keep, now lit with orange lanterns. Gray found himself searching their faces, looking for Mura. Impatiently, he picked up his pace, racing through the courtyard and heading towards the Great Hall.

A Vision of Death

Vera knelt before the fire. She warmed her hands on the flames, but the cold was bone-deep. She couldn't stop her body from shaking. She looked over her shoulder.

They sat in a small room. It was bare, save for a wood chair whose legs and back she had already used for kindling. An entry at the far side of the room showed a black night. She loathed the night, for there was nothing to do but think about but her ravenous hunger and the biting cold. Somehow in the day, she could distract herself from the pain of her gnawing gut.

Within arm's reach, Kirin lay fast asleep. He was curled, arms

wrapped around his small body, shivering in his sleep. Her heart panged. Why did he have to be so quiet? So unassuming in his pain and suffering? With every waking moment Vera felt her anger and bitterness grow. But Kirin never said a word. Instead, he merely pushed forward. Twice he had nearly been caught for stealing a loaf of bread for the two; and the price for theft in Farbs was steep—the loss of a hand or even death was the toll for quick fingers. And still, he would smile and give her the bigger half. She envied his perseverance.

Quietly, she removed her cloak, wrapping it around his tiny, gaunt frame when a figure entered, head scraping the ceiling. Immediately, her heart darkened. She pressed herself against the wall. "Who are you?" she asked.

It spoke and the walls quaked, "A nightmare." The voice was like thunder. She couldn't see its face within its hood, but she knew it was smiling. It loomed, its frame nearly filling the room with malevolence.

"Leave us alone! If you're looking for food or money, we don't have any…"

"Enough," it said coldly, cutting her off. "This is a dream. Break this foolish illusion, Vera, or I will break it for you."

As if waking, she looked around. Instead of rags, she wore her midnight black dress with its long slit at the top of her thigh. Instead of the cloak around Kirin, it was the thick cape she had fashioned from the hide of a disobedient verg. She shook her head, and rose to her feet. She eyed the man before her, and suddenly it all made sense. He'd found her. A dark dread, a thousand times more terrifying than before seeped beneath her flesh. She breathed and it misted in the suddenly frozen air.

"Kneel," he breathed.

Without hesitation, she pressed her face to the hard clay ground. "Master…"

"A touching image," he said, head turning to take in the small room, "You disappoint me."

"Master, I live only to serve… I—"

He interrupted her. "You still have feelings for him, don't you?"

She looked up, catching his gaze. He meant Kirin. "He is nothing to me," she seethed.

"Truly," he replied, eyeing the cloak that warmed the boy.

"A dream and reality are far different things," she retorted.

"Is that so? He tried to save your life that day, but still you wish to finish him and retrieve Morrowil?"

Vera neared the sleeping Kirin. Grabbing the ruby-throated dagger from behind her back, she smoothly unsheathed the blade and drove it towards his chest with a cry. The boy gasped, eyes opening as blood spouted from his chest. Vera cut with ruthless precision. Two cuts. She severed the major veins and his eyes flickered, closing as the last of his breath fled. "Do not doubt me. Nothing matters but the blade. I will bathe in his blood before it is done."

The figure sneered, but still she couldn't see his face. He waved his hand and the boy disappeared like smoke. "That is yet to be proven." Suddenly his fist clenched, muttering beneath his breath, and terror filled Vera.

Her hand tingled as if a flame was embedded just beneath the skin. "What are you doing?"

"You didn't think your betrayal would escape my eye, did you?"

"No! I simply tried to…"

"Your orders were simple. You were to follow the Kage." His form grew bigger, nearing, words rattling the room.

"I did as you commanded! You told me—"

"SILENCE!"

Vera trembled, feeling her mind bend as if unhinging before his presence. "I... What do you want of me, my lord?"

"I want you to obey. I saved you that day for a reason. It seems I was wrong to have done so. You've failed me." He flicked his hand and suddenly a fire burst upon her hand. She watched in horror as scarlet flames consumed her flesh, eating her fingers one at a time, burning her alive.

She screamed, "What is this?"

"I'm undoing what I did so long ago."

"No," she cried, "Without your spell, I will die!" The flame continued to burn, reaching her wrist, eating at her arm. Fire lit the walls, burning the small room and the dark man remained still. "Please, save me! I was simply trying to find the boy! The Kage are wrong! We must think ahead of him!"

The figure lifted a hand.

The flesh-eating flame stopped, but still the room's inferno burned until her face was drenched in sweat. She tried to think, tried to form words in her frantic mind. "He... he will evade the Kage, he is smart and there are others on his side, helping him. At this rate, we will never get the blade."

"Then what do you propose? How would you take the blade? Speak quickly."

"We use the dark army to flush out the boy," she said.

His head tilted, stalking forward like a hungry wolf. "Go on."

A small smirk creased her face as she gripped her white-boned wrist in agony, "To catch a rat, you must first scare it from its nest. Burn its home to the ground, then the flame and smoke will push the rodent from its hovel towards waiting arms."

He lifted his hand and the scarlet flames danced around her bone arm. "Speak plainly. My patience is already at its limit."

"The boy is in Lakewood, use the Kage and the rest of your minions to siege the town and flush him out."

"And if he escapes?"

She couldn't help but grin wickedly, "Then I'll be waiting and we shall spring the trap upon our little rat." One way or the other, Kirin, you will be mine.

The looming black figure was silent, and then a dark laugh echoed off the walls and the flames danced. "A foolproof plan, it seems."

She bowed her head lower. "I live only to serve, my lord."

"No," he said and dark power filled his voice, "you live only because I allow you to, and I will ensure that you continue to do so."

Vera gasped as a chill entered her—it sunk beneath her flesh and gripped her bones. "What are you doing?"

"Insurance," he said and closed his eyes. Vera watched as a single thread of the element of flesh appeared, drawing from her skin. It was blindingly bright with power. Suddenly, like a spider's web dissolving before a flame, it evaporated. The figure looked up. She felt her blood freeze. Dark-red peered from his cowl and into her soul, as if his eyes were globes of blood. "It is finished."

Her skin glowed translucently. "What is this?" she asked, touching skin that felt soaked in oil.

"You have two weeks to kill the boy and obtain Morrowil."

"And if I fail?" she asked.

"The potent threads I wove long ago to keep the darkness at bay are unraveling. If you fail, or your sentiments towards the boy are untrue, then the darkness of the blade will eat at you. The remnants of Morrowil's magic will consume your flesh bit by bit until the death I spared you from takes you once again. And this time, there will be no returning from the grave."

Abruptly, Vera had a flashing memory of a dark night.

The room was filled with broken furniture and dead bodies. Blood ran across the stone—it was her own. She eyed it in confusion as she rose to her feet, a strange spell coursing through her veins as she eyed the tall figure before her.

"Who are you?" she asked, looking up at the terrifying form—he was taller than any mere man. Instead of clothes, black flames wreathed his wide-frame. A demon... her mind whispered.

"You may address me as 'my lord'. I have spared you from death, Vera. But the price is your life. You will be my servant from now until I release you, if I so choose. If you fail me, however, you will regret your salvation from death, for I will show you a pain this world has never known."

She pushed the memory aside, returning to the moment.

"And… when I succeed?" she said, choosing her words confidently despite her rising terror.

"If you obtain the blade, the spell will return and you will once again be spared from true death."

Vera nodded, feigning confidence. Before she could respond, he spoke. This time his voice thundered in her skull, rattling her to her core and she closed her eyes, grabbing her head to keep it from splitting in two. "Find the boy, and take Morrowil, or die. Now go, but do not think I will be far. I am watching you always. And if you ever betray me again, this visit will seem a pleasant dream."

When she opened her eyes, he was gone. The fire before and flames upon the wall died in a rush and suddenly the nightmare collapsed.

Her eyes snapped wide. Darkness enveloped her. Nearby, she felt Drefah's presence. The huge wolf's fur ruffled from a breeze. Otherwise, the night was quiet. Separated from her Niux's camp, the snarls and grunts of sleeping vergs and saeroks were distant. There was a faint glow beneath her blanket and she lifted her covers.

Upon her arm was a deathly light. Her whole body stiffened as she raised her hand to stare at fingers no longer flesh, but bone. Abruptly, the light faded, seeping back into her skin, but she felt it—waiting in the shadows, slowly eating away at her until there was nothing left.

Soul-burning purpose and the desire to live filled her. Hot tears rolled down her cheeks as she stared with hollowed eyes into the distance. It's simple, she told herself reassuringly. Vera knew what she had to do. She would warm herself in the blood of Gray, giving him death in order to spare herself.

And in the end, she knew a final truth the dark figure did not name. Once I gain the blade and become its owner, I will no longer need the spell… the power of the blade will return me to my true form, and not even the gods themselves will defy me.

The Great Hall

Gray reached the doors of the Great Hall. The sound and flow of commotion guided him towards the chambers like a fish in a stream.

The doors burst open, and a torrent of cheer flowed over him. A group of drunken guards stumbled out. He sidestepped them as he took in the spectacle of the hall. Huge, ornate pillars ran down the center and flanked long rows of oak tables. Each table was filled with guards and commoners, eating and drinking while servants hustled.

Gray scanned for Mura as he moved through the tables. The hall was raucous. The clink of plate and fork, and the chiming of frothy mugs set his nerves on edge, and he jumped at a round of sharp laughter. Nearby, a group of men and women danced to the tune of a flute and drum. The noise and bright lights jarred him. He looked around feeling eyes on him.

Abruptly, he heard a scream, and he twisted towards it. A bearded man with a greasy smile grabbed a passing waitress. Several men including two nearby guards watched the flailing woman, jostling one another in amusement. Gray moved to help the woman, and stumbled over a chair, causing a string of curses from those nearby—but before he was halfway to her, the brown-haired waitress laughed and batted her aggressor away while fluttering her lashes. The men he had bumped into watched him as if he were mad. Pulling up his cloak, he wove his way to the corner of the hall looking for a seat to calm his frayed nerves. What's going on? He thought, his heart thumping. What is this feeling?

In the corner, beneath a flickering torch, he found an empty table where the din of the hall was reduced to a low hum. He took a deep breath. I'm jumping at every little thing. Something tingled beneath his shirt, and as he reached for the pendant a voice spoke.

"Is this seat taken?"

"No," he said retracting his hand and looking up. There stood Mura with a wry smile. Gray leapt from the bench and embraced the hermit, lifting him from the ground. The man grumbled good-naturedly, but Gray paid no heed. Mura felt real and solid.

"I see you've not lost your strength," Mura said, rubbing his ribs with a laugh.

"Where've you been?" He exclaimed. The man wore a tan shirt and brown pants, and in place of his usually tattered shirt, he wore a snug black tunic. A few scratches marred his cheek and forehead, but he looked nearly unscathed.

"I've been here. When you caused your little raucous over there I spotted you. Is everything all right, lad? You look as if something is nipping at your heels."

"I'm all right now," he said and motioned the man to sit. So caught up in the moment he failed to notice that the hermit had placed a steaming dish upon the table. It was filled with cubes of lamb, buttery rice, and two thick slabs of bread. The smell of spices rose from the plate hitting Gray's nose, and his stomach twisted in knots. "I've never smelled anything so good."

Mura chuckled. "Fool boy, I figured you hadn't eaten since I last saw you."

"You're not too far off."

"Well dig in!" He exclaimed pushing the plate towards him. "I've had my fill, several times over," he said with a wink, and when he saw the look on Gray's face, he added, "I'm not going anywhere. Eat and then we'll talk," he insisted, pushing the plate closer.

Gray was only too happy to oblige, and as he finished the last savory bite, he looked up. "Is there more?"

Mura laughed, and then smoothly caught the attention of a waitress, signaling for another plate. "Well, I'm glad you haven't lost your appetite."

When Gray had his fill, he pushed the plate away. "What happened, Mura?"

"Back in the woods, or after?"

"Both. I want to know all of what happened until now."

Mura nodded. "Then I'll need a drink," he said, and again smoothly snagged the eye of a barmaid and ordered two pints. She returned carrying two frothing mugs. Preparing his long-stemmed pipe, Mura spoke, "After I watched you fall over that cliff's edge, I feared you were dead, but I never let myself believe it for a moment."

Gray took a long draught, wiping foam from his upper lip. "And I prayed for you. But how did you survive?"

"By tooth and nail," Mura answered. "A verg is a difficult thing to kill. A Nameless, however, is another thing entirely."

Gray breathed through his teeth. "You killed a Nameless?" Nameless were fabled beings, rarely mentioned in the stories. They were more evil than a hundred vergs.

Mura tampered down the pipe's contents, and took a long draw. As he exhaled, smoke billowed. "I killed the verg, but not the Nameless. I was lucky enough to escape its dark blade with my life. A Nameless is no mere creature of the Wasteland. It is far worse. In truth, I had heard only stories, and did not believe they existed until that day in the woods."

"What are they?" Gray asked, leaning forward.

A round of sharp laughter went up at a table of gamblers. Mura continued when they quieted. "They are dark beings from another age. Some say they aren't even living, and perhaps never were. They shift from shadow to shadow like a dark breeze, and can mist from thin air. Most legends say they can't be killed. From older elvin stories, they are said to be once-Reavers—those who wield magic beyond the gates. During the great war, dark Reavers twisted their own form and a new enemy was born… the nameless."

There was another bout of laughter, and a stream of curses erupted from the nearby table. Gray shook himself, pushing away his drink.

"Now it is my turn," the hermit said as he leaned closer. The torch on the wall behind them flickered, casting Mura in a ruddy orange light. "What happened to you my boy? How did you get away?"

At Mura's words, Gray flinched, remembering the verg, the wolf's bite, and what came after. "I fell."

"...from the cliff?" Mura whispered, incredulous.

"Somehow I survived. I still don't exactly know how." Gray continued, "When I came to, I remembered what you said and I followed the Silvias River." He paused as a barmaid passed their table, tucking her long blonde hair behind her ear. It reminded Gray of Karil. "By the way, how do you know Karil?"

The hermit took a drink from his pint. "You mean, how do I know an elf? But I suppose both are good questions. Finish your story, and I shall tell you mine."

"There's not much left to say," he said with a shrug. "I made my way through the forest, and..."

"What is it?" Mura questioned.

"I met a woman on the border of the woods and we were attacked."

"Who was she?" Mura asked.

"I'm wondering that myself," he said. "Her name was Vera and she came from across the gates. She said she knew me, but I didn't trust her. Then again, she saved me."

"From across the gates? Interesting," Mura said as he refilled his pipe.

"There's one more thing," he said. "I saw Kail."

The hermit choked, coughing smoke. "You what? He's alive?"

"I'd say so," Gray said, fingering the cut the Ronin gave him upon his cheek.

"So it's true... What in the seven hells happened?"

Gray tried to remember Kail's words. "He warned me... Something about the sword, and at the same time, he was pained by its touch. Then he left in a rush."

"Just like that?" Mura whispered, "He didn't try to kill you?"

Gray shook his head, still deeply confused by it all.

Smoke billowed as Mura exhaled in disbelief, "A Ronin come to life... I fear I will not believe it truly until I see it for myself."

"I would not wish that upon you," Gray said. "I fear it would be the last thing you see."

"You might be right. Did the man seem mad as the stories say?"

Again, he shook his head. "He seemed driven, as if by some dark purpose."

Mura scrubbed the stubble upon his chin. "This raises many questions. I will tell Karil of this news. That you were attacked so close to Lakewood worries me greatly. Lakewood is short on men as it stands. Half of them are patrolling the streets and watching the wall, and in truth, many have been too scared to take up their duties. Karil has done her best to light the dark corners of the town, but we must still be wary. Which reminds me, do you still have the sword?"

"I had to leave it with the guards."

Mura inhaled deeply on his pipe, and let the smoke puff out the corner of his mouth. "We must get it soon."

Gray admitted not having the blade at his side was odd. Somewhere along the way he had grown strangely attached to it, but Mura looked to be hiding something. "Is something wrong?" he asked.

"Let's just say, it's better for the sword to be in your hands."

He leaned forward. "Mura, what aren't you telling me?"

The hermit tapped his pipe, emptying its contents, and placed it back in his pocket. "I suppose it's time to tell you all I know," he answered. "Three years ago, I was on the other side of the gates. I lived in Eldas, the great Kingdom and home to the elves. At that time, a prophecy was uttered, one that would change the course of history. It was the prophecy that was destined to be the hope against the Return." He paused, his eyes distant as if remembering and he took a long draught of ale. Gray knew of the Return. It was what all people feared—it was the Ronin's return from the dead to finish what they started and leave the world in ruins. "It feels like a lifetime ago, but I can still remember her voice as she spoke the words."

"Whose?"

"My sister," Mura replied, and then looked up with a smile. "She was the prophet. The one who named you." Gray's fingers curled, balling into fists as he listened. "Our meeting was not chance, Gray, but that does not make me any less glad for it. You are an integral part of the prophecy. Three years ago, I came to my sister upon her deathbed. She instructed me to go to the Lost Woods, to wait for the one prophesied. I left everything I knew, crossed the gates with the aid of the elves, and made a home in the forest. There I waited for you."

As Gray listened, a memory filled his vision of a dark night. Rain soaked through his tattered tunic, and his wet cloak clung to his cold limbs. He looked down. A sword was gripped loosely in his hand. A flash of lightning lit the forest. He saw dried blood upon the blade. Thunder roiled, shaking the ground when he smelled smoke. Gripping the blade, he followed the scent, weaving through the shadowy trees. Orange light shone through the branches. It was the light of a fire seen through glazed windows. A hut. Safety at last.

He returned to the moment. It had seemed sheer luck that he had stumbled upon Mura's hut. But now he knew it was more. It was all intended.

"Are you all right, lad?" Mura asked. He rested a hand upon his arm, displaying the same warmth he had shone him so long ago.

"It's a lot to take in, but it all makes sense. Why are you telling me now though? You knew I sought the answers to my past." He couldn't keep the frustration from seeping in. "Why have you held it from me all this time?"

Mura's face went distant. "If you only knew how many times I wished that I could. But the prophecy demanded that you not know. It required that you live your life until the day it demanded you. My sister insisted upon that in her dying words." The hermit took another long draught from his drink. "Though truthfully, I had my own reasons as well. I wanted you to become the person you are today, unhindered by the burden of your prophecy. That is to say, I wanted you to have a moral compass that was true—I couldn't do that if you thought it was for some alternate purpose, than just simply to be yourself."

Frustration and confusion rose inside him and he pounded the table. Others nearby looked over, their conversation slowing. Gray waited until they looked away, and spoke, "I just want to know who I am, or who I was."

"You were born within Farhaven, but beyond that, I cannot answer your past. I wish I could."

"But I don't want this—any of it. Why would the prophecy choose me?"

"I know not, but oftentimes, we do what we must, until our fate reveals itself."

Gray felt for the pendant beneath his shirt. "I never asked for this…" The metal bit into his palm, but he held it tighter. A man in red and black livery wove through the tables, making his way towards them.

"Yes?" Mura inquired as the man approached.

"Apologies for the intrusion, but the queen seeks you," the messenger said in a low tone.

"Is it urgent?" Mura asked.

"There is trouble. I was told to find you without delay."

The hermit gave a deep breath and he turned to Gray. "I must see to this, will you be all right?" He nodded, and they clasped forearms. "I will see you soon, my boy, and we will talk more." With that, the hermit rose and swiftly followed the messenger out of the Great Hall.

Alone now, Gray settled back into his chair. Everything Mura said still churned in his head. "Prophecy," he whispered aloud, but it sounded more like a curse.

And at a nearby table, the commotion was picking up, as voices grew heated.

He felt violence in the air.

A Rogue's Luck

Darius rolled a die across the ridge of his fingers, holding his breath, his other fist clenched beneath the table. At last, the seven dice on the round wood table stopped their roll.

Seven ones.

He let out a strangled gasp of surprise. "Seven," he said. All the other men grumbled and threw their coin, sitting back into their chairs. All except one.

Across the table, old Bueler eyed him with one squinted eye. "Had I not known all your tricks, Darius, I'd think ya was cheatin'."

"What can I say?" Darius shrugged. "When you're lucky, you're lucky."

Bueler snorted, "Aye—the Ronin's own dark luck."

Darius was startled by the comparison. He hadn't heard them mentioned by name since he was a boy. He laughed uncomfortably and looked around the table. The other men looked equally unnerved by the name. At that moment, a group of shapely women passed closely by, flirting with the gamblers. Thank Lokai. Best make use of this. Darius pushed back his chair.

"Hold on!" Bueler croaked loudly. Darius saw the coin-seeking women hadn't fazed Bueler. Instead, the man's dark eyes narrowed, looking like small, angry lumps of coal. "Not going to let a man have another chance at his money?"

The others turned. Darius froze, half-risen from his seat. He knew where his dagger lay. He could get to it in the blink of an eye, but he didn't move his hand. He didn't want to fight nine men, not for a foolish wager. He debated giving the coin back, but something in Bueler's eyes suggested the man wasn't wholly interested in the loss of silver anymore.

"Settle down, Buel," said Farley in his rumbling voice. He was Lakewood's blacksmith, and his brawny arms attested to that, as they barely fit inside his tunic. "No use getting worked up. It's just a game. And if you start a fight at the festival, the council will have your head on a pike." Bueler didn't seem to care. He stared at Darius with growing rage. He wasn't sure about the others, but Bueler's mind seemed more for blood than coin. The man was different tonight, a darker glimmer in his eyes. And while Bueler surely couldn't fight, the fool could work the others into a lather. Once in his life, Darius had seen a mob form, and a man had died as a result. It was a terrifying thing what the irrational power of rage and numbers did to a man. It was time to work his charm, before things got any worse.

"My apologies, gentlemen, while I would love to stay and chat, it is just far too glorious a night to waste simply tossing dice, even with such fine company." He bowed deeply, gesturing with his one hand, and with his other slid a portion of his earnings into his coin purse, leaving most of the heavy coins on the table—more than enough. Darius gestured to the coin. "A token of my appreciation. Until next time..." He turned, hiding a smirk. That should work, now to—

"Oh, you're not going anywhere," Bueler called. "Not this time."

Darius heard the scrape of wood as the other men slid back their chairs. He cursed inwardly.

"Turn and face us, you scoundrel!"

Slowly, he turned, and saw the speaker. It was Bueler's lackey, Ruben. Ruben was big, and while not as big as Farley he was still twice the width and a good hand taller than Darius. Moreover, the man's face reflected his many fights and foul temper. A scar ran across his missing left eye and down his mouth, leaving it in a perpetual sneer.

Don't look the bull in the eye. It'll only anger it. He turned his gaze down and flashed his most disarming smile. "Look, this is clearly a misunderstanding. If you want another game, all you had to do is ask... I'm ready to lose my coin. That is, if you're man enough to take it. Now sit, sit," he ushered, "The next round is on me." He looked around for a barmaid, but as the tension grew, a clear gap was dividing between them and the others in the hall. Dice! Where are they when you need them?

"No more games," said another.

Darius tried to slow his beating heart. "Surely you're not going to start a fight in the Great Hall itself? A man of your intelligence, Bueler, would see the folly— "

"Shut up!" Bueler said, sliding his chair back, "Enough talking! Even your silver tongue won't save you now."

"You're mine first, rogue," Ruben voiced as he kicked a nearby cask, knocking it out of the way and causing a cascade of stacked barrels.

"You! Don't move a muscle!" A voice shouted from behind.

Ruben paused in his tracks and Darius twisted to see a young man striding towards him. Gray, he remembered. Gray shoved aside a stool, stomping towards him, his face a thunderhead. Darius backpedaled closer to Ruben. He was caught between a hammer and an anvil.

Gray grabbed him by the scruff and yanked him up. "You! You left me!"

Darius grabbed Gray's hands, trying to pry them off, but he had as much chance as prying a nail from hard oak. "You're angry, I can see that, but you don't understand."

"Oh, I understand perfectly," Gray replied with a crazed light in his eyes.

"And just who are you?" said Bueler, squinting one eye at Gray.

"Back off, old man," Gray snapped.

Bueler recoiled, eyes widening.

"What did you just say?" Ruben sneered, stepping forward.

"Gray, you don't understand," Darius said in a fierce whisper, so only his friend could hear. "This man will hurt you and me. Just do as he says."

Gray ignored him and looked to Ruben. "I said back off," he repeated slowly as if the man were daft. "This is none of your affair. It's between me and the rogue."

Bueler gave a cruel-looking grin. "Ah, but that's where you're wrong. This is the last time that swindler will cheat any of us of our hard-earned money. We're taking back what's ours out of his hide."

"Whatever he owes you, he owes me more," Gray growled. Ruben stepped forward. As he did, Gray released one hand, reached inside his coat pocket and shook his head.

Ruben froze, looking down his broken nose at Gray. "That better be more than a pig-sticker you're hiding, because it's going to take a lot more than that to stop me."

Suddenly what Gray was doing dawned on him. He realized the grip on his collar was only so tight that it looked painful. Hiding a smile, he decided to play along. "I'd do as he says," Darius told Bueler and the others, as if afraid for them.

"There's nine of us, and only one of you—those aren't good odds, friend," Bueler stated, though he looked less certain now.

Gray laughed as if it were a trivial matter. "I'm a reasonable man, so I'll compromise. You can have him after I'm done, if there's anything left. But if you attack me now, I swear, I may not take all of you, but I'll leave my mark deepest on you," he said, his gaze resting on Bueler.

There was a long pause as men fingered their concealed blades. Ruben stepped forward, and Bueler put a hand to the man's chest, "Wait," he ordered. The big man stopped. Bueler eyed the hand in Gray's coat. "As long as he gets what's coming to him," he said with a twist of his upper lip.

"Oh, you can be sure of that," Gray said and turned, throwing Darius ahead of him.

They rounded the corner into a hallway just out of sight of the Great Hall, and Darius breathed a sigh. He laughed softly, punching Gray good-naturedly in the arm. "Dice, nice going! Where'd you learn that trick?" He looked around. The hallway, lit with several torches in iron sconces, was empty of people.

"Who says it was a trick?" Gray asked, raising a brow.

Darius swallowed uncertainly. Gray's stern features broke and he laughed, jabbing the rogue in the ribs with an elbow. Darius chuckled as well, but this time wondering if his friend was a tad crazed. Perhaps I was safer with Bueler and his big oaf. "Well, thanks either way," Darius said. "And I'm sorry about leaving you before. I thought they were after me. Imagine my surprise when the guard snagged you."

"Don't worry about it," Gray said, "It wasn't your fault."

"Good, glad that's settled. What happened to you? It doesn't look like they roughed you up too much."

"No, I'm fine. I was taken to see someone, and a good thing too, they led me to the man I was looking for," Gray replied.

"So you found your friend?" Darius asked when he felt a sudden sharp pain on his ear. He wailed, twisting to face his assailant. Blue eyes met his. He blinked in surprise, quickly taking in the pretty face. She had fair skin with a petite nose and a sprinkling of freckles across the bridge. Her looks were nearly enough to dampen the pain. But he knew that face, and as a result, both his attraction and fear immediately fled. "Dice! Let go of my ear, Ayva! What are you doing?"

"No," she fumed, "What are you doing? Thinking you can get away from me when you and your pals shattered two of my best casks?"

"What are you talking about?" Gray asked.

Ayva, still with a firm hold on his ear, shot a finger around the corner and to the gambler's table where mead frothed from two big oak casks.

Darius cursed. "Look, Ayva, it wasn't my fault."

She snorted, yanking his ear higher and he yelped. "I don't believe that for a second," she said angrily, and looked to Gray, "And who are you?"

"Gray, meet Ayva. Ayva, Gray." Darius said through his teeth. "Now let me go!"

She nodded curtly in greeting. "Curious friend you have here, and what in the seven hells of Remwar are you two doing over here?"

"What does it look like?" Darius growled, "And keep your voice down, will ya?"

"Hiding like a couple of bilge rats, is what it looks like," Ayva said.

Gray grabbed Ayva's arm and pulled her further around the corner, out of the open and away from the attention of the gamblers. Darius took the moment to shirk off her grip. He stepped back, rubbing his ear.

Ayva brushed off Gray's hand and glanced around the corner at the men who had settled back into their gambling. "What's going on? And you two better start speaking soon or I'll call those men over here—I won't hesitate," she warned.

"Those men accused Darius of cheating," Gray began.

"Bueler was acting like a downright fool!" Darius added.

The two shot him a fierce look. He fell silent, grumbling under his breath as Gray continued, "Before anything too bad happened, I pulled Darius away by reassuring them that he was mine first."

"I could have told her that," he snorted.

"Well, I see why you're hiding. And that's either pretty brave, or pretty foolish of you," Ayva said to Gray. "Bueler is an old fool like Darius said, but a dangerous one at that, and he's the guard captain's uncle." She looked to Darius, raising a brow. "Accused of cheating? Why doesn't that surprise me?"

Darius scoffed. "I never cheat."

She waved it off with a hand. "Well, I don't want trouble any more than the next person, but as I see it, I'm still down two barrels, and it's at least partly your fault," she said with a hard eye in his direction.

"No it isn't!" he replied, "Like I said, I did nothing but…"

Gray clamped a hand over Darius' mouth. "What he means to say is we'll gladly replace the cost of the barrels, seeing as we were a part of the incident." He let his hand go and Darius wanted to protest. There's no reason why we should pay, but judging by the look in Gray's eyes, he didn't think he'd win this fight.

Ayva watched Darius, and he flashed a toothy grin in reply. "I couldn't have said it better myself," he lied.

She bit her lip. It was normally an attractive feature of hers, but right now it only annoyed him. "I suppose that will suffice," she said and she ticked off numbers on her fingers, "Let see, two barrels of Redsmead, and the weight of each was somewhere around ten stone… that's around ten silvers, give or take."

"How about take! Are you kidding?" He exclaimed.

Again, Gray shot him a withering look. Darius sighed and fell back against the wall, crossing his arms over his chest. Gray answered, "Sadly, Darius is right. I don't think either of us has anything near ten silvers."

"Maybe if we were kings," he mumbled to himself.

Ayva smoothed her white apron and smiled. "I figured as much. In that case, perhaps you two can help me get some new barrels from the inn since you destroyed those. These men are rowdy as is, but without drink? Soon the scuffle you prevented will seem a mere drop in the bucket."

"We'd be glad to help," Gray said before Darius could object.

Darius looked between the two, arms crossed. "Oh, delighted," he replied mockingly.

"Great! Than follow me, the Golden Horn is my father's inn. It's not far away."

"Come on," Gray said, grabbing his arm.

Grumbling, he followed and together they took to the side hallway, avoiding the gamblers and moving out of the Great Hall. He watched Gray pull up the hood of his cloak, and glance from right to left as if stalked by something much greater than the thugs in the hall. Watching him made even Darius jumpy, and he found himself looking deeper into the shadows as well.

Nameless

With Ayva and Darius at Gray's side, they reached the inn by way of a back alley. He noticed the cobbled street was rutted with two well-worn tracks from the use of many carts. A merchant's lane, Gray suspected.

"You two stay here," Ayva ordered. "I'll be back with the horse and cart from the stable." The alley was narrow and the stone walls were lined with big oak barrels stacked high. A door on the far wall led into the inn. All of it was lit by the ripe moon.

Darius shuffled next to him, looking guilty with his hands stuffed in his pockets.

Gray glanced up when he heard the clopping of hooves on stone. Ayva returned leading a horse and cart. With her instruction, he started to load the heavy casks. The rogue begrudgingly helped. Soon the cart sank under the weight.

"You two can handle the last two. I'll be back in a moment. I'm just going to explain the situation to my father," Ayva said and then bit her lip. "Wish me luck."

"Good luck," Gray said.

Ayva smiled and disappeared through the inn's door.

He turned to Darius, and then glanced to the last barrels. "Shall we?"

Darius grumbled under his breath. Together, they picked up the oak and iron-strapped barrel. Gray's muscles strained. "These are heavy," Darius groaned. "Why are we doing this again? I feel like I'm a part of some sort of charity."

Gray replied with a wry laugh. "I think someone had the brilliant idea to get in a fight."

"Bah, I was merely the victim of circumstance."

"A victim of greed, more like," Gray mumbled beneath his breath.

Darius snorted, "Don't blame me for being clever at dice."

He shook his head, figuring that arguing with the rogue was futile.

"If someone sees me right now, there goes my hard earned reputation," Darius griped. "I've got an idea. If someone does see us and asks, we're stealing these, and not helping, agreed?"

"I'm not aiding your ill-famed reputation. I'm sure you're good enough at that on your own," he said as they picked up the last barrel. Darius slipped, nearly dropping the cask. "Watch it!" He said, struggling with the bulk of the weight. The rogue picked up his slack, but still his eyes were riveted to the roofs around them.

"Did you hear that?" Darius whispered.

"I didn't hear anything. What was it?"

"I'm not sure," the rogue said, shaking his head. "Must be my imagination."

"Too much ale?"

Darius chuckled, but something in his face still looked troubled.

They threw the last barrel in, closing the latch on the cart to prevent the load from rolling out, and as they did, something brushed his shoulder. His muscles tensed. In the corner of his eye he saw the look on Darius' face and he nodded. "I felt that," he whispered.

"Maybe it's just the wind," the rogue replied, backing up.

Gray reached for his blade and realized it wasn't there. "I don't think so," he said. From a hidden pocket, Darius extracted a broad arrowhead dagger. Together they watched the shifting shadows. "Stay close," Gray commanded.

Silence filled the alley.

"I think it's gone," Darius said with a breath of relief.

As he spoke, a black mist formed in the air on the nearby rooftop. Then, in a flash, the dark mist vanished. They twisted as it reappeared on the black-tiled roof to their right, then again to their left, too fast for the eye to follow.

"Dice, what in the seven hells is that thing?" Darius whispered.

He knew exactly what it was. A Nameless. He backed up against the stone wall of the alley, pulling the rogue with him. "Stay against the wall." The thing continued to move, faster than light, flashing from the rooftops to the ground, circling them. Gray looked to the door. It wasn't far, but something told him they wouldn't get to it in time.

The carthorse whinnied in fear. In a flash of black, the sound was cut short. A gruesome noise rent the air, like claw or teeth ripping tender flesh. A gurgling scream from the horse cut through the night.

Darius trembled. "Gray…"

The sight was obscured by the cart, but he saw flashes of dark cloth, moving furiously, as if ravaging the animal.

"We must run." He grabbed the rogue by his tunic, and lunged for the door. A rush of wind threw them against the wall, halting their advance. Gray twisted.

The Nameless perched upon the cart. Its cloak wavered in the night, black strips of cloth dancing in the wind. It was nearly invisible in the alley's shadows. All save for its gaze. Stark white pupils held him, glowing inside its black shroud.

"What is that thing?" Darius whispered.

"A Nameless." As he uttered its name, it leapt from the cart, landing lightly upon the ground. It raised its arm. In its hand, mist formed taking the shape of a blade. The edge gleamed in the full moon. Frantically, he looked for a way out, but there was none. The door was too far. The only way out of the alley was around the Nameless. He leaned towards Darius and spoke, so low he could barely hear his own voice. "Be ready to move when I say."

Darius' eyes were wide, watching the creature. "What in the dice are you thinking?"

"There's no time, just listen. The Nameless moves in the shadows. If I can fight it in the light, I should be safe." At least long enough for you to get help, he thought. "When I say so, stay in the light and don't stop running."

"Like hell I'm running while you stay and fight," Darius snapped, and gripped his dagger tighter. "You just tell me what to do."

He was glad for the rogue's stubbornness.

"I am here for only you," the Nameless said, pointing its blade at Gray. "But I sssuppose you can both die." Its voice sounded like dry rasping leaves. A black tongue ran across sharp, bloodied teeth and it lifted its phantom blade.

"Not another step!" the rogue threatened, waving his shiv, a blade a third the size of the Nameless' sword. "The next one will be your last," he warned.

The Nameless gripped its dark blade tighter, knuckles cracking. "Do you even know what I am, human?"

"No," Darius replied, "but I don't need to know how to make a sword, to know it will cut. And if you take another step I'll show you."

"Fool," it laughed, "no mortal blade can kill me."

Gray realized the rogue was buying him time, and he searched for another way. Behind the Nameless he saw the cart, filled with its barrels. He eyed the latch that held the barrels in. If only he could reach it. Gray pulled with his mind, wishing he was close enough, but even if he lunged, it was too far.

The Nameless drew closer. "Enough talk. Time to dieee." In a blur it reappeared, striking at Darius. The rogue raised his dagger in a flash. The two blades collided. Immediately, Darius cried out in pain, gripping his hand and falling to the ground. Calmly, the Nameless turned to him. His jaw clenched, as he pressed further against the wall. He looked past the creature to the cart. He pulled with his mind, again, desperately reaching out. If he could only…

Suddenly, the latch clicked and the heavy barrels tumbled out. The Nameless twisted in surprise, but the weight and speed of the barrels were too much. They collided with the creature. Gray dove out of the way as the casks crashed into the wall and exploded. Wine sprayed through the air and soaked the ground a dark red. Gray looked up. The Nameless was nowhere to be seen. He ran to Darius, and the rogue groaned. "Are you all right?" he asked.

Darius stood shakily. "I feel as if I just ran headlong into a wall, but I'm all right."

The Nameless misted in front of them. Before they could move, it backhanded Darius. The rogue hit the wall with a thud. At the same time, the creature swung his phantom blade at Gray. He rolled to the side, but the Nameless strode forth. He saw a thick strap of iron from a broken cask. He leapt for it, gripping it as the Nameless drew near. And with all his might, he swung at the approaching creature. The Nameless moved lightning fast and grabbed the iron. A smirk twisted its dark mask. Gray strained. He held the iron with every ounce of strength. The iron bent and steam hissed, rising from it as if the creature's grip was acid. Gray's hands burned, and he let go in a rush.

In the corner of his vision, he saw Darius move. He looked back, holding the creature's attention. The rogue neared, brandishing his arrow shiv. Gray smiled. The Nameless' eyes widened in curiosity, and Darius cried out as he stabbed the creature in the back.

The Nameless' body convulsed and it disappeared in a rush.

"Did we get him?" the rogue asked as he sagged. As soon as Darius spoke there was a sound like the hiss of steam. It filled the night, sounding from everywhere. Laughter, Gray realized.

"Arroganccce," the Nameless hissed, echoing in the air. Gray twisted, searching for the origin of the voice.

Darius tensed at his side, pressing against the wall fearfully. "The blade went in, how in the seven hells is it not dead?"

"The arroganccce of your kind amuses me. Two thousand yearsss I have roamed this arid heap and still you dare to ssspit your pitiful ignoranccce at me."

Gray moved to the center of the street. He stood in the light of the moon. Puddles of dark wine pooled around his feet, staining the stone like blood. "Come out!" he shouted.

"What are you doing?" Darius replied in a fierce whisper, beckoning him back. "We cannot fight this thing!"

"We can't escape either," he answered quietly. "When I say so, run and get help." He looked back to the dark rooftops, still hearing the horrid laughter. "Show yourself!" Fear pounded in his veins.

Abruptly, the Nameless' laughter cut short. In the silence, Gray heard blood pump in his ears. "Run!" he shouted and was glad to see the rogue sprint away. At least he's safe.

A mist suddenly appeared before his face and a blade arced, jutting from the black vapor, crashing down. He dove, but he was too slow. Something sparked in his mind. It cut through the thick barrier and as it did a bright gold light burst. Gray saw forked lightning shoot forth. It connected, blowing the Nameless back, and the creature slammed against the wall. His mind churned. What had he done?

The Nameless lay in a heap against the wall, its black rags singed. Smoke rose from its still form. The lightning crackled and vanished. As random and sudden as it had appeared, it was now gone. The alley was dark again. Gray staggered, catching his breath as he looked at his hands. He looked up. Against the wall, the Nameless twitched. It's still alive.

"Imposssible," the creature seethed in anger as it slowly staggered to its feet, rising to its full height. Smoke still snaked from its body. "He sssaid you would not have your powersss yet."

"Powers?" Gray questioned. As soon as he did, he regretted it, as the Nameless' expression shifted from fear to one of confidence.

It laughed. "I sssee. Then, you do not know how to wield it. Not yet at leassst."

The Nameless misted and Gray saw what was coming. He sprinted towards the door. The wind parted. He leapt to one side and the black blade slammed into the ground where he had been. Twisting, he watched the phantom sword lance toward him, this time too fast to evade. He closed his eyes, waiting for the blade to pierce when steel rang.

He opened his eyes to a tornado of movement, a blur of white and black. The two collided, jumping from roof to roof, materializing from thin air as their swords tangled. His eyes could barely keep up with the blur. Whatever it was, he knew someone or something was fighting the Nameless, and what's more they were keeping pace.

Abruptly a blood-filled scream rent the air. Twenty paces away the black mist appeared. The Nameless. The creature stood, motionless. Then it crumbled to its knees and evaporated. As it disintegrated it hissed a single dying word. "Ronin…" And it was gone, as if it had never existed, leaving behind only its midnight black garb.

The white blur appeared in front of him, and the shroud fell, eddies flitting into oblivion. A man stood in its place. He held a sword loosely in one fist. Gray recognized the wanderer-like clothes. The man pulled back his hood and long gray hair fell, draping across his broad shoulders.

"Kail," Gray whispered. The man looked up. He sucked in a breath as furious scarlet eyes took him in.

Kail's eyes turned upward, and Gray followed them. From behind the clouds, a wine-red moon appeared. Kail turned, as if to leave, showing his cloak. An emblem of the twin black swords, crossed and faded, was emblazoned upon his back.

"Wait," he shouted, reaching out.

Without turning, Kail paused. "They are coming. Be ready," said a voice on the winds, and then he was gone.

Into the Darkness

Gray watched the rooftops. As he did, hands grabbed him, pulling him back beneath the inn's eaves. Turning, he saw it was Darius and he breathed a sigh.

"Sorry," the rogue said with a smirk, "I couldn't just leave you to get yourself killed." The black cloth of the Nameless fluttered from a gust of wind. "Dice, you killed him. How—"

He ushered Darius to silence and motioned to the rooftops.

"Looks like we've found you at last," said a voice in the dark.

Before he could react a second voice sounded from the rooftop to their left.

"What are you doing, Maris? We were told to inform the others at once when we found him."

Gray followed the voices, his eyes straining in the dark, when the first voice replied, "Ah, you never let me have any fun, Baro. Besides…"

"We're already here," said a dark whisper and a man stepped out from the shadows. He was slender with fitted gray breeches, and a long matching vest. Diamond-shaped vambraces were etched with the symbol of a sun. His heavy white cloak brushed the ground. In the moon's dim light, he saw that the man wore a white cloth mask that obscured all but his cold blue eyes. One thing was certain. This man was far more powerful than the Nameless. "Where did he go?" The man asked.

In the corner of his vision, Gray saw Darius' grip tighten on the dagger behind his back. Gray caught the rogue's eye and shook his head.

"I wouldn't," said another voice in the dark. A fourth voice? How many are out there? Darius let out a sudden yelp as his dagger clattered to the wet ground. The rogue rubbed his hand as if burned, as he searched the darkness.

Gray stepped forth. "What do you want? Who are you looking for?"

"Das de rah hand da," said the voice in the dark.

"We will not torture the innocent, Seth," the masked figure said. "I will only ask this once. The man who saved you from the Nameless, what did he say? And do you know who he is?"

"Kail," he answered. "And he said nothing."

"Gray, what are you talking about?" Darius asked. "You saw Kail?" In a flash of red, a shadow appeared, and Darius crumbled to the wet stone. A man stood over him with a condescending look, his sword held in his loose grip.

Gray fell to his friend's side. "What did you do that for?" With a cold sneer, the man turned. He wore a cloak with an insignia of a red flame. "Answer me!" Gray yelled, ready to lash out.

"Was that really needed, Seth?" said the voice upon the rooftops—the one that first spoke. "I've seen a cerabul drop from less."

Seth shrugged. "He knew nothing. He was only going to cause more trouble."

Gray's fists clenched and a breeze swirled around him. He counted the voices again. Two on the rooftops, two on the ground. Four. He knew he couldn't take that many, but he wouldn't go down without a fight.

"Move aside, Seth," said the white masked man. Though the words were barely a whisper, authority rang in his tone. Gray paused. Reluctantly, Seth stepped out of the way. The man knelt beside Gray, removing his fingerless gloves. "May I? I will not harm him."

"How am I to trust you?" Anger seethed inside him.

"Unfortunately, you have little choice," the man replied. "Please." Gray moved back slightly. The man closed his eyes and put a hand to the back of Darius' head. "Your friend will survive. He is merely unconscious," he said and rose to his feet, replacing his frayed gloves smoothly. "Let's try this again. What did Kail want from you?"

Gray shook his head, kneeling in the cold, wine-soaked street. "I told you the truth before," he said and rose to his feet, "For the life of me, I don't know what he wants. He is both savior and demon. At one moment he seems to want me dead and in the next he saves me. And truthfully, from where I'm standing? You seem more of a threat than Kail."

Omni's gaze bore into him. "You know more. Speak the whole truth, or I will listen to my friend in the shadows. I do not wish to harm innocents, but much is at stake."

Gray cursed inwardly. Somehow the man could read him like a book. He remembered what Vera had said about Kail and the sword. "He seems to be after the sword, and yet...when he touched it last, it caused him pain," Gray replied.

The man's ice-blue eyes widened. "So Kail does not have the sword?"

He was curious at the man's surprise. "No."

The masked man turned, speaking to the shadows. "You all can come out now."

Shadows moved upon the rooftops, and figures dropped, landing silently in the street. Each rose to their full height. Lit by the moon, he took them in from left to right. The first had a shock of white hair, and wore an amused expression. Dual blades protruded above his shoulders. To his right, stood a man with a barrel chest roughly the size of a horse. Next to him, a man squatted on the balls of his feet, watching Gray with apathy, and beside him, stood another, who was covered head to toe in dark gray and tucked away in the shadows, lit partially by the moon's light. Standing behind the others were two men, one shorter with a curly beard and carrying a sword and shield. The other was taller with a hooked nose and a lantern jaw.

One, two... Eight men, he counted and suddenly, it all clicked. Maris, the Trickster. Baro, the Bull. Hiron, the King-Slayer. Dared, the Shadow. Aundevoriä, the Protector. Aurelious, the Confessor. He rattled their names and titles off in his head from left to right as he backed away. Every one of them appeared just like the stories—living legends in the flesh, all minus Kail.

The Ronin.

"You're all supposed to be dead," he whispered.

They ignored him, turning to the cloth-masked man. Omni, Gray now knew, adding his title to the rest. The Deceiver.

"What does it mean, Omni?" Baro asked in his rumbling bass.

"It means our friend is far more than he appears," Maris answered as he leaned against the wall, and cleaned his nails with a dagger. Upon his back was Masamune, the legendary blade. The stories said it had seen endless blood and couldn't be shattered.

Another spoke, Hiron, the one on the balls of his feet. His trademark dual daggers sat at either hip. Gray knew their names well—Calad and Láidir. "Te dá theobh le gech scéal," Hiron whispered, then spoke aloud, "Then this also means the Traitor is truly not the rightful bearer of the sword."

"We cannot presume that yet," another replied—Aundevoriä. He stood next to his taller brother, Aurelious. Aundevoriä's famed sword, Durendil, sat on his back, its wire-wrapped handle protruding over his shoulder. The stories formed in Gray's mind, and he found himself watching it all in mute disbelief, as if it were a dream.

"It is the only thing we can assume! He is no longer a Ronin. His betrayal made that clear," Seth replied, striding forth.

Gray recognized him as the one from the shadows—the one that wanted him tortured. While most of the Ronin were tall, Seth was taller. Each wore colored vests of subtle hues, what he remembered the stories called a haori; Maris' was forest green, Aundevoriä's the color of slate, Dared's black as night, Omni's silver, Hiron's white like snow, Baro's a dark, steely gray, Aurelious' was flesh-colored, and Seth's haori was a fiery red. His vest matched the blood-red sword at his hip called Heartgard. Seth, the Firebrand, he recalled. The rest of each the Ronin's attire was dark earth tones, blending with the shadows.

"The boy may be lying," Hiron said.

"You don't have to believe me, but I'm not lying," he replied. He looked to Darius, hearing the rogue's labored breaths. "I told you what you wanted to know, as promised, now leave us be."

Omni spoke, watching him, "He speaks the truth, but the extent of it is still a mystery. We can, for the moment, assume Kail is not in control of the sword. As a result, it seems he is no longer our leader."

A gamut of emotions flickered across the other Ronin's faces, too varied and convoluted for Gray to decipher. "That he no longer binds us would explain why I have not felt his presence for over a year."

Maris spoke, "That explains the emptiness I sense."

"I've sensed it too. We all have. But what about the boy?" Baro asked, rolling his massive shoulders.

"Kill him," said Seth, raising his sinuous blade—a red flame ran across Heartgard's surface. "He is of no use."

Fear shot through Gray. He stepped back, searching for a way out but the Ronin surrounded him from all sides. Squaring his shoulders, he stood his ground. He would fight with every morsel of his being if he had to, though he did not think it would be a long fight.

Maris unsheathed his dual blades from his back and the ring of steel filled the alley. "You were already advised against that path, Seth. Do not press your luck."

"Keep quiet, Maris," Seth snapped. "If I have to watch your back from the Kagehass and scout for the traitor, I might just choose to drop one of those responsibilities."

"Careful, Seth, you're sounding like him now," Baro rumbled, stepping forward.

Omni spoke calmly, silencing the bickering legends, "The boy is useful. And we do not kill innocents, Seth. If I am forced to repeat myself, I will be very displeased."

Seth's lip curled in disdain, but he fell silent.

"Then what now, Omni?" Maris asked eagerly, sheathing his blades. His fingers flitted at his side—the man's infamous habit.

Omni looked away in thought, while the others watched, equally expectant, including Gray. "More answers and only more questions," the Ronin whispered. Omni looked up at last. "We take the boy. Leave the other one—he serves no purpose and may only be hurt."

"I'm not coming," said Gray, standing beside Darius, "I'm staying with him."

In a sudden flash, Omni disappeared. Gray flinched. In the same instant, he reappeared, an inch away from Gray's face. Now, his eyes within his white mask were orbs of blue fire. "You will come, or your friend will die. Those are your choices."

Gray returned the glare. "I thought you didn't kill innocents," he said, mustering his voice.

“Not unless I have to,” Omni answered.

At last, he looked away. “What am I to do?”

“You have been hiding one last thing.” Omni glanced to Gray’s hand. “Your hand has been itching to touch a sword ever since we arrived. I believe the sword you do not have, is the same one we seek. Take us to the sword, Gray.”

“Someone approaches,” Hiron said abruptly.

True enough, an echo sounded in the alley—footsteps on wet stone. Omni grabbed Gray and dragged him to the alley’s wet walls. Gray watched as the other Ronin disappeared before his eyes, shifting into the shadows.

* * *

Ayva opened the back door of the inn.

The cart sat in ruins, broken barrels littered the ground, and red wine ran through the cracks of the cobbled street. She growled beneath her breath. She should have known. Trouble always came in threes. Once the wise, twice the fool, thrice the blind, she quoted.

“I heard voices,” she called. “I know you’re out there!” Silence. Why are they not showing themselves? They didn’t seem like thieves. Surely it was just an accident. She spoke again, trying to hide her fear. “Gray? Are you out there?”

“Ayva?” A voice called, stepping forward and a face materialized from the shadows.

“Gray, thank the heavens!” she said with a breath of relief. “I knew someone was here. Why didn’t you respond? You scared me out of my right mind!” Then she paused and fixed him with a hard look. “What happened here?”

He grabbed her shoulders and she flinched. “Ayva, go back into the inn, right now!”

“Gray, you’re scaring me. What are you talking about?”

“There’s no time to explain! Listen, go now, it’s not safe here!”

Anger rose inside her. “Where’s Darius? If this is some kind of sick ruse then you can just—” The clouds shifted, and she saw a body in the shadows. “Darius!” She ran to the rogue’s side, falling to her knees. “What happened? What’s wrong with him?” She touched the rogue’s head of unruly hair. It was wet. She gasped.

Gray pulled her to her feet. “Darius is fine, I promise! He’s only unconscious, but if you don't leave soon…" He cut short as the nearby shadows moved again. Ayva tensed, as others stepped out of the darkness.

Eight men... She tried to form words, but nothing came out.

"It's too late, Gray," said a figure wearing a white shroud. "She stays."

Distantly, Gray said something at her side, but Ayva didn't hear as a man cloaked in black and red with a scarlet sword, flashed a demonic grin. A sudden dark light came to his eyes and his blade roared alive, hissing red flames.

"Ronin…" Ayva whispered in a cracked voice and fell into darkness.

* * *

With the Ronin at his side, Gray moved through the alleyways. The alley was dark and quiet, lit only by a wax-colored moon high above. The moon scuttled amid clouds, as if trying to hide. Gray understood that sentiment. He waited to run into a townsperson; waited for the shrieks of terror as a man or woman turned the corner to find the Ronin, nightmares of mankind, striding down the dark alley, but strangely they met no one. Instead, the alleys were empty. He judged they were closer to the outskirts of the town now, and some ways from the festivities of the center green. The quiet streets seemed unnatural. The figures that strode beside him with deadly grace didn't seem to notice. He wondered if a person did appear if they wouldn't simply kill them. Legendary slayers of men, he thought with disdain.

"You shouldn't worry for your friends so much," Omni said at his side, as if reading his thoughts.

Gray kept his voice low, but couldn't keep the heat from it. "Why did he do that to Ayva?" he said, glancing to Maris. The man paid him no heed, moving like a wolf in the shadows.

"Your friend will awake. If she had cried out and attracted unwanted attention, then you would have true cause to worry. Besides, this way, she is safe and far from harm." The Ronin stared straight ahead as they maneuvered through the dusky street. "In a few hours, both she and Darius will wake up with only a bump, and a memory of something they won't believe."

"We're here," he said at last, turning to the Ronin. Before them was a guard tower he had seen on the way in. It was a high-roofed building of white stone that hugged the town's wall.

"So the sword is in there?" Maris asked.

"I'd assume so. That's the only tower I've seen, and that's where he said they were taking the blade, to the tower. So, what's your plan? I'm pretty sure it's guarded."

"Well, we're just going to saunter up and ask them in a sweet voice if we can have it," Maris answered.

He scowled. The man was beginning to get on his nerves.

Omni grumbled beneath his cloth mask. "Get on with it, Dared."

Dared was so utterly silent, Gray had forgotten that the last Ronin was even with them. Tall and handsome, with thin lips and dark, emotionless eyes, Dared looked truly the description of a man lost in immortality. He threw down his pack and Gray noticed his cloak and its insignia. Two crescents of a moon united in a circle, one part light, and the rest dark. Kingdom of the Moon. Dared riffled through his pack and pulled out a coiled strand of rope and something metal that had three rods of steel.

Gray leaned in curiously. "What is that?"

"A kri hook," Maris explained, sounding as if it should be obvious. He took it from Dared and flicked his wrist, and two of the flat metal rods flipped up on invisible silent hinges. They locked in with a click. With one arm, Maris lobbed the hook. It landed in a crenel in the battlements at the top of the roof, thirty paces up.

"Up you go," Omni said to Gray and motioned up the wall.

"Aren't you coming? Can't you get it easier yourselves?"

Maris laughed, "And risk our own hides?"

Omni looked to Maris and the man cut short his laughter.

"If we're discovered we'll have a whole city in an uproar. If you're found stealing your sword back, it'll only be mischief," Omni explained. "We'll keep the alley safe for your return." And make sure I don't run away, Gray thought.

He turned, barely believing what he was doing, grabbing the rope, and he climbed hand over hand. When he reached the top, he looked back down. The Ronin had vanished.

A stone turret sat upon the roof, looking over the town of Lakewood like a sentinel. Gray slowly crept up to the watchtower, staying low, and peeked over the lip of the stone. The turret was empty.

Climbing inside, he found a ladder. It led down and into the guard's hut.

What in the seven hells? He wondered again. First the stories come to life, and now I'm about to risk my life for them? But the sword was his, and he wanted it back. He paused upon the tower, looking out, knowing they were out there somewhere, watching.

Then, with a deep breath, he descended

Arrival

Gray grunted as he landed on the balls of his feet. He rose and brushed himself off, looking around the small room.

It lacked any décor, aside from a few crude tapestries to cover the stone walls, and several weapon racks filled with wooden weapons. The hearth before him still glowed with orange embers, and on the nearby table he noticed a half-eaten loaf of bread. He reached out and touched it. Still warm. They'll be back soon. I'll have to hurry. There was only one door in the room, his only option was forward. Tiptoeing across the room, he grabbed a wooden spear off a rack and approached the door.

He pushed open the heavy door and entered the hallway. There are others near. It was the same calculating voice that told him Vera was more than she appeared. Cautiously padding through the hallway, he came to a split.

One hallway led straight ahead with a series of doors on either side. Laughter and voices emanated behind the nearest one. Suddenly the door flung open. Gray threw himself to the wall. A guard in chainmail appeared. Bright light poured forth from the room. The guard tossed words with those inside, and then closed the door with a thud, cutting off a chorus of laughter. With a deep belch, the man stretched and moved down the hall, away from Gray.

The other hall snaked, winding down and smelling of pitch. Clutching the wooden spear tightly, Gray followed the flickering torches. He reached the end of the hall and saw a giant cast-iron door with more bracketed torches flanking its side. It stood wide open. Cautiously, he neared when he heard grumbling and grunting from inside. He gripped the spear tighter and slipped into the dim room.

Kneeling in the darkness with his back turned was a small gangly man. He mumbled angrily, as if arguing with himself. Gray moved closer and watched as the man, hunched before a giant chest, fumbled with a large ring of keys. In the light of the torch, he saw pockmarked cheeks and silver rings in his ears. It was the trader whose cart he had snuck upon at the gates of Lakewood. Erebos.

"Merhass! Which stinking one is it? If I find out you lied, I'll wring yer' filthy neck," Erebos grumbled, oblivious to his presence.

Gray saw something dark pool around his feet. The torch light resolved its red tint. Blood. He turned and in the shadows was a body. He approached, keeping his eye to the trader. The man on the ground, a guard by the look of his armor, was still alive. With a look of anguish the guard reached out, gripping Gray's ankle with surprising strength. Gray wanted to tell the man it was going to be all right, to impart strength in him, but before he could, the guard gurgled, choking on his own blood and gave a final breath.

"Are you finally dead?" Erebos asked and twisted, squinting like a creature unaccustomed to light. Gray lifted the spear. The trader squawked, and flung the set of keys towards him. Gray batted the keys from his face, giving the man just enough time to grab a metal blade. In the lurid light of the torches, Gray saw the small man's dark eyes and sickly pale face.

"I don't want to fight," he said hastily. "We can both drop our weapons and…"

"Shut up!" Erebos snapped, and then tempered his voice as if afraid of others hearing. "You just say that because I have the real weapon. Who are you? Did the Shadow's Hand send you? And answer quickly or I'll cut you!" he jeered, thrusting the dagger.

Gray dodged the blade and answered, "No one, I don't know what you're talking about!"

"No one? Then you're of no use, and no one will care if you die,"

Erebos replied.

"Fine!" He said quickly, before the man could move. "I didn't want to tell you, but..." He dropped his hands and assumed his most confident tone. "Drop the blade and I'll tell you all. I swear." He stood tall, and swallowed, towering over the little man. "Believe me when I say, if one drop of my blood is spilled you will see justice, and the Hand will not be kind." Gray watched as a sudden light of recognition entered the small man's beady eyes.

"Then you mean to say you are of the Kin, as well?"

Gray was more cautious to accept this title. Though he didn't see any choice. "I am, now give me the blade, and slowly."

Erebos shook his head. "But she said I was the only one… I was to get the sword before they arrived and deliver it to them by hand. That's what she said! She promised me," he voiced, as if pleading. He looked up, his face a mixture of confusion and betrayal. The look was replaced by a sudden mask of rage. "She promised me!" he shouted, spittle flying from his mouth as he rose to his full height—far taller than Gray imagined.

He cursed, having guessed wrong. "Calm down, I was…" he searched for a word to not offend the man, but found none. "I am not the Kin!" he said at last, but the man's eyes were wild, as if consumed with only the desire for blood.

Erebos strode forward, raising his dagger.

"Worth a try," Gray whispered beneath his breath, gripping the spear tighter.

The trader circled him. "Ah, I was worried for a moment, but I see it's simple now. If you are of the Kin, I have only to kill you and the oath will be mine," Erebos said with a crazed laugh. He tossed the blade to his other hand and slid it along the inside of his forearm, then licked the bloodied steel.

Ambidextrous, the voice inside Gray's head shouted. Suddenly, time slowed as a picture was painted, not so much in real scenes, but in feelings, deeply embedded, moves and strikes and counters—all of it against warriors that fought with both hands, and all of it as if he had done it a thousand times before. Ambidextrous fighters are always more skilled at attacking than defending, the voice said. Strike first and you will have the advantage.

Gray's eyes snapped open as the man lunged. The dagger dove

for his stomach. Gray lifted the spear in the nick of time. The blade clipped the wooden haft in two.

Attack! The voice commanded, fusing his limbs with energy. He ducked, the blade whistling over his head. He charged forward. Erebos swung again, swiping at his neck. In the last moment, he flipped the spear around, and rammed the splintered end through the man's jutting jaw. It happened so fast that Erebos' expression hardly changed. His small eyes split wide in surprise and his blade clattered to the ground. With a gurgle, he fell to his knees, dead.

Dazed, Gray dropped the spear and moved to the door. The hall was empty. He listened for any sound. Nothing. Turning back, he snatched the metal ring of keys from the ground. He fumbled trying to match one to the chest's ornate lock…words sounded inside his skull. Often the smallest of keys unlocks the greatest of treasures, Mura's voice echoed.

Gray found the smallest iron-cast key and slid it into the chest's slot. It slid home with surprising ease. He laughed in surprise, and with a twist and a clicking sound, the lid popped open. With haste, he moved aside weapons until he uncovered it. A polished gem amid

rough-hewn rocks, Morrowil. In the light it appeared simply a perfectly forged steel blade. Suddenly, whispers bounced off the stone.

Quickly, he untied the white cloth from around his waist, and wrapped it around the sword again, then strapped the bundle to his back. Silently, he treaded back down the hallway. At the split, he turned left, and as voices neared, he swiftly slipped out the nearest side door without a breath.

Luckily, he found himself outside. A soft rain fell and mist covered the ground. He glanced left and right. Nothing but dead-end alleys. Straight ahead, the narrow alleyway bisected with the main avenue. Distantly, he heard sounds of the festival, but otherwise, it was deserted. He stepped forward when the mist parted. Figures stepped from the shadows.

"Omni," he said. "You scared me, where did you come from?"

"You should be scared," another said from the shadows. It was Seth's voice. "Did you think you could evade us so easily?"

"Aye, I'm wondering what you were thinking as well," Maris inquired.

"I wasn't thinking anything. I simply needed another way out."

"Did you have trouble?" Omni asked.

"There was a man there already."

"Did you kill him?"

"He attacked me. I had no choice." As he said the words, he realized the breadth of what he had just done... It had been easy. Something about that terrified him.

Maris slapped him on the back. "Good, I only hope you did it silently."

Seth stepped out of the shadows, anger in his stride. He had a sharp nose, dark eyes, and long black hair, and carried Heartgard, as if ready to unleash it at any moment. "What in the blight did you do that for?" He snapped. "Was your goal to alert the whole town? Why don't you just announce yourself as an intruder while you're at it?"

"You've been less than subtle in your deeds as well, Seth," Aundevoriä replied. Seth shot him a look, fingering his blade. Aurelious took to his brother's side.

"Silence! Enough, you three," Hiron said. "Let the boy respond."

"No one was alerted, there is no need to check," Gray said.

"Was it your first kill?" Omni asked, touching his shoulder.

"I'm not sure," he answered truthfully. "That is, I can't remember."

Maris, rolling his dagger through his fingers, sheathed the blade and looked up. "Well then, that sounds like an interesting past you have."

"A tale for another time," Omni said. "The man you killed, what was he doing when you found him?"

We were searching for the same thing, and I'd seen him before."

"When?"

"Entering Lakewood," he said. "He was the cart driver. A trader named Erebos, he called himself. He helped me get in, though unwittingly. I snuck onto his cart after the gates were closed. The man seemed suspicious at the time, but I never really thought much of it."

"Just now, did this Erebos say anything?" Omni questioned, blue eyes glinting in the mist.

"Other than wanting the blade? He didn't make much sense. He seemed mad."

Omni gave a nod and looked to the dark sky. "Most of them are, driven by their desire and the false promise of immortality from their masters." Omni gripped his blade in one hand. "If you are telling the truth..." The Ronin paused. "Did he call himself anything?"

"Kin," Gray said, remembering.

All around, the other Ronin tensed.

"What does it mean?" he asked.

Maris spoke from the recesses of his hood, his voice dark, "Shadow men or women. They are agents of the dark beings. They've called themselves many things over the ages, but now they are known as the Kin. They appear before Shadow's arrival."

"It means they are coming," Omni announced. "The Kage are near."

THE KAGE

As the words left Omni's mouth, a scream rent the air.

"They are already here," Hiron whispered.

With a metallic ring, Maris unsheathed the dual blades from his back, dashing towards the sound. The other Ronin followed.

They sprinted out of the alley, and a figure crashed into Gray, sending him to the ground. In the tangle, eyes met his, filled with terror. The man scrambled over him, stumbled to his feet and continued running. Gray turned. A wave of darkness towered over the stone gates. It surged higher engulfing all it touched.

Guards leapt from their posts upon the gates and fell to the ground far below. More guards threw spears into the seething black only for them to disappear. Shrieks sounded, and then cut short as men were swallowed whole by the darkness.

The wide gates gave a sudden thud, pulsating like a throbbing heart. He stepped back. Again, the thud echoed, and the doors bulged under tremendous pressure. He twisted, and looked down the road behind him. In the corner of his vision, he saw the Ronin. Their faces were hard, their feet planted firmly.

"It's them," Omni's words cut through the screams.

Gray saw an aura distort the air around each Ronin—a gold aura wreathed Omni, Hiron was wrapped in a cerulean hue, and Seth seethed a fiery red, flames licking at Heartgard's surface. Nearby, Dared's eyes were rimmed in black, soaking in the darkness. Aurelious and his brother, Aundevoriä stood side by side. Aurelious' blade, Stice, was changed, no longer metal, but a pale white as if made from bone. Aundevoriä, on the other hand, held Durendil, and the blade now looked made of granite. He gripped a marble shield in his other hand.

Gray unsheathed his own blade from his back, the white wrapping falling to the ground. The blade glowed a blinding silver.

Hiron gripped his dual daggers, "This is it. Be ready."

Seth roared over the screams, "Let them come!"

Baro looked grim. His meaty fists gripped his giant war sword. "Fight together! Side by side!" The doors shuddered. A loud crack split the air and the gate burst, showering wood and stone. From the haze, nine figures cloaked in black strode forth. They rode dark steeds, the beasts' eyes rimmed in blood. Malice surrounded them. In their armored fists were long, cruel blades.

Gray's hands wrung tight around Morrowil's haft until it hurt. Darkness seeped beneath his skin, and he saw a thin vein of black slink across the sword's surface.

"Maris, take Gray and run! Save the villagers!" Omni shouted.

"No, I can fight! " Gray shouted in return.

"Perhaps another time," he replied. "For now you must help the villagers escape."

"Seems you live another day, boy," Maris said, grabbing his arm. Gray yanked his arm free when the earth shuddered and he was thrown to the ground. He looked up as the walls crashed down. Saeroks, vergs and Nameless flowed over the rubble.

A guard, his legs broken, moaned and tried to crawl to safety. A saerok strode forth from the dark pack. In a swift motion, it cut the man's throat with one-long claw silencing his cries, and as if on command, the dark army moved forth.

Maris grabbed Gray's cuff and pulled him up. "You're coming, now!" He dragged him away when a sudden mist appeared. A blade slashed at his face. Gray was slammed in the shoulder as Maris took his place and parried the Nameless' blade. The Nameless took form and their blades moved in a blur of steel, striking, parrying and evading with impossible speed.

The pendant burned against his chest. He gripped it and words flowed through him. The sword is what they want! No matter what, you must not stop! The tone was both familiar and elusive. But the truth was clear. Gray stumbled to his feet and ran, flying around the next bend. A hundred paces ahead, he saw the clearing and the villagers. They danced and laughed unaware of the chaos that approached them.

As he glimpsed the colored tents, he shouted at the top of his lungs, "Run!" Yet he was too far away, and the music and cheer drowned his voice. His legs burned and he shouted again. This time, his words carried as if by some strange purpose, "RUN! Flee for your lives!"

At his amplified words the villagers turned. The music cut short. Fear and panic spread in their faces. Gray turned and saw the hordes. Saeroks and vergs charged, loping on all fours. He held his ground gripping Morrowil tighter when the ground shook with a terrible boom. Suddenly, there was another explosion and the house on his right erupted in shards of wood and fire.

He shielded his eyes and when he opened them a huge timber hurtled towards him. At the same time, he heard Maris call his name. Upon the roof, Gray saw another figure. Red eyes flashed amid the chaos as the timber came crashing down.

* * *

Cries of terror filled the air.

Gray's skull rang and he tried to make sense of the world. He put a hand to his head and saw blood. Skin deep, a voice said reassuringly. Assess your surroundings.

He was in a courtyard, and at the center, was a large oak on fire. Maris lay motionless beside him. He crawled to the Ronin's side. The man's white hair was soaked red. His chest wasn't moving. Panic rose in him until a voice guided him, and he placed two fingers on the man's neck. A throb. He was still alive. Before he could breathe a sigh of relief, he felt the rush of wind, and looked up.

A figure stood on a burning branch. The man's cloak wavered in the wind.

Kail.

An explosion shuddered the buildings, and he was thrown to the ground. When he looked back, Kail was gone. Suddenly, the flames upon the rooftops were snuffed, and darkness slunk over the courtyard. Fear gripped his heart and he clutched his chest. Slowly, he twisted.

Standing in the center of the yard, wreathed in darkness, was a nightmare. He wore plates of black armor, as if molded to his towering frame. Upon his broad shoulders, sat round, heavy pauldrons, one with a jutting spike.

Gray's eyes flashed to Morrowil. Too far, a voice warned.

The Kage spoke, "For two hundred lives of mortal men I have lingered in darkness and shadow. Waiting. Now, at long last, the gates will be breached, and Farhaven will know true terror."

"You cannot use the blade without me," he answered. "I know the prophecy."

With heavy steps, the Kage neared. Gray's heart hammered in his chest. With one mighty fist, the nightmare gripped Morrowil. Smoke rose from its armored hand in billows. A burning stench filled the air. The Kage's head turned towards him calmly. "What do you know of prophecy?"

Gray spoke in a fearful whisper, "I know the blade is mine. It chose me."

"And yet, the blade and the prophecy will be the death of all you know." The Kage released Morrowil and loomed over Gray, a giant shadow.

"You lie…"

Lost in the abyssal darkness of its hood, he saw a flash of red and felt the Kage's hot breath on his face. "It is a prophecy that rides between salvation and destruction. It is a fool's hope."

The Kage withdrew a huge blade and black lightning crackled across its surface. He raised his arms high in the air, and the blade plummeted. Suddenly, blinding light seared Gray's vision, wind rushing over him. The Kage's blade hovered above his face, its point scraping his skin. Thick white eddies encased the cruel sword, as if holding it suspended in midair.

A laugh sounded, reverberating from the rooftops.

"Ronin…" The Kage hissed.

A voice shouted in Gray's head. If you value your life, run now…

Gray backpedaled, but then saw Maris. I can't leave him…

Then stay and die.

At the same time, the bonds of wind holding the Kage's blade burst. The sword hurtled towards his head, and a thunderclap of wind blew Gray back. He hit the wall. When his vision cleared, he saw the Kage and Kail, their blades entangled. Wind flowed and strange energy rattled the air. With a gust, the two flew apart.

Gray looked between the two.

The Kage's hood had blown back. White hair. Red eyes. He looked to Kail. The Ronin's white hair tousled in the wind, and his eyes gleamed, a burning red. The same face… The nightmare was a mirror image of Kail if he had died and risen from the grave. His face was pale with missing chunks of flesh, and his eyes were black orbs with red centers.

"How valiant," the Kage growled. "Saving the one who is destined to take your place."

"You mistake me," Kail said, gaze flashing to Morrowil. "Morrowil and your death is all that matters. And both are within my grasp now."

The Kage sneered. "You never were the hero, were you? Tell me, how was it to watch that woman die within your arms? How did she look upon you when you failed to save her?"

The wind spiked, and Kail bellowed in rage. His blade flickered, but just as fast the creature parried. Again and again he hammered down, a blur of flashing metal, but the Kage's blade was there at every turn. Abruptly, in a blur of wind, Kail disappeared. In his place golden bolts exploded from thin air, and pelted the nightmare. Chunks of metal flew from its armor. The Kage thrust out a huge hand, and a gust of wind blew a hole in the stone wall, raining rocks on the Ronin. Kail disappeared beneath the cloud of dust and rocks, but reappeared attacking ever harder in a whirlwind of strikes and parries, too fast for Gray to follow.

As the battle grew, the wind raged harder. Gray felt himself being lifted from the ground. He gripped the oak's trunk. His pack was stripped from his back, sucked into the whipping winds. He saw Maris, his body being dragged by the building storm towards the fight.

A cry rent the night.

Kail knelt, blood gushing from his shoulder. But through his tangle of white hair, the Ronin sneered, pressing a hand to the ground. A hum resonated in Gray's gut. Holding onto the tree, his arms began to shake. Suddenly, the tree's roots burst from the ground. He fell to the earth showered with dirt. Kail bellowed, throwing his arm. Like an arrow, the huge oak hurtled towards the Kage. In the last moment, the nightmare swung his sword. A crescent-shaped gust sliced and the tree was cut in two. The halves flew to either side of the Kage.

Gray seized a stray root as the wind pulled harder. Swiftly, he tapped into his mind and felt the swirling ball of air. He gripped it. Uncertain, he took strands of air and wrapped them around his boots, and his feet rooted to the earth.

Another round of explosions sounded, heightened by a peak of screams. Gray fell to Maris' side, threw him across his back, and ran. He paused at the edge of the courtyard, and turned towards the legends, but all he could see was a tornado of dust and swords. At last, he turned into a narrow alley.

Cries filled the air and smoke stung his eyes. With each step, the weight of the Ronin threatened to buckle his legs. Yet he pressed onward, fear propelling him as he moved towards the black skyline. Over it all, he heard the thunderous ring of swords as the legends clashed.

Fire and Chaos

They sat just outside the town's walls and Ayva's eyes burned with the heat of the orange flames. The last thing she remembered was fainting. When she awoke, she was on the back of a steed, behind a tall figure. A Ronin. He had set her down once they reached a safe distance from the chaos and fire. She now stood watching everything she knew go up in flames. Out of the corner of her eye, she saw Darius. He was still unconscious on the back of a Ronin's great warhorse—Baro, she reminded herself. The names from the stories came to her easily.

She looked back towards Lakewood, and prayed, watching the flames that threatened to burn the world. Smoke burned her lungs and stung her eyes. You love that inn more than your own daughter, don't you father?

Ayva surveyed her companions. The Ronin sat silently on their steeds. Apart from them, a tall man rode a midnight black stallion. He wore a grand cloak and his hood pulled forward to hide his face. At his side was a woman, slender and also concealed in a scarlet cloak and a fitted riding dress. She rode a perfectly white mare that seemed out of place in the dark chaos. Beside the woman, upon a brown gelding, was an older man with gray streaked black hair. His calloused hands gripped his reins and he had a pained expression as he watched the flames.

Suddenly, the Ronin who had carried her out of Lakewood yanked on the reigns of his massive steed. It was a creature larger than any Lakewood breed Ayva had ever seen. The Ronin spoke, “We cannot wait any longer, Omni. They would have come by now.” Ayva matched his name to his face. Seth, the Firebrand. The one with a temper like a raging fire.

Ayva stepped forward to speak up, but Omni was first.

“We will not leave Maris behind,” he ordered. Though she knew Kail was supposed to be the Ronin’s leader, Omni looked to be in charge now. The stories said he was the elusive right hand to the infamous Kail. “And, unless you’ve forgotten, the sword is still with the boy. I shouldn’t have to remind you that if the blade falls into the hands of the Kage, all is lost.”

Ayva looked back to the inferno, and she saw a flash of movement at the gates. “Look!” she shouted, pointing.

The older man started forward. “Can you see them, Rydel? Is it Gray?”

“It’s them,” the tall man replied. “Maris and the boy.” Ayva couldn’t see how he could be certain. They were much too far to recognize.

The woman in the scarlet cloak spoke, “We must go to them.”

“What are we waiting for?” Ayva asked.

“It might be a ploy,” Omni said.

“But they need our help!” she argued. “We can’t just watch!”

The Ronin didn’t move.

“Let’s go,” the old man said, spurring his horse towards the two men.

The scarlet cloaked woman started to follow, but her companion gripped her arm, stopping her. “I know what you want,” the tall man said.

“Let me go, Rydel,” the woman replied in a clear voice.

“And what if it’s a trap?” Rydel answered. “Saving them will not absolve your guilt, Karil, and the Lando did not shed blood and die for you, just so you could fall here. Would that be your gift to them?”

Karil ripped free of his grip. “They risked their lives, if I can’t do the same, I don’t deserve what they’ve given me. I have to try,” she said, spurring her white mare.

At the same time, Seth wheeled his horse. "Grab hold," he commanded. Ayva reached out and the Ronin pulled her upon the horse. "Now hold on." She nodded against his leather tunic, circling her arms around his waist.

"Seth, stay here. It's too risky," Baro, the biggest Ronin, rumbled.

"The girl is right," Seth said. "Seems the women and the old man here are the only ones with any guts." Seth dug his heels into his mount's flanks, and they galloped after Karil, and in the direction of the two figures. The wind in her face, Ayva held on, pressing her cheek against his broad back.

As they neared, she saw Gray. He was dragging Maris. She recognized the Ronin's flames of white hair just like the stories. Upon seeing them, Gray collapsed to his knees. Suddenly, from behind them, more dark figures stepped over the shattered rubble of the gates. Their faces became visible. They made it. Relief rushed through her as she recognized them. As if a tap had been opened, the villagers poured through the gates. Ayva dismounted and ran to Gray's side. His face was streaked with blood and a sword was strapped to his back. His gray cloak hung loosely around his neck, its edge frayed in blood.

She helped him lift Maris as the old man joined their side. "Are you all right, lad? Are you injured?"

"I'm all right, Mura."

Many of the villagers were hurt, but they pressed forward, knowing what was on their heels. This close, Ayva felt the full heat of the flames. It singed her hair and she coughed from the smoke.

Gray shouted over the roar of the flames, "We need to get these people out of here. The Kage are close! They are held off by the flames, but it will not hold them long!"

Seth eyed the villagers. "We cannot save them all!"

Gray let Ayva and Mura take the weight of the Ronin and abruptly seized Seth's bridle. The tendons in his arm rippled and Ayva was taken aback by his ferocity. "We can and we will!" The fire raged as Seth looked down at him. At last he gave a nod.

A bout of flame erupted from the gates, shooting towards the villagers. Seth spurred his horse, racing to meet it. He whipped out his blade that burned a fiery red. The fire collided with the Ronin and Ayva cringed. Yet instead of charring the man alive, the spurt of flame funneled into the Ronin and his blade, as if absorbing the fire. There was another fiery burst, even bigger, and the flame channeled into Seth. "Run!" Seth said, "I can't absorb much more!"

Suddenly Aundevoriä was at Seth's side. With a roar, Aundevoriä slammed his sword down, and Ayva watched in amazement as stone swelled from the ground, forming a barrier of earth between them and the flames.

"Let's give the Kage something to worry about," Seth said to Aundevoriä. Aundevoriä gave a wicked grin. Seth raised his blade and the flames rose even higher, turning scarlet buffeted by the giant wall of rock.

Meanwhile, the other Ronin yelled orders, herding the villagers onward.

Omni appeared, his warhorse rearing from the bursts of flame. "Give him to me!" he ordered, nodding to Maris. Ayva with Mura's help hoisted Maris up, setting him gently upon the big steed. Omni motioned to two Ronin and they approached, grabbing Ayva and Gray. "Get them out of here!"

"Wait," she shouted, "Let me go! I need to find my father!" She searched the faces of the crowd, but Hiron pulled her away. She tried to wrestle free, but it was no use. The Ronin's grip was like a shackle. In the chaos, she saw another Ronin grab Gray.

"We can't hold them off forever!" Aundevoriä bellowed, "Run now!"

And with Hiron holding her tightly, he spurred his horse and they fled. She screamed, fighting even harder as she watched Lakewood shrink. Only once they reached the top of the hill did Hiron stop and turn. Pain and sorrow filled her heart. A growing black smoke lay over the land. What was once Lakewood was now an inferno.

"Gone," she whispered hoarsely.

Hiron's eyes caught hers. The Ronin lifted one hand to the sky and his sword blazed a brilliant cerulean hue. The sky cracked with the sound of thunder. She felt wetness upon her cheek, and she held out a hand. Rain. Thunder boomed again and the rain became a downpour.

"My tribute to your father," Hiron said quietly. "No man's final resting place should be one of fire and chaos." And the Ronin turned, following the others. Yet beneath the thunder of rain and fire, Ayva still heard the sharp cries of death.

Koru Village

They moved for days, over the rolling hills and through small thickets. Gray rode with Dared. When they moved through the groves, he took Morrowil from his back, holding the blade tightly, fearing more beasts lay in wait behind each shadowed tree. But as always it was quiet, as if the world had been abandoned. He didn't trust the quiet. Yet one thing was certain. They never stopped moving. The villagers seemed spurred by the same fire, as if the Kage were only a breath away.

Ayva and Darius were silent as they traveled. Ayva especially. She hadn't said a single word since Lakewood, and her eyes seemed fixed vacantly on the horizon or staring through the pommel of Hiron's saddle. Gray wanted to comfort her, but he didn't know what to say. He couldn't imagine what she was feeling.

Nearby, Karil rode on her white mare. Rydel was at her side upon his dark stallion. Though they rode beside the other villagers the two seemed from a different world with their elegant beasts and fine clothes. Yet the others didn't seem to notice.

Darius was sullen, occasionally mumbling to himself or clutching at his dagger in his black rags. He wondered if the rogue had lost someone as well. Darius rode with Baro, who reminded him of a mountain with legs. His biceps were twice the size of Gray's thighs, and he imagined the man could snap necks with a single squeeze.

"How's your head?" Gray asked at last, unable to take the silence of the woods.

Darius felt his head with his mop of unruly hair. "Ah, it's not bad. Suppose it looked worse than it was. But don't think I'll be taking any dark alleys anytime soon."

Gray chuckled when he sensed something ahead. "There's something beyond."

Mura rode a dark brown gelding on his left. "What do you sense, lad?"

He couldn't explain how, but he felt a connection to the ground beneath him. As the wind blew, he felt the lay of the land. He could feel the trees become rolling hills, and beyond, a large rise. He sensed something different. "I'm not sure what it is, but it seems man-made," he answered.

"Maybe it's help," Darius said hopefully.

"It's a village," Dared answered, sitting before Gray. The man had not said a word until now. He was so silent Gray sometimes forgot he was riding with someone. No, not someone. A Ronin.

"It must be Koru Village," Darius said, rising in the saddle. "It has to be."

"I would not be so quick to rejoice," Baro said in his deep rumble. Gray noticed his meaty fists gripped his reigns tightly. "Something doesn't feel right."

"A darkness," Dared agreed in an ominous whisper.

As the words left his mouth, and they reached the last stand of trees, each of the Ronin's well-trained warhorses nickered, dancing nervously. Then it hit. A gust of wind rushed over the crowd, stinking of rancid meat. The smell hit him like a cudgel to the side of his head.

It was the smell of death.

The villagers retched and shielded their noses. He crested the hill and at the end of the hill's slope, he saw Koru Village. A circle of wooden-poled walls was practically all that remained. The once burgeoning town was nothing but charred blackness with spotted orange glows from fading fires.

Men and women ran towards the village, heedless of danger. The Ronin sat on their steeds, impassive. Gray reached out to stop them when he felt a hand on his shoulder. The hermit gave him a look and he understood. There was no danger now.

Around the village, spreading for a mile radius from the walls was a black stain. "What is that?" He asked.

"The enemy's mark," Mura replied.

They reached the town's entrance. The small entry looked as if dark titans had wreaked havoc. The gate's hinges were shattered and black, doors missing as if blown away. An enormous piece of wood blocked the entrance. Dared motioned for Gray to dismount. He stood beside Darius and Ayva. His legs felt awkward from days of travel upon horseback, but he was glad to not be sitting anymore.

The Ronin motioned the villager's back. Omni stood alone. A golden glow grew in the center of the wood beam, shining like a small sun and the log lifted from the ground. Whispers sifted among the crowd. Omni threw one arm to the side, dismissively, and with a sudden burst, the log flew, tumbling across the hard ground.

Omni strode into the decimated village, the other Ronin close behind. The villagers followed, if more slowly. Ayva swallowed and glanced towards him. Gray felt her fear, but he kept his face a mask and moved with the crowds.

Aundevoriä and Maris stood like stone sentinels on either side of the gate. Maris' head was now bandaged, wrapped in a strip of cloth. The villagers hedged around the Ronin, but Aundevoriä and Maris didn't react. As he passed, Maris shot him a look. He felt small under the cold scrutiny of the legend. The man gave a nod, as if in thanks. He returned it when there was a tug on his sleeve. Ayva clung to him, her eyes wide. He followed her gaze and horror rushed over him.

Bodies were everywhere. They littered the ground and hung from the splintered walls. A group of villagers parted revealing rows of poles. Upon each was a skewered head, expressions twisted into masks of terror. Ayva averted her eyes and pressed her face to his shoulder. "Gods, why?"

Darius shook his head in mute horror. "This is hell."

Maris appeared at Gray's side. The Ronin looked upon the scene with knowing sorrow. He spoke quietly, as if unwilling to disturb the dead, "In the Lieon, thousands of these poles littered the fields of battle. Always, they incited terror. They served their purpose too, for when the Kage appeared at the gates of the Great Kingdoms, many didn't even put up a fight. Narim, the Kingdom of the Moon, Dared's homeland, even lowered their gates in hope they would be spared."

Ayva eyed Dared, who in his shadow rags sifted a handful of dirt though his fingers.

Gray shook his head. "How can anything or anyone do this?"

"The Kage are not human and true evil knows no limits, Gray," Maris said.

He saw a woman leaning against a building. She looked untouched, huddled with her arms around her legs. Darius knelt before the woman. A subtle breeze tousled her brown hair, revealing a gaping hole in the side of her head. The rogue stifled a gag.

Gray smothered a cluster of glowing red embers in the dirt with his boot. When he lifted his foot, he saw the remains of a tiny black doll. He bent to pick it up.

"I wouldn't," Maris said. "The Kage's mark is upon that thing." The blackness suddenly moved. Gray snapped his hand back. There was a ring of steel as Maris' sword, Masamune, leapt from its sheath and stabbed the doll. A shriek escaped as the darkness withered and vanished. Maris sheathed his sword. "Be careful what you touch," the Ronin said and moved away, joining the others.

Mura appeared at his side. "Lad, are you all right?"

He loosed a breath he didn't know he was holding. "I'm fine, but what was that thing?"

Mura held his staff in both hands, watching the nearby buildings as if the taint was everywhere. "The darkness is somehow attached to the Kage and their powers. It's thought that they use it as a second sight or that shadows come to life and the darkness has a mind of its own. No one knows for certain. If anyone did, it would be them," Mura said, nodding to the eight Ronin upon their steeds, "but for now, be cautious before touching anything within these walls. Agreed?"

"Agreed," he said.

Ayva nodded, and Darius shoved his hands in the folds of his clothes. "Dice, I'd be fine leaving this cursed town right now, and never seeing it again."

Slowly the villager's rose, forming a crowd. Omni addressed the scattered men and women, "Gather yourselves. If you choose to follow, we travel north to Death's Gate. But make your choice quickly for the enemy has made theirs, and they will not stop until you meet the same fate as the people of this town." He gestured to the bodies and the villager's shifted nervously.

Seth spoke, "You may very well fear us if you listen to the stories, but we are real, and so is the danger that you now face."

"What chases us?" A man in the crowds asked.

Baro's voice boomed over the sea of heads. "Nightmares of men known as the Kage who pose as us." Whispers roared anew, but Baro's voice continued, cutting them off, and Gray was jostled among the crowd as they leaned in. "They are the piece missing from your stories, and the true evil of the Lieon."

"How can we believe you?" A voice shouted in reply.

"You have no choice," Omni said. "The Kage aim to destroy every living thing in Daerval, until they find the item of their desire."

The villagers looked at one another, whispering and stirring anxiously. A woman spoke defiantly, "Even if we did believe you, Daerval is not defenseless. The lands will come to our defense!"

"The enemy has taken every city from the Eastern Kingdoms to the western plains, and now Lakewood. What you hope to defend, no longer exists," Omni said.

A pandemic of voices replaced the Ronin's. Shouts and whispers of denial and anger, while disorder roiled among the villagers. Gray fought to stay near Darius and Ayva.

"How can that be?" A voice amid the crowds asked.

"Their dark army is larger than before when the nine kingdoms with all their might failed long ago. There is nothing to stop them."

"And what about you?" A woman asked.

"They mimic our powers, but they are whole and we are not. As we stand, we cannot defeat them," Omni answered.

An explosion of voices erupted.

"Impossible!"

"There must be something we can do!"

"We have to run!" another voice shouted. Others cried the same, and the crowds swelled.

A man strode forward. "Cowards!" he roared. "You are all gutless cowards! We can fight! I, for one, will not run!" He stood like a barbarian, his large chest puffed in defiance. He had no one around him, Gray noticed.

"Reven, your family is gone, and I weep for you, but mine is not, and I will not lose them to suicidal plans!" Another snapped.

"They are coming! We have to go!" A woman shouted, and others began to cry out as well.

"And follow the Ronin? Surely there must be another way!"

"We all saw the enemy first hand! They are nightmares! We must follow the Ronin. They will protect us!"

A voice rose above the rest. "The Ronin are evil! They can't be trusted!" Gray followed the voice and saw a small wiry man robed in layers of rags. Eyes turned to him, and he scuttled quietly back into the thicket of the crowds.

"What about Tir Re' Dol?" someone shouted. Gray turned, recognizing the voice, and saw Darius. He stood, perched on a fallen beam to see above the heads of others. "Surely Tir Re' Dol is safe!"

"We must flee to Tir Re' Dol!"

"Tir Re' Dol is gone," Seth said, silencing the rising shouts like a thunderclap. "Reduced to a mountain of ash and charred stone. If your so-called great capital was sacked in one night, you don't stand a chance. Even if you did, there is nothing to fight for. What you know as Daerval is no more."

"You said they seek an item," a woman asked. "What item?"

"Yes!" said another, "Perhaps if we give them this item, they will stop!" Others spoke up, agreeing avidly.

Gray clutched Morrowil tightly.

Omni glanced to him out of the corner of his eye. "No," the Ronin said, "If they gain the item, then even Farhaven will be destroyed. You have but a single choice. If you follow us, there is no certain safety, but we will protect you as best we can. If that is your decision, gather supplies for a journey north. Bring blankets, food, water, and anything else you can find that you will need to survive. Spare all else. We move before the sun sets."

Gray watched the faces of those around him, and he saw uncertainty. At last, he looked north. Beyond, were mountains that reigned like spires of ice, and beyond that, sat the monolithic Burai's.

"I don't believe it," Darius whispered.

"Daerval can't be gone. An entire land can't be taken without a fight," Ayva said.

Gray wasn't so sure. Suddenly, the crowds stirred, life rippling through the throng. The villagers rose, and without ceremony stripped the deceased of their possessions, the very same bodies they had wept for only moments ago. They scattered, gathering cloaks, blankets and other necessities. As they moved, they slowly gained purpose.

"We should help," Ayva said. She seized Darius' arm, and headed towards a large burned building in the center of town.

Gray followed. They approached the fallen structure. Inside, he rummaged for supplies while Ayva and Darius went up the rickety staircase. A sign amid the broken tables read, "The Willow Yen Inn," and he propped it upon the hearth's mantelpiece made of thick yen wood. It was the only thing that seemed unharmed. It seemed right leaving it there.

Ayva came charging down the stairs. Behind her, Darius stumbled with clothes brimming from his outstretched arms, bags strapped around him like a packhorse. He laughed and Darius shot him a grimace. Outside, they counted their luck.

Ayva listed their bounty. "Three packs, clothes, a sack full of dried salted pork, as well as two blankets and several skeins of water."

"Not bad," he said.

"Pssh, no help from you," Darius replied shoving him.

Gray scoffed, feigning injury. "That's not true, I helped."

"Sure, if sitting back while I did all the hard work is helping," the rogue said.

Ayva shoved a leather pack into Gray's hands and another in Darius'. "Here—stop your bickering," she said and then gave a toss of her hair. "We all know it was all my work anyway."

Darius rolled his eyes, and then they quickly divided the rest. Gray filled his pack with clothes and water, and strapped it to his back where Morrowil was already placed. Once they were done, they made their way back to the villagers.

Ayva paused, looking around. "Where's Darius? Wasn't he just here?"

Gray scanned the soot-streaked faces. What was he doing? Sight-seeing? Every building was toppled and charred, so all the alleyways were blocked, every exit but one. It led deeper into the ruined village. “Let’s find out,” he said, and Ayva followed him. Most of the structures rose no higher than their head, but a few still loomed precariously.

In the corner of the village, huddled against a wall, were four terrified horses on the verge of bolting. Darius knelt before them.

“Darius what in the seven hells of Remwar are you doing?” Ayva whispered. “You’re going to be trampled.”

Darius held up a hand and a sprite young mare the color of snow whinnied and reared onto its hind legs sending a shower of hooves. Darius remained motionless. Slowly, he stood. He approached the creatures while issuing soft words, and slowly put a hand out toward the stallion. It had a black coat, and a white blaze. The creature’s dark eyes watched him. Then at last, it bowed its neck and let him stroke his muzzle.

Ayva sighed in relief.

“You’ve got to give it to him,” Gray said.

Darius looked back with a smug grin, “Not bad, right?”

The snowy mare was the perfect height for Ayva, and beside it was a plain brown pony. But there was one that stood alone, a chestnut stallion with a golden mane. He flicked his head and snorted in warning. Gray approached.

“I wouldn’t,” Darius advised. “That one is mad.”

The horse snorted rearing up on its muscular hind legs. Gray pressed out a hand. In the horse’s wild eyes something swirled, the chaos of the scene that had destroyed Koru village. Gray stretched closer, and lashing hooves skimmed his head. He reached into the back of his mind and wind whipped around him. A hoof scrapped his cheek cutting a shallow groove.

Ayva and Darius cried out. “Wait! It’s all right,” he said speaking to the thrashing horse. “I understand.” He reached out a hand and touched the stallion’s velvety nose. The animal’s muscles flexed revealing daunting strength.

Darius breathed through his teeth. “Nicely done.”

The animal nuzzled his palm. The fear in its eyes was gone. “I guess this one is mine.”

“It’s as if they’re meant for us,” Ayva said. “What are the odds?”

“My lucks not run out,” Darius said and leapt onto the black stallion.

Together, they found saddles and rode to the village square. Gray dragged the stubborn pony along. Out of the corner of his vision he saw a flash of gray cloth. He swiveled in his saddle. Wind rustled debris through the empty street.

Ayva and Darius looked at him. "What is it?" she asked.

"I felt something." His eyes scanned the destruction, and he turned the corner. A verg's head stared at him with an expression of frozen horror—mouth twisted and black eyes peeled wide. It had a face like a bloated man's head, but with leathery gray skin and too-big eyes. Jagged teeth sat inside a wide mouth, its jaw like a cliff. It sat on a blood soaked wooden post. A few threads of wispy hair fell from its pate and stuck to the blood. The cut at its neck was clean; the skin hadn't even puckered yet.

Ayva put a hand to her mouth and turned away.

"Who could do this? And what is it doing here?" Darius said.

"It's a message," Gray whispered, peering into the distance, as if he could pierce the walls.

"What kind of a message?" Ayva asked.

"Who cares? It's a dead verg, that's all that matters, and I don't plan on sticking around to find out," said Darius. "Come on, Gray."

But the glint of metal caught Gray's eye. He neared and saw that a small dagger pinned a fragment of gray cloth. He grabbed the edge of his own cloak. A small swath was cut from the corner. He wrenched the fragment free from the dagger, and they matched perfectly. Glancing over his shoulder, he saw Ayva and Darius had already moved away. He crumpled the cloth scrap in his hand, and turned away from the gory head.

They reached the village square and saw the others were already moving. They formed a long train out of the village, following the dusty trail northward.

Gray anxiously rubbed the cloth between his thumb and forefinger. He debated telling the others, but decided against it. What would he say? The betrayer of mankind is trying to kill me? No, he had no idea what Kail wanted. But whatever it was, it was between him and the traitorous Ronin.

Approaching the others, he handed off the brown pony to the nearest couple with a small child. He caught up with Ayva and Darius. Mura, Rydel and Karil were at their side, and all of them were just short of the Ronin. He swayed in his saddle while his thoughts churned. The ruins seemed to be full of lurking shadows. Kail was out there, somewhere. To take his mind off it, he decided to name his steed as they passed through the last shattered gates. He looked down at the stallion.

Fendary? Fendary the Stormbreaker. Fendary the Sentinel. Fendary Aquius, a High General during the Lieon had supposedly fought the Ronin. As the stories went, he had only a hundred men to the Ronin's nine—which side won was a mystery in the stories, but the fight alone solidified Fendary as a legend. However, now that was all mixed up… truth and fallacy, who was good and who was bad, all blended together. No, he thought, patting the horse's flank affectionately. That name doesn't fit you.

Fael'wyn, the word came to him. Strangely it seemed right, familiar somehow. Gray nodded, for the first time feeling that he had a companion, someone to share his troubled thoughts with. Looking up, Death's Gate soared in the distance. It was as if they summoned him.

A Clash of Heroes

They traveled for days. Gray watched the land change after leaving Koru Village. The grassy hills turned to the flat lands of the Yimar Plains. As they rode, Gray witnessed more of the Kage's devastation.

The land was scarred, flayed by an army of hooves and tracks from machines of war. Anything green was charred and shriveled, the roving hordes burning all in their path. Several times Gray skirted pools of inky black, remembering Maris' warning.

Once or twice, they spent a cold night in the shelter of a partially ruined farmstead. Gray slept inside a small farmhouse, like the others, but the smell of death kept him awake. After that, he preferred sleeping on the ground under the sky. Still, he had trouble sleeping. He tossed and turned with nightmares of a burning Lakewood, heads stacked on poles, bloody vergs, and bloated bodies.

One morning as he was riding beside Ayva and Darius, fingering the gray scrap of cloth he'd found, a shrill scream broke the morning air, cascading over the hills.

"What in the dice was that?" Darius asked, watching the skies.

The villager's all around were equally frightened, whispering amongst themselves.

Maris appeared from thin air at his side, watching the sky with narrowed eyes. The Ronin wore a light green vest, what the stories called a Haori. The man looked just as he had imagined with piercing eyes, an angular face, and white flames of hair.

"Well?" the rogue probed.

"A dragon," the Ronin answered.

"A dragon? I thought they were just stories," Ayva said breathless.

Maris smirked. "Like us?"

"Do dragons serve the Kage?" Gray asked.

The Ronin looked to the turbulent morning sky. "Yes, but it was not always so. Once, long ago, they were divine creatures detached from the affairs of the mortal races—elves, dryads, human and their kin. Somehow during the Lieon, the enemy turned them, and over time they lost their immortality and much of their magic. Now, the once grand beings are mindless beasts by comparison—hounds of the enemy who fetch and kill at the Kage's whim."

"They won't attack with you and the others near, right?" Darius asked.

"I doubt it," Maris said. "But it is worse than that."

"What do you mean worse? How can it be worse?" the rogue said.

"Dragons are the Kage's eyes and ears. Their cries have a greater purpose."

Gray spoke, a cold seeping beneath his skin and chilling his bones. "They are giving away our position by sound."

"Flaming dice," Darius cursed.

Ayva pulled her blue cloak tighter, "How close are they?"

Maris glanced to the horizon. "At this pace? The enemy will be on us before daybreak."

"And the others know this?" he asked.

The other seven Ronin rode ahead, conversing quietly.

"Well aware," Maris said.

Darius shook his head, "Then what are they going to do? They have a plan, right?"

Maris was silent.

Mura approached. Gray was glad for his company. The hermit rarely seemed to leave Karil and Rydel's side of late.

"Maris?" asked Ayva.

The Ronin swayed in his saddle. "A long time ago and just over those hills lay the town of Mesia." Gray and the others followed his gaze, seeing only shrouded green hills. "Lush gardens enclosed by white stone. A different breed of people too—their hearts too big for their small frames. And the taverns," he gave a fond sigh, "I didn't think I could ever grow tired of the Green Tavern or the sounds of laughter that sifted among the rafters."

"Maris," he said. The Ronin looked to him. Gray was speechless. Those were not the eyes of the living. Ahead there was a loud commotion, followed by the ring of steel. Maris spurred his horse and Gray, the others at his side, kicked his heels and followed.

The shouts rose as they pressed their way through the crowd to see the Ronin. The seven men faced one another gripping swords and arguing loudly.

Mura broke the tirade, striding forth, "What is going on here?" the hermit bellowed. "If you haven't noticed, the enemy is behind us."

The legends turned to him.

"Leave it be, old man," Aurelious said.

Gray's ire rose. "No, he's right. What do you think you're doing?"

"What does a boy know of such things?" Seth said.

Maris grabbed him. "These events are far over your head, Gray.

Leave it be," he said in a cold whisper.

He shrugged the Ronin's grip off and strode forward. "Call me young, but I'm smart enough to see a fool's trap. By fighting amongst one another you're playing into the Kage's hand."

"You know not—"

"Quiet, Seth. Let him speak," said Omni.

Gray swallowed his trepidation and raised his voice, "This is what the enemy wants. If you destroy yourselves then their job is already done."

"Then what do you propose?" Aurelious asked.

Gray searched for the words, but the truth was he didn't have an answer. "I'm not sure…"

"Perfect," Aurelious said. "This is what we get for listening to a boy's plans for salvation."

"And do you have a better idea, brother?" Aundevoriä asked.

Aurelious growled and a chorus of shouts erupted as the Ronin fought once again.

"Silence!" Baro boomed.

The Ronin quieted and Baro stepped back, Omni taking the big man's place. "We must face the simple truth," he announced, "If we continue on this course our death is sealed."

"Then what are we doing here?" Seth questioned. "We've saved them, but we can do no more. They are slowing us down. At this rate, the Kage will catch us. The enemy will not stop. Shall their death be ours as well?" he asked, pointing to the fearful men and women.

A silence descended over the crowds.

"It is true," Hiron said suddenly. Omni looked surprised by his words. "I'm sorry Omni, but for once I agree with Seth. We returned from the realm of the dead for one thing. That one item was and always has been our main goal. You said it yourself, all else is trivial by comparison." Hiron turned to look at Gray. "We came for the sword and we found it."

All eyes fell on him. Gray stepped back. All of a sudden, he was not ready to hand over the blade. It was strange… though part of him loathed Morrowil, something felt wrong about giving it up.

"I made a promise to these people," Omni replied.

"A fool's promise," Seth sneered.

"Watch your words, cur," Baro snapped, baring the bright steel of his giant sword, Iridal.

Hiron spoke, "As usual, Seth does not know his place, but he is also right. A promise is no good if you're not alive to keep it, Omni."

"I hate to admit it, but the fire-head has a point," Dared said, breaking his silence.

"Then what are we waiting for?" Aurelious asked roughly, moving towards Gray.

Gray tensed, reaching for Morrowil.

"Stop, Aurelious!" Omni ordered, but Aurelious didn't slow. Omni flung his hand and a blinding beam of light shot from it. Its light encircled Aurelious like a rope of gold and tied him to the ground.

"Let me go!" Aurelious raged, trying and failing to reach for his sword.

"The blade is out of our hands now, Aurelious," Omni said, "Let it go!"

Aurelious seethed against the golden bonds, "That is not your decision!" he shouted. Luckily, he seemed restrained. Gray sagged with relief until he saw Seth approach out of the corner of his eye.

He gripped the sword in his hands.

Aundevoriä stepped between him and Seth.

"Back away from the boy, Aun, or I will make you," Seth said with cold fury.

"The blade is not yours to take!" Aundevoriä said and a giant earthen hand rose from the ground. Huge rock fingers curled around Seth. The Ronin sliced, but more shot up in their place. With an angry shout, Seth plunged Heartgard into the ground. The hand of earth dissolved in a bout of flame and Gray shielded his eyes from the blast, and then ran to help Aundevoriä.

Maris grabbed his arm, holding him back.

"Let go! They are fighting over the sword! I can end this!" he tried to pull away, but the man held him tightly.

"It's not your fight," Maris said.

"What then? Shall I do nothing while others fight and die for something I hold?"

"I will not let you risk yourself. The sword and you are more important than any one of us."

"Take it!" Gray said, offering the blade, "If you take it, they will stop."

Temptation glittered in Maris' eyes. "I can't…" he replied. "Morrowil is yours."

Gray broke free of Maris' grip when roots sprung from the ground. The thick tubers wrapped around his legs, pinning him. Aundevoriä loosed another cry, a behemoth hand of rock shuddered from the earth. The ground swayed, but the vines held him in place. Villagers cried out and ran. Seth growled and a fire bolt shot from his hand. It hit Aundevoriä and created a cloud of dust. Gray held his breath until Aundevoriä rose from the smoke, clothes smoldering. He gripped a marble shield in one hand and a stone sword in the other.

"Stop this madness!" Omni shouted, and another beam of golden light shot forth, racing towards Seth and Aundevoriä. Yet Baro spurred his huge mount, leaping before the beam. The two collided and the big Ronin grunted as the light hit his broad back, wrapping around him like a huge snake. Baro raised his massive arms and the gold band burst.

Seth was almost to Gray, though Maris stood between them.

Gray gripped the blade tighter, readying himself when suddenly his hands grew hot. The hilt seared until he felt his flesh being fused to the sword's grip. He gasped, at last letting go. In a burst of flame, Seth disappeared then reappeared, swiftly reaching for the blade. Wrist-thick roots sprung from the ground and snatched Seth's arm.

"Back away from the blade," Maris said. "We are your brothers—this is not right!"

"Don't speak to me of bonds! You betray us all! The sword is everything, yet you let a boy hold it!" Seth bellowed.

"He is more than just a boy, can't you see that?" Maris replied.

Seth raised his arm. "If he is more than simple fire will not hurt him."

Gray pulled at the vines harder, trying to flee.

"Stop now, Seth, before you get someone killed!" Maris shouted.

"And what is one life compared to thousands?" Seth growled. "We will all die if the blade falls into the hands of the Kage!"

"Listen to reason. You cannot hold the blade!"

A blast of fire shriveled the roots holding Seth's arm. More roots sprung up, even bigger, trying to pin the angry Ronin, but more fire met it and Gray shielded his eyes. Suddenly too powerful to contain, the fire shot into the crowds. Pandemonium erupted. Ayva was blown back by a blast, falling to the ground. He shouted her name, but still the vines held him, Morrowil trapped against his body. He clawed at the thick tubers with his free hand, but it was no use. Heat washed over him as fire rained down upon Maris, the man now shrouded in an emerald aura. A ball of fire ricocheted off and raced towards Ayva. Darius leapt from his horse, diving before the fireball. The rogue's cloak erupted in flames, and Darius flung it from his back as more fire rained down.

Gray watched, his anger rising. It surged, building like a tempest. "No more," he seethed, rising to his full height and the roots sloughed from his arms and legs, falling to the ground. "Enough!" He bellowed and a gust of wind sent all to the ground. All but Maris and Seth. Striding forward, Gray grabbed Seth by the throat, holding him in midair. The fire and roots stopped in a rush. Gray's fist tightened, limbs shaking.

Seth choked, glaring with hatred. Fire wreathed the Ronin's body, growing and he lifted a burning fist.

Gray gripped the man's fist and a gust of wind snuffed the fire. "No more," he breathed and dropped the Ronin, falling to his own knees, dropping Morrowil. The wind that swirled around him was too much to hold. Exhausted, he let it go and it dissipated into thin air. Gaining his senses, he looked up slowly. All around the Ronin wore looks of shock.

"The boy holds the power of wind…" Dared announced.

"Miraculous," Hiron breathed.

"And more than that," Baro rumbled, "He is a natural—the Banished Element is not easy to hold."

Aundevoriä tapped his stone sword to his marble shield and the two melded as if one. "At last, another wielder of the flow," he said and thrust the now metal blade into the earth, bending to one knee.

Dared knelt beside him, and Hiron did the same.

"Please, don't," he pleaded uncomfortably, ushering them to their feet.

Aurelious rubbed his shoulder and knelt. He pressed a fist to his heart. Gray forced himself not to shirk under his scrutiny.

Seth rose to his feet, wiping blood from the corner of his mouth. "Have you all gone mad? What is this?"

"Perhaps we were wrong, Seth," Aurelious said. "Kail's powers and Kail's sword. It seems only right… The boy was meant for the blade."

Seth's face was a thunderhead. "You all cow to his meager power, but it changes nothing! In the end, even Kail was not worthy of Morrowil, or did you all simply forget that as well? The blade does not belong in the hands of a boy!"

"Then you try to touch it," Maris retorted quietly.

Seth eyed him as if it were a trick, than slowly, he strode forward. "If it is my duty to do what you all cannot, I will." Seth knelt and reached for the blade. As he touched its handle, he unleashed an anguished cry. The Ronin fell to his knees, and his eyes rolled in his skull. He threw the blade as if tearing it from his grip and the Ronin's whole body sagged, hand trembling.

"Don't you see?" Maris asked with fury in his voice, "None of us can touch it!" he said and kicked Heartgard towards the still sputtering Seth. "Morrowil has chosen the boy, whether you like it or not."

Roots twined around the blade and lifted it towards him. "Take it,

Gray. It's yours." Gray grabbed Morrowil, sheathing it firmly upon his back. A shiver coursed through him, glad to have the blade once again.

"That still leaves one thing unsettled," said Hiron. "What about the Kage?" He sounded as if he was wondering about the weather, not questioning the unstoppable dark horde that bit at their heels. "They are still almost upon us. And even with the boy's power, assuming he is able to summon it again, we still stand little to no chance against the enemy."

"That is why we must part ways," Omni announced. "We must lead the Kage away. Only then, will the blade be truly safe from the enemy's grasp."

"And where will we go?" Karil asked, joining in. "What is left that the Kage have not burned to the ground? From what we have seen, Daerval is all but gone."

"There is still one place that is safe," Omni answered, "A place hidden amidst the mountains, untainted by time."

"Are you sure it still exists?" Mura asked.

"What still exists?" Gray said.

"The Shining City," Karil replied.

Omni whipped out his sword and drew lines in the dirt. "The road leads north, between valleys, and at last to a range of mountains. From there, the road to the Shining City is treacherous. It is icy with steep falls, and much of it has been worn with time, but if you can make it to the mountain's peak, you may find a safe haven," he said, stabbing his sword at the summit of the drawing upon the tallest mountain.

"Where will we part?" Mura asked.

Dared, the ever-silent Ronin answered, "Not far ahead, there's a fork in the road. There we can lead the Kage astray."

"You can't leave," Ayva said suddenly.

Darius shook his head, and lowered his heated voice, "They just nearly killed you! You still want them around?"

Ayva's fists gripped her split riding skirt. "What will we do without them? You know as well as I, the Ronin are the only thing between us and the Kage."

"Not the only thing," Omni answered, looking to him. Gray felt the hot weight of eyes. Luckily Maris spoke, attracting their attention.

"I will stay as well," Maris said abruptly. Gray watched tremors of surprise pass among the other Ronin's faces, but most of all he watched Omni. In that moment, a thousand emotions passed between Omni and Maris, far too complex and subtle for Gray to decipher, but then it was gone and Gray wondered if he was seeing things.

"So be it," Omni said at last. "You will stay and keep them safe, fulfilling my promise, and we will ride to face the Kage, once and for all. "

"That is all I ever asked," Seth said with a fierce light in his eyes.

"I think it was always meant to come to this," Baro said, gazing to his brothers.

Dared and the others echoed the sentiment.

"As long as the blade does not meet the hands of the Kage, than we have succeeded in our mission," Omni declared.

The matter settled, the Ronin mounted their steeds and turned north, and the villagers followed. Gray took his reins from Darius quietly.

"Are you all right?" Darius asked.

Gray merely nodded, too overwhelmed for words.

"What was that you did?" Ayva asked.

"I'm not sure," he answered truthfully. "I just saw you being hurt, and it happened."

"Well, whatever it was, thank you," Ayva said sincerely.

"You're welcome," he said with a smile.

"And what about me?" Darius huffed, "I think I might have had some part in—"

Ayva reached up, cutting Darius off. The rogue recoiled as if about to be slapped. Instead, she grabbed his head in both hands and gave his cheek a hard kiss. "Thank you," she said, pulling away with a coy smile.

Darius cleared his throat. "Of course, I mean… it was nothing." Gray felt a sting of jealousy. Mostly though his mind was consumed with thoughts of what he had just done.

Fael'wyn's reins twisted in his hand. He wasn't sure what to think. He had seen the looks of the Ronin. They had looked to him as if he was one of them. The thought was too much to handle and he

shoved it aside. After a stretch of riding, they came before the two paths Dared had mentioned.

Gray slowed Fael'wyn to a halt and looked down both as far as he could. One path veered left, into small thickets of vinewoods and nettlebranches. The other path veered right, towards the Shining Mountains where the frozen blue caps never melted. Mura had told Gray that one of the Great Kingdoms still lurked in those mountains, but other rumors said that the Shining City had fallen long ago. Between the two paths, Death's Gate loomed in the distance—huge stone gates nestled between the giant Burai Mountains.

"So, a hidden city is in those mountains?" Darius asked skeptically.

"That's what they said," Ayva said, still sounding afraid.

The rogue laughed sardonically. "Well, let's just hope the Ronin are the only ones who know about this hidden kingdom."

"And if the Kage do know about it?" she asked.

"They will finish what they started," Gray answered morbidly. "They'll destroy the rest of Daerval and us along with it."

"Dice, way to lighten the mood," Darius grumbled.

"Then we flee to Farhaven," Ayva said, looking up hopefully.

"And how do we get through the Gates?" he replied as he clutched the pendant beneath his shirt. It was strangely warm against his chest once again.

"I don't know," she said, then insisted, "But there has to be a way."

Suddenly the sound of voices drew his attention. He rode to the head of the train and Ayva and Darius followed. As he approached, he saw a circle had formed.

"What's going on?" Ayva whispered.

Gray shrugged, and saw the Ronin sat upon their mounts in an arc, while the villagers, Karil and the others completed the other half. Omni dismounted suddenly, and strode forth. He stopped in the center of the large circle and beckoned to Gray. Curious, he obeyed. Ayva shot him a curious look, but he ignored it and approached.

Omni stood patiently, his cloak with its symbol of a golden sun wavering.

He stopped before Omni, feeling the pressure of eyes.

"This is where we part ways," the Ronin said in a voice just loud enough that only he could hear.

"Why are you telling me?" he said uncertainly.

"Because you are now their leader."

"Me?" he questioned, until Omni's stare made him swallow. "No offense, but there must be a mistake. What about Karil?" he asked, looking over his shoulder at her. She sat regally upon her white mare beside Rydel. He looked back, "Even Mura is a better choice than me."

Omni shook his head, "None of them hold the sword. The blade chose you, and you alone."

"But I don't even know why I was chosen."

"Nor I, but Morrowil does. Trust the sword. More importantly, trust yourself Gray. You were born to lead. They will all listen to you. However, you must believe it first, or no one else will."

"What if I don't want to lead? What if I say no?" he asked hesitantly.

"We cannot deny our fate or our destiny. And yours is to lead. From here on, you are on your own until you make it to the Shining City."

"And even if this hidden city does exist, what then?" he asked. "The Kage will just return—if they can't be stopped now, no one will ever be safe."

Omni placed a hand upon his shoulder. "You are wise to question the future. Sometimes, however, we must do what we can, until we can do what we must."

He shook his head. He didn't know a thing about leading, and somehow he was expected to guide the villagers to safety?

I will help, a voice said.

He froze. Kirin. Turning, he closed his eyes. Get out of my head, he ordered. I am no longer you.

Ah, but I am you.

Gray felt his mind tearing, fear rising from the voice's sudden intrusion. You will not decide my fate.

I can help…

I don't want your help!

We can lead them, Kirin insisted.

"No!" he shouted, silencing the voice at last.

He was afraid of losing himself to the voice… afraid to be overtaken and then be nothing more. Just as Kirin was lost to himself, couldn't the reverse happen? He shivered and looked back to Omni. Luckily, it all had happened in a moment, but the Ronin looked confused by the sudden outburst.

"You will deny your fate?" Omni asked.

"I would lead, but not if this path is simply one of death and

misery."

"Enough," Omni said and gripped his collar. He pulled Gray close, whispering in his ear as all watched, "Listen closely. That blade on your back is more important than you, than us, than anything. You fear for their lives, but they are trivial in comparison. And if we stay, it is only a matter of time until the Kage overtake us. Once they do, they will kill everyone, including you. And once they pry the blade from your dead hands, all will be lost. They cannot possess the sword."

"But why me?" he asked, pulling the blade from his back, "I still don't understand! Shouldn't it have chosen you? You're a Ronin."

Omni shook his head. "The blade was once Kail's, our leader. Believe me when I tell you, that sword would only choose a powerful and righteous owner and it chose you. But all that matters is that you alone can carry it, and so you must.

"If it's any consolation, I was there the day Kail was given Morrowil. Initially, he rejected the blade, fearing the responsibility and doubting his role as well—perhaps Morrowil admires a reluctant leader as opposed to a willing tyrant."

The mention of Kail sent a tremor in Gray. Omni was right, yet to be in that man's footsteps… He gripped the sword, both honored and afraid of its choice. Morrowil was his.

He met Omni's gaze at last. "What would you have me do?"

"For now, get the villagers to the Shining City," Omni instructed. "Once we have led the Kage away, we shall meet you. Until then, be vigilant. And most importantly, guard the sword with your life."

Gray gripped the blade, and then looked to the villagers, including Ayva, Darius and Mura. "I will do all I can to prevent the sword from falling into the hands of the Kage, but know I cannot choose the blade over a life."

"That is your call. Though I fear that choice might be forced upon you before the end." Omni's cloth mask wrinkled in a smile. The first he had ever seen from the man. "Good luck, Gray."

Baro replaced him. The big man grasped his forearm, engulfing it in one mighty grip. "I knew you were an interesting one. Till' next we meet," the man rumbled, a grin splitting his red bearded face. He turned, showing his cloak with its insignia of a black and white blade, joining his brothers.

Gray looked to the Ronin, each giving a slight nod of farewell.

Hiron spoke, "Our time was short, and I wonder if this is how it was always meant to be, but meeting you seems no coincidence. I have a feeling we shall meet again in one way or another."

"I hope so," he said, suddenly afraid he would never see the Ronin again.

"I still don't believe the blade belongs in your hands," Seth said, "but at least you're wise enough to hold it with pride."

"I'm wise enough to hold it with fear," he answered.

Seth snorted, "Perhaps even wiser. Do not die until next we meet, boy."

"And the same for you," he said, and meant it.

Maris laughed, slapping Gray's shoulder. "I like your fire, boy. I'm already pleased with my decision. This shall be fun."

"Are we done here?" Seth said.

"We are," Omni said, nodding to Dared.

Dared stood before the two paths. Silently, he motioned Gray over. Cautious, he went to the Ronin's side. Dared took off his glove and placed one hand to the earth. "Closer," he instructed. Gray neared and the Ronin seized his ankle. "Stay still." Swallowing, Gray was as still as stone while Dared closed his eyes.

Suddenly, the ground vibrated and a strange hum filled Gray, his body tingling. White wind swirled around Dared's arm, until it engulfed his whole body. Suddenly, the wind burst and slammed into the ground, and footprints were stamped into the earth all around them. Gray followed the imprints, thousands of feet and hooves as they stretched north. The deed done, Dared released him and slipped his glove back on.

"How did you…" he began.

Dared smirked. "You mean, how did you? Kail's progeny indeed."

Gray's knees shook, wanting to buckle. Putting it together, he realized he was even more drained than before. The sun slipped above the horizon, casting the seven legends in shades of gold and scarlet.

"Das reh vo menihas," Maris said with his eyes locked to Omni.

A flash of emotion passed between the Ronin and Omni abruptly strode forward, lifting his white shroud. As he did, a fall of long auburn hair tumbled out, framing a slender neck and a strikingly beautiful face of a woman. Without warning, she leaned towards Maris and kissed him deeply. Maris returned the kiss just as passionately. Gray wanted to turn, but he couldn't help himself and he watched, awe-struck. Omni pulled away at last, replacing her cloth-mask, showing only her slender blue eyes once again. Then, in a swirl of dust and sand, Omni raced north, the other Ronin at her side.

"I didn't see that coming," Darius whispered.

"Nor I," Gray replied, shaking himself. This whole time, Omni was a woman… A female Ronin, and a beautiful one at that, he thought. The stories had never mentioned it. However the stories were full of flaws, including the false nature of the Ronin. In a way, Omni being a woman wasn't that surprising to him. He recalled the way she moved, graceful and deadly. She was truly a Ronin.

"Now that I think about it, I always knew there was something off," Darius said.

"Liar," Ayva retorted.

"Am not!" the rogue said.

"I saw something, however," Ayva said, lifting her chin. "She always seemed stronger than the rest, and I see with good reason now." Gray laughed, and together with Maris, they watched until the Ronin were a spec on the horizon.

"Well then, what now?" Ayva asked, turning.

She looked at him expectantly, as if waiting for his next words. The villagers, Mura, Karil, Rydel, and even Maris waited for his cue. Glancing into the sun rising in the east, Gray glimpsed the imposing white-capped spires. "East," he announced and raised his voice for all to hear, "We make towards the Shining City."

A Decision

The sun blazed high in the morning sky.

Vera tugged her dark cowl forward as she stood at a fork in the road.

One road lead east towards looming ice-capped mountains, and the other led further west, through ruined towns and away from Death's Gate. Both paths were bare of tracks—as if the Ronin, and the villagers had simply disappeared. Wouldn't that be convenient? She thought, not believing it for a second.

The Kage stood before the two paths as well.

All nine sat upon deathless steeds. They were garbed in dark armor with seamless, overlapping plates like a snake's skin, and deep black cloaks that hid their faces. Grass burned and shriveled to ash with each stomping hoof from the Kage's mounts. Steam breathed from the steeds flaring nostrils. Behind the Kage, the dark army roiled and Vera's eyes scanned the restless horde.

Endless rows of beasts trundled and contended for rank, gnashing and clawing at one another. The Kage's army blotted out the hills. It was a black stain on a once-green land. In the distance she glimpsed dark war-machines, crudely made, rising above the swarming masses. Even to Vera, the sight made her heart clench with fear. A human emotion, she thought disdainfully.

Vera stood removed as she preferred. Behind her, Drefah sat on his haunches. Beside him, stood the remaining few of her pitiful niux.

The leader of the nightmares, Malik the others called him, leapt from his huge mount. He was even taller than the others and wore a huge armored spike affixed to his right shoulder. Darkness flowed from him as he moved, defying the blazing sun. He knelt to the earth, his dark armor crunching as he sniffed the air like a feral beast. Every action of his unnerved her. Malik twisted and his burning stare fixed her. “Come, Vera,” he rasped, not aloud, but sounding inside her skull.

Vera suppressed her terror and obeyed.

Darkness breathed forth from the hood as Malik looked down upon her.

“How may I be of service, my lord?” She replied, hating her servile tone.

“Kneel,” he ordered.

She fell to one knee.

“Lower,” he commanded.

Wordlessly, she bent towards the soft earth.

His dark armor rustled as he knelt beside her. Vera noticed a handful of dirt in his armored fist. “Smell.”

She sniffed and gagged. “The flow. It’s the smell of wind,” she said in surprise and disdain. Wind was the outlawed element, and practically a myth within Farhaven. It was by far the most powerful of all elements, perhaps even stronger than the darkness she wielded. She had no idea it even existed, save for Kail the traitor… Kirin, she realized, nails biting into the flesh of her palm. She looked to the two paths and thrust a hand to the ground, summoning the spark. A veiled smile twisted her lips, seeing the footprints that were no longer there. “Their prints lead west. It looks as if they attempted to cover them up. It was done with the power of wind. A foolish mistake, my lord. Wind is too powerful an element to dissipate in such a short time.”

Malik made a grunt she took for agreement from within his deep cowl. “Their scent leads west as well.” He glanced over his shoulder to his other eight brethren on their dreadful steeds, as if confirming to them what had just transpired.

The dark army suddenly moved, roiling forward like a monstrous snake.

"We head west then?" she asked over the stampede of boots and rattle of armor.

"Where the sword goes, we go," he replied.

Vera glanced away concealing her rage. The mere thought of the sword in their hands made her stomach twist and her dark power rise inside her. When she looked back however, her face was smooth. "Am I done then?"

Malik lunged, snatching her throat with impossible speed. Vera gasped. She grasped the giant hand, prying at his fingers, but it was no use. With inhuman strength he hoisted her from the ground like a doll and he rose to his full height. "No, I am not done with you. I grow tired of your disobedience, but I rather like your cunning. What to do with you? You desire to kill me, do you not?" Malik reveled in her surprise. "To have you at my side is a nuisance and yet…"

"Let me go," she gasped.

Malik watched silently. Her vision dimmed and she flailed for her power, but it was no use. It was like reaching for a breath of air under an ocean of water.

"I…will…serve," she voiced with her last breath.

Darkness flooded her vision, body convulsing. Malik flung her to the ground. She grasped at the fetid earth as her sight slowly returned.

"Yes, you will," he whispered, so close she could smell his rank breath. He grabbed her hair. She winced, looking up at him, seeing only his pale, thin lips twisted in a sneer. "You are mine now. You will not leave my side from now on."

No! She cursed. All my plans useless. I will never wrench the sword from Kirin's grip, and if I do, I will have to hand it over. Suddenly she realized… "Does he approve of this?" Vera asked. "I very much doubt it would please him to hear that his pets are taking matters into their own hands and disregarding his orders."

"The idea was the dark lord's own," the nightmare hissed. "Disagree and die." Rage filled Vera's vision as her nails clawed at the earth. "Gather your niux. I will see you at my side shortly," he said, roughly brushing his armored hand across her smooth cheek. The skin cut and a thin red line of blood dripped onto her hand. He released his grip on her hair, throwing her down. His black cloak whisked as he mounted and rode towards the front ranks.

Vera watched the army roil forward, leaving dust and black smoke in its wake. Her anger was gone. A cold fire replaced it.

The ruby-throated dagger was in her hand, a familiar comfort but a frail imitation of her desires without the sword in her grasp. She eyed the trail. Something is not right. The voice that always pulled her closer to the sword told her that there was deception at play.

"Mistress?" Drefah asked, appearing at her side.

"It's a trick," she whispered.

"But I smell the sword-seekers as well," the wolf growled. "Their foul stink flows west."

"The trail is false. The sword took another path."

"How do you know?" The wolf asked.

It would be impossible to explain to the wolf the voice that spoke to her. In truth, she didn't even know what it was. Perhaps it was him? Or even the dark magic she had given herself over to long ago that promised to make her a living god once she possessed the power of the sword. She wasn't even sure herself how it worked, but it did, so Vera said nothing as she turned and looked east. The Shining City. The last Great Kingdom in all of Daerval waited in those vast mountains. The last bastion of hope. A smile suddenly lit her perfect features. Just the kind of foolish fancy for a hopeless rabble.

"We go east," she commanded, her voice filled with the promise of death. "Gather those who are loyal and those who seek the rewards of slaughter. We travel to the Shining City and to its demise."

"But the Kage?" Drefah asked, eyeing the thundering army that moved west.

Vera wiped at her cheek, and looked with disgust at the blood that now stained her hand. "By the time they discover I am not by their side, it will be too late," she said and licked the blood from her fingers. Soon, I will taste your blood, dear Kirin.

Burning Memories

The inferno burned and screams rent the night air.

Karil looked for a way to run, but every path was shrouded in fire. Her eyes watered from the heat of the conflagration. Hanging lanterns that flanked the forest path suddenly burst, and she shielded her eyes with a cry. Thundering cracks sounded above, and she looked up. The buildings suspended in the giant trees were collapsing. She ran for her life when the ground shook sending her sprawling. She gazed up as fiery wood and branches plummeted towards her.

Karil awoke in a violent rush. Real, she thought, gripping the coarse wool blanket. With a breath she looked around, remembering where they were.

Bodies surrounded her wrapped in blankets. They were inside the destroyed village of Moonville, a town just shy of the road to the Shining City. It was a small village. She remembered seeing it on the maps of Daerval in her many studies as a girl. All elves were trained in lore of both worlds, but only the king's daughter was expected to know it all. She recalled those days fondly, studying the maps of Daerval. Back then, she could scarcely imagine a world without magic. A world beyond Farhaven. She would often wonder how humans, like her mother, lived without the spark running through their veins. They lived such short lives she had always thought. Yet now she knew that they did so much with those brief lives. She did not feel sorry for them, knowing the paradox in which they lived—for each short human moment was filled with enough life, that three hundred long years of elvin lifespan could not replace. One was not better than another, they were merely different.

Though Karil could not make out all the villagers in the darkness, she knew there were more among them now. Upon entering the town, she had been surprised to see a few surviving souls step forth from the burnt ruins. Only a few hadn't joined them. She shivered, remembering those hollowed men and women; for all life in their eyes had been crushed by the terror of the Kage, like a boot upon a burning ember, leaving them mere husks.

There was a slight breeze. "I'm all right," she answered before he could speak.

"I will be the judge of that."

Like a gust of wind, Rydel appeared from the shadows. He removed his hood, and knelt before her. His great black cloak, while shrouding the rest of his form, did nothing to hide his powerful shoulders and muscular neck. The elf's long, sharp ears protruded through his shoulder-length dark hair.

Sometimes the suddenness of his presence unnerved her… No, she caught herself. She would not let herself run away with mistrust and fear, especially not to those closest to her, and definitely not to him. He was and always had been her greatest ally and friend.

Rydel put the back of his hand to her forehead, and she brushed him away, though before she did, she was surprised at its softness. A slight tremor ran through her again, and his eyes narrowed. "You do not seem ill," he admitted.

"I told you," she insisted, gathering her cloak around her shoulders. "I'm all right. It was just a nightmare. We all get those."

The elf looked into her eyes reading her, as he always could, but he could not refute the firmness of her tone. She dearly loved those pale blue eyes—they chilled others to the bone, but to Karil, they were warm. At last, he relinquished. "Full elves do not get nightmares," he said, resting on the balls of his feet. "We sleep dreamlessly. I suppose the nightmares are from your human side."

"I envy you," she said quietly. Karil had seen her father sleep.

The great elf's lids never fluttered once, as if he were dead. The thought made her choke, fists clenching.

Rydel looked at her intently. "If I could take them I would."

Karil changed the subject, ignoring another shiver. It reminded her of her mother's vision, of prophecy. At least I'm not burdened by that gift, she thought. "Is it safe?" she asked, looking out into the waiting dark.

The darkness seemed somehow comforting, like a warm blanket that she could not see beyond, but she knew how deceptive that could be. Squinting, Karil could only make out the nearest sleeping forms and the outlines of buildings. Shattered remnants of what were once buildings, she amended. It was sorrowful sleeping upon the ground where the blood of innocents had been spilled, though now it was only hard-packed dirt, the earth long ago had soaked in the fallen, embracing them, much like the final rights of all elves.

"It is silent, and your uncle keeps watch for now," he said, motioning to a faint outline that sat perched on top of a ruined tiled rooftop. He looked out over the flat desert terrain and sparse brush. "He has a keen eye, but I feel we are unnecessary."

Karil knew what he implied, for Maris, the Ronin, kept watch as well.

"There is nothing wrong with another set of eyes. We still do not know if the Ronin's deception worked," she said. However she knew Rydel inferred much more. Even now Karil could see keener than the others humans around her, and Rydel, even sharper still. Likely in the pitch of black the elf could resolve the tree line two hundred paces from where they slept, though she knew that was not what her companion meant.

Rydel bent to stoke the fire that had grown cold in the night. "He does not need eyes to see… It is the flow. He senses me long before I arrive, and always knows what we've been doing." The man paused, looking out as a slight breeze rustled a nearby tree's leaves. It reminded her of the boy's powers. She narrowed her eyes. Gray's still form lay twenty paces away, sleeping between his two friends. Light and flesh what she wouldn't give to know exactly what that boy is destined for…

"What was the nightmare?" Rydel asked abruptly.

"The same as the rest," she answered hollowly. "Eldas burning and my father's death replayed a hundred times. The worst is the visions of Dryan on his rise to power." Her hands clenched the blankets, remembering. "The tyrant's crusade spreads like a disease, infecting the woods and beyond. I watch each time as elves are slaughtered for rejecting Dryan's cause. Thousands upon thousands," she whispered hoarsely.

"Simply nightmares," said Rydel in reassurance, but even he held a note of uncertainty.

"Our world is dying," she retorted sharply, staring into the shadows and looking north. "Dream or not, I can deny it no longer. We must cross the gates and soon, or all will be lost. I must get home," she whispered fiercely.

"And what then?"

At last Karil smiled, "Then, I have a plan. Then, my dear friend, we wage a war."

Rydel's thin lips curved. It looked sinister in the shadows.

She knew the odds of what they would have to fight as well as him, but she had planned it out, and most importantly, it had to work. She prayed to the spirit of the forest, let the pieces fall together as I see them, and I will ask of you nothing else, she vowed.

"But for now, we aid the boy as the prophecy demands," she continued, with a silent prayer to her mother, and Rydel nodded, listening. "Above all, we must not let the sword fall to their cruel grasp, for it is a part of my plan as well," she said. Karil saw far beyond the still shadows that surrounded her, beyond the outlines of buildings and even beyond the Gates too far to see.

"Then we will not let it fall," said Rydel, "and we will see the boy protected, no matter the costs."

"Soon, we will see our people, and justice will be served."

Sacrifice

Vera truly hated this type of work. When she killed, it was quick and often painless. The need for precision always made her seem cruel, and she did not think herself so. Of course she was not foolish or misguided enough to think she was benevolent. Long ago she had left behind foolish notions of kindness and weakness.

Vera's mind focused back to her work at hand.

The white-haired woman screamed a bloody cry as Vera shoved the dagger deeper into her gut. The woman gasped sharply, trying to catch her breath. Vera paused patiently as the woman sobbed. She watched the light in her eyes, careful not to kill the woman before the ritual was complete before continuing. It was tedious work, but without careful attention it would all go to waste.

Slowly, methodically, Vera twisted her ruby-throated dagger. She cut left and then up, severing the small tendons from one another and scarlet blood, dark as Sevian wine poured forth.

Lifeblood, she thought, licking her lips in triumph.

Vera retracted her dark blade. She loathed the next part, but it was necessary. She plunged her fingers into the soft intestines and the woman gasped, body convulsing against invisible tethers. Vera ignored it. Her powers kept the woman in place. Shaping her hand like a goblet, she scooped up the dark blood, raised it to her lips, and she drank deeply. She gasped as sights filled her mind, memories as if her own.

Standing aside, Silvia watched as the ragged men and women graciously accepted blankets, skeins of water, and whatever food she and her followers could spare. Again, she wished she could give them horses, but all the livestock were slaughtered or eaten by the creatures in the siege. She watched as they piled the supplies on their horses and on their backs. A flicker of something beat inside her—a shred of envy at the veil of hope they still carried.

Soon enough, the lot was packed and ready. They bade her thanks, and began their long trek east. Why anyone would travel to those cold mountains was still beyond Silvia. Then again, there really was no safety or sanity left in the world. One place was just as good as another.

Silvia looked. She took in the young man before her. He was an attractive youth with tan skin, a sharp nose and a fierce intelligence burning in his green eyes. He looked nearly the Age of Passage. Were he a Milian, she imagined he'd be courting the girl of his choice and nervously preparing the Speech of Acceptance to her father.

"Again, thank you," he said sincerely.

"No need," Silvia replied softly, cupping his cheek. She thought he looked like her son, if taller and broader of shoulder.

"Are you sure you will have enough food and water to make it through the winter?" the girl to his left asked, compassion in her eyes. She was tall and pretty and Silvia thought the two were a match, but the charming, if mischievous-looking one at their side made her wonder.

"There is no answer for the future anymore, but we will make do. I wish you all the best of luck," she said.

The young man extended his hand. It was ice cold. Such cold hands for such warm eyes. The pretty girl was speaking again, but Silvia was barely listening. Her mind drifted to thoughts of her Barner once again, and she swallowed back the tears, busying herself by smoothing her tattered, blue dress.

Most of all however, she avoided the scrutiny of the young man's other companion. He was tall and forbidding, with hard features. He wore strange clothes, even for Lakewood folk. Silvia always tried to be as calm and flowing as her namesake, the river, but this man truly scared her. She averted her gaze and looked back to the young man who resembled her son and saw a strange black mark on his wrist. He saw her look and tugged at his sleeve to hide it. At the same time a shred of gauze from the clothe bundle on his back fell and she glimpsed the sheen of silver.

The sword.

The word rung through Vera's mind, echoing from far away and she grasped at it. Vera gasped, returning to her body and her surroundings. Bodies littered the ground and hung from the low wooden wall, its splintered poles like jagged teeth. Drefah at her side, watching guardedly, making sure none of the other beasts approached.

"What did you see?" he questioned.

"The woman aided Kirin and the others."

The wolf's ears flattened against his head. "The boy was here?"

Behind, her army stood, watching from a distance—like curious children she thought. In her meditative state she was weakened and though they feared her, she did not trust the beasts. Thus she made sure that Drefah stayed at her side, ensuring no other beasts neared. She could never turn her back on them.

Their numbers had grown since their departure from the Kage. Her once small group was now tripled in size, she thought with delight. And still growing… More saeroks and vergs joined their ranks daily as they marched towards the promise of death and destruction.

"How do you know the boy was here?" Drefah asked, pressing his curiosity.

Vera turned her attention back. She knelt and wiped her bloody hands on the woman's rumpled dress. "Lifeblood is a powerful force. In the right hands it can divine certain answers," she said simply, though it was far more complicated than that.

"Then where are they now?" Drefah asked. His lips curled back revealing teeth the length of small daggers. A gruesome grin. "What does the woman's blood tell you?"

Vera picked up her now bloody jeweled dagger, hating its gaudiness and answered, "I do not need her blood to know where they are headed."

"What do you mean?" Drefah asked.

"I already knew that the boy and the villagers were headed to the

Shining City."

Drefah shook his massive head, "Then why did we travel to this stinking town?"

Vera's eyes narrowed, "You doubt my methods, my pet?"

"No mistress," Drefah's ears wilted, looking away. "I was only curious."

Vera smiled, a twinge to her perfect lips, and answered, "I needed to know that the sword was with them. Kirin must die, but if the blade is not with them, then all of it will be pointless. And secondly, the road to The Shining City is barren and icy. There will be no forest beasts to feed on." Vera paused for emphasis. "Our army will be hungry."

She looked to her army, and knew the beasts' sharp ears had heard. This time, the creatures responded without fear. They rose on their haunches, tall and imposing, showing fearsome rows of teeth. Vera waved offhandedly towards the dead carcass. She moved away and the beasts roared in reply, attacking and fighting for the warm flesh.

Drefah followed at her side, "Forgive, Mistress. I will not doubt your wisdom again."

"Curiosity was the death of me, my pet. I would be careful," Vera looked away, ignoring the slop and grind of flesh and bone, gazing towards the frozen blue peaks. The Shining Mountains. "I will see you soon, old friend."

The Lost Road

Gray slowed to a halt. Ahead the road spiraled up into the bowels of the Shining Mountains.

Ayva and Darius stopped at his side. Karil and Rydel were on his other side. Their pointed ears and slender eyes barely visible from inside their deep hoods. Behind them, the villagers fanned out.

Up close, the Shining Mountains scraped the heavens, white and blue frost clung to their craggy spires. It seemed an endless mountain range. Seeing them in the distance, the mountains reminded him of a blue spine, rising from the land of Daerval—but now that image fell short.

"I never thought they'd be so big," Ayva whispered. "They're beautiful." Her light blue cloak framed her soft face as she sat on her white mare. Part of Gray thought she looked too fragile for all the harshness that surrounded them, but he reminded himself that she was tougher than most. Looks can be deceiving.

"It's just ice and rocks," Darius mumbled, shifting in his ragged black clothes.

Mura clasped his shoulder. "You did it. The Lost Road, the path to the forgotten kingdom, The Shining City. A sight I never thought I'd see."

"We did it," he replied and with others close behind, he led the procession to a patch of grassy ground at the foot of the mountains. Maris rode up from the back trail. Again, somehow Gray sensed the man's arrival before he even appeared. Gray glanced to the trail from where they had come and saw no evidence of footprints. It was a clean swath of dirt as if no one had ever ridden there. It still amazed him.

"This will do," Maris announced, eyeing the surroundings approvingly—a tall stone sat in the middle of the withered grass. Gray assumed it was a relic from the Lieon. The Ronin pointed to the foot of the mountains where a stone hollow was carved out of the mountain as if dug by a giant's hand.

"Give the word. Feel free to inspire hope, but do not fool them. We cannot stay here long. We depart at dawn."

"They are cold," he said. "Many of them will want to make a fire, can I at least give them a chance for some warmth?"

"Just for tonight," he said at last. "Let them know that upon the mountain it will be all too noticeable."

Gray turned to the villagers. They looked like apparitions filling their tattered clothes, but he saw a flicker of hope in their eyes, and he wouldn't take that away. "We will camp here for the night," he announced. "Rest well, but be ready to move at first light."

Most looked reluctant, but dutiful before turning to set up camp.

"They really listen to you," said Darius.

"Aye," Mura agreed with a note of pride.

Turning to Maris, he knew the man's eyes were fixed on Death's Gate in the distance. The Ronin's thoughts were clearly for his brethren, and Gray wondered how the other Ronin fared as well.

Maris looked to Karil who was as exotically breathtaking as ever upon her white mare. "Set them in that hollow over there. It will provide sufficient shelter for tonight."

Rydel looked taken aback by the order. Karil put a hand to his muscled forearm. "Relax, dear friend. We all have our part to play if we intend to survive."

"You two can help her," Maris added, eyeing Ayva and Darius.

"Gladly," Ayva said and Darius grumbled with a nod.

Maris turned to Mura.

"And for me?" the hermit asked.

"You, old man, set up watch with the elf. Keep an eye to the outskirts of our little camp. Alert me if you see anything," he ordered. Mura's brows furrowed obviously detesting the title old man. Gray couldn't disagree. Mura's age, while a mystery, could not vie with the Ronin. A Ronin was immortal, or so the stories said.

Maris turned to Gray as the others began to set up camp. "Come," he bid, heading towards a small thicket.

"Where are we going?"

The Ronin didn't answer as he rode silently away.

He spurred Fael'wyn. Gray was all too aware of whom he followed, a Ronin. He shivered and looked over his shoulder to see Ayva watching him from afar. He held her gaze, until he slipped into the thicket of bamboo and beyond.

* * *

Ayva watched the two enter beneath the strange forest of tall green poles. What in the seven hells is he doing now? She thought. Why does he trust him like that? She shivered, thinking of the Ronin with his white flame of hair, ice-blue eyes and sly gate, the man, if he was a man, reminded her of a wolf. What could Maris want with Gray?

"Thank you," an elderly woman with curly gray hair said, taking the blanket that Ayva absently extended.

"You're welcome."

The woman set up her bedroll beside a man and a little girl. She watched as the man helped the little girl into the bedroll, tucking her in and planting a kiss on her forehead. For a moment, she remembered her father tucking her into a warm bed with crisp clean sheets. He would hum her favorite lullaby as she drifted off to sleep with the scent of sweet spices and the tang of hops from the kitchen.

Ayva shook her head, pushing the memory aside as she wiped her eyes. She looked again to the forest. Nearby, Mura cursed, singeing his hand upon the fire.

"Mura…"

"Yes?" he asked, looking up, burnt fingers in his mouth.

She realized she actually couldn't tell how old he was. Lines marked his face, alongside his fall of gray and black peppered hair. However, his eyes were a mystery that spoke of years of wisdom, but full of youthfulness.

"You've known Gray for sometime… Why?"

"You mean why is Gray, Gray?"

"Exactly."

The man laughed. "I'm afraid that's a difficult question to answer. In truth, the boy has always been a mystery. Even when I first met him. Even more so back then, really."

Ayva bit her lip again as she knelt by the man's side. In the corner of her vision she saw Darius working with two young boys, helping them set up their bedrolls. The small boys seemed eager to please.

"Where did he come from?" she asked.

"Farhaven," Mura answered, and as he spoke, he waved a hand over the piled sticks. A fire sparked, lighting the twigs.

She gasped. "You can wield it too?"

Mura gave a self-satisfied nod. "Yes, I have the spark, but only slightly. All those from Farhaven have a touch of the spark, though not many but the elves, Reavers, or Dryads can wield it. And to answer the question, whatever Gray can do, and wield is far different."

The spark, elves, dryads, Reavers… Ayva's mind spun with the words, and images flashed in her mind. She was filled with questions and wasn't sure which to ask first. "Then you're from Farhaven too, just like Gray."

"From the land of the elves."

"Eldas?"

Mura nodded with approval in his eyes. "Indeed," he said excitedly, "Very impressive, not many in Daerval know such things."

Ayva warmed under the praise. "Yes, well, I spent my life in Daerval, but my father always said that my mind was elsewhere." Again, the thought and memory of her father caught her off guard, and her voice failed her. Mura seemed to notice. When her throat lessened its constriction, she spoke, "My mind lived in Farhaven." It was her father's words.

"A fine place for a mind to live," Mura said. His hand touched her shoulder, and she looked into his warm eyes. She could easily see how Gray loved this man. He appeared gruff on the outside, but kindness radiated from him.

She cleared her throat, "But you're not an elf."

Mura chuckled. "No, I am not, but one does not need to be an elf to live within Eldas."

"I heard differently," she said. "I thought it was elvin law that humans are forbidden to pass the borders of the Relnas Forest and enter into the Kingdom of Eldas." Again, she read surprise in his eyes and delighted in it.

"How do you know all this?" he leaned forward, the fire dancing in his features. Nearby, Ayva overheard an old woman telling a story, ushering the children to sleep.

"Gray's not the only one with a mysterious side," she said.

"Indeed. Well then, you're right again. However, consider the phrasing of your own words. Humans are forbidden to pass the borders of the Relnas, but one could be born inside without passing through, correct?"

"You were born inside Eldas?"

"I was," he said. "I am an exception to the case, for that and other reasons."

"That's amazing! To be born within the city of the elves, you're so lucky. I can't even imagine the stories you must have. Sometimes I wish that I was born an elf." She realized it sounded silly, but Mura just looked at her, not indulgingly, but interested and she continued her confession. "Other times, in my dreams, I see myself as just a cloud and I whisk beyond the Gates to see what lies beyond Daerval."

Mura smiled genuinely, "That sounds like a lovely dream. When the imagination has no answer for the unknown, what you see must seem limitless. Modesty aside, however, Farhaven is a world just like you imagined. A world of magic and one without limits."

Ayva's heart nearly burst hearing those words. "I knew it!" she said, gripping her skirts. I must sound like a little girl. "So, you knew Gray from Eldas then?"

"I wish," Mura said, tossing another stick into the fire and brushing his hands, "Perhaps it would be easier to understand the boy, or at least to be able to help him with his answers, but I only met Gray once I came to the Lost Woods, so I don't know where he lived in Farhaven, but he has the mark of a Reaver."

"A Reaver?" Ayva asked. "You mentioned that before, I've never heard of it."

Mura stared into the fire. "Casters and wielders of magic, the spark. They are few but powerful. They live in the great city of Farbs, but reside in the restricted and infamous Citadel, a great black keep in the heart of the desert city. It is the hub for all the human kingdoms, the capital and a great bastion of power, wealth, and knowledge."

The words again flowed through Ayva, conjuring images. "Gray lived there then?"

"Likely, but he is nothing like a Reaver. Nor does he wield the power of one."

"I don't understand," she said. "It's all magic, is it not? And why not a Reaver if he bears the mark?"

Mura shook his head, as if realizing whom he was talking to. She saw the look in his eyes. It was the same look her father got sometimes—like he was trying to piece out a puzzle in his mind. "Of course not, my apologies."

"No, I want to know," she pressed. "Please."

Mura pulled out an apple from his pack. He carved it as he talked, offering a piece to her. "Let's see, where to begin? The power of a Reaver is the power of the eight elements, fire, water…"

"… stone, moon, sun, flesh, metal, leaf," she finished.

"Ah, very good," he said waving his knife with emphasis. "But did you know that each element stands for a kingdom?" He raised a sliver of apple, as if to simulate one of the kingdoms. She shook her head. "They were nine empires of old, called the Great Kingdoms that held sway over all the lands. Each element represented one of these cities. They were the famed cities destined to unite the world in a time of bloodshed and bitter conflict. And they accomplished this. For five hundred years, the lands knew peace, creating the age of the Lieon, or the Everlasting Peace. In the end, it was not meant to last." He bit into the slice of apple. "These same kingdoms broke the sacred alliance and shattered the world."

"The Lieon," Ayva whispered. Mura nodded, chewing. Something about the numbers didn't add up to Ayva, but she held her peace, captivated.

Mura prodded the fire, then looked up. "My mind wanders from my point. What was I saying? Ah, yes, the power of the Reaver. It stems from the eight elements, and they harness them with varying degrees. Their ranks split up as Neophytes, who wear gray, and then the infamous Reaver, who wear the scarlet robes. It is a title gained after many years. Some Reavers may only don their robes at the age of ninety or a hundred, and some never—it is a very difficult challenge to live the life of a Neophyte, let alone pass the Seven Trials."

All of it was a mystery in Ayva's ears, and she only feared Mura would stop.

"Of course there is a final rank, that of Arbiter—only three Arbiters exist, and some say, ever have. They live thousands of years, having harnessed and obtained a level of the spark that some say is not feasible for mortals. Rumors abound that they uncovered ancient powers and now give their souls to the dark. For that and other reasons, many nations fear them and the magic of the Citadel." Ayva shivered, and slid closer to the fire. "Needless to say," Mura whispered, "Reavers and those from the Citadel do not seem like Gray's sort."

Ayva threw a stick into the fire, absently chewing on the apple slice in thought. "I see…"

"Moreover," Mura said, staring deep into the fire, "the power of a Reaver is not what he wields." The orange flames snapped, as if soaking in the story as well. "Reavers wield all eight elements, but the forbidden ninth—that of wind. The banished element. A power far greater than all the other elements that died out long ago in all races, and some say never existed, except in one man. The traitorous Kail." Mura stared out towards the bamboo woods. "And now two."

"Gray," she whispered.

Darius approached, lumbering under the weight of sticks filling his arms. "Where's Gray?" the rogue asked. Mura grumbled and Ayva fell silent. Darius snorted, "With the Ronin again?" He tossed the kindling upon the ground.

Twirling a scrap of kindling between her fingers, she watched the bamboo woods. Nearby, the villagers had all settled down and a deep night was sinking in. Where are they? She shook her head. "Stubborn fool," she muttered, throwing the tinder into the fire. Making me worry like a girl waiting for a dance.

Darius looked towards the forest, "I don't get it. Maris is so worried about roving bands of nightmares and they are still out there?"

"Are you worried about Gray?" Ayva asked.

"No," he said quickly, sounding flustered, "I'm worried about us, I mean, the villagers." He grumbled and composed himself. "The Ronin, our supposed fierce protector, is out gallivanting in the woods. What good is that?"

Ayva hated to admit it, but she agreed and eyed the shadows. What if the dark army is out there right now?

Karil approached, offering comforting words, or answering questions to villagers as she passed, and all seemed to listen and trust her Ayva realized curiously. She approached, moving like flowing water. "You have to trust him," the elvin queen said.

"How did you hear us?" Ayva asked incredulous.

"An elf's hearing is quite different than humans," she replied. Karil knelt at Mura's shoulder but looked to Ayva as she spoke. "He will come back. You must trust him to do the right thing."

Rydel appeared, pulling back his heavy cowl. She hadn't seen him approach, but it didn't surprise her. The man was quieter than a shadow. Tall and imposing, she was afraid of him, but equally intrigued. "It is only natural that he spends so much time with Maris," he said. "The boy and the Ronin hold a strange connection, something ancient it seems."

Mura grumbled again, "Not natural."

"I agree," Darius said.

She couldn't argue with Rydel, for Gray did seem tied to Maris. A Ronin. Darius shook out a blanket and handed it to her. She accepted it with a smile and then pointed to the mountains ahead, dark and imposing in the night. "Why is the road we are following called the Lost Road? I've heard you call it that several times now."

"A good question, with a dark answer," replied Karil. The elf pulled back her hood and motioned for Ayva and Darius to sit beside her. Ayva was taken by her features—her tall pointed ears, sharp nose, high cheekbones, and silver eyes. She was breathtaking. Darius seemed equally taken. Again, a sliver of envy shot through her.

Karil spoke, "The story is short and bittersweet. The road at one time led to the Great Kingdom of Hoalin, or the Shining City as many call it now, the shining bastion of all the Great Kingdoms in this land, said to exist even before the Gates. During the Lieon, as one of the destined nine Kingdoms, they fought for the safety of the lands of good. Then it came time for the Shining City to send their famed war leader, Menithas, to the frontlines when Eldas was under siege. He and his army did not show. It was a betrayal of the deepest kind. Thousands of elves died."

"If the Shining City had fought, would the war have been won?"

Darius asked.

"Many think so," said Karil. "It has been many years since then, but few in Farhaven have forgotten it, and least of all the Ronin, I expect. Their hatred for those who had a hand in their death so long ago still burns red hot, even deeper than the elves. The only thing they loathe more is their once-leader."

"Kail," Ayva whispered the legend's name and the flames crackled and sputtered.

"The Betrayer," Darius cursed.

"He is known by many names, Betrayer among them," Karil said. "Soulless, Dark One, Traitor, but none are more well-known than the infamous Wanderer. One day perhaps history will know the true reason for his betrayal."

Ayva couldn't help but feel the ominous weight of the following silence.

"We should all get some sleep," Rydel announced, breaking the silence. "I will take first watch, and then Mura."

"Then I," Karil said.

Rydel looked like he wanted to argue. "Then you, my queen."

"Then me," said Ayva.

"Three should be enough," Rydel replied.

"Aww… nothing for me?" Darius asked with a feigned look of disappointment.

Mura winked at Ayva, "I'd gladly let you have mine my dear, but middle shift is definitely the roughest and I don't sleep much anyway."

Karil spoke, again, softly, "Get some rest, Ayva, and you as well Darius. I'm afraid we'll all need it in the coming days."

With that, they moved to their bedrolls, Ayva settled in beside Darius and even closer to Gray's empty spot. Though as she lay there, she was restless. She knew Rydel and Karil were right, but she couldn't stop thinking about what Mura had said. She glanced up and east, to where she knew Gray had wandered. Above, a spray of stars lit the night, casting soft light on their camp. The crackling campfires lulled her, and after days of hard travel, she found her restlessness overcome and her lids like weighted shutters. She drifted off to sleep, her last thoughts of distant lands and legends.

The Nexus

Keeping one eye on Maris, Gray watched his surroundings as they wove through the haze of mist and bamboo. Beneath him, Fael'wyn nickered. He stroked his mount's neck, understanding the creature's unease. Anything could hide within that mist.

Before him, Maris rode confidently. Gray eyed his swaying cloak and the insignia. It reminded him of his own, yet different. Instead of his two crossed swords, Maris' bore the mark of a simple leaf.

Abruptly the Ronin stopped. They stood in a small clearing now, and green and black stalks of bamboo encircled them. The mist was thinner here. A white layer coated the ground and swirled around Fael'wyn's hooves.

The Ronin dismounted. "Get off your horse."

Cautiously, Gray obeyed and approached.

"Discard your blade."

"Why?"

"You will not need it," Maris replied. "Its powers will confuse your own for now. And in the future if I command you to do something, you will do it without question."

He was taken aback by the Ronin's sharp tone. Hesitantly, he grabbed the haft of the sword and threw it aside. The Ronin grasped Masamune, his famed blade, and threw it. The blade twirled end over end, sticking into the ground.

"Now what?"

Maris gave a wolf-like smirk. "Now, I'm going to teach you to maintain the flow." The Ronin bent his head and there was a low hum. The mist pulsed. Gray's blood stirred as a faint green aura sheathed Maris' limbs. The Ronin raised his head and Gray took a step back. Maris' pale eyes now glowed an ominous green.

"How did you do that?"

Maris' eyes dimmed. "When a Ronin finally learns to control his power his eyes will glow according to their gift when he embraces the flow."

Gray remembered Kail's red eyes.

"I will not mince words with you, Gray. If you control too much of the flow, you will die, but if you fear it, it will control you. It is essential that you learn where you stand quickly, or you will be a victim to your own power. I know you're afraid of who you are, but you must conquer your fear before you can maintain the flow. You must face your past."

"But I can't remember anything!" he said angrily.

"Ah, you can't remember who you were, not who you are."

He looked to the sword on the ground, "I've heard the same before, but what if my power still feels my hesitancy?"

"Then you must give in."

"Give in?"

"Give in to the power that lies within you. There is a wall before you, Gray. You are trying to go left, right, up or down, to push the wall, or pull it. Instead, imagine there is no wall and walk forward."

With a breath, Gray shut out his surroundings, and delved inward, probing the corners of his mind. It was different this time, like reaching his hand through shining glass. Just as before, the swirling ball of air appeared, glowing in his mind. He opened his eyes.

The swirling ball of wind now floated in the palm of his hand. He looked up and a note of surprise flashed across the Ronin's face.

"Very good," said Maris, as he approached.

Gray's concentration wavered, and sweat beaded on his brow.

Maris circled, continuing, "If you can do that, I assume that you likely have found your source. That may save us some time."

"My source?" he asked.

"What some call the nexus, it is what you draw your power from," the man answered. "It is what you just pictured in your mind and what the power of the flow feeds on. For each Ronin it is different. I, for instance, see a leaf, Seth, a flame, but no one Ronin's is the same."

"The flow… is it only the power of the Ronin?" Gray asked.

"Correct. Reavers, magic wielders from the other side of the gates, wield the spark, not the flow. Some are powerful too, but it is not the true power."

"What's the difference?" he asked, still holding the floating ball of wind in his hand.

"The flow is the essence of all elements, whereas the spark is but a sampling. There is an old saying, 'Ki are the eyes of the world, the spark its hand, and the flow its soul.' Aside from the power of Arbiters, the highest of their ranks, there is no comparison."

An owl shrieked and the power in Gray's hand died, air dissolving across his palm.

Maris' eyes narrowed. "I see. Your power is pitiful and hard to hold. Then your true power can only be summoned under dire need."

Gray bristled, but said nothing.

Maris summoned a breath, and a giant ball filled his palm like molten green fire. Angry and alive, the whole glade was illuminated by its glow. Maris made a fist and the ball disappeared. "The stronger you are, the more of the flow you can hold. I know my limits, but I've had the luxury of a thousand years of practice. You, on the other hand, do not. You will have to learn quickly. You will master the flow here and now." Gray's heart beat wildly inside his chest. "What comes next is of terrible importance. This once, you must summon every ounce of the flow that you can hold."

"Assuming I can, what will that do to me?" Gray asked.

"I have heard it described a thousand different ways. To me, merely touching the flow is bliss and fear, like holding a flame that burns my hands, but ignites my soul. For you however, holding all your power may feel worse than death."

Gray swallowed. "What happens if I don't?"

"If you do not fill yourself to the brink, you will always fear what is inside you and it will never truly be yours to hold. It takes many years to acquire a relationship with your source, your nexus, but we do not have that luxury. We will have to force it."

Gray looked to the ground. Strangely, he trusted the Ronin. Why would he suggest it if he did not think me capable? But why risk it? Was it not two days ago that I didn't even know I held this power? At last, he smiled and looked up. "I'm ready."

Maris nodded. "To trigger it, I will have to attack you, and it will have to be an attack that requires you to defend with all your power." Gray's fists clenched at his side. "But that is not enough," continued the Ronin, "after you block the attack, summoning your power by need, you must make it yours. You may lose your mind up until that moment, but if you ward off my strike, you then must come to your senses and gain control of the raging fire inside you to truly make it yours. With that much of the flow inside you, it can be only contained by your sheer will, or you will die."

"I understand," Gray said.

"Then let us begin," Maris said and closed his eyes. Bright green flames suddenly roared to life, coating the Ronin's limbs. Gray threw up his arms, shielding himself from the flaring heat. He glanced down and saw the mist shudder when the air crackled and the hairs on his arm stood on end. Leaves floated, rising from the ground. Puzzled, Gray touched one and startled as it snapped, sizzling as if on fire. Fear pounded in his veins and he saw Maris through the haze.

The man was a flame of green, burning like an emerald sun. Green filaments pulsated from his center, making the nearby stalks bend. All the air in the glade rushed towards Maris, but wind coated Gray's feet and anchored him to the earth. Roots burst from the earth all around him, undulating as if with a mind of their own.

Maris raised his arm and a flaming green spire shot towards Gray.

Gray cried out, bracing himself when his world dimmed… Power roared inside him, but it was too much. He was useless against the storm rising inside him. He grasped, reaching for control, but his vision clouded completely and he fell into the abyss.

No! He raged. But it was no use as his voice dwindled, too small for even him to hear. Lost in a world of white, there was no pain, no anger, simply a shroud of endless pale… time and space of no consequence. A thousand years or a single moment might have passed. Something was oddly pleasant in that vague notion. Emptiness. He could finally give in… love and hate, life and death… none of it mattered in the ashen world. All strife and struggle faded. Even existence was of no concern. Simply a fleeting memory.

Fight it or die! A voice pleaded. And as if thrown into a lake and drowning, he fought, scraping to hold a single thought.

Maris—the name was an arrow to his conscience.

Gray opened his eyes. The world was a blinding white and gold, so bright it hurt. His whole body felt aflame and everything Maris said came back to him in a rush. He knew he was being overtaken by his power.

In his mind, Gray saw his nexus. It was alive and growing. Air sparked from its core, forking like white lightning. Gray reached out a mental tendril and then recoiled as if burned. He lunged, throwing himself onto the crackling ball of wind and cried out as it burned, but he held on. Light burst from every seam in his body, but still he held. Then at last, the nexus' slowed its expansion. Listen to me! He ordered. Grudgingly, the lightning stopped and it shrunk, returning to its normal size until it was quiet at last.

Distantly, he felt the damp earth and he opened his eyes to see eddies of white and gold wind flow back into him. All around, stalks of bamboo lay shattered, felled from the might of the clash. Then he saw the Ronin.

Gray rushed to Maris' side. The man knelt upon one knee in the middle of the glade, his head bent and cloak draped over his still form. As he reached the Ronin, Maris looked up. A thin line of blood ran from the corner of his mouth, and his green eyes looked drained, but otherwise, he appeared unharmed. His hair stood on end like flames of white and he gruffly wiped the blood from his lip.

"Are you all right?"

The Ronin rose to his feet with a chuckle. "To face the Kage, the foul legions of the Endless War, and then to die by the hands of a boy?" He cracked his neck with one hand. "It would take more than that."

Gray sighed in relief when he sensed something behind him and turned. Morrowil lay quietly upon the ground.

"You feel the sword's presence don't you?" Maris grabbed the blade, and pain filled his eyes. Gray accepted it with open palms. "Morrowil is truly yours now," he announced. "That was the final test. It recognizes you as its owner."

Gray examined the blade. "There is one thing though. When I was overtaken by my power, a voice called out to me. Was that you?"

Maris shook his head, confused. "No. I was already overcome by your defense, which was, admittedly, slightly more than I was expecting. Perhaps it was the old you."

Kirin… Despite his last encounter, his old self was still in there, and it had saved his life. Thank you, Gray thought inwardly, feeling very peculiar giving praise within his own thoughts. Still, he would have to be wary of his second-self; for he had no idea if it was truly good, or simply sought their mutual survival. He looked down and his grip tightened. Morrowil, he thought, speaking its name in his mind, accepting the blade at last. It felt right in his hands, finally.

"Get some rest," Maris said. "You will need it. The power takes far more out of you than you realize, and tomorrow will be a long day."

"That's it?" he asked.

"That's it," Maris replied over his shoulder. "Now, leave me be."

Irritated at the man's sudden terseness, Gray mounted Fael'wyn, but paused at the edge of the clearing in annoyance. "You know for a moment there, I saw a human side to you…"

"Then that was your mistake," Maris said callously.

Gray swallowed the cold words.

"You fool yourself with friendships, Gray. The boy, the young girl, even the old man… You risk their lives needlessly. We can hold no attachments. They only hinder us, and cloud our judgment. In the end, a Ronin is always meant to be alone," Maris said.

"Then I am not a Ronin," Gray said.

Maris laughed coldly, "No, you are not. For if you care about them, you will let them go before you destroy yourself or them. Now, enough lessons for today. Go."

Gray snorted and turned. As he left the glade, he looked over his shoulder to see the Ronin standing like a statue in the shattered glade.

A Fated Man

Darkness was fading as Gray laid his battered body on the ground between Ayva and Darius. A bit of rest is all I need, he thought and within minutes he was drifting off. Moments later, something woke him. He ignored it, grasping for the darkness of sleep when the voice came again.

"Kirin..."

Gray opened his eyes. He wasn't sure how long he had slept, but it was still dark. Sleep beckoned and his lids grew heavy once more, memory of the voice fading.

"Kirin!"

His eyes snapped wide. "Who is it?" he called, but there was no answer.

Around him he saw the rumpled forms of the villagers. He looked on either side and to see Ayva and Darius still deep in slumber; the rogue's hand still clutched the dagger hidden in his jacket. Again the voice came. But this time, the sound of his name hummed in his ears like an echo in a cave.

He rubbed the sleep from his eyes and rose, covers falling. The cold crept beneath his skin and he snatched his blanket, curling it around his shoulders. The voice echoed again. Grabbing his blade, he stepped over Ayva. He watched the rise and fall of her chest, careful not to wake her.

Tiptoeing through the maze of bodies, Gray stepped past the last sleeping villager into the darkness beyond the camp. With every step, the pendant grew hotter upon his chest. He ignored it and raised his sword, which glowed silver, lighting the way.

"Kirin…" the voice called again. In it, he heard affirmation, as if it was telling him that he was going the correct way. Soon enough, he stood before the bamboo thicket where he had trained. Shrugging the blanket off, he stepped forward into the mist. The voice led him left, and right, and then left again, weaving through a labyrinth of fog and bamboo. Maris was nowhere to be seen.

At last the voice stopped.

A figure stepped out of the shadows, tall, slender, and in black.

"Vera. You're alive! But how? And how did you find me?"

"Our bond." On his wrist, Gray saw the mark crawl and writhe in the light of the sword. Vera spoke again, drawing his attention, "Even if we both weren't Reavers, I could find you anywhere, Kirin."

"Gray," he corrected remaining at the edge of the enclave. "I'm no longer Kirin."

"If you insist."

He shook his head, "How did you survive?"

"Are you disappointed?"

"No, I just…"

She approached, her perfectly sculpted legs flowing out of her dark gown as her hips swayed. "By luck."

He swallowed. "What happened?"

Vera's eyes lingered on the blade and a strange look darted across her flawless features. Gray pulled the sword away and her eyes flickered back to his. "Yes well, it wasn't easy," she said as she pulled back her black sleeve. Gray recoiled from the sight. Where her first two fingers once were, there was now merely bone. The flesh had been peeled off and a gruesome gash ran up her arm.

"How?"

Vera casually dropped her sleeve, hiding the wound as if to spare him. "At first, when you ran, most of those creatures followed you. In that moment, I gathered enough power to cast a simple spell of light which blinded the rest of the beasts and allowed me to escape, so I thought…" she paused. "The creatures caught up with me.

That's when they did this."

Gray choked, imagining the horrific scene. "And they let you go? I don't understand."

"They tortured me, but it was not me they wanted," she said calmly.

A shiver traced Gray's spine. "What would they want with me?"

"Are you really so naive, Kirin?" Gray gripped a fistful of hair and eyed the glowing blade in his hand. Morrowil. "He searches for you with every ounce of his being. He wants his sword back."

"Kail," he whispered.

Vera hissed at the mention of his name. "You invite darkness by invoking his name—he is the wanderer and nothing more."

He shook his head, "No, it doesn't make any sense, Vera. I saw him. I told you back then, he didn't take the blade. In fact, he did the opposite… He warned me of its dark power."

Vera laughed, it echoed through the woods, it was beautiful but cold and derisive, "Oh sweet Gray. That you question and doubt his methods is simply a tool of diversion… And when you put your faith in him fully, only then will you realize the depth of his madness and the error of your ways. There is a reason why he is called the traitor of mankind. So no, he may not take it now, but he will have it. And once it is his, the world will drown in the darkness of him and his brothers."

"His brothers… Are you implying he is a part of the Kage?" Gray asked.

"A mere part?" she laughed, "As much as one's heart is only a part of their body."

"He is their leader," he whispered in realization. How can that be?

Vera gripped his arm. "But you don't have to worry… I didn't speak a word, for I would never betray you."

"Why not?" Gray shouted, pulling away from her. "You should have told them everything! They could have killed you!"

Vera looked hurt. "Kirin, you don't remember?"

"What are you talking about?"

Her violet eyes narrowed, her face pained as if wounded. "I see… I will show you then why I protected you just as you once looked out for me." Before he could react, she snatched his wrist. Suddenly, his mind was filled with a vision.

The air was warm and the sun blazed high in the sky. They sat on a grassy bank, just outside the tall city walls. A lone oasis in a dune-filled desert. Their legs dipped into the warm water. Kirin's stomach rumbled in hunger. They hadn't eaten in days. "I'll find a way," the little girl said at his side abruptly. "Soon we'll have all the food we want and no one will ever hurt us again." She turned to him gripping his hand. "I promise." And Kirin squeezed back.

Flash.

They stood in a packed room as a man spoke, fear pounded in his veins. He shifted in his ragged street clothes that fit loosely on his small body. A powerful voice boomed off the stone walls. Something at his side grabbed hold. Her hand. He looked at her small round face. Her tiny palm was warm and sweaty but he couldn't be more thankful for it. He gave her a look of confidence, and saw some of her fear fade. Kirin looked back. He would be strong for her, as she had been strong for him.

Gray's eyes snapped wide, and the images fell. The shrouded forest was unchanged, and Vera was right before him. She was the same, and the same fire still burned in her striking violet eyes. He looked to the sword in his grip. "I trust you, so then what am I to do with this?"

"You must keep it safe. It is prophecy."

"Damn the prophecy!" he shouted. "That's all I ever hear!"

A fierce light entered her eyes. "Understand Gray, you can't give up, for the wanderer must never gain control of the blade. With the power of the sword, he would be able to cross the gates and tear the world asunder."

He hid a shiver and grabbed Vera's hand, pulling back her black sleeve to eye her mutilated fingers.

"Did you hear a thing I said?" she questioned.

"Does it hurt?"

She snorted, amused. "You haven't changed at all, have you? Just like back then." Her other hand came up, brushing his cheek with her soft, but cold fingers. She lifted his head to stare into his eyes. "You do understand, don't you? Kail must never touch the blade."

Gray pulled her sleeve down, hiding the wound again. "This was my fault, but I will make it right," he vowed as his eyes fell to the blade in his hand and his grip tightened. "Kail will not so much as set eyes upon it as long as I hold Morrowil."

"Good," she whispered in a husky voice. "That is what I wanted to hear. You are truly something, Kirin." Nearing, Vera pressed body against his. It was firm, yet soft. Gray didn't move. Delicately, she grabbed his face in her hands and kissed him deeply. At last, her soft lips left his and he returned to the moment, finding his breath. "Goodbye, Kirin."

Vera turned and he grabbed her arm. "Don't go."

She smiled, her eyes full of promise, and his cheeks grew hot, "And where would I stay?"

"In the camp, with us," he answered.

Her fingers grazed his cheek. "You mean with you? In your tent?"

Though his blood grew hot, he met her gaze evenly, "Where else will you go?"

"The woods are shelter to those who seek it. I am no wilting flower, Kirin. I'm more than capable of fending for myself. As for why I cannot join you? It's a story as old as time eternal. Reavers and Ronin simply don't mix. Maris would kill me as soon as I stepped foot into your camp."

"But you said I am a Reaver. Besides, Maris isn't like that. I could reason with him," he pleaded.

Vera shook her head with a soft tsk. "The comparison is unjust. You are a Reaver, but you are different than anything this world has ever seen. And Maris wouldn't listen to reason once he saw me. If you care for me at all, this you must trust me on." She paused. "One more thing, if the Shining City is not safe, you must flee to Death's Gate."

He turned away angrily. "Is that part of my prophecy as well?"

"My dear Kirin, you are the prophecy."

Gray felt his hands curl into fists at his side, rage coursing through him. He wanted to denounce the prophecy, to convince her to stay, or tell her he didn't care about his destiny. But when he turned back, she was gone and only the silence of the misty bamboo forest remained. All he could think of was Maris' last words. Perhaps I am destined to be alone…

As if in response, Morrowil glowed brighter. Gray held the blade close. The sword breathed its silvery luminesce, beating back the shadows. It was now truly his companion, he realized. And as he left the clearing, wrapping the blade back in its cloth, a dark glint shimmered across its surface. He looked again, but it was pure silver. Just my imagination.

Through the last stand of trees, he saw the glow of campfires and he halted at the tree line, bile rising in his throat. He felt no desire for the warmth of others this night; he wanted only to be alone. He slunk down, resting his back against a nearby asp tree. Wrapping himself in his cloak and cradling Morrowil, Gray found solace in the shadows and a strange dreamless sleep.

A Figure in the Snow

It had been several days since Gray had seen Vera in the bamboo forest. As they traveled he focused on the treacherous road ahead, trying to distract himself from thoughts of prophecy and the like.

The Lost Road looked as if it had not been used in over a millennia. Higher and higher they traveled winding and twisting. The mountains were thick spires of ice. Their scope and size weighed on his shoulders and he saw others wearing the same look of awe. The soles of the villagers' boots wore thin. Several times Gray pulled men and women up from the ground, urging them not to stop.

Now they made camp at a cliff's edge high upon the winding path overlooking the land below. With dawn fading, Gray wove through the last stand of villager's camps. There was a heavy mist in the chill air reminding him of the bamboo forest. He pulled his cloak tighter. A storm is coming, he knew, feeling it in the air and he moved quickly towards the promise of fire and a warm blanket.

He saw Darius and Mura in the orange glow of a small campfire. They sat on rocks playing a game of cyn. Ayva watched, brows knit in consternation. He glanced to the board and noticed Darius was losing, again. The majority of the pieces on the board were Mura's usual white poplar figurines, opposed to Darius' dark oak. Gray smirked. Mura had bested him more than a few times at that blasted game.

Avoiding the glowing lantern that swung from a withered tree, he made his way to his pack, hoping for a bit of cheese or even dried bread, his stomach hollow with hunger. Several wool blankets were rolled tight and stacked alongside the bags that held their remaining supplies. A teakettle sat on the fire and whistled softly. Despite their vagabond lifestyle, Ayva had managed to make the camp feel like home.

She turned and smiled at him. Throwing back his hood, he returned the gesture, when Mura made a swift move on the board.

"Ah lad, you're back! How's the weather this morning?"

Gray shrugged off his damp cloak with a shiver, "Worsening."

"And scouting? Did you or the Ronin see anything?" Darius asked without turning.

"Nothing but ice and wind." It was not the least bit comforting to him however, and he had been on edge all morning, feeling as if things were hiding in the shadows.

"I coulda' told you that," Darius mumbled.

Mura tugged his dark cloak tight. "Good, good. No news is always the best news when it comes to that sort of thing." He motioned Gray to sit. "Come have some tea lad. It takes the chill off." Gray grabbed a blanket and wrapped it around his shoulders.

"I hope we reach a village soon," Ayva said. "There's little left in the way of bread and now we're dry as a bone as far as meat and cheese goes."

Mura grunted his agreement, "Aye, let's hope."

Gray listened to the sound of the howling wind. Something Maris had said still churned in his mind. "The storm is stronger than it should be at this height and it will let up only when it decides." The way he made it sound… as if the wind was something more. His stomach growled loudly and the others turned.

Mura raised a furry brow, "Have you eaten, boy?"

"I really haven't had time. Come to think of it, I don't think I ate much last night either."

The hermit shook a sausage-thick finger. "You fool, you're going to faint if you don't eat something. You're going to learn to take care of yourself, even if it's the death of me."

Ayva was ahead of him, pulling a half-loaf of frozen bread from the hard ground. Gray suppressed a grimace. The ice kept the mold at bay, but all remnants of taste were sapped in the process, and it always left him hungry. Gray remembered a time when he took for granted a simple loaf of bread. Still, he thanked her, knowing it was the last of their supplies.

"The Kage… how close are they now?" she asked.

"There was no sign, Ayva. Don't worry," he said as he took the cold bread from her. "Maris believes the deception worked. The path is clear from here on. We'll be safe all the way to the Shining City." Somehow Gray felt as if he was trying to convince himself more than her.

"Aha!" Mura exclaimed, making both Gray and Ayva jump.

The hermit reached across the board and picked up the slender figurine at the back, a piece shaped like a man sitting in a tall chair. He plopped it boldly on Darius' slim corner, then wiped the last dark oak pieces from the board.

Darius gave a sly look and he knew that expression. The rogue picked up the short, stout piece; it appeared to be a cloaked fat man holding a coin purse. Skipping it across the board, Darius knocked over the figurine in the high-backed chair with a clunk.

Ayva leaned forward. "Wait, I don't understand. How did you do that? You were about to lose, weren't you?"

"He sacrificed his Followers to get to my Mark. A rogue's trick," Mura grumbled, scrubbing his peppered beard.

"Say what you will, but it did work, and on you no less," Gray said.

Darius nodded smugly. "That's right. What he said."

"Bah, true enough," the hermit admitted.

"Apology accepted," Darius said, "Now where's my coin?"

Mura batted the rogue's hand from the air, "Fool rogue." Gray noticed the remark held an affable touch and he remembered the days when it was only him and Mura. Somehow they seemed so long ago and nostalgia ran through him.

Darius rubbed his hand like a wounded cub. "Oh well, nothing to spend it on anyway. Not until we get to the Shining City at least. Dice! I'm not one for drinking usually, but I've never wanted some warm spiced wine so badly in my whole life." He leaned back and folded his hands behind his head. "What I wouldn't give for the light of a common room, the laughter of men and women, a good bard's tale soothing me to a nice, drunken stupor, and perhaps some warm company on my arm. Both arms that is of course. They'll have to compete for my attention. It'll be tough. I'm quite choosy and I won't want to disappoint either of them."

With the back of his boot, Gray casually knocked him over, ending his rant.

The rogue yelped and fell into the blankets. "Gah! What was that for?"

"I think I regret backing you up."

"I still don't understand," Ayva said, eyeing the board.

Darius leaned back, owning his newfound position. "It's quite simple really. Everyone is so focused on the battle that the war is often taking place right beneath their noses." He pantomimed snatching it from the air.

"Wise words." All four turned at the abrupt voice. Maris stood on the edge of their campsite. With his hood pulled back, his white hair blended with the snow behind him. His features were hard, breath misting in the morning air. "Pack up," he ordered. "Have the villagers ready to leave shortly." He turned as if to leave then glanced back at Gray. He knew that look. He was being summoned. Maris turned and disappeared as mysteriously as he'd entered.

"Why is it that I always feel we are in the dark?" Darius questioned. He got up and gathered up cyn pieces, dropping them into a leather bag.

"Because we are," said Ayva. "What is he having you do that's so important?"

"I've told you. I'm helping him scout. Why are you two so suspicious all of the sudden?" Gray asked.

Ayva grabbed a blanket, vigorously shaking and folding it. "How can we not be, Gray? Did you not see what just happened?"

"What's that supposed to mean?"

"What do you think it means?" Darius asked as he angrily cinched the bag of cyn pieces.

Gray raised his hands defensively. "Look, I really would like to pretend that I know what's going on here, but I have no idea what you two are talking about."

"Of course not," said Darius.

He replied calmly, "If you have a problem with Maris, talk to him,

I don't see—"

"Are you really so blind, Gray?" Ayva asked. "What makes you think he'll talk to us? He has no need for us. He only wants you."

Gray tossed the heel of the bread. "Why do you both care so much? Honestly, I don't complain when you two laugh and have private jokes in front of me, or talk about times in Lakewood that I have no idea about. In fact, now that I think about it, I guess I'm the only one who does have something to be angry about."

Darius laughed unkindly. "So you didn't grow up where we did, who cares? I'm not going to change the things I say just because of that. And it's easy to make private jokes you don't get if you're never here."

"Listen, I don't know about the rest of it, but Darius is right about one thing, we barely see you," Ayva said. "It's like you're too good for us."

"Is that what this is all about? You think I'm too good for you?"

Mura spoke gruffly, "Enough! All of you stop your bickering. Gray is simply aiding the Ronin for now. Besides, once we get to the Shining City this hard road will be behind us and we'll all feel a lot better."

"I don't need this," Gray said, grabbing his wet cloak.

Darius jumped to his feet. "Go then! No one is stopping you. Then again, a Ronin's lapdog wouldn't notice either way."

"Darius that's enough," Ayva said.

His fist clenched at his side. The rogue thrust out his chin, as if daring him to take a punch. At last, he released his fist and strode away.

"Gray, wait!" Ayva shouted, but he was already gone, moving into the camp. Snow fell, but it did not cool his blood. What do they know? They just don't understand, He kicked at a patch of snow. They can play their dicing games and make their stupid jokes while the whole world topples down around them for all I care.

Ahead, he felt the Ronin's presence. Maris stood waiting at a little place above the camp, on the rise of the winding trail. Already, the fire in Gray's blood was beginning to cool, but his annoyance seeped out as he asked, "What is it?"

Maris looked into the white beyond, as if his eyes could see through the flurries of snow. "It was told to me once that with the power of the wind one can sense the presence of others. I need you to do that for me."

"I've done it before, but I thought you can sense others also?"

Maris turned, looking troubled. "I can feel those who move along the ground with the power of leaf, but this presence is blocked. I have a feeling yours might just work."

Nodding, he delved into his mind. Summoning the nexus was easier now. The swirling ball of air floated forth and he traced the same threads, as the Ronin called them. Abruptly, the world was illuminated, not by sight, but by feel. Whatever the wind touched, he could see. With the rising turbulent winds, he imagined this would be easy, but guiding his power was like trying to grasp a feather in a storm. He had to strain to see through the smoke of the campfires and the swirling snow. Tiny bright lights flickered in his mind, glowing as clear as day. Villagers, he realized. When he had a marginal handle on his power he asked, "Where did you want me to sense?"

"Go north."

He obeyed and Darius words flashed in his mind, irking him—the thought of him as Maris' lapdog, but he shoved it aside and pushed forward.

Most of the trail ahead was a haze of white, but he pressed on, flowing over rock and ice. Suddenly a presence pinged, smaller than a gnat. Veering towards it, he saw a tall figure standing upon a rock, but obscured in the blur of wind and snow. A flash of scarlet red pierced his soul and pain erupted in his head. He cried out, vision shattering. He opened his eyes to see his gloved fingers gripping the cold snow. Maris knelt over him with a worried look. "Are you all right?"

"I think so."

"What did you see?"

"A hooded figure standing upon a rock. I saw red eyes."

Maris didn't react. "How far away?"

"I couldn't tell."

Maris rubbed his jaw then gave a smirk. "No matter. You surprise me, boy. You're even more talented than I anticipated."

"Was that?" Gray couldn't say his name.

Maris offered a hand, helping him to his feet. "Kail," the Ronin supplied. "It was a shot in the dark, but I figured if anyone could see if it was him, it would be you. Your powers are remarkably similar. It seems I was correct."

Gray rubbed his head as he gained his feet. "I don't think I was so lucky."

"You think he let you see him?" Maris asked. Gray nodded. "I should have figured. The Traitor is clever. More than any man I've ever known—a fact I owe my life too, and perhaps my death as well."

Though he had heard the stories, Gray could scarcely imagine what happened those many centuries ago to cause such rift. "Then he is the one that is changing the weather and causing this cursed storm?"

Maris rolled his knife through his fingers. "It could only be him."

Wind tugged at his clothes, howling through the passes. "How can he be so powerful?"

"This?" Maris raised his knife, gesturing to the brewing storm. "This is but a fraction of what he can do. This is a lover's caress for him. If he wished it, the wind would not be so gentle," Maris shook his head. "I don't know why but he is making each step upon this mountain a hard-fought one, yet for now, he has still made it feasible. Let's just hope he doesn't bring the mountain down upon our heads."

"What do we do?" Gray asked.

Maris slammed his knife into its sheath. "Nothing we can do. We must continue to move forward. Keep an eye on him if you can, but do not stray too far north—I don't know the extent of your powers, but he does. He was the strongest of us all, and he's had more than a millennium to hone those skills. We must keep you safe." Maris spoke over his shoulder as his cloak flapped in the storm. "Gray, do not let your friends get to you. You will need each other in the days to come." With that, the Ronin headed back towards the camp.

Gray tried to pierce the haze of white with his gaze.

A voice sounded, blending with the wind. "I am coming for you…"

* * *

Over the next few days, Gray searched intently for Kail, though he never saw him again since that moment with Maris. His vision of wind saw only what his eyes did, endless sheets of snow and ice. He found himself spending less and less time with Ayva, Darius and the others, but they didn't seem to mind. A few times he sensed eyes on him, and he looked to see Ayva watching him. Otherwise, he watched as his friends laughed and talked as if he was never there and the gap between them grew greater and greater. Instead, he spent his time with Maris. When the gales of snow, sleet and ice, would get too heavy, they would have to find shelter and make camp or be swept from the mountain. In these moments, Maris would tell him stories of the Lieon, of ancient battles, generals, and the Great Kingdoms. Moreover, he would instruct him on the ways of the flow. And with the aid of the Ronin and hard work, his powers expanded slowly but surely.

One morning, scouting just as normal with Maris at his side, Gray reached out with his heightened senses, expecting the usual when his senses stumbled. The feeling of the mountain was gone, as if there was a void in the world where there should be more snow and rock.

"What is it?" Maris asked.

Gray spurred Fael'wyn, deciding to find out. As they turned the bend, the screen of white cleared unveiling what he had sensed. He pulled Fael'wyn to a sharp halt. His cloak whipped fiercely, as the raging wind threatened to pull him down.

Ahead, the lost road came to an abrupt end.

The path fell away, and an abyss a thousand leagues deep and fathoms wide replaced it. In the distance, beyond the chasm, Gray saw the road begin again. Maris was silent at his side, and Gray realized that the Shining City might as well have been destroyed for they would never reach it now.

The Golden Walkway

The world fell endlessly before Gray. Beyond the chasm, the icy trail of the Lost Road continued, impossibly out of their reach. Mura clasped his shoulder, turning him. "Come back from the ledge, boy."

"It's all right," Gray said. He didn't tell the hermit but the wind coursed around his feet and rooted him to the ground like leaden boots, just like in Lakewood.

"What are we going to do?" Ayva cried over the wind.

"Gone," Darius whispered.

He spoke, still eyeing the chasm. "We cannot turn back." Others turned to him and he continued, "There must be another way. We did not come all this way to be stopped here."

Darius clutched his black rags against the wind. "I don't know if you've noticed, but it's a giant abyss. We're stuck. There is no way forward."

"Then we must find a way."

Ayva spoke with a sudden fire, "Gray is right. We cannot give up! This mountain is full of passes. I saw at least a dozen on our way. One of them has to lead to the Shining City!"

"They are all ancient, dead passes," Mura answered. "There is only one path that leads to the Shining City and that is the Lost

Road."

Maris appeared. Gray watched as all eyes fell to the Ronin. The legend spoke in a voice loud enough for all to hear, "The old man speaks the truth. This is a dead end."

The crowds erupted in shouts. "What are we to do?"

"There is no more food!" another shouted, "We must go forward!"

"No, we must turn back. We are cold and hungry! If we stay, we die!"

The villager's cried out, a dozen voices echoing their fear.

Gray ignored them. He heard something in Maris' tone and he eyed the man. The Ronin, though usually impassive, sat upon his mount with an unaffected look.

"I need to speak with you," he said as the villagers argued. Maris quietly dismounted, and Gray pulled him aside. He spoke in a low tone, too low for others to hear, "Answer me, and tell me the truth, did you know this was a dead end the whole time?"

"Yes," Maris said.

Gray's heart dropped. "Why? You lead us all the way here for nothing?" Maris was silent and anger rose inside him, "Do you have any idea what you've done?"

"I know exactly what I've done. This was a test."

"What are you talking about?" he said feeling his muscle's tense.

"This is what you've needed. Omni knew it as well."

"You're not making any sense, speak straightly," he said, confused and angry.

"Don't you see? Finally, you have an opportunity to conquer your fears and face the limits of your true power. And here it is," the Ronin said giving a broad swipe of his arm, gesturing to the impassible chasm.

"You can't be serious. That's what I am to you? A test?" he said with disdain, and suddenly he loathed the legend, "You tricked me. You took us all this way merely for a game of power."

"No," Maris said calmly. "This is much more. If you do not see that, you will never be able to fulfill your destiny. You must learn to wield and know the limits of your power or you will never be able to face the Kage."

Gray shook his head. "I don't care about that if it's at the cost of others. Don't you see how many lives hang in the balance?" He pointed to the many behind him, "These are innocent men, women and children, or are they merely figures on your board as well."

Quicker than light, Maris' snatched Gray's outstretched wrist. He squeezed it until it felt as if the bone was going to snap. "Watch your tone," the Ronin breathed. "I've faced more death and suffering than a thousand men combined, and I will not be lectured in the ways of empathy. Lives always hang in the balance. It is the knife's edge we must walk. Sometimes, you must risk a great deal to do what is needed. Now is one of those times."

He held the man's gaze until he could no more. At last, he pulled his arm away, rubbing it, "What are you asking of me?"

"Simple. You must bridge the pass to save those you care so dearly for."

"I am not a Ronin," Gray retorted, "How am I supposed to do that? Besides, you're their leader, not I."

"Yet you speak like one," he said, squelching Gray's fire with the truth in his words. He looked away and Maris continued, "You are their leader, Gray. Trust yourself and the nexus will guide you. Besides, your abilities surpass anything I can do. You are Kail's progeny."

The mention of the traitor and his connection made Gray shiver. Far away, a flat landing of rock and ice was barely visible—where the path began again—like an island of ice. A lump rested in Gray's throat as he spoke, "You think I can do this?"

"I do."

"Tell me how to begin," he replied.

"Summon the nexus, and then give into it. The spell should weave itself."

"Is that all?" Gray asked.

Maris gave a wolfish grin, "Just know you will have to summon more power than you've ever wielded before; far more than you had within the bamboo forest. It will shake you to the core. You're going to feel like you just ran a hundred miles and your body was pummeled the whole way. If it doesn't break you."

"Break me?"

"Drawing too much of the flow will kill you, or drive you to insanity."

"Thanks for telling me now."

"Better late than never," Maris said with a sly grin.

Gray nodded, "I'm ready then." He strode forward, and Ayva and Darius came to his side.

"I know that look," Ayva said fearfully, "Just what are you planning, Gray?"

He gave her a reassuring smile, which only seemed to heighten her look of uncertainty. He turned and looked to the villagers, who suddenly quieted. "There is another way," he voiced. The villagers leaned in, trying to hear.

"Summon the nexus," Maris said at his side.

"Why?"

"Kail had the ability to speak with great volume and I remember the threads. I cannot weave it for you, but I can show you," Maris said. Gray agreed and the Ronin touched his temple. Gray stiffened, dragged into a sudden vision. Thousands of dead bodies littered the streets of towns. Villages, farms, and fields on fire, and vast cities of stone crumbled before his eyes. He realized it was the memories of the Ronin. Maris redirected the images, and Gray saw Kail standing upon a hill before the other eight Ronin. The legend addressed a vast army upon the rolling green hills. He watched as intricate webs danced in Kail's hand. The spell took the form of a cone, summoned before his mouth, visible to only those with the power. The threads abruptly tightened and Kail spoke, his words booming.

The vision broke and he opened his eyes. All of it only took a mere moment. Maris flashed a wink, stepping back. He faced the crowds. He realized how he stood. It was just like Kail before his army. However, Gray's own army was much smaller. Moreover it was not trained soldiers, but villagers, men, women and children. However, in a way, the two armies were exactly the same. The villager's bore the same stubborn look. Their strength was quiet, yet unmistakable. Gray lifted his head, gazing over the crowds as he extracted threads of wind from the air. He formed them as he had seen Kail do. He pulled the threads tight.

He spoke, addressing the villagers, "I will lead us to the Shining City—" he faltered, startled by the power of his own voice. Each word boomed, flying over the crowd and reaching every ear. He spoke again, adjusting his volume, "There is another path, but you will have to trust me."

Ayva leaned in close and whispered, "What are you planning?"

Darius gave him an uncertain look as well.

The villager's whispers grew.

"Do you trust me?" Gray asked.

"Of course," Ayva answered.

"We're with you," Darius said, "We always have been. But whatever you have in mind, it better be good."

Gray winked, hiding his doubt, hoping he did have what it took. Slowly, he turned back to the divide, leaving the villagers to whisper and watch. He stepped to the edge, placing his toes to the rocky lip. Bits of rock fell away, tumbling endlessly. They clattered and echoed off the cliff's walls until there was no sound. He wasn't sure what he was doing, but it seemed right. This close to the edge, wind pummeled him from all sides. Zephyrs flowed around him like hands, strong and alive, gentle and furious. He teetered, and threw his arms out when a strong hand clasped his outstretched arm. Mura was at his side, holding him.

"Some things never change," Mura grumbled, a smile beneath his grimace.

Gray felt another hand, and saw Darius holding his other arm.

"Need a hand?" the rogue smirked.

Gray turned to the drop and delved inward, closing his eyes. His power flooded him and his body shuddered. The hands on his arms tightened. He gave in to the nexus and watched as threads unraveled, twisting, and weaving together. More! his mind demanded. He took it all and the wind from the abyss poured over him, feeding the nexus. The swirling ball expanded beyond his vision. A fearful voice whispered, warning him, but he pushed it aside and drew more. He heard Maris' voice, "Drawing too much of the flow will kill you, or drive you to insanity."

He shrugged the words off. Instead, he wove the threads faster and faster, seeing a tapestry of wind form in his mind, so intricate and dense it appeared spun by a thousand looms. All the strands coalesced and his breath caught as he realized the pattern was complete. He reached out, willing the strands to lengthen and bridge the gap. Tightening his fist, the last threads snapped into place like a taut rope.

Slowly, his world returned.

His heart hammered and golden light filled his vision. He heard gasps from all around. Mura and Darius released his arms, and he let them fall as he took in what stretched before him. A bridge of golden light spanned the long abyss. The surface appeared solid, like hammered gold, but beneath the flat surface currents of air flowed. The whole thing was wide enough for two carts with horses to walk side by side, and room to spare.

Gray took a deep breath and he stepped out onto the walkway.

"Gray!" Ayva cried.

His foot landed firmly. The surface was harder than dirt, but more yielding than steel. He took another step, and then turned, looking back. "It's safe," he announced and the villagers burst into cheers, the sound loud enough to shake the mountains. He grinned and Ayva and Darius rushed out to meet him, stepping onto the golden walkway.

"You did it!" Ayva said jumping into his arms with a hug and he laughed as well.

Darius grabbed his shoulders, shaking him, "Dice! That was amazing!" He said and bounced on the balls of his feet, testing the golden surface.

Over Ayva's shoulder, Gray watched as others made their way onto the bridge, glad they were excited and not afraid. Ayva released him, "What is this thing?" she asked, touching the ground and gasped, "It feels warm. Is it wind?"

Gray nodded.

"Isn't that what Kail wielded?" Ayva asked.

"Dice!" Darius cursed, "You're as powerful as the Blight Seeker!"

Gray swallowed, feeling sweat flash on his forehead and palms. He knew that name, as did many—it was one of Kail's many names, including the Traitor, and the Betrayer of Men.

Ayva punched Darius' arm. "Don't you ever watch your mouth?" She turned to Gray. "It's really amazing. I'm not sure how you did it but…" she touched his arm, and she looked as if she was about to speak when several villagers approached. They clapped him on the back and thanked him. Wisely, the villager's kept clear of the edges. Mothers clutched their children with both hands and men steered away others who veered too close in their excitement.

Mura pushed his way through and embraced Gray. "Lad, one day we're going to have to talk about what just went on there."

"One day, I might understand it as well." A terrified cry erupted in the cheering crowds—it was soft, but he had heard it clearly. The others hadn't. They laughed and smiled, unaware, obviously not hearing what he had. "Quiet!" he shouted and his words boomed, silencing the villagers. The cry came again, shattering the quiet and Gray spotted a little girl shrieking and pointing to the sky.

Gray followed her hand and saw huge beasts hurtling towards them, diving right at the crowds. "Dragons!" he shouted and the world exploded into chaos.

Maris grabbed his cuff, "Tell them to get down!"

"Down! Get down!" he bellowed, using his amplified words.

Men, woman, and children, fell to the walkway's surface, pressing their bodies against the flowing gold. The dragons roared and swooped down, snatching several men and women too slow to get down, piercing them upon the point of their talons. Gray turned to Ayva and Darius at his side. Ayva gripped his hand, and Gray's heart pounded as the dragons circled.

Maris spoke calmly, "Time to act, Eminas. We will all die if we do not move. We must get to the other side. Give the command now!"

Gray summoned his voice. "To your feet! Spread out and get to the other side!" The command rose above the chaotic chorus of screaming. He turned to Ayva and Darius. "Keep low and don't stop moving!"

Ayva grabbed his arm. "Wait! We'll follow you!"

"Lead the way," Darius said.

"Stay close." He turned and unsheathed Morrowil as he dashed into the fray. There was a bestial cry and he watched as the dragons descended, diving from every angle. Ayva and Darius at his side, he ducked and dodged slicing talons. A maw snapped towards him, lunging for Ayva. He cried out, slicing down with Morrowil, but the beast pulled back and beat its colossal wings. The wind buffeted Gray, throwing him but Darius grabbed his arm, pulling him forward. They sprinted onward, the wind of the heights thrashing from all sides.

An old man stumbled, and then let out a strangled gasp as a huge, sword-length talon protruded through his chest. The old man looked down, his face a mask of shock. Before Gray could react, the dragon lifted the man from the ground and flung his carcass into the chasm. Another dragon flew overhead, and he dove to the ground assaulted by a gale of wind. The dragon's thick beating wings took men and women from their feet, sending them to the ground.

Lying flat on his stomach, anger and panic surged inside him and he gripped Morrowil tightly as he leapt to his feet. He watched the villagers dash for the opposite ledge, spread out along the golden walkway. Ayva and Darius were nowhere to be seen. He seemed to be the last one. He looked behind to make sure and dread filled him.

A dragon hovered above a child. It was the little girl who had sounded the alarm. The beast reached, clawing for the girl and Gray gave into the nexus. He threw his hands out, pulling with every bit of his power. Thick bolts of air struck the beast and it staggered. The creature released a guttural roar, diving at the girl again, but the bolts gave him just enough time. He dove first, grabbing the girl in a roll and coming up swiftly.

Ahead, more dragons rained down. One swooped low, its talons colliding with a group of running men and women, sending them clear off the golden bridge. Their screams echoed as they fell. Several dragons picked off stragglers, the loud clang of their talons against the golden walkway pierced his ears, ringing like steel.

He turned back to the huge beast as it faced them, blocking their path. Without taking his eyes off the creature, he spoke softly to the little girl, "I need you to be brave," he said, glad his own voice came out steady. "Can you do that?" Her big eyes and small face stained with tears looked back at him, and she nodded. "Good, now climb onto my back and hold on tightly."

The dragon clawed the walkway, snorting and hot steam billowed from its flaring nostrils. The little girl climbed onto his back. Gray checked to make sure the nexus was still there. It sat, waiting. He drew it, asking for more power, and letting it fill his limbs. The girl's arms tightened in fear around his neck as eddies of wind surrounded them, coating their skin.

And Gray ran.

The beast roared and charged, ripping through the air. Its huge talon swiped at him, impossibly quick for the beast's size. He skidded to a stop. The razor-sharp spears missed by a hairsbreadth and a gap formed between the creature's trunk-like hind legs. He dove, the power of the wind aiding him, but the creature was already moving. Its huge maw snapped at the little girl on his back. In midair, the heat of the creature's breath was on his neck. He cringed, yelling as he slid. The barbed teeth pinged off the little girl as if hitting a coat of steel armor. The dragon recoiled. The effort of the shield sapped Gray, and he let it drop. But he was already through the gap and running.

He heard the beating of wings and glanced over his shoulder to see the beast rise into the air and follow. Gray poured wind around his legs and arms, forcing it to his will. The threads came together seamlessly before he knew what he was doing, and he flew like the wind. At his side, he saw the horses. They stampeded, nostrils flared in panic. Their fear gave them wings as they galloped at full speed, yet Gray kept pace until he reached the train of villagers and joined the crowd.

Through the spread of people he saw Mura. Ayva and Darius were at his side. The hermit wielded his obsidian scimitar, fending off a snapping dragon. Further ahead, Rydel was miraculously riding one of the beasts. His dagger was pressed into the dragon's thick, scaled neck as the beast beat its immense wings, trying to toss the nimble elf. The other dragons came from all sides, showering them with talons and deadly fangs, killing left and right. Gray's eyes scanned as he sprinted, until he found what he was looking for—Maris.

A hundred feet ahead the Ronin stood at the golden walkway's end. His hands shook, lifting towards the sky. Gray watched as suddenly, bouts of rock fountained from the mountain overhead, catching a dragon as it rose. It shrieked as its wings were smashed and it fell to the abyss below. Ducking and dodging, Gray reached Maris. The Ronin spared him a look. Maris touched his arm and Gray gasped, sucking in a breath as energy filled his limbs. When he opened his eyes, he saw the Ronin sagged—the weight of what he had just done clearly visible.

He helped him to his feet, shouting over the chaos, "What did you just do?"

Maris gripped his collar, pulling him close, "I gave you what's left of my power. You can do more than I. Now, go, save them!" He yelled, pushing him away.

Gray let the little girl down, handing her to the Ronin, "Watch over her," he said, and then turned. He let the nexus fill him. The power was overwhelming, far greater than ever before. It blinded him, and his knees nearly buckled as it coursed through him. With his vision bathed in golden light, he ran.

As the dragons struck from all sides, he raised his hands and golden white shields struck back. The first dragon connected, crashing into the shield as if crashing into a wall. The monstrous weight of its body thudded against the shield like the slap of meat, snapping bone and tendon. Gray grunted under the weight, but ran on. More dragons dove, attacking the running villagers, and he flung out his hand again. Filled to bursting with the power, more shields sprung to meet them. Talons pinged, ringing like steel against steel; and where the claws struck, rings of gold spread like sunbursts.

Two dragons dove from both directions, claws aimed for a cluster of women and children. Gray erected a giant shield over the huddled mass, and then channeled the voracious winds upward. The dragons' wings caught the upward draft of air. Their paths shifted and they slammed into one another, breaking bones and falling onto the waiting shield. A rush of cries sounded from behind. He twisted. The dragon from before, the largest beast, clutched a man in its talons. He sprinted. In his hand, he compressed a ball of air until it was denser than an orb of steel. The beast's jaws engulfed the man's head. Gray screamed a bestial cry that matched the dragon's roar and let the hardened sphere fly. It streaked through the air, thudding into the huge dragon, and pierced its scaled hide through the chest. The beast groaned, dropping the man in its claws and then fell, smacking the bridge and spiraling over the edge.

The mountain rattled once again. He turned back and an avalanche of rock crashed into the last dragons, puncturing their wings and pummeling their thick bodies. The creatures fell, tumbling endlessly into the icy chasm.

A quiet settled.

Gray fell to his knees, breathing heavily as he scanned the crowds.

Ayva and Darius rose to their feet. Closer still, Mura withdrew his obsidian sword from a dragon's corpse with a dour look, flicking black blood from his blade. Karil and Rydel were at his side. Safe… and Gray breathed a sigh of relief, though as he looked around, he felt a wave of guilt and sorrow. The villager's sobs reached his ears, many kneeling at the walkway's edge, eyeing the empty abyss.

In the end, there were no cheers or shouts of victory, just the heavy howl of wind.

Threads

Snow gusted and Gray held his cloak closer as he rode beside Maris. To his right was the cliff's edge. It was a sharp drop of ice and snow, devoid of trees. As usual while scouting, he and Maris rode ahead of the villagers. It was a ritual that he had come to enjoy. But this morning, something seemed different about the Ronin. The man had said little since they had first set off. Now, a dark silence sat between them.

It had been two days since the golden walkway and the horror of the dragons, and though the grief of the scene had not left, Gray did not think that was the reason for the silent tension. Something else troubled Maris, and he feared it greatly.

More icy wind assaulted them and Fael'wyn snorted in annoyance. He was grateful that Fael'wyn and the others horses had instinctively followed them across the golden bridge, escaping the claws of the dragons. He stroked his mount's neck. He knew Fael'wyn must be as tired and cold as he was. Hold on, he thought, at least for a bit more. When we get to the Shining City, then you can have all the food and warmth you want. Fael'wyn's ears pricked and he nickered softly as if acknowledging.

Ahead, the Ronin stopped. Gray pulled his reins to a halt.

"I can't continue with you," Maris announced abruptly. Gray

was speechless. The Ronin's hood was down, unveiling his flame of white hair. Dark brows hooded his slender eyes, but his face looked sterner, more resolute than normal. He often reminded Gray of a fox. His cloak was draped to one side of his big stallion and he could just make out the insignia of a leaf, what he now knew to be the sigil of the Great Kingdom of Eldas.

"Why not?"

"Ahead lays your path, but mine is elsewhere. You must know, I am truly glad and honored to have been at your side for this long in your journey. You have learned more in a matter of days than most learn in many years." Gray averted his gaze, unable to take the rare gem of praise. He did feel as if the days of training under Maris, hard as they were, eventually bore the fruit of success, hardening him, and his power. The nexus and the wind were becoming more familiar each day. He grew stronger; wielding more than he thought was possible. He didn't want it to end.

"But why now, when we are nearly there?"

"That is why I must go now, before we reach the Shining City."

"I don't understand," he said, confused. "Besides, the villagers need you, you can't simply abandon them."

"They have you now to watch over them."

Gray wanted to say something to make the man stay, but he didn't know what—in truth he feared there was nothing he could say. "You can't go," he said at last.

"It is still strange hearing such things. It's been a long time since anyone has wanted the presence of my company." Maris gripped his shoulder. "Trust yourself, Gray. The nexus burns like a fire within you."

Gray's cold fingers tightened on his reins. "Without you, I'm alone. I'm different."

The Ronin raised a brow. "I believe I know more about being an outcast than you, and you are not one. You, out of all people, have taught me that we are never truly alone. Besides, the rogue and the girl? They have lost their homes and the ones they love too."

While he knew it was true, he felt a thread of frustration, like an ember burning just beneath his skin. He didn't know how to explain it. "You don't understand. It's this power, it's this title, it's all of it… with you here I am—I feel more normal."

"But you are not normal."

"And that is exactly what I fear."

Maris spoke into the silence, "I know what you fear, but you are not Kail, Gray."

The simple words struck a chord, and his jaw clenched as he looked away, unable to meet the man's stare. "And what if you're wrong?" he whispered. "I have the same powers, the same sword, why not the same fate?"

"You may share similarities, but you are nothing like the man. Besides, your friends do not see darkness, but light."

"But they have not seen what I've seen," he answered. "I've seen the darkness inside me." He grabbed his sword and shook it in his fist, "I've seen this blade, my blade, according to you, wet with another's blood, and I know nothing of it!"

"You have a choice before you, Gray. To live in your past or embrace the present, you cannot do both."

"It's not so easy," he replied.

"I said it was a choice," said Maris. "I did not say it was an easy one."

He turned his gaze on the Ronin. "Have you forgotten your past?"

Maris' gaze turned stony. "My past is much longer than yours, wrought with thousands of years of death and destruction, but also with memories of life and joy. I will not stand here and tell you that those memories are buried and gone. I still grieve the lost, and in my darkest hours, I wish I could relive certain moments and change their outcomes. So in the end, I am much like you, but what I can tell you, is with every dark inhale I may take, I let out a breath of life. I do not fear my darkness anymore."

"But I am terrified by mine…"

Maris gripped Morrowil, and pain roiled in his eyes. He pressed the sword to Gray's chest. "Then if the blade came to you in darkness, show it only light." The Ronin turned.

"Wait," he called. Maris stopped, cloak wavering. "Will I see you again?"

"We shall meet again, in one realm or another," Maris said. "Remember, when one thread ends, it's only waiting for another beginning." Maris looked to his wrist. "I almost forgot. There's something I've been meaning to tell you. That mark of yours, it's the mark of the Devari."

"But… I thought it was the mark of a Reaver."

"Who told you that?" Maris asked.

Not wanting to reveal Vera, he conjured a lie, "A book I read, one of the stories."

"The book was wrong. While they both live within the same walls, and the marks are fairly similar, a Devari and a Reaver are worlds different. Reavers are men and women who control the spark. They are respected and feared throughout Farhaven, though many are corrupted by their greed for more power."

Gray's curiosity spiked as he remembered what Vera said. "The book also said that Ronin hated Reavers."

Maris grunted. "True, but again taken out of context. There is no great love for Reavers from any who remember the true events of the Lieon. They were our magic against magic, but many of them sided with the enemy, selling our secrets, and in the end it resulted in a great schism."

Gray nodded. "But what is a Devari anyway?"

"An elite group of warriors who can hear keener, and smell sharper, as well as sense the presence of others. They also have the peculiar ability, for a small moment, to inhabit the body of one nearby and feel what they feel."

Gray was speechless. "Are you saying that is who I once was?"

"It's at least a good start," Maris said.

"Where across the gates?"

"Within the great desert city of Farbs, in a dangerous place known as the Citadel, where all but Reavers and Devari are forbidden." The Ronin looked over his shoulder with a sly smirk. "I hope that helps," he said sincerely and turned, riding into the haze of white. Just like that—he was gone.

In the distance, Gray heard the crunch of snow. He reached out with his mind. He sensed Ayva's quiet steps, Mura's firm plodding, Darius' sly gate, Karil's smooth tread, and even Rydel's almost silent stride, as well as the hundreds of villager's behind them. As he opened his eyes, he remembered Maris' words and glanced to his wrist. The ability to sense others.

Darius was the first to appear. The rogue coughed into his ice-rimmed gloves, "Where's the Ronin?"

"Gone."

The rogue cleared his throat, "I think I misheard you, did you say Maris was gone?"

He turned, eyeing his friend with a smile. Darius' mop of disheveled brown hair was matted down by white snow. "I did. He just left."

The rogue scratched his head, confused, "Well, is he coming back?"

"We are on our own now." Gray eyed the trail ahead as if he could see the Kingdom of Ice around the bend. He knew he would see Maris again. And Kail was out there too. He couldn't forget that. "Just another thread waiting to begin," he whispered into the wind.

The Shining City

Gray slouched in the saddle. He listened to the sound of hooves on the road as he faded in and out of sleep, when he glimpsed an image of white stone. It was only a flash, but it shone brilliantly like a white gem. He jolted upright.

Mura rode at his side. "Well, good morning." Gray rubbed his tired eyes. "I'm glad you're awake, lad—I think you ought to see this." The hermit raised his staff and pointed.

Gray's jaw dropped as he looked ahead. In the distance, sat a massive city of snowy white against a crystal blue sky. Towers like brilliant flutes shimmered, rising impossibly high, while long bridges suspended by mostly air stretched between the spires. A great alabaster wall surrounded the grand kingdom.

Up and down the wide dirt road, murmurs of amazement rippled through the scattered villagers. The trail of refugees buzzed like a kicked bee hive.

Immense, Gray thought, to seem so vast and tall from this distance. Clouds hung in the sky above. Their gigantic shadows not enough to darken even a pocket of the crystalline city.

"What do you think?" Mura questioned, swaying in his saddle upon his dark gelding.

"I never thought it would be so big. It's beyond breathtaking."

With the coolness of dawn fading, Mura shed his cloak and stuffed it into his saddlebags. "And yet, it is but a small glimpse of what it once was."

"What do you mean? How could this be anything more?"

"What you see before you is only one of the cities that once comprised the mountains, and only part of the Kingdom of Ice."

"Part?"

"Long ago these mountains were filled, all of it the Kingdom of Ice. It was a sprawling fortress with each city, just like this one, connected by colossal bridges, so long and wide they appeared as if made by magic. Sadly, now this is all that remains from the Kage's path of destruction during the Lieon."

Looking at the city before him, Gray couldn't imagine anything grander. "I've read the stories about the Great Kingdoms, but this? How can men make such a thing?"

"It was a time of legends, thousands of years of knowledge and wisdom accumulated to create a world at its very pinnacle," Mura said and shook his head. "No, I'm afraid it has been a long time since anything like this has been made. Sadly, many of the great builders are lost to time. However, many of the nine Great Kingdoms still exist. If only you could see Eldas, Kingdom of Leaf. It is a city of wonders, where lights are suspended in the ancient monarchs whose branches reach the heavens," he said excitedly and then sighed.

Looking at Mura, he felt a twinge of sorrow for the man, for a moment glimpsing what the man had left behind. "You've lost a lot for me. I'm truly sorry, Mura."

"I'm not," said the hermit and winked. "I would make the same decision again in the blink of an eye, my boy."

Gray smiled, hearing the sincerity in the man's voice. All along the road, the people laughed and smiled as they stared at the fortress-like city. For once, they let down their guard. He watched as men grasped their neighbor's shoulders, and women talked excitedly, while children pointed, trying to gather their elder's attention as they hopped on the balls of their feet. It was infectious and he found himself smiling as well, caught up in their good cheer.

Mura leaned closer. "Before we enter, my boy, there is one thing you must know. The people of the Shining City are proud, but their pride borders on conceit. They know no better because they are cutoff by the collapsed passes to the west, the pass you bridged, and they have been that way for the past two thousand years, since the war of the Lieon."

Gray scratched his head in thought. "If that's the case, then it will be hard to convince them of the danger they're in."

"That will be the trick of it," he said. "They are stubborn to the bone. Moreover, we are the first outsiders they've seen in a very long while. In the past, other towns, including Tir Re' Dol sent messenger doves in an effort to establish some form of cooperation, and the city's king, Katsu, not only refused, but sent back hawks with the severed heads of the doves. He proclaimed that if it were possible for men to be sent he would do the very same thing."

"How can someone like that become king?" Gray asked.

"Do not be so quick to judge a man's character, for I suspect Katsu may not have been so foolhardy when he rose to power. Though with time, power corrupts many. If he held a hint of pride or arrogance before, with the rule of an isolated land, it has only worsened." Mura's eyes narrowed, "Suffice it to say, this will not be an easy task."

Gray thought Katsu sounded like an arrogant fool; then again, power did change people. He glanced to his hand that held Fael'wyn's reins, eyeing the sinuous black tattoo. The nexus whispered in his mind, but he pushed it aside, swallowing hard. Somehow and somewhere along the line, Gray now was responsible for the villagers, and if Katsu wouldn't see reason, he wasn't sure what he would do. He felt the sword on his back and itched to grip its dark red handle.

Ayva and Darius rode up alongside him. "My eyes, look at that!" the rogue exclaimed with a lopsided grin as the sun gleamed off the soaring walls.

"It's beautiful," Ayva whispered. She cast Gray a sidelong glance. Contrary to her shy smile, her blue eyes flashed before she turned away. They neared, close enough to see the guards walking on the high ramparts of the gates.

"Dice…" Darius muttered

Ayva kicked him in the shin. "Watch your mouth, there are children around!"

Darius mumbled beneath his breath, when men on horseback approached. Gray squinted under the glare of the gleaming armor. He eyed their sharp, burnished halberds and heavy helmets that must have sweltered in the sun. Their mounts snorted, cantering briskly, obviously fresh from the stables. The two parties came to a halt, a stone's throw apart.

A rider with a plume upon his helmet rode forward. "I am Captain Mashiro, commander of the High Guard, servant of the righteous King Katsu," he said in a strange accent, clipping his words. Then he paused, eyeing the procession. "Who leads this rabble?"

The few villagers at the head of the line turned to stare at Gray. Reluctantly, he nudged Fael'wyn forward and spoke, "There is no one leader among us, but many. We seek entrance to your fair city."

Karil appeared at his side with Rydel beside her. Surprisingly, she looked untouched by travel. While he felt as if he could fall asleep for a week, she looked well rested. Her fall of blonde hair, tucked behind her elvin ears, was brushed to a shiny luster and her scarlet cloak looked as if recently washed.

"Who are you and how in the light's realm did you cross the pass?" Mashiro questioned.

Gray wasn't sure how to answer when Mura appeared at his side. "The pass was bridged when we came across it. There is no longer a divide between the Shining City and the world," the hermit shouted in reply.

This news seemed to rock Mashiro, but he answered in a steady voice, "What is it you seek?"

"We come from the west, from Lakewood. We have dire news and seek council with King Katsu, immediately. These people need only the shelter of your high walls."

Instead of answering, Mashiro turned to his armed party, and they conversed in lowered voices. Gray wished he had a way to hear their words.

"What on earth are they discussing and why is it taking this long?" Ayva questioned, restless.

"This isn't good," Darius grumbled and shifted in his saddle.

Gray looked back to the armed entourage when a voice skittered across his awareness. Listen… He paused, and the pendant grew hot on his chest. Suddenly, the nexus pulsed within his skull, swirling eddies of white forming in his mind. Gray listened and the nexus filled him. Suddenly, threads wove in his hands. Feeling almost as if his power was not his own, it flowed through his limbs, into his fingers tips. Yet he knew it came from him. The threads wove together, thin ribbons of light blended with wind. Then they abruptly tightened.

He reached out a hand instinctively and the wind flew to the armed guards. Then as if ladling water, he cupped the words, catching the vibrations in the wind and bringing them to his ear.

"What if it is a ploy?" said a guard, watching the crowd.

"A pretty big ploy if you ask me. Look at them, they're near dead," another replied.

"It doesn't matter," Mashiro countered. "You know the rules. Outsiders are only permitted under orders from the King or from Councilor Tervasian."

Mashiro twisted, looking set on a decision, and Gray knew the answer. But before the man could speak, he raised his voice. "Mashiro, we are hungry and exhausted. If you have a shred of compassion in your body you can see that, and I doubt Tervasian would approve of this.

Even from this distance, Mashiro visibly rocked back on his horse, stunned by his words. "You are under order of the Councilor?"

"The Councilor himself," Gray bellowed. He tried to hide anything but his conviction. Gray felt sidelong glances of uncertainty from Karil and the others. He didn't look back, hoping they would continue to play along.

At last, the guard captain raised a hand. "Approach alone!"

Gray turned to Karil. "Come with me. It might help our position."

Karil simply nodded. "Stay here," she ordered to Rydel. The man looked liable to argue for a moment, but at last bent his head.

As they approached, the captain flipped back his gleaming steel visor to unveil deep-set eyes and a beard that encroached high upon his cheeks. The men ringed him like a fan of steel. When they were a cart's distance away, the captain spoke. "That is far enough! I said alone, how difficult was that to understand?"

"You fear a lone female, captain?" Karil asked.

The man grunted. "It is clear trouble follows you. Why should I let you in?"

"Look for your own eyes, the danger is not from us—many are women and children, and they are starving. We can move no further. You would deny them?" Karil said.

The captain looked at the crowd. Gray saw his hesitancy and he leaned towards Karil, speaking in a low breath, "I have an idea."

"I'm all ears at this point," she whispered.

"Reveal yourself."

Without question, Karil pulled back her scarlet hood and the guards gave looks of shock.

Seizing the moment, Gray spoke, "It was told to me that your people, this city, once had an opportunity to aid those in need long ago. Instead, they hid, cowering behind their high walls and forsaking all bonds. Thousands of elves died that day. Do you seek to repeat history, Captain? Or do you wish to rectify a tragedy and redeem the honor of your people?"

Mashiro eyed him a long hard moment, but only when he looked to Karil did his face soften. At last, he turned to his men, "Give the command. Open the gates."

His men clapped fists to heart. Shouts were relayed and massive chains rattled. The giant double doors slowly opened. Upon the door was a huge teardrop of white and Gray recognized the symbol.

It was the flame of the Kingdom of Ice. One of the nine elements that stood for each Great Kingdom. The same symbol Hiron's cloak bore. Gray watched as the excited villagers were herded towards the massive gates.

"What just happened there?" Darius said, nearing. "That was crazy, I was sure we weren't going to get in, but then from out of nowhere they started barking orders and jumping like milk-fed stable hands!"

"Watch your words, Darius. If they hear you and change their mind it'll be more than me that will want to have your hide," Ayva admonished, and then leaned in close. "What did just happen there?

How'd you change their mind, Gray?"

Darius scowled.

Gray motioned them to quiet as Captain Mashiro approached wearing a grimace. "These men here will see to an inn for you six." To the men he said, "See them to the Dipping Tsugi."

"And the villagers?" Gray asked.

"The rest will be given provisions in the Common District, and shelter will be found or made. That is all I can do."

"Thank you, Captain," Mura said.

Mashiro squinted into the light of the sun near its zenith. "A man will come for you before sunset, if the king is willing to see you."

"If?" Darius questioned.

"This is no light matter, lives depend on this, Captain," Mura cautioned.

"And I will present your request with the fervor you have shown, but it is his Majesty's decision whether or not to see you." Mashiro turned to leave. "If that is all–"

"Wait," Karil interrupted, "Let me come." The captain's eye narrowed. "Take me with you, to ensure the King understands the weight of this matter."

"So be it," he said at last.

"I am the queen's personal guard. I go as well," Rydel said. He sat ramrod straight on his horse, and seemed unlikely to back down.

"I will not take a whole procession unannounced to his majesty, King of the Shining City, last of the Great Kingdoms. You will stay."

"He will not be coming," Karil interrupted. She turned to Rydel and lowered her voice to a whisper though Gray overheard, "Pick your fights my friend. You know this is possibly more important than any of us. The king must be informed of the real threat—the Kage. I can protect myself. Please don't worry. See to the others and secure us an inn. Keep them safe."

Rydel never took his eyes off the captain. Finally, he gave a slight nod to Karil.

"We leave now," the captain said. He spurred his horse, and with the guards in tow they made their way through the gates and towards the king, their hopes riding with them.

As Gray watched them leave, a small weight lifted from his shoulders. He had gotten them this far, and it had seemed impossibly hard. The next step was out of his hands. He felt suddenly exhausted. He swayed in the saddle and at the same time Fael'wyn danced to one side nearly toppling him.

"Whoa! Easy there!" Darius called. "Dice, are you all right? I don't know about you, but I could use a cold brew and from the looks of it, you need a good night's sleep."

Gray laughed. "I'll take you up on that, but if I do sleep, you think you can stay out of trouble on your own?"

Darius' words were suddenly cut off by a long, continuous creak from the doors, ushering all to silence as the city was unveiled.

Spellbound

Gray gawked at the scene before him.

Houses lined a paved road of ivory brick, the smallest of which could fit ten or more of Mura's simple cabins with room to spare. Each roof was a colorful mosaic of blue, green and yellow clay tiles with eaves elegantly curled like fingers, and tiled spines like vertebrae. Straight ahead was a channel of turquoise water that ran crossways to the street. A white bridge spanned it, leading deeper into the warrens of the Shining City. But first and foremost, Gray noticed the people.

Farm carts and wagons ran back and forth along the smooth road. A line of men came to and fro from a giant white and blue marbled building with thick columns and a series of stairs, the tallest and grandest of all the nearby structures. They jostled jute sacks over their broad shoulders, piling them onto a large boat that sat in the channel.

Darius whistled through his teeth.

The sharp ping of a blacksmith's hammer rang in the distance, soft music filtered from the inns, and the sounds of trade flooded the air. Those closest to the gates stared fearfully or in awe at the ragged newcomers.

"Well, no use wasting time here, right?" Darius said with a breath of excitement.

Gray urged Fael'wyn forward and the others followed. Side alleys branched from the main road that led to green courtyards lined with trees bursting with pink flowers, stone benches, and viewing pools. Upon the canals, slender boats skimmed along the water, brimming with trade goods, sacks of flour, stone bricks or even squawking geese. The men or women who manned the boats carried slender wood poles to urge the vessels along. Here and there, the canals fed to quiet pools where other boats sat moored. The water reflected the white city around them.

"Light, this place is beautiful," Darius said. "I wonder what the inn is going to be like. I'm so used to the hovels of Lakewood." The rogue's eyes were wide, as if he were already picturing the pints of frothing beer and smiling waitresses.

"Lakewood's inns weren't hovels," Ayva replied.

"Have you seen where we are?" Darius scoffed. "This is what a city is supposed to look like!"

Ayva's brows furrowed. "You're a fool," she said. "The Golden Horn had twice the heart and warmth of any place here I'd bet."

"Sure, sure," he replied.

"Take it back, Darius," she said.

Gray kicked the rogue's calf, hoping the fool would realize that he was touching a sore subject, and at last he threw up his hands, "All right fine! Sheesh, the Golden Horn was a step above the others, but they all were ..." Darius saw Gray's look and he coughed into a hand. He spoke again, softer, "Look, the Golden Horn was great, but all I'm saying, is by comparison, I'm pretty sure—the Golden Horn excluded—the rest of them will look more like Mistress Sophi's outhouses than inns. Speaking of which, I think I'm ready to take you up on that drink you promised me, Gray."

"Interesting, I don't seem to remember a promise like that," he replied.

Darius slapped his back, "You've had a lot on your mind. I forgive you."

Gray laughed when an image flashed in a nearby alley. Twin swords. He pulled Fael'wyn short, gazing down a dark alley mashed between two marble walls, but he saw only shadows.

A hand clasped Gray's shoulder and he startled.

"Gray?" A soft voice asked. Ayva's light blue eyes met his, creased with concern.

"I thought I saw something, but I guess I was wrong."

Darius shrugged. "Well, that's good enough for me."

"Are you sure you're all right?" Ayva asked.

"I suppose I'm just tired. My eyes were simply playing tricks on me."

"All the more reason to get to the inn and get some rest."

"And don't forget that drink!" Darius said.

Gray hesitated. "You two go on ahead, I'll be there soon."

"Come on, Ayva, I've had enough cursed fresh air for the rest of my life." Darius turned his horse towards the stone gates ahead, following the tail end of the villagers.

Ayva paused a moment longer, until Gray thought she wouldn't go. At last, she turned, "Join us soon," she insisted as she guided her mare after Darius.

Gray dismounted and ducked into the shadowed lane. No harm in being cautious. The alley was quiet after the bustle of the streets. He searched but saw nothing, when he suddenly saw a scrap of light blue cloth pinned to the wall. Ayva's cloak, he knew, heart pounding, feeling it between his fingers.

"A symbol that you trust too easily," a voice echoed in his head.

Gray knew that voice. "Where are you?" he called. Dark maniacal laughter replied, echoing off the walls. "Show yourself, Kail," he shouted as the laughter grew.

Again the voice sounded inside his skull, "You endanger their lives. Why?"

"They stay of their own free will!"

"Free will or not, can you live with their blood upon your hands?"

"You're wrong," he said, shaking his head. "I can protect them!"

"But can you protect them from yourself?"

"I would never! I would die before I caused them harm!"

"A fitting answer," Kail laughed. "For only when you are gone will they be safe."

"Enough!" he bellowed and unsheathed his blade with a sharp ring. A sudden pain lanced through his arm. He fell to his knees, holding his trembling hand. Gray watched in horror as dark tremors writhed beneath his flesh, crawling like black snakes.

"You see? It's too late… The darkness has found you. Now it will not let you go."

Gray threw the blade and it clattered against the wall. Still the dark tremors swelled, and his arm bulged as the black veins grew. Mad laughter filled the alley, ringing in his ears. Desperately, he pulled for the nexus, praying it would dull the pain. The nexus appeared, shrouded in black as if dipped in a pool of ink. He plowed through the darkness as if trudging through a mire of sludge. The black tremors wormed their way into his chest, but he pressed onward. Suddenly, he lost sight of the nexus altogether. Still he dug, searching amid the darkness. At last, he touched a tendril of light. He gripped it tightly, and his power filled him. In a burst of light, the nexus shattered the black mantle. He opened his eyes. The tendrils in his arm retreated, moving back into his skin and then disappeared altogether.

Cradling his limp arm, Gray caught his breath. Slowly, he unfurled his clenched fist. Gouges marred his flesh. Marks where his nails had bit deep into his skin. There, resting in his open palm, was the blue scrap of Ayva's cloak, stained in blood…

Kail's voice echoed off the marble walls. "You are alone."

The Stonemason

The Dipping Tsugi, Gray read the swinging sign above his head. His grip tightened on Morrowil's hilt. The blue cloth was now tied to his sword's handle, reminding him of the legend's words, and of what he had to lose. Gray sheathed the blade with a shiver, taking his mind off thoughts of Kail as he took in his surroundings.

The Noble's District, he recalled, remembering the street sign he had read as he passed through a large entryway. As he had climbed, rising through the tiered city, the roads had grown steadily less crowded. Now only a thin stream of people strolled along the pristine white roads. Most were robed in flowing gowns of layered silk with bright and jarring colors, others in oiled-leathers, while thick pelts draped their shoulders—wealthy merchants and rich traders, he assumed. There were no more hawkers or peddlers. Moreover, he studied the buildings. There were few shops here. Most appeared to be sprawling villas with verdant trees, arched terraces, and carved statues. Inns dappled the wide street as well, their roofs reaching several stories high and gilded in silver or gold. They bore fanciful names like The Siren's Song, and The Silver Harp. Gray couldn't remember seeing anything this extravagant in all his life.

He turned back just as a lanky, blond haired stable hand came running from around the corner of the inn. The boy looked exhausted. He handed Fael'wyn's reins over. "Take good care of him and see he's well-fed," he said, flipping the boy a coin he had won in a game of cyn with Darius. Best use of the rogue's coin I can think of, he thought.

The boy looked at the silver coin as if it were dark magic. "I've never seen coin quite like this before," he said, his voice the reedy whine of adolescence.

"It's real, I assure you," Gray said.

"Where are you from?" the boy asked.

Gray debated lying, but at last he saw no harm in it—the King would find out soon enough. "Far away. A place called the Lost Woods. It's a long ways south from here," he answered.

"So it's true," the boy whispered, "The others said it was so, but I didn't believe it."

"Others?" he asked.

"Ah, just the other stable hands and some of the waitresses. And I thought they were teasing me again, but they looked mighty shocked themselves. Then you're with that scary lookin' crowd that just came in? How in the light's realm did you get pass the great gap?"

"It's a long story, perhaps another time." Gray moved towards the inn's door.

"Wait, hold on," the boy said.

"Yes?"

"Then you're here to see the King?"

Gray nodded. "What of it?"

The boy bit his lip nervously as he eyed the nearest people, waiting for them to pass. "A word of warning then," he said, lowering his voice, "be wary of the king's advisor— Tervasian. It's well known that he has the ear of the king. Both of them. If you plan to get anywhere with Katsu, you will have to convince Tervasian first."

Gray remembered that name—it was the same one the guard had uttered. Councilor Tervasian… "Thanks for the advice."

"Sure thing, and thank you," said the boy with a wink, pocketing the coin, and with that he took Fael'wyn away.

As Gray turned toward the inn's door, he heard a sudden commotion and the door slammed open. A body came barreling out and crashed into him. The two fell, toppling head over heels into a pile. Gray hit his head and something sparked—a vision flooded him.

Baked sand filled his nostrils, his lips parched. Before him was a dark castle, rising from the tan desert. The vision shifted and he was in a vaulted room of black stone. He was not alone. A slender woman stood confidently before a mirror, dressed in scarlet red robes. Her hands glided over her form. Gray looked down and saw his own coarse brown robes. He looked back up. The woman eyed her reflection with pride. She had just done something… something noteworthy. She turned to look at him and called his name. But it was not his name. Her delicate wrist stretched towards him, but there was something else in her grip. As he reached out to touch her, smooth fingertips brushing his, she screamed. Suddenly she was on her knees and blood was everywhere. There was a scream and he gasped and the room plunged into darkness—thick feelers crawling up the walls and consuming everything they touched. The bloodcurdling cry continued. Gray wanted to tear his ears from his skull if it would stop the sound.

As quickly as it came, the vision vanished. Gray took a sharp breath. It couldn't have lasted more than a few seconds. His head throbbed as he regained his senses, and the white paved street of the Shining City settled familiarly around him. Nightmares from my past…

An angry voice shouted, "And stay out you lout! For the last time, keep yourself to the Commoner's District!" The door slammed shut.

Gray sized up the man before him. Lines creased the corner of his eyes and deeper lines ran from his nose past his mouth. His drab clothes identified him as a laborer like the ones Gray had seen at the docks, but his clothes had a touch of finery. He spotted flared cuffs with a bit of dark embroidery. Gray guessed the man was perhaps Mura's age, but he wore his years with less grace than the hermit, like an ill fitted coat.

The man turned towards him, a woozy smile through his scruffy beard. "Yes? What do you want?" he grumbled. "I am not for sale, you know."

"What? You ran into me…"

The man belched, raising a fist to his lips. His words came out heavily slurred, "You find me handshome. Why else would ya' be giving me that come hither look, lass?"

Looking around, Gray saw there were other people on the street, but they were all too far to hear.

"Shhh, no no," the man said, overriding him. "There's no need to be coy!"

"Uh..."

The man raised his fist to the sky, "But alas, it cannot be. I am woefully sorry, you have to understand, my dearest madam. I am betrothed only to my work!"

Gray put his hand in his hair and shook his head, this time with a laugh. He bent down and grabbed the man by his clothes, pulling him up. All the while the man complained. "I've never seen anyone as drunk as you," Gray laughed. "First off, I'm not a woman. And second, what has got you in such a state that you're this drunk by midday?"

The man rubbed his eyes, peering through his heavy lids and then rose to his wobbly feet. "First!" he said, raising a finger and then paused to belch. "My apologies. You are definitely a man..."

"I'm glad we got that settled."

"...But you are a very pretty man, so you are to blame as well. Second!" He raised his third finger, interrupting Gray. His expres-

sion became deathly serious. "I am no ordinary drunk. Though I am very drunk, right now. I am Balder, chief of the Stonemason's Guild."

"Stonemason's Guild?" Gray asked.

"You do not know of it?" Balder said in shock, "Everyone knows us! Where have you been? You do have an odd accent." He dismissed it with a gesture. "No matter, I will inform you then. The Stonemason's Guild is the most powerful of all the guilds in the Shining City, and I was its chief!"

Gray narrowed his eyes, "You said you are its chief before."

"What? Oh that's right! Am, its chief, am. What did I say? Never mind that! I have an idea, what say you and I go for a drink. So you know, my apprentices always pay for the first round. It's custom, but I'll get the next one, of course."

Gray tried to interrupt, but there was no opening in the man's ranting.

"—You know, it used to be free for me. All the innkeepers clambered to give me a drink. Sometimes I'd repay them with a bit of the finest touchups on their establishment. Of course, only after rack-ing up a wee little tab," he nudged him confidentially. Balder's eyes flickered to his wrapped sword. "Say, what's in the wrapped bundle on your back? Mind if have a look?"

Gray ignored the comment. "Why did you get kicked out?" he asked, looking to the inn before them.

"I just made a remark, nothing big, just a simple observation about the innkeeper, Hitomi, and her own guild The Tavern and Inn. I'd be careful of that one if I were you," he said and then reached for something in his jacket, extracting a flask and bringing it to his pursed lips.

He grabbed Balder's hand, "No more."

The stonemason's face turned beet red. "Who are you to…" he said and paused, clasping a hand to his mouth as he twisted and threw up.

Gray groaned. "What am I to do with you? You're much too drunk to be wandering the streets."

"No no, I feel much better now," Balder muttered, wiping his mouth.

Gray eyed the stonemason. If the man was truly the chief of the stonemason's guild, he would surely know the layout of the Shining City. Perhaps even know of a way out…

Balder was now appraising the stonework of the nearby planter where he had just vomited, ranting really at the bricks. "No, this is all wrong. Not vertically staggered, and… what is this, a saerian bond? Who built this? Were they blind? Or perhaps it was done at night, with a blindfold, and a spoon instead of a chisel. This is practically rubble!"

Am I really planning on leaving? Gray wondered. When he saw Balder reach for the flask again he dragged the man to his feet. "I can't have you wandering into some dark alley and getting robbed, or worse."

Balder harrumphed. "I am the chief of the Stonemasons' Guild! I built this city from the ground up! Anyone who robs me will find justice at the end of a sword. Now enough of this nonsense, let's find another tavern. Do you know of the The Green Hoof or the Red Maid? The Red Maid is good, but the The Green Hoof is better."

Agreeing while Balder talked, Gray led him to the door of the inn.

"Wait wait, not there!"

"Keep your mouth shut and stay behind me, it'll be fine. My

friends and I are under the king's protection."

"Hogsfeet! His majesty's protection? Who are you?"

Gray grumbled, "The name's Gray, now are you coming or not?"

"All right all right, no need to get upset," Balder said and gave a suddenly impish smirk, looking not at all drunk. "Say, you sure you aren't a woman? Because you're just as pushy." Gray shook his head wryly, shoving the man through the door and leaving the cold streets behind.

The Dipping Tsugi

As soon as Gray opened the door, a burly voice bellowed, "What's he doing here?" Gray noticed the speaker who stood on the other side of the room. He was a bear of a man with a huge, blocky frame and a face like misshapen putty from too many bar fights. He had a hooked nose that crooked one way and then the other. A thick scar made a jagged line across his trunk-like neck, from where someone had obviously tried to garrote the behemoth and failed. "I just kicked that laggard out!" The shout cut through the noise of the common room. Balder tried to duck away, but Gray held him in place. The big man pushed his way through the tables.

Gray stepped in front of Balder.

"Tell me why I shouldn't knock the two of you flat," growled the brute, raising his meaty fist.

"Relax," Gray said with a gesture. "He's with me, just let me explain."

"Relax, he says," a silken smooth voice spoke, ringing with authority. Gray turned and saw a woman who stood behind the counter. She had shiny black hair pulled back in a twisted bun, and held in place with a stick. Her face was mature, not old, with smooth skin and hard eyes. The only lines she bore were those of sternness around her lips and eyes. He recognized them because it was just like Mura. The woman continued, "I am quite relaxed. Now answer quickly or I'll let Dorbin have his way. Who are you and why do you bring this man back into my establishment?"

All eyes in the room were now on Gray. Even the harpist stopped playing and watched. The room was dead silent. He swallowed and approached the woman with the heat of eyes upon his back. Dorbin put a huge hand on Gray's shoulder, stopping him. The woman nodded and Dorbin withdrew it.

"My name is Gray, and I'm here under the protection of the King," he said and gave a nod, behind him. "If you don't mind terribly, I'd rather not draw this much attention."

The innkeeper smiled thinly, a show of politeness. "You are with the others then?"

"I am."

"Chrissa," the woman called prompting the harpist to play. The band took up their odd stringed instruments and Gray glanced over his shoulder. The strange but pleasing music drew the crowd's attention once again. The woman flicked her eyes. The hulking Dorbin backed away, stepping into the shadows of the common room. "I apologize. We are not use to such esteemed guests."

Gray hid a breath of relief. "No apologies needed…" he paused, searching for a name.

The woman gave a small bow. "You may call me Mistress Hitomi, Gray-sama."

Gray noticed Hitomi did a good job keeping her eyes from the stonemason, but he saw the fire in her expression was still there. It was evident she hated Balder. The stonemason, however, was oblivious. His eyes danced from the harpist to the slender and fast-paced barmaids and Gray hid a sigh—the man was beginning to remind him of Darius. "If I promise he will cause no more trouble, can he stay?"

"Strange company you keep, but if you insist," she answered.

"Thank you," he said sincerely, "And the others?"

"The rest of your company has been seen to. Your rooms are upstairs." She pointed to the polished banister of rosewood that led to the second floor. "Yours is the second door on the right with the honorable Darius-sama. Your friends are in the library, waiting for word from his majesty. It is quiet there and you can talk. If it would please you, you may join them, I will have dinner brought in."

"Sounds perfect," he said, hoping to smooth their rocky start.

Mistress Hitomi motioned to one of the young barmaids and the girl approached. Gray took in her form fitting red silk dress and she flashed him a less-than-coy look. His cheeks grew hot. "Come with me," she said and Gray followed, dragging Balder. They entered a short hallway, which led to a simple oak door. "Your friends."

"Thank you," he replied.

She smiled and bowed away.

Gray put his hand on the smooth knob and paused, realizing the others would likely question his new friend and wonder why he had brought him. Gray couldn't let them know he was contemplating leaving. He turned to Balder. "Listen, the others are a bit choosy when it comes to company. If they ask, tell them I invited you along because you know something about the king and his councilors."

"Like what?"

"I don't know, lie if you have to. You already seem to have a talent for exaggeration."

Balder rubbed his chin. "Are you sure these are your friends?"

Gray growled. "Can I trust you?

The man shrugged, "I suppose that's easy enough. Is that all?"

"And no flirting, man or woman." Balder opened his mouth to reply when a shriek resonated from within. It was loud even through the thick oak, and Gray threw open the heavy door.

The Keeper of the Silver

As Gray opened the door, he was pulled, guided by a force that flowed over his arm. He flung the door wide, and it crashed against the wall. Quickly, he scanned his surroundings.

A long, rectangular table spanned half of the large library. Candles were spread out across its polished surface, casting dark shadows across the room. His friends turned to him in surprise. Ayva, the closest looked shocked at his intrusion while Mura scrutinized a cluttered pile of books in front of him. “A nice entrance,” he said. “A bit extravagant and reckless but…”

“You fool, you nearly broke the door,” Rydel said.

Gray cleared his throat, “I heard a cry. What happened?”

Mura grumbled, still riveted to his book. “A little misunderstanding.”

Ayva, her brown hair tied back in a long ponytail, gave an apologetic wince. “That was me. I’m sorry. You see, I can explain though. I was reading through this book,” she raised the dusty tome. Its spine was cracked and it had faded gold trim. On its title it read: The Lost Covenant. “I just came across the most interesting thing. It’s hard to describe. Let me show you.” She beckoned him over.

Balder hovered over Gray’s shoulder impatiently. “Ahem. Aren’t you going to introduce me?”

"Everyone, this is Balder. Balder, everyone." He gestured with a hand and went to Ayva's side. She motioned for him to take a seat on her right. In the corner of his vision, Gray saw Mura introduce himself. Balder shook his hand. It gave him a chance to rattle off his long title.

Ayva sidled her chair closer, near enough he felt her warmth. Despite days of travel, she smelled pleasantly of spice. "All right, see here?" She pointed to a thin strip of writing. "The whole book is written by a man who never mentions his name, except for right here." She pointed to an inscription at the bottom that read:

-Renald Trinaden, Warden, and Keeper of the Silver.
16 A.L of the Second Age.

Balder gave his lengthy introduction to Rydel. "Master Chief Balder of the famous Stonemason's Guild, at your service, dear elf. We don't get many of your kind in this city, in fact, I'd venture to say almost never!"

"Who is this man?" Rydel questioned.

"He said he had insight into the king and his councilors. I thought he may be of use," Gray answered quickly.

"I do, indeed!" Balder said. "In fact, the King and I were once best friends!"

Gray cursed inwardly. Why did the man's claims have to be so grand?

"Is that true?" Mura asked.

Balder puffed his chest, "Why, I'd swear my title on the claim!"

Gray coughed suddenly and the others turned, eyeing him curiously. He rubbed his throat and eyed Ayva's water, "Mind if I? Sore throat," he explained, she nodded, and he took a long draught as Balder continued.

"We go way back, the King and I, course' I didn't call him King back then! 'Viv,' I called him, though he hated it. Vivius course' is his first name. Vivius Katsu! Strange name, don't you think?" The man was good, Gray admitted.

"I suppose so," Mura laughed. "It is a pleasure to meet you. You are a valuable ally indeed. We have dire news for the council and his majesty, perhaps you can fill us in on what to be wary of before the king."

"Gladly!" said the stonemason, and he leapt into a long tirade.

Gray distracted himself, not wanting to catch another one of Balder's lies. He turned to Ayva. "You were saying?"

Ayva shook her head, gathering her senses, "Right, well, at first I thought 'the silver' might just be referring to his money or something along those lines. But when I continued reading, the title kept coming up. I realized it was something different. He referred to it as if some sort of entity."

Gray scratched his head curiously. "An entity… what is this book about?"

"Right, sorry, I'm jumping ahead of myself," she said. "From what I can tell this is a journal. Renald writes about guarding his country Eldorath, which based on the map sketched…" she flipped through pages quickly, finding a page with an ancient looking map. It was Daerval by the outline, but with all the strange city names and markings it made it almost impossible to tell. "Here," she exclaimed, pointing to the word Eldorath on the borders of the Lost Woods. "You see? Our friend Renald actually lived right where Lakewood is! Or was…" she winced, and let out a breath.

Gray didn't know what to say, and tried to think of something to comfort her when the hermit spoke. "You're quite the natural scholar, dear girl. One to rival the elders of Eldas, or the seven sages of Newarth."

"I couldn't just wait around," she said, her head already back in the book. She continued, "And it gives me something to do, besides this stuff is really relevant I think."

"So you said 'the silver' meant something different? What does it mean and what does it have to do with anything?" Gray asked.

"Gray! What happened to your hand?" she exclaimed, eyeing the wound upon his palm.

He snapped his hand back, "It's nothing. I fell on my way here." Gray pointed to the book again, "Go on." In the corner of his eye, he noticed Ayva's cloak and saw it was missing a piece and his fists clenched.

Her brows furrowed, but she continued, "Yes. All Renald talks about is his duties. The way he writes about it, he sounds like some sort of elite guard. Nearly every other word is about his duty to 'protect the Silver.'"

Gray shrugged. "So why couldn't that be about money then? He wants to protect his wealth, or someone else's wealth. Guards do that kind of thing."

She shook her head adamantly, "No. Not these men. When he talks about it, the silver sounds like the most vital thing in all of existence, like humanity depends upon it being safe."

"You sound like you know what it is…"

Ayva gave him a serious look. "Perhaps. You see, Renald talks about 'knights of the old code.' I think he means the Ronin."

Across the table, Mura perked up. Even Rydel looked up from polishing his curved dagger.

"That is a fearsome name," Balder said.

"It is a name that only evil should fear, and with good right," Mura said sharply.

"Continue," Gray said. "This man, you said he mentions the Ronin?"

Ayva pulled the book closer, "Often. Here, listen to this." She flipped back to the first page, carefully holding it down as she read:

The lands are now stripped and salted, and all who would remember those courageous battles are nearly gone. The horn of valor calls in the distance, echoing over the flat plains. Men and women rise from the ashes. But few remain who remember those knights of the old code.

I have not seen them, but know they exist, slipping between the shadows of our vision. At times I think I can feel them, a sensation rises between the blades of my shoulders, but it is gone each time I turn. They are unknown to a world that has forgotten the true meaning of a warrior.

-Renald Trinaden, Warden, and Keeper of the Silver
16 A.L of the Second Age."

"That is a rare find indeed my girl," Mura said.

"Someone else must have thought so too," Ayva said and gestured to a torn page. "The page is ripped in two, which means we only know the half of it."

"What's 16 A.L?" Gray asked.

"16 A.L is after the First Age," Rydel stated calmly. "It literally translates to 16 years after the Lieon."

Mura shook his head in amazement. "Indeed. That fact, along with the desolate description of the lands, Renald seems to be a warrior in the chaos and aftermath of the Lieon. At the end of an age, and turning point of another. If I'm not mistaken, it seems our friend Renald is a Devari." For a mere moment, as he spoke, his eyes passed over Gray, but then it was gone.

"What's a Devari?" Ayva questioned.

"An ancient warrior," the hermit answered, "They still exist too, on the other side of the gates, but in past times, there were more of them. The Devari took orders from only one group of men. The Ronin."

Balder cursed beneath his breath.

Gray tensed, Devari…

All others turned to him and he realized he had spoken aloud.

He cleared his throat. "What else do you know about the Devari?" he asked.

"The Devari were elite warriors," Mura said, "almost a class of their own in the Lieon. When the Ronin were at their most revered, the Devari were thought only one step shy of holy. They held certain powers, like their leaders, for they were the guardians of the Ronin, having sworn a sacred oath. However, I assume at the time Renald writes, the Lieon has already occurred, which means the Devari and Ronin's bond was long broken."

"Why was the bond broken?" Gray asked.

"No one knows for certain," Mura said. "The bond was shattered during the war, when the Ronin were deemed betrayers of mankind. Many called it The Great Schism, when the Devari left the Ronin."

Gray had a sudden memory. "Maris… he said something about a schism between Reavers, Ronin, and Devari."

Karil nodded. "It is said the Reavers were a part of The Great Schism, but again, the annals of time have left out what happened exactly. You would have to ask the Ronin about that, I'm afraid."

Gray wished he had. "The stories say the Ronin turned against their own, slaughtering those they were sworn to protect. But I always knew that wasn't true… What happened so long ago? Do the elves know?"

"Some. It is well-known that half of the Great Kingdoms turned against the Ronin," Rydel said.

"Why?" Ayva asked.

"Because an object they were entrusted to guard was stolen," Rydel replied.

"What was it?" Gray asked.

"A sword," Rydel answered.

Darius scoffed, "The Lieon was started over a cursed sword?"

"It was no ordinary blade," Rydel replied. "It was one of the nine great swords, each entrusted to a Great Kingdom in a forgotten time. The blade of leaf for the Kingdom of Leaf, moon for the Kingdom of Moon, metal for Metal, ice for Ice, and so on. The blades were a symbol known throughout the land, each a sigil of peace to bind the nine kingdoms together in peace. When the sword was stolen, the peace was broken."

"Which sword was stolen?" Gray asked.

"Omni's blade—the sword of sun, stolen from the golden city of Vaster."

It made sense, Gray realized. He had seen Omni's current blade. It wasn't unique like the others, just a simple piece of steel. "Omni didn't have the blade when last we saw her. She couldn't have stolen it," he said.

"It was treachery," Mura answered in a heated voice.

Ayva whispered in realization, "And who else to take the fall then the guardians of the blade."

"Exactly," Mura said.

"Who stole the blade?" Gray asked.

"A deep and dark power, something insidious."

"Worse than the Kage?" Ayva said.

Rydel's eyes narrowed. "Much worse. I fear it is a darkness that has had its teeth sunk deep into the lands for centuries, both Daerval and Farhaven. It is the same dark machinations of those who killed Karil's father and put our lands in chaos."

Silence settled as Gray took it all in, trying to connect the many pieces as his thumb absently rubbed the insignia on his wrist.

"A dark history," Mura said. "One absent from the stories."

Ayva cleared her throat, drawing their attention. "There's one last thing. Something I forgot to mention. I was still curious about 'The Silver,' but he never says what it is. Almost as if he's afraid to reveal its identity in his own journal."

"But you know don't you…" said Mura.

"I cheated. I read the end, but still it said nothing about the silver." She flipped through the pages as she talked. "But then it had a few blank pages and on the very last page I found this…" Ayva read aloud:

"At times, I find myself drawn to thoughts of the enemy of long dead and the silver calls to me. Twice I have opened the chest to see it glow divine silver. And though, I am enchanted by its call, I fear its evil."

Gray let out a breath. Mura leaned back in his chair, while Rydel muttered what sounded like a soft, flowing Elvish curse. Balder, however, only harrumphed. "What's all the commotion about?" said the stonemason," I don't see anything so special about that."

Silently, Gray withdrew the cloth bundle from his back. He let the wrapping fall, unveiling the sword. The blade glowed blinding silver.

"Hogsfeet! That's… that's… it can't be," Balder stammered in disbelief.

"Morrowil," Gray answered. "The blade of wind. Kail's sword, the leader of the Ronin and Betrayer of Men."

"One of the swords? I thought they were just legends!"

"Like the Ronin?" Mura asked quietly.

Balder glared. "Yes, like the Ronin. Gah, curses, I said it!"

"The blade of wind is more powerful than all the others combined, or so the stories say," Rydel said. Gray's eyes were locked on the sword and its radiant hue when a knock came on the door, hard and swift. Several jumped at the noise.

"I don't think the Kage are going to knock," Mura informed them and then looked to Gray. "I'd put that away, my boy, quickly now," he instructed as he rose. Gray swiftly sheathed the blade. The hermit opened the door and four petite barmaids with straight black hair moved into the library. In their hands they juggled platters, dishes of food, and frothing mugs. Mistress Hitomi was the last to enter.

The stern innkeeper began to direct in a different language—the same the waitress had used. It was brusque and commanding. The barmaid in the red dress from earlier placed a steaming plate of rice before Gray and gave him a sly look. He smiled in reply. Ayva pinched his arm.

"What?" he asked.

Ayva spoke beneath her breath, "You can close your mouth now."

He shrugged. "What? I'm just being respectful."

She rolled her eyes with a breath, mumbling something about "men" and "hopeless."

They finished and Mistress Hitomi signaled with a hand to her side and the girls filed behind her as if it were an orchestrated dance. When all was in its place, the innkeeper spoke, "Tonight's dinner is tender roast duck breast glazed in Tsugi's own famed sweet meruu sauce, with grilled vegetables, and a traditional Hrofi side dish of glazed rice."

"Hrofi?" Mura questioned. "That city hasn't been around in over two thousand years.

"You're right," she said. "Very astute. You'll notice most of our customs date back to ancient times, seeing as we've been isolated these many years. If there is nothing else? Onne—" she said to the four women and turned to leave.

"Wait," said Gray. Mistress Hitomi paused. "If you don't mind, I was curious about your books. It's quite a collection."

Mistress Hitomi glanced at the dusty books fondly. "It has been a hobby of mine for as long as I can remember."

"Collecting books?"

"Rare artifacts" she corrected. "A piece of history, if you will. It just so happens that books are the best resource to our past." Gray felt a twinge of regret as he remembered the tome that Mura had shared with him… back in the Lost Woods. Mistress Hitomi continued, "Where else can you learn about the Lieon, elves, and Farhaven all at once?"

Ayva's eyes grew wide. "Where did you get all of them?" she asked.

"I earned them, one by one," she said fondly. "It started with a curiosity about languages. Then one day I stumbled across a certain book that led me down a different path. Soon I was collecting a very… distinctive sort of text. The rarest, most valuable kind—the kind that contains stories, which likely only the elves know." She glanced to Rydel. "Stories about the Ronin." Those in the room exchanged silent looks.

"You're not afraid to say that name?"

The innkeeper gave a subtle snort. "You will find it's quite hard to usher me into silence. Forgive my bluntness."

"I understand," said Mura. "You are a wise woman."

Mistress Hitomi looked like a bird with her feathers ruffled, but her cheeks took on a spot of red. "Perhaps more stubborn than wise." She then turned, taking in the well-sized library with its many packed shelves. "Every book you see here has been bartered or bought from all over Daerval from the dark corners to the light." At his side, Gray saw Ayva, and he half expected her to squeak with delight or awe.

Mistress Hitomi continued. "Searching for them became as much a passion as reading them—each time I found something new, something almost no one living knew about. Some were dark deals, and they nearly cost me my life, but they were all fair trades," she insisted.

"Indeed," Mura commented.

Gray took in the dusty tomes with a newfound appreciation for both the books and their intriguing innkeeper.

"I see you found one of my favorites," Mistress Hitomi said, eyeing the book in Ayva's hands. "A very rare one too. You have quite the eye." Ayva warmed under the praise, smiling shyly. With that, Mistress Hitomi turned to leave and the four waitresses followed her out like ducklings in a row.

Gray was famished. He picked up a pair of thin sticks. Out of the corner of his eye, he saw Mura, Balder and Rydel use the two sticks in perfect unison. He followed suit and deftly grabbed a piece of duck. Satisfied, he popped it into his mouth and nearly groaned in satisfaction—it was perfect, juicy and tender. Every bite was delicious. The glazed rice was slightly sweet and tangy, and the vegetables were fresh and grilled to perfection. Though he couldn't lie, he probably would have devoured a heaping plate of mush and been content at that moment.

"You should see the stables, Gray," said Ayva abruptly, putting down her sticks. "They alone are three times as big as my father's whole inn and gorgeous—I hope our rooms are half as clean. The wine cellar alone could probably fit The Golden Horn."

Gray smiled, "I'll have to check them out. Where's Darius?" he said suddenly, realizing the rogue was nowhere to be seen.

"Drinking at a nearby tavern I'm sure," Ayva said with an irritated huff. "When he heard that everything was free, because we're the king's guests, he had to find the fanciest place."

At that moment, the door flew open, and Darius came barging in as if on cue. "Worthless!" he exclaimed loudly. "All of it, worthless! Rotten fake money!" He threw a clattering of coins upon the tabletop. Gray picked up one, fingering it. Along its band and on its surface were small strange symbols, unrecognizable lines and curves, like the other signs he had seen in the city. The coin was as light as a feather in his hand.

"Where'd you two learn to open the door?" Mura muttered with a harrumph. "There's such a thing as a knock."

Darius shrugged, still shaking his head in annoyance, "I won ten games straight before I realized not one person in this place has any real money. It's all that tin junk or whatever it is. But it's definitely not gold," he vented as he bit down on a shiny piece and made a disgusted sound, throwing it on the table with the rest. "It even tastes bad."

"I could care less about the money," Ayva said. "Besides the books, and the stables and this whole inn, and the people, this entire city is amazing. I've never seen anything like it."

Darius snorted. "I've never seen so many people, and dressed so finely. I'll agree with that much." He shut the door and took a chair backwards, next to Balder. Darius introduced himself with a rough handshake.

Rydel pushed his plate towards Darius. "Go ahead," said the elf.

"Not hungry?" Gray asked.

"No elf can eat the flesh of another animal," Rydel replied.

"Well, then don't mind me," Darius said and dug in, shoveling the food into his mouth. With his other hand he gestured with a cooked carrot. "Say, what'd you all think of that Mistress Hitomi?"

"Stubborn as a mule, but not hard on the eyes," Mura answered, picking his teeth.

"I'm not sure how you can even look at her like that," Darius said. "She's got a mantle of stiffness wrapped around her so tight it looks painful."

"It's easy to look at any woman for their beauty," Mura rejoined.

The rogue shrugged. "Well, she gives me the shivers, right down to my bones."

"Do you think we can trust her, Mura?" Gray asked.

"I'm not certain," said the hermit. "She seems to be holding much back, as are we. Until the King makes his choice, you have to understand we cannot feel for these people, Gray. It's not wise. It is still possible that he may fail to see wisdom." Another knock came on the door, hard and fast, sounding more urgent than before.

Mistress Hitomi stuck in her head. Gray noticed the hulking frame of the brute, Dorbin, hovering close behind her in the light of the hallway like a second shadow. "His Majesty is ready to see you. His messenger awaits," she announced.

The Shiroku Palace

The messenger led them through the ivory-paved streets at a quick pace. Together, with the others at his side, Gray ascended the tiered city.

Blue flags waved majestically on the tops of buildings, proudly displaying the symbol of the Kingdom of Ice, a white flame of ice against a dark blue backdrop.

As Gray rode, he passed richly garbed men and women. Each was draped in robes of deep purples, or rich reds. The people of the Noble's District walked along garden paths in small groups. Many of the men were plump with heavy jowls and smooth skin, while the women were slender with thin eyebrows like painted lines. A few of the men's polished pates shone in the fading light of dusk. The plush borough was serene compared to the bustle of the lower city. As their entourage whisked past, the men and women turned and cast the galloping strangers curious stares. Brows rose in surprise until Gray thought they would come off their foreheads.

Ahead, he watched the messenger's back. He was a man of rank, dressed in white and blue, wearing a tabard with the symbol of ice. When he had summoned them, their mounts were already waiting before the inn. Now he matched his urgency by pressing his horse hard.

They came to a sudden halt as the white road ended.

"The Shiroku Palace," the messenger announced.

Before them was an alabaster palace. It was vast, blotting out the setting sun and dwarfing the nearby villas. Fluted columns, and detailed frescos adorned its front and Gray glimpsed flying buttresses in the distance. At its pinnacle, was a large golden dome that reflected the sun's rays.

Two straight rows of stern-faced guards, decked in full plate, led to the palace's doors, which themselves were enormous plates of silver. Handing his reins to a nearby guard, Gray dismounted. Fael'wyn's hide sweated with a thick lather. He strode forward.

"Wait!" the messenger cried, "You must wait!"

Gray didn't slow. Darius, Ayva and the others quickly dismounted and joined his side. He approached the massive doors and several guards hastily broke rank and opened the huge metal doors just in time. As he strode down the spacious hall, he surveyed their surroundings.

Niches were carved into the hallway. Each nook was filled with curious objects: there were low flat tables of polished wood with slender vases made from swirling-pink stone, helmets on stands, slightly curved swords of varying size in elegant racks, a painting of falling cherry blossoms, and large rice-paper hangings with deep black brushed symbols. Beneath his feet was a vibrant blue and purple carpet. Guards flanked them as they moved. On every passing corridor he saw more guards and the insignia of the Kingdom of Ice. He remembered Mura's words. The Shining City was but a fragment of the once Great Kingdom. The notion was hard to believe.

Ahead he saw another pair of doors, this time gilded with gold. The guards at the door were dressed in white tabards with dark blue trousers.

"Your weapons," a guard demanded, motioning to a nearby table.

"So be it," Mura answered.

Gray hesitated while the others withdrew their blades. He stepped back from the others, hoping the guards wouldn't notice his bundle as a weapon.

"What's that on your back?" said a tall guard.

The messenger approached, breathing heavily, having caught up with them at last. "Hand it over," he ordered, breathless. Grudgingly, Gray unstrapped the sword. Luckily, the guard simply threw Morrowil into a pile on the tables with the others. Only then did the guards unbolt and push open the heavy gold doors. A chorus of voices assaulted them. Inside, hundreds of rows of balconies were filled to the brim with people—men and women dressed in layered robes.

All eyes turned to Gray and those at his side, and whispers filled the room.

"Dear Lokai," the rogue muttered.

The huge circular floor gleamed with red-veined white marble. At the heart of the room a symbol of ice was inlaid.

The messenger pushed ahead. "Quickly, give me your names and where you hail from, so that I may introduce you to his majesty." Gray provided the only answer he knew, and the man said in a booming voice, "May I introduce to his Majesty, the eminent King Katsu, the honorable Rydel-sama and Mura-sama of Eldas, High Kingdom of Elves, Darius-sama and Ayva-sama of Lakewood, and Gray-sama of the Lost Woods." He finished with a deep bow, his head nearly skimming the ground. The man's impressive voice had filled the room, and now a hush settled over the vast chambers.

An Image in Fire

Gray strode to the center of the room with the others at his side. In front of them were marble stairs with wide steps leading to a cavernous throne. Rows of servants stood at either side of the marbled throne.

"Welcome…" King Katsu said, his voice both deep and commanding.

Gray appraised the man known as King Katsu who sat in the throne. White robes hung from his frame, the design and fit much like the other citizens, only with more layers. He had a white patch of hair beneath his lower lip, a trimmed mustache, and straight white hair that fell to his shoulders. Karil stood at the side of the king, and while she was still in her simple forest garb, she didn't look a bit out of place.

"Mor 'in dunindas. Forgah 'l sendria tu va varius," Mura said and knelt. He grabbed Gray's sleeve, yanking him down, and the other's knelt as well.

"Rise," Katsu said. "You speak Yorin well, if a bit rusty. Food or drink?" The servants began to move forward with trays piled with food, as well as silver and gold pitchers and chalices.

Mura raised a hand, stalling the servants. "Thank you, but if we could move to pressing matters."

The king nodded. "You have come a long way. Your urgency is not taken lightly." King Katsu studied them. "But before I hear what you have to say, I will ask you a question and I hope for a sincere answer. Your friend has filled me in on your journey and the danger that follows you. From all counts, it seems you and your friends have brought death to the doorstep of my fair city and have endangered my people. Is that true?" The nobles in the stands whispered, a dark hum.

Mura spoke, "You are not wrong, yet…"

The king's powerful voice overrode him. "Then why should I help you? Make no mistake, I have already heard the pleas of your fellow traveling companion, so do not rant about the claims of a dark army."

"Claims?" Gray repeated, incredulous.

The king turned, brows arching, "Excuse me?" he said. Gray was rooted by his scrutiny and scathing tone. A chorus of shuffling sounded as those in the balconies shifted and followed Katsu's gaze, examining Gray.

A tall man rose from the gallery on Gray's right and spoke, "Who is this man who dares to interrupt his Excellency?" He wore robes like the others of deep blue, but was distinguished by a stole that looked like a thin ribbon of white.

Shouts erupted from the balconies.

"What is your name?" a man called.

"Speak!" said another.

Ayva and the others swiveled to each new, harsh voice.

Mura grumbled beneath his breath, "You've done it now. Well, go on, answer the mob."

Gray rose to his full height. "I am Gray," he said loudly. "And if you want someone to blame, blame me! I am the one who led the villagers over the impasse."

The tall dignitary, who stood first, spoke again, "You led them over the impasse? I see. Then you were the one who lied and used my name to Captain Mashiro."

Councilor Tervasian, he remembered and swallowed, "If I lied, it was only to save the lives of many."

"And at the same time, risk a whole city and its people. How valiant," Tervasian answered.

Gray remembered the stable hand's words, but he would not argue with a fool. He directed his focus to the king. "Listen please, you point fingers and blame, but as we speak a dark army moves towards this city! Whether or not we brought them here does not matter, the danger is not us, but the Kage!"

Tervasian shrugged, "Yet perhaps this is another lie."

Gray ground his teeth.

"The councilor is correct," King Katsu proclaimed. "The greater question is, can you even be trusted? Who is to say this isn't a trick? Perhaps you and your friends are even allies with this enemy?"

"That's ludicrous!" Ayva shouted, "How can you say that? Hundreds have died to come here, and at the hands of the Kage! They killed my father!" Tears filled her eyes.

"Moving words, but still I see no reason to trust you," the King answered.

The councilor smiled toward the king, a sleek, greasy look. "His Excellency is most correct. Furthermore, this council demands to know how you crossed the impasse."

Gray ignored the man again, his blood pumping, "How do you not see the truth? We are few and they are many! The Kage are coming. Fighting with one another is useless and only serves to aid them! If not for us, at least see reason for your own people!"

The councilor spoke again, "You speak stirring statements, as does your queen. Still, the fact of the matter is, what cause do we have to believe there is a threat? The council does not take action on mere hearsay. So far, all we've heard is children's tales of the Ronin coming to life."

At the word, cries gushed from the galleries like a floodgate being opened.

"Fables!"

"A cursed name!"

"They are real!" Darius shouted in return. "And it's not the Ronin to fear! It's the Kage. If you can't see reason, you are all fools and cowards!"

Tervasian continued, his calm mask breaking as his face twisted in anger. "Fools are those who expect others to listen to children's tales. Fools are those who bring down a cursed name like that. Fools are you, who try my patience and the king's with no proof of this threat!"

Karil descended the plinth, as the fearful whispers and shouts echoed off the walls. She turned to those in the balcony. "You want proof?" she said, voice ringing with crystal clear authority.

The King raised his hand and silence fell over the grand chambers, "I will allow you one last chance to make me believe your claims." Gray noticed councilor Tervasian. He wore a look of disdain and he wanted to wipe the look from the man's face.

Karil whispered to Gray, "I may need your help." He gave a curious nod and she closed her eyes, placing a hand to the white flame upon the marble floor. Her brows drew down and sweat dotted her forehead. Suddenly, a fire sparked, sprouting from the stone. Whispers of fear and awe suffused the wide chambers. The flames grew to form a large pane like a sheet of orange glass. Coldness radiated from the flame. Still, it grew, large enough for all to see in the hall. Karil's legs trembled and she called his name. He reached to grab her, but Rydel was quicker, catching her before she fell.

"What do you want me to do?" he asked anxiously.

"Contain it," she whispered, face strained.

Gray could see now that the flames from the fire were beginning to snap outward hungrily. She was losing control. He reached for the nexus and a flood of light entered his vision. Focusing on the roaring fire, he reached out. Strands of golden air shot from his fingertips. The strands stretched like flowing water over the rampant flames, and the tongues of fire were contained and shielded like a sword being sheathed.

Karil stood straight with Rydel's aid, "Thank you."

Gray stepped back. He looked to Ayva and Darius. Their mouths were wide, mimicking the rest of the chamber. On the marble dais, even the King watched in wonder.

The guards at the tall doors and behind the dais, shifted their halberds in their hands and clutched their curved swords threateningly, ready to move at a mere word from their king.

"What is this?" Katsu questioned.

"Proof," The elvin queen replied. Karil turned to the flame, lifting a hand. An image appeared in the fire, and gasps filled the chambers. Men and women laughed and danced in an open green field. Suddenly, screams echoed from inside the flames as they were slaughtered by the rampaging horde. The screams reached a peak as flames enveloped the town.

"What is this place?" the King asked, stricken.

"Lakewood," Ayva answered.

"A small taste of what has already passed, though I'm not done," Karil said loudly for all to hear. "Observe!" The red flames roared. Nine cloaked men flashed within the window of flames, riding dark steeds with an endless army at their back. The balconies erupted in chaos.

"The Ronin!" voices murmured.

"No! The Kage!" Karil shouted. The image of the Kage vanished and was replaced by horrific scenes, one after another… Charred streets, bloated bodies, ruined cities. Karil spoke, "All of these are images I have seen, events already come to pass. This is what you should fear!"

The faces of the dignitaries grew in horror with each fiery red vision.

"Enough!" The king shouted finally, his words bringing an end to the images.

The man's face looked ghostly white. Gray couldn't help but take some satisfaction in the king's rattled visage. "Now you see the truth."

Councilor Tervasian laughed. The condescending sound filled the vast chambers. "That is all?" he said snidely, "The cheap tricks and witchcraft of an elf? What sort of truth is this?"

"Silence!" The King bellowed. Tervasian quieted, but glowered at Gray. "Let's say we believe you," Katsu continued, hands gripping the arms of his ornate throne, "If we do, and those images are real, what would stop them? How am I to protect my kingdom from this evil?"

"No one knows how to destroy the Kage," Mura voiced, "but their army is composed of vergs and saeroks, and they bleed and die just like you and I."

Rydel stepped forward. "You have to make a stand here. Gather your men—with your numbers and your high walls, you should be able to, at the very least, hold out against the dark army. They cannot bring siege weapons in the high passes. You can fight them!"

The dignitaries in the balconies looked to the King in his deep-seated throne. He rose and spoke, "I will protect my people! The Shining City will prepare for war! As for you six, you will be confined to your inn."

"Confined?" Karil exclaimed.

"If I could leave you with your dark evil and spare my city, know that I would throw you from my walls at this moment. However, it seems too late for such things. As it stands, you will stay out of the council's way. As for your villagers, they are not welcome. They may stay tonight, but they must leave tomorrow—the way they entered. Fail to heed my word and see yourself forever locked below the keep!" Other dignitaries in the stand seconded the motion. Tervasian watched Gray with a snake-like grin of satisfaction.

Gray strode forward, eyeing the guards, ticking off how many there were. Fifteen. But he had already seen more throughout the palace. He wasn't sure what he was doing, but he felt tendrils of air swirling at his fingertips as his eyes fogged with rage. He wanted to grip the sword and unleash its power.

Mura gripped his arm, holding him back. The hermit shook his head.

"Leave us now!" The King commanded, "The council and I have much to discuss." The stone-faced guards approached with hands upon their pommels. He eyed the hermit and at last released his power. Flanked by steel, with the others at his side, Gray was led out of the vast chambers, dark whispers at his back.

A Hallway of Gold

In the west, the setting sun lit the dark keep. The open hallway glowed from the sun's rays. Between the shadowed pillars and far below, Gray glimpsed the vast city.

Baked-clay houses were crammed together, sprawling into the distance. Colorful stands lined the many streets. In the heart of the city was a domed castle, easily twice as big as the Shiroku Palace. More buildings just as massive could be seen in the distance, growing like mountains in a sea of cream-colored buildings. Where am I? Gray thought, standing in the corridor's orange light. He looked down and saw flaxen robes. The coarse weave was strangely familiar.

No use standing here, he thought and started forward. He moved through the hall that led to a wide set of stairs and he took them two at a time. He passed a few more halls when he realized what seemed so strange about the place. There were no people.

Abruptly, he stood before a door, hand upon the doorknob, though he couldn't remember putting it there. Dread suddenly filled him. The last thing he wanted was to open the door. He tried to let go, but panicked as his grip tightened. His hand twisted and the door swung open.

A young woman knelt in the center of a dark room while black tendrils seeped along the ground. They pooled around his boots and flowed into the hallway. The woman clutched something at her chest. Morrowil. Malevolence sprouted from the sword. The woman reached out, pleading for him to save her life, but Gray was rooted to the ground, helpless. The light faded in the woman's eyes. This is a dream! This isn't happening! He shouted to himself, begging to wake. This is a dream! he shouted louder. Suddenly, he stood before the woman. He looked down and saw he gripped Morrowil, hands coated in blood.

The woman gave a breathless whisper, "Why?"

No, he said in horror, trying to back away.

Suddenly voices sounded from behind. Gray twisted to see men dashing down the hallway, swords raised. A gong rang, echoing in his ears—the alarm had been sounded. It was too late. He yanked at his legs, trying to pry himself free, but he was stuck. He wanted to throw Morrowil, but the blade was fused to his hand. The men drew closer, their face's becoming clear.

Everything flashed, and the woman and the room crumbled.

"Ren…" he whispered.

Gray awoke.

He knelt before Ayva, gripping his blade. Morrowil hovered a breath away from her slender throat. He froze, muscles rigid. Ayva's eyes fluttered, sleeping. With held breath, he pulled away. His arm tensed and seized. Panicking, he pulled harder. A black tendril slithered beneath his flesh and he watched the muscles in his arm ripple. The sword hovered closer. "No," he begged in a whisper. Ayva rustled in her sleep, rolling over and the razor-sharp blade skimmed a lock of hair. Gray opened his mouth to wake her and stopped… He couldn't risk it.

He reached for the nexus. But where it once sat, there was only an abyss of darkness. The nexus was gone. Beneath him, Ayva moved restlessly again. Frantically, he moved deeper into his mind until he saw a glimmer of light. He felt pain but ignored it, racing towards the light, but the closer he got the farther it seemed. Panic rising, he opened his eyes to see tendrils slithering over his limbs, their touch like cold fire, burning. His whole body was nearly consumed in living darkness. He held back a cry of anguish as the darkness reached for his neck. It was too late. He couldn't touch his power, and even if he could, it was clearly engulfed by the darkness. His mind desperately searched for a way out when something burned against his chest.

The pendant.

With his free hand, Gray gripped it as the darkness slithered into his mouth. He fumbled, straining to twist each piece, frozen fingers working like wooden pegs. Leaf, moon, sun, he flipped the halves into place. The darkness coated his lungs and he choked. The pendant slipped from his hand and darkness slithered over it. He wiped it with his thumb as he gasped for a breath. Stone, water, flesh… His vision faded. The last three pieces clicked into place. Suddenly, a brilliant light burst from the pendant. It shattered the darkness binding his limbs. The inky blackness skittered to the shadowy corners of the room.

He sucked in a desperate breath. Ayva shifted but slumbered, unaware. Slowly he pulled away, rising to his feet with shaky gulps of air. He looked at Ayva and decided. Silhouettes ghosted behind the paper-thin door and he froze. When they passed, he rose and began wrapping his sword. No time to waste. Dawn was only hours away.

Beside his bed upon the floor was a set of new clothes, neatly folded, compliments of Mistress Hitomi. Quickly, he dressed, throwing on the dark green tunic and black pants. He strapped his sword on his back, and pulled on his tattered gray cloak, then grabbed his pack but stopped. If anyone spotted him with his pack it would be a clear sign that he was leaving. He scanned the room when he saw the window.

He cracked it and looked out upon the main street of the city. Chill air hit his sweat-soaked skin sending a shiver down his spine when boots upon stone sounded. He ducked as a file of guards marched past. When their footfalls faded, he carefully lowered his pack onto the slick blue tiles. It slid, landing upon the road with a soft plop. Behind him, Darius sniffed. Gray tensed. At last, he heard the sound of snoring and he turned to see the rogue gripping his dagger in the folds of his worn rags, eyes closed.

Gray looked at his friends one last time. Despite his sorrow, he was glad, for he would never be the cause of their suffering again. In the end, Kail was right and Maris was wrong. He was alone.

He slid the paper door closed, tiptoeing down the hallway. Passing a screen door, he heard Mura's saw-like snores, but he moved on. The hermit would take care of the others now, he knew, feeling content.

No noise came from the common room, but as he descended the stairs he spotted Mistress Hitomi quietly polishing pewter mugs from behind the throne of her rosewood bar. "Can't sleep?" she asked scrubbing an already immaculate mug.

The rest of the common room was vacant, seats and tables empty, waiting for the new day. He took particular notice of the corners of the inn, but didn't see Dorbin, the hulking brute, anywhere. They were alone. "Bad dreams," he confessed truthfully. Mistress Hitomi took in the bundle upon his back, but without his pack, he could have just been out for a late-night stroll. "I wanted to thank you for the kindness you've shown my friends and me. We'll be out of your hair soon."

"Ah yes," she said sadly. "Now that the king is exiling your friends, the refugees from Lakewood."

"How'd you know?"

"I have many eyes and ears. They keep me informed," she said mysteriously. "You definitely are a strange bunch. You know, others might be mad at you for getting the whole city in an uproar like this."

Gray heard the rattle of boots as another file stomped down the street. "And you?" he asked, calmly. "Are you upset?"

"Why should I be?" she shrugged, "You only told that fool Katsu the truth."

"Well, I can't take all the credit."

Mistress Hitomi raised a single brow, "Yes, your companions. I know many people in my line of business, but I've never seen friends quite like yours."

Gray swallowed down the knot in his throat. He tried to change the subject, "I was wondering, was there any food left over from tonight?"

"Some. The roast is all gone, but you can have the vegetables and rice. I'll get one of my girls to bring it out to you." Gray thanked her and moments later a girl came out with the food conveniently wrapped inside a small polished wood box tied closed with strings.

He moved towards the door when Hitomi asked, "Where are you headed?" He said nothing and she smiled, returning to polishing her mugs. "Watch yourself. I have a feeling you can handle that sword of yours, but I don't like bad things happening to good people, and I get a sense of that in the air."

His sword was bundled in cloth and unrecognizable. "How did you know…"

"That you wield Morrowil?"

He froze.

"I saw the blade's shimmer through the cloth," she said. "Those books of mine are not just for decoration."

"Does anyone else know?"

"Unlikely. Like I said, I am inquisitive, but I'm not so base to flap my tongue, and I doubt any in this city would know what I know. Besides, I've a sense whatever you're involved in is far over my head. Though if I could, a bit of advice?"

He nodded.

"When all seems darkest, trust yourself, for the power we carry is not in some item or sword. It lies within." She tapped her chest, and then shrugged as if she were telling him the weather. "That's all."

"You are a wise woman," he said quietly. "Mura was right." With that, he turned and took to the night.

* * *

Gray breathed a sigh of relief upon seeing his pack, and he threw it on, sliding his sword beneath.

The streets were quiet, but he could hear the rhythmic march of more soldiers in the distance, nearing. Standing in the shadows, he wondered who knew about their confined status. It seemed unlikely that every solider knew at this early stage, but he didn't want to test his theory.

Sticking to the shadows he took the nearby alley. Slipping around the corner, he came to a three-way fork surrounded by moonlit sakura trees, their flowers a dim red in the night. On either side, sat quiet marbled houses. Gray settled on the alley before him, paralleling the main road, which would lead him to the gates of the city. When he heard a voice.

She held his face with twisted lace,
Close enough to kiss and not enough to miss,
But instead of a sweet old pucker,

Ole' Tompson got a sucker!
Duck and dodge she did, and ran away
With his whole pay, to find some other fodder!

A figure shifted in the shade of one of the trees, and a face appeared. Balder. In one hand, he nibbled on a strange fruit, and in the other he held a ceramic urn.

Gray strode forward, "What are you doing out here?"

"Evening," Balder said and gestured to the starless sky. "I often sit here to watch the moon. I think the real question is what are you doing out here? And what's with the pack?"

More boots echoed in the distance and Gray swiveled to the sound.

"I see," Balder said slowly, "Well then, where are we going?"

He ignored the question. "Are you going to tell the others?"

"Only if you don't tell me where we're going."

"I can't tell you, Balder."

"I see. Then let me ask, just how are you planning to get out of here?" The stonemason leaned back against the tree, resting his hands behind his head. "I suppose you could have done whatever it was you did before to cross the impasse, maybe two hours ago, but that time has passed. By now the gates are locked down tighter than a Landerian seal of marble, and crawling like a kicked hornet's nest with soldiers. They won't let anyone through, especially not someone held captive by order of his majesty."

Gray scowled. He knew the stonemason was right, and he also knew he was hiding something as well. "How do I get out, Balder?"

"What makes you think I know a way out?"

"You claim to have created this city from the ground up. Surely you know a way out."

"Ah, so now you need the grand stonemason?" He said and brushed his coat. "Recognition at last!"

"Balder, I don't have time for this! The others could find out I'm missing any moment."

The stonemason tapped his lips in thought. "You're right. From the little I've seen, I'd guess that boy and young woman would follow you to Death's Gate itself. But what is this plan of yours? Some sort of heroic solitary undertaking?"

"Does it matter?" he asked.

"They will be upset that you left them, you know that."

"There are things at work you don't understand, Balder," he said quietly, "I have to leave."

The stonemason peered at him curiously. "I see. Those eyes of yours have taken on a different set. It seems you've found what you were looking for. So be it, I will help, but first I've a request. Would you mind terribly saying my full title?"

Gray gave a deep bow, twirling his hand. "Balder the Magnificent, the most glorious of builders, who would never use a saerian bond, and is the true leader of the prestigious Stonemason's Guild… would you please help me?"

Balder raised the ceramic urn to his lips and a clear liquid sloshed out. Then he stood and threw the urn against a nearby tree. It shattered noisily. "No more of that tonight, got to keep our wits about us. No time to waste chatting either, let's get going!" The stonemason set off down the road, opposite where Gray had been planning to go.

"Where are you going?" he called, "That only leads into the city."

Balder looked over his shoulder. "You were planning on going to your own arrest. Now do you want to know where the secret tunnel is or not? Likely, we'll both be captured and thrown in some dank cell, but it's worth a try." Gray shook his head and ran to catch up, and together they moved through the moonlit alleys. He was torn as he followed Balder. Should I trust the man? He wondered as they avoided a small patrol of guards. A darker voice answered, do we have a choice?

Balder moved towards the main street and Gray caught his shoulder, "There are soldiers swarming out there. If any of them know of the king's order, I'll be caught instantly."

The stonemason winked, "It's better to hide in the open, than be caught in the dark and thought a thief."

Reluctantly, Gray released him.

"Into the lion's den!" Balder said, and with that they moved into the crowded streets.

The Sodden Tunnels

Striding along the white-paved road, Gray watched the torrent of soldiers.

To their right, a file of armed men ran closely by them, their boots chiming as one as they went the opposite way. Their silver plate gleamed in the moonlight, the white flame of ice bright upon their breastplates, while swords jostled at their waists. As they passed, Gray inched deeper into his cowl, hiding his face.

Night was fading, and in the sky the clouds turned pale, lit a faint pink from the rising sun. "Will you look after the others?" he asked Balder, as another file of guards on horses passed.

"Look after the others?" Balder harrumphed. "What do you take me for, some kind of wet nurse?"

People all around were beginning to open up their doors to their large villas, or look down from high balconies. Women in night-gowns, bare-chested men and small children watched the commotion fearfully. "If you're thinking you can come with me, you're wrong," he replied.

"Come with you? No thank you. The Shining City is my home. Besides, I have other things I need to see to," Balder said mysteriously.

"Can you include watching over the others in those plans? Please, as a favor to me."

The stonemason grumbled incomprehensibly before finally relenting, "I suppose."

Gray gave a nod of thanks and together they made their way to a large square. In the center of the bazaar was a statue. Standing taller than all other buildings, it depicted a king holding a sword over an opponent with a flame of hair. He shook his head, puzzled by the familiar image when a voice caught his attention.

A round man upon a podium announced in a deep voice, "By order of his majesty, the honorable King Katsu, a new decree is set upon the citizens of the glorious Shining City! Any man able to bear arms must report to Captain Isamu in the barracks of the Noble District. All other citizens are hereby ordered to remain indoors." With Balder at his side Gray left the square, the man's proclamation fading.

They reached a fork in the road. On the left, the wide stone street wound up towards the palace, and before him was a stone wall. It crawled with finger-thick ivy. In the center was a stone door. On either side of the door, iron brackets burned with small fires. Above, the golden dome and Shiroku Palace threatened to fall down on their heads.

"That's it?" he asked.

Balder whispered under his breath. "Look at the guards." Four stone-faced soldiers stood stationary with halberds nearby the small door. Balder was right. It was far-too curious for four soldiers to guard a single door.

Another file of armored soldiers ran past. For the briefest moment, in the darkness of a soldier's helmet he caught the glimmer of scarlet red eyes. He caught his breath. Kail? But the man was gone like a dream as the file mixed with other groups and headed down the road.

"Snap out of it, Gray. Quick, turn your back and look over my shoulder, but pretend like we're talking."

"We are talking," he said, still searching men's faces. Up here, it was almost a constant flow of men coming up and down the wide white road, clothed in plate, mail and sword.

Balder sighed. "Yes, but pretend like we're talking about something other than what you're staring at, and wipe that anxious look from your face."

"What look?"

The stonemason's thick gray mustache twitched as he talked, "That look that says, 'I'm planning on tricking the guards behind us and escaping.'" Gray looked away. "Not at the ground! At me! Look at me!"

"How are we going to do this?" he asked, trying to look calm with the thousands of soldiers storming around them. He watched a great ballista made of wood and metal, mounted with a giant spear twice as long as him. It rattled down the street, pushed by a group of men with shields. In the distance, men climbed spiral stairs on nearby towers and gongs rang stridently.

"One last chance to back out. Are you sure you are up for this?" Balder asked, his eyes shifting.

"I'm ready," he said. His voice was steady.

Balder's mustache curled. "Good. There are a few things you should know first though. When you enter, if by some miracle I get you in, it will be dark, and it is very long. It is full of many turns. If you have a choice, always go straight, the other paths are dead ends, I think."

"You think?"

Balder shrugged. "I'm not sure, no one has ever taken them; at least not in a thousand years. Some say they are shortcuts to places that exist no more, some say they extend deep into the bowels of the mountain, taking weeks to traverse. Anyway, the right path should take a full day's journey. Don't get discouraged."

"I don't know how to thank you, Balder."

"Don't thank me yet. This will not be easy. From what I've heard, those men are under strict orders to attack anyone who even comes close," Balder said and paused. "One last thing, not many people know it but my real name is Jiro. Balder is my last name."

Gray ran a hand through his hair with a chuckle, "If it's all the same, it would be hard for me to view you as anything but Balder."

"Balder is just fine. Now, I'm going to create a distraction. When I do, and if it's enough, the guards will leave their posts. Use that window of opportunity to get in, but make sure no one sees you."

"What are you going to do?" he asked. "If you get caught…"

"I don't plan to," Balder snorted. "I plan on destroying something

I've thought an abomination since the moment I finished it. Just watch for your window. Now go stand over there until it happens," the man said, pointing to the outside of a quiet inn.

He grabbed Balder's arm. "If I don't see you again…"

The stonemason winked. "Then the safest of travels, Gray." With that, he jaunted off in the other direction.

He waited excitedly as he watched the crowds of soldiers pass. He imagined he was a small stone in a river, easy to overlook. Suddenly there was a thunderous crash. The sound shuddered the streets as if a building had collapsed, coming from the way Balder had gone. Soldiers hurried to the scene. Gray was impressed at the extraordinary shockwave, and he anxiously watched the four remaining guards. They peered at one another in uncertainty.

Please, he thought.

They exchanged a signal and three of the four took off down the street, leaving one behind. Gray cursed. He didn't have a choice. He started walking towards the stone door, not quite sure what he was going to do when he got there. The soldier eyed his approach. Another crash, louder this time, shook the streets, pounding in Gray's ears. He threw himself to the ground, along with hundreds of others. More soldiers rushed to the sound and gongs rang, clanging through the streets. This time, the last guard left his post running to the sound.

Gray stuffed his hands into his pockets and hurried towards the door. He reached it and looked around. The surrounding soldiers were still too busy to notice a young man in a dark corner. The door was solid stone. Gray saw iron handles indicating that it took several men to move the giant block. He put one hand to the door and called on the nexus.

Filaments of air slid between the crack of the door, probing. The crack was nearly seamless and Gray cursed. How do I move the door, if I can't fit any more of the power inside? He paused. Perhaps I don't need to… With a breath, Gray extracted thin threads of wind. Carefully, he slipped them between the slim cracks. Then, gathering all of his remaining power, he let it flow, pouring into the crack in one swift burst, thrusting filaments of wind until it overflowed. Wedged by the wall and the door, the power expanded. Abruptly, the door scraped open—not much, though just enough for Gray to enter sideways. Without wasting a moment, he slipped inside.

There was a loud bang, and darkness filled his vision. The door had shut. Panic shot through him. He twisted in the darkness, reaching out with the power. He felt for the crack in the door. His blood ran cold. There was no seam. He was trapped. A cold sweat broke out on his skin. How can that be? He probed with his power, searching frantically for the crack in the door, but after a while, he could deny it no longer. The slit in the stone was gone.

He tried to control his breath and backed away. Darkness enveloped him. His heel hit something and he tripped, tumbling backwards, landing in something wet. Terror rose in his throat. A voice echoed in his skull, Stay calm. Use your breath and center your thoughts.

At the same time, something brushed his leg and he snatched it back. "What was that?" Silenced echoed as he listened to his own shallow breaths. At last, he took a deep breath. "Just my imagination," he said aloud. As if in reply, a sound came from the darkness, like a chill breath. Gray resolved the words.

The sword.

Suddenly he remembered the sword and its glow. Hope flashed inside him. He unsheathed the blade from his back in a rush. It blazed silver, pressing back the darkness; though the silvery light illuminated only a few feet before him. He leaned forward, his eyes searching. At the edge of his vision he saw shadows moving, twisting and blending.

"Give us the sword," a voice whispered.

"What do you want with it?"

"Give it to usss," it answered and the darkness shifted.

A familiar voice within his skull spoke forcefully, Use the pendant, boy! Now!

The eerie breath spoke like a thousand soulless voices, "Give usss the sssssword..."

"It's mine!" Gray replied, his grip tightening on the blade, "Be gone!" Silence answered his words. Something touched his boot. He flinched and thrust the sword downward, shining its light upon the ground. In the gleam of silver, a dark black mass slunk upward, reaching his ankle. Gray kicked at the darkness, smashing down with all his weight. The dark mass evaded his foot and shot higher, reaching his calf. In panic, he tried to kick the boot off but the darkness lunged. It gripped onto his other foot, pulling him to the ground and the air was knocked from his lungs. He lifted the blade and watched as black tendrils crawled higher. The silvery light of the sword dimmed as a black vein snaked across its surface. He twisted and pulled at his bound legs, but to no avail. The darkness scuttled higher. It burned through the thick layer of wool. Suddenly the ground writhed as if alive and he knew it was everywhere.

More tendrils of darkness crept across the blade and the sword's light vanished.

Dark Deeds

Maris watched as Gray slipped through the stone slit, disappearing into the ancient tunnels. Meanwhile the Ronin was lost in memory.

It was a dark night. Like phantoms, they gathered in the quiet stone courtyard. He looked to his eight brothers in arms; all silent, cloaked like emissaries of death and justice. The message from Hiron was urgent—King Endar of Runile, a city within the Kingdom of Ice, had turned, betraying the nine kingdoms and was attempting to flee that night. They waited until a group of hooded men appeared from the shadows. Maris smirked. The king and his men watched the darkness in fear, unaware of the eyes that watched them as they slipped into the tunnels. Wordlessly, with his brothers at his side, they followed. The scent of the betrayer king and his guards was sharp and full of terror. They chased down the King and his guards, meeting them at a juncture. The men froze at his voice. Endar turned. He still remembered that face—round eyes like glass beads and a wide, slack jaw. In the flickering torchlight, the king's skin was pale white, drained of blood. The traitorous King knew what their appearance meant, just as he should have known the moment the fool committed his act of betrayal. The roar of Maris' blade, and the others filled the dark caverns.

Maris suddenly returned to his body. He squatted on the balls of his feet, standing upon a stone roof, looking out over the town square that was roiling with unrest. He shook his head, still remembering the blood that had been spilled, and the valiant attempts of the king's guard. Always a shame when good men die for a wretched man's cause.

Below, guards ran to and fro, their bright plate made him squint as dawn replaced night, looking more like shiny, armored playthings than soldiers. At the same time, nobles attired in rich silks and heavy brocade watched from the safety of their homes while torches were lit and orders were shouted to find the intruders.

It was the chaos that followed the crazed man's act. Maris shook his head. He wasn't sure if it was bravery or stupidity or a mix of both, but Gray's foolish friend seemingly got away with it. Either way, Maris was quite grateful for the man's deed. He rubbed his chin, eyeing the now shattered statue that lay in ruins upon the white paved stone. He could still see half of his face, or what he assumed was his face lying upon the ground like a cracked melon. He held out his hands like a picture frame, bordering the face in his mind.

"No, no, no, the features are all wrong," he declared with a sigh. But why? He wondered, scratching his chin. Maris cocked his head, embracing the leaf. The stone lay a hundred paces away, but his vision narrowed. He saw the face more sharply as if he were standing before it. "Yes, see? That's it—the nose is far too broad and my chin is sharper than that, surely," he said and squinted. "But the hair isn't half bad," he admitted. He fanned his hair upward in taller spikes, trying to imitate his likeness. The statue of the king that had been in the act of vanquishing him now lay in complete ruins—only a glimpse of the stone hand with its encrusted rings still intact.

Maris turned suddenly somber, eyeing the tunnel and where the boy had gone. Is what I did right? To hell with prophecy, he always said, then why did I abide by it this time? Because the Traitor was right. A torrent of emotions assaulted him. What would the others think if they knew I had conspired with the Traitor? He knew that was the least of his issues. He didn't care about himself. The fate of much more was in the balance.

"It had to be done. The Knife's Edge is too important to ignore, and the boy too young to set his own course," he said aloud. Yet to decide the boy's fate and play him like a puppet was wrong. Maris had trained Gray with pride, and knew his talents. He was just like the Traitor, in nearly every way. One day the boy might even surpass the legend, for he had seen a glimmer of the boy's potential, and it was vast.

Putting his hand to the rooftop, he embraced the leaf as he had done countless times.

He raced forward through the city, along the earth, feeling the streets that trembled with soldier's boots. He moved past the white gates, back from where they had come, along the icy paths. Suddenly, the ground pulsed. Maris tensed. He pushed forward. It shuddered again, far heavier than anything he had felt before. He pressed on until he found what he dreaded. His senses shook as the raucous stampede of hooves clambered, shaking the mountains all around—at its side, was the scrape of claw, and dark metal boot, marching forward. Heading north.

His eyes snapped wide and slowly, his breathing settled. He looked over the rooftops, and past the vast walls. He still felt the ground thundering with the march of war.

They were coming.

A Dark Way

In the pitch black, Gray heard only his frantic breaths as the dark presence slithered up his legs and burned his calves like fire.

"Give it to ussss," the darkness hissed, echoing off the walls.

Gray thrashed, but the more he struggled, the tighter the darkness squeezed. Use me! A voice shouted, and the pendant burned. He lunged for it, when pain lanced through his arm. He realized he still held the sword and threw it from his grip, grabbing for the pendant. The darkness crawled higher and he panicked without sight, trying to decipher the symbols.

"I can't see!" he bellowed. Then feel, the pendant whispered.

Gray felt the raised bumps in the darkness. A half-moon, a teardrop, a flame. Moon, Ice, and Fire. Those three were all touching. He made his first quick twist. A leaf, a blade, and a heart. Leaf, Steel, and Flesh. Second twist. Faster! His mind shouted, time running out. In a flush of panic he twisted it one way and then another, trying to remember the pattern he had made that had unlocked it before. But as he continued to twist, he lost track. The darkness slid over his heart and pain flooded through him. In the same moment, something grabbed, tearing the pendant from his grip. Fighting his way through the muck, he clawed for it, searching wildly. He dug through slime and muck until his fingers grazed something solid, and he ripped it free. The darkness oozed over his face, down his nostrils and over his lids, burning like fire. In a sudden movement, the slithering dark squeezed. Gray gasped, feeling as if a hammer had been dropped upon his chest, bones cracking beneath the weight. He rubbed the pendant's surface.

Moon. Ice. Fire. Leaf. Steel. Flesh. Stone. Seven, he counted with his fumbling fingers. All were turned, but one. What was the last one? He thought, trying desperately to think through his rising fear.

"Diiiieee," said the soulless voice. An image of Omni and her burning blade flashed. Sun! And Gray twisted the last piece in place. He flinched as light blazed forth from the metal disk, blinding him. The darkness shrieked. It sizzled like water thrown upon a hot pan, steam rising as it shirked from the golden luminescence. Gray thrust the pendant forward, lighting his legs and torso. The darkness recoiled and fled, sluicing from his limbs. At last, it retreated, climbing the muck-covered walls, and fading into oblivion.

Gray watched in shock. He gained control of his breath and after he was sure the darkness was gone, he fell back with a slump. Upon the pendant, all the symbols had coalesced, forming the symbol of wind.

He waited for the pendant to answer, but it was quiet now. Slowly, he rose, grabbing Morrowil and gathering his remaining strength. The pendant still glowed in his hand, lighting the way several paces ahead. He peered beyond and saw more darkness. But with the light of the pendant in his hand, he felt safe. He took several steps and looked back at the door.

Ayva, Darius, and the others would just be getting up now to see an empty bed. They wouldn't find him now. He turned from the door, and peered into the gloom, hoping he had seen the last of that strange darkness. No use waiting around here. He thrust the pendant ahead like a beacon and started forward. As he walked, the pendant illuminated the tunnel. It was no wider than both his arms outstretched. Thick layers of pale green slime stuck to the walls, obscuring any sign of stone. Some slime was putrid and wet while other patches were dry and lifeless, centuries old.

Fear of the darkness always lurked in his awareness. At times he heard a sound like tiny feet scraping in the distance, but it didn't sound like the darkness from before. He shivered and thrust his imagination to the back of his mind, as he kept moving. Time blended in the murky half-light of the tunnels. He had a feeling that it wasn't later than midday, but he could swear he had been walking for days. His ears popped as he moved deeper and deeper into the core of the heavy mountain. At one point, when his feet dragged like steel boots and his lids grew heavy, he found a dry spot, put the glowing pendant in his lap and stole a few moments of sleep. He awoke to the same murky darkness. He knew it hadn't been long, but he berated himself for wasting precious moments, and with renewed vigor he took to the tunnels. A few times he came to a four-way divide. He would pause and peer ten paces down the right and the left, but always take the path straight ahead. He wondered what was down those side paths, thinking about the strange scraping sounds.

And suddenly it ended.

He found himself before a large flat stone. He reached out, feeling for a seam in the stone, but this time, he realized not only was there no seam, but the stone itself was a part of the mountain. He threw all of his weight against the wall, and pushed with a grunt. It didn't budge. Reaching into the recesses of his mind, he withdrew a sliver of wind, feeling the stone's joints, looking for where he could apply pressure, but there was nothing. He pushed harder, slamming his body painfully into the flat stone. With each push, his fear and anxiety multiplied, until his breaths were short and jagged, and sweat rolled down his face. He forced his mind calm, but failed. "I won't be stuck down here!" His voice reverberated off the cramped walls, emphasizing his solitude.

Gray began to feel the heavy mountain, its thick stone and endless tons of dirt weighing down above his head. His chest tightened, and with a shudder, he imagined it all collapsing upon him. Words filled him suddenly.

Our power lies within us… Hitomi, he thought.

He took a calming breath, and then another. Turning, he walked. When he was at least a hundred feet from the dead end, surrounded in darkness, he began to run, until the run became a full-fledged sprint. He pictured the nexus inside. As he charged, wind followed him. For a brief flash, an envelope of golden light encompassed him, urging him forward. At last, his shoulder rammed against the stone and the earth shuddered upon the impact. With a crash, he burst through and tumbled headfirst. He twisted his body into a fast-paced roll and flew over the falling chunks of stone, dirt, and other rubble.

Coming out of the roll, he stood, a bit shaky and looked back. At his feet, stood the foothills tipped with melting ice. His gaze rose, taking in the full scope of the towering mountains. Turning, he looked at the dusky valley rolling with tufts of dry grass and sparse, hardy flowers. He heard wind. It sounded loud after the long quiet of the tunnel. The absolute silence of the tunnels had unnerved him. He was glad to be out from underneath the weight of the heavy mountain. He looked towards Death's Gate, when a screech sounded.

Perched upon a rocky crag was the hawk. "Motri… is that you?"

The bird cocked its head sideways, its burnished eyes examining him. It let loose another screech.

Gray shook his head with a laugh, "I have no idea how you got here, but I'm glad to see you." He looked north and raised his arm. "I'm headed that way. If you want to join me, I'd appreciate the company. It's a pretty long road." The bird had proved its intelligence before, and though it couldn't understand his words, he sensed it knew the meaning behind them. Still Gray was glad there was no one there to hear him.

The hawk merely ruffled its golden plumage.

"Well, I'm going north now," he called, walking backwards. The hawk remained. He sighed, and at last turned. Putting his thumbs beneath the pack's straps, he headed north along the weathered valley.

Night faded, and morning came. As he walked, he nibbled on the food that Mistress Hitomi had given him. The Shining City's mountains sat behind him, far in the distance now. He imagined the hawk back there, and wished he had the bird's company.

He didn't feel tired, but as he walked he began to grow thirsty. He coughed at the dusty feeling in his mouth, swallowing his own saliva. The feeling in the back of his throat grew to a burning thirst. He ate a few flowers that he knew to be safe, but they didn't stave his thirst. It grew worse. He licked his lips, and the roughness of cracked skin made him wince. He envisioned diving into a lake and drinking until his belly swelled, but the images didn't help. All he saw was bone-dry rocks and stretches of dry land, when he glimpsed a glimmer on the horizon.

As he got close, the sound of rushing water was loud. A sigh escaped his parched lips. He stumbled towards the sound, and minutes later saw the great rushing Sil. Falling to his knees at the green bank, he scooped handfuls of water and drank deeply. When his thirst was fully quenched and his lips no longer stung, he looked up. Blocks of gray stone hundreds of times bigger than him lay on the grassy bank. Two square pillars rose to heights taller than any building in the city, just fifty paces away.

In the gushing current of the Sil more behemoth blocks rose, sticking up from the deep-running water. Far across the great river, more impressive blocks of stone lay toppled. Thin tubers and green vines had already begun to trail up the massive hunks of stone.

A memory came to him at the sight, something Darius had said, "Piddler Lane, the main road of Lakewood. Follow it north, and in a fortnight, it will lead you to the famed Bridge of Suns, which is only a short jaunt from Tir Re' Dol itself."

"The Bridge of Suns," he repeated, eyeing the now dilapidated crossing. Well, if Darius was right, he was getting close. Gray did not spend long in grief at the Kage's total destruction. After filling up an empty leather skein with the crystal clear water, he looked upstream. A loud screech drew his attention upward. Perched upon a broken pillar, was the hawk, watching him with an inquisitive tilt to its head.

"Well, welcome back," he called. With a hand, he scrubbed the back of his head in thought. "I need to find a bridge, one that's preferably not destroyed. You don't see anything from up there, do you?" he asked.

The hawk peered out over the landscape from its lofty position, its golden-feathered head swiveling, and then looked back. Again, its head tilted.

"No, huh? Well, guess I'll just have a look myself!" he said and hefted his pack, heading upstream. He looked up with a smirk and saw the hawk, circling overhead as expected. With a laugh, he picked up his step. Each time he glanced up, the hawk was there, as if watching over him. A ways up, behind a shroud of vegetation, Gray spotted a small rope bridge that skimmed the surface of the Sil's quick waters. Somehow, the Kage's hand had missed the bridge.

Gray crossed the rickety bridge. The landscape shifted. Looming on the horizon were dark storm clouds that threatened rain. He traveled for several more miles before he came upon a large grassy cliff. In the past, he had poured over Mura's many maps. If the maps were accurate, the greatest city this side of Death's Gate lay beyond that precipice. But an ill feeling rose inside his gut as he approached the edge, and the scene struck a knife blow to his heart.

The earth was charred for miles, and lying in the stain of black were ruins as far as the eye could see—fallen towers, broken walls, jagged walkways, and shattered bridges. Smoke rose from the ashes, thick black plumes that blotted out the blue sky. Those were the dark clouds of rain he had seen. He fell to his knees in disbelief.

In the distance, tracks of an army scarred the earth, the only thing that was clearly identifiable. Quickly, he got to his feet, wiped his eyes and searched for a way down the steep ledge. He found a less steep section and half-tumbled, half-ran down the dirt cliff.

By the time he reached the ruins, shadows stretched. A pale moon cast the ruined city in a sickly luster. Slowly, he moved through the ruins, his cloak dragging in the rubble. His throat clenched as he wove between the fallen buildings. The wind switched directions and suddenly the stench of burnt flesh filled his nostrils and he gagged. "Who could do this?" There was no answer, only the eerie silence of the dead. 'A short jaunt from Tir Re' Dol.' The words and Darius' cheerful tone rang in his ears.

He looked for signs of life amid the ruins, but he couldn't stifle his wrath, and he didn't want to. It burned like a furnace inside his gut. He stopped in the darkness. The sun had set fully, and as he had done in the tunnels, he unsheathed the pendant and twisted the symbols to make it glow. With the sudden flare of light he saw what stood before him and his stomach lurched.

Ahead, was a mountain of bloated bodies—men, women, and children. Ravens, their coats like ink-drenched shrouds, crawled over the pile of carcasses. They cawed and pecked, their calls a rising cacophony. Gray's blood pulsed as the birds screeched and fought for scraps.

Picking up a piece of burnt timber, he swung at the closest raven. The bird took off in an explosion of feathers. He swung and they cried in rebuke, but refused to leave. Out of the corner of his eye, a shadow darted. He threw up the timber defensively, but sharp talons scored his arm. Suddenly, another blur shot down from the night sky, brighter than the rest, and the mass of black feathers collapsed.

It was the hawk. "Motri!"

The hawk turned to the others and attacked in an exchange of wild talons and sharp beaks. As the last raven flew off, he caught his breath and a figure stepped out from behind the ruined wall.

The figure was half-lit by a shadowed moon. It loomed head and shoulders over Gray. Its broad shoulders hunched inward as its barrel-chest heaved in short, eager breaths. Gangly arms nearly skimmed the ground. Gray watched its claws that gleamed like tarnished daggers.

"Saerok…" he breathed.

Fox-Like

"I thought that might attract you," the saerok said in a sinister hiss.

Gray delved into his mind reaching for the nexus. In his panic, it eluded him. He felt nothing, only a black void. An even deeper panic set in. On his back, beneath his cloak, was the weight of his bundled sword. He couldn't reach it in time.

"You humans sicken me, the stench of your arrogance. But you are weak creatures," the saerok hissed, extending and retracting its claws rhythmically. "You realize how weak you are, do you not? Your large stone cities, your shiny skin you call armor. All of it, a lie! You are frail things."

Suddenly Gray's arm shook with tremors of darkness. Panic took hold. Not again. His heart thundered inside his chest as his back pressed against a wall. "Why are you here?"

"I knew more would come, so when the others left, I stayed."

Gray tensed as the creature took a long step forward. "But why kill me?" he asked, trying to delay the beast.

Rope-like muscles rippled beneath a thin layer of fur. "It's simple. You are weak, so you should die." The saerok lifted its gangly arm and the hawk appeared with a cry, lashing at the saerok's eyes. Using the precious moment, he scrambled to his feet and ran. Behind him, he heard the hawk cry out in pain and he glanced over his shoulder.

The hawk was nowhere to be seen, and the saerok was gaining on him, loping on all fours impossibly fast. Gray tore through a ruined archway and turned again. He skidded, one hand sliding along the ground as he took the corner. The saerok's gangly arm swiped at him, skimming his head. Gray turned, taking another path and dread filled him. It was a dead end. The creature loomed in the corner of his vision, gaining ground. Gray sprinted, not slowing as the wall approached. In the last moment, he ducked. The beast flew over his head and slammed into a stone wall and rubble crashed around him.

He rose, not wasting a moment to see if the beast survived. As he sprinted, he peered over his shoulder. The saerok shook off the rubble, and rose to its full height. With a rumbling snarl, it took to all fours again, loping faster than any horse. Gray veered, sprinting down the maze of ruins, trying to slow the beasts' momentum. Still the saerok gained with astonishing agility until he felt it hot on his back. He dove and gave a strangled choke as it gripped his cloak. Gray kicked and swung. His cloak pin broke, and he dashed behind the wall.

310 The saerok landed with a thud in front of him—it had taken the ten foot wall in a single leap. The beast ran its claws along the wall, creating a thin screech. "You cannot escape me! No human has been a challenge. But I'm going to enjoy eating your flesh. The others left, the fools, heading south to the city that shines. But, I knew more would come."

Gray summoned a smirk despite his fear, "The people have been warned. This time you will fail."

"I think not. Your own precious kind will let us in and my brothers will bathe in their blood!"

Our own people will destroy us… In the last moment before the creature struck, Gray reached for his blade. He pulled it from beneath the pack in one fluid motion. The saerok grinned, eyes widening for the final blow. With the power of the wind, the white cloth fell from Morrowil. The wind flowed over his arms and encased the blade giving it an impossible burst of speed. The creature's eyes flashed wide as he sliced its chest, cleaving the beast from neck to groin.

The sword's tip fell to the earth, limp in his hand. A soft rain fell from the night sky, coating the ruins of Tir Re' Dol and the saerok who lay in a mangled heap. He knelt and cleaned the blood from Morrowil in a puddle of water.

There was a movement, a small rustle of something behind one of the squat walls. Gray's pulse jumped, his senses spiking. The nexus came, and his power filled him, golden and dark. He threw his hand to the noise and a bolt of air flew from his fingertips. The corner of the wall shattered.

There was a frightened scream and a voice called, "Gray! It's us!" Two shadowy figures appeared from behind the wall. Darius stood with his hands raised, and Ayva stood behind the rogue, watching Gray fearfully.

"Ayva… Darius…" Tendrils of wind quickly fell from his fingers. "I didn't mean to…" his legs trembled and gave way, falling to his knees.

"Gray!" Ayva shouted, and the two rushed to his side. "Light, are you all right?" she whispered. He nodded and she smacked his arm, "Fool! Rushing off and getting yourself nearly killed! What did you think you were doing?"

"How?" he asked looking between the two.

She ignored him. Her eyes turned to the corpse behind him, mouth parting.

Darius cursed, flinching, "Is that a saerok? It's even uglier than the stories say! It looks like something from a nightmare."

"It is a nightmare," he answered, and then shook his head, "what are you two doing here?"

"You killed that?" Ayva said, her blue eyes wide. "Are there anymore?"

"I don't think so," he said. Suddenly he remembered the hawk. Motri had saved him, buying him time to flee the saerok. "Motri…"

"Who?" Ayva asked.

"There was a bird, it saved me," he explained.

"A bird saved you?" Darius scratched his head. "Where is it now?"

"He was back there a ways, near the dead," he said, trying to rise. "I think he's hurt."

"Go check," Ayva said to the rogue.

Darius grumbled but sprinted off, returning moments later. His face was drained of color as he wiped his mouth. He looked like he had recently vomited. "I saw the pile of bodies. The smell… I've never seen anything so awful. But no hawk."

"He was there," Gray insisted. "I'll check myself."

"I checked everywhere," Darius replied in anger. "There was no dicing bird, just blood and bodies! Did you take a blow to the skull?"

"I'm sure it simply flew off to safety," Ayva said. Safety… The word shot through Gray with a flush of fear. The Shining City. He groaned and tried to get up again. Ayva pushed him down easily. He felt so weak. Is it from using my power?

"Let me go," he growled.

"You're obviously hurt. You're not going anywhere," she replied.

"I have to warn them!"

"Warn who?"

"Everyone!" he answered, "They're in danger!"

"Of course they are," Darius grumbled, he nudged Ayva, "See? I told you, he clearly hit his head."

"You don't understand," he said in frustration, "The saerok said our own people will let the dark army into the city. Mura and the others will be slaughtered!"

Darius cursed. "Treachery."

"And what do you plan to do?" Ayva said, gripping his collar. "It took us two whole days to travel here. Unless you plan on flying, there's no way you would reach the Shining City in time to warn them!"

"She's right," Darius said. "What are we supposed to do?" Gray shrugged the two off and rose to his feet unsteadily. "I'm all for half-schemed plans, Gray, but what you're saying is plain suicide!"

He closed his eyes in anger, knowing they were right. "What can I do? I can't just abandon them," he whispered.

Ayva's hand touched his shoulder. "Trust Karil, Mura, and Rydel," she replied. "They will take the villagers and the others to safety."

"How are you so certain?"

"Well, how do you think we got here?" Darius asked.

Gray shook his head, "How did you?"

"We had a little chat with Mistress Hitomi," Ayva explained. "She knew about the Sodden Tunnels. Awful place by the way." She shivered. "We couldn't have made it without the torches she lent us to light the way."

All of it made sense and he breathed a sigh of relief. He would have to trust the others. However, it didn't answer one thing. He had left to keep them safe. He closed his eyes as exhaustion caught up with him. "But why?" he asked, "Why did you follow me?"

Ayva answered with a shrug, "You're our friend, and we're in this together."

It sounded so simple. But they didn't know what was inside him, the darkness that waited. He thought about what he had nearly done to her.

"I'm afraid you're stuck with us," Darius said, gripping his shoulder.

"It seems so," he said with a smile.

"So, it's settled! Where are we headed?"

"The Gate," Gray answered.

Darius choked, "Dice! The gate? Why don't you just say Remwald, or the gates of the underworld! It'd be the same thing!"

"It's our only salvation," he said and looked north, "And if the others make it out too, that's where they'll be headed."

"When they make it out, you mean," Ayva corrected.

Gray prayed she was right. Together, they turned and looked north. In the distance, beyond a vast stretch of desert, the black towers of Death's Gate rose, dark and looming. "Farhaven…" Darius breathed, staring at the Gate. "I can't believe it."

"Wait 'til we get there," he said.

A Deserted Night

Ayva snuffed the dwindling flames of the campfire as dawn broke.

It was the second day of their journey after leaving Tir Re' Dol. Each day had been filled with swift travel across plains of grass. They now made camp on a wooded hill. It was the last patch of green before an endless sea of desert. The Sobeku Desert, Gray had said. As they covered ground, Ayva's mind raced with the stories she had heard as a child about the land of magic. Farhaven…

"Sleep well?"

She startled, jumping at his voice.

Gray was sliding his bundled sword between his pack. From the first moment she had seen him, she sensed he was not from this side of the gates. In his ragged cloak, he looked a wanderer, shrouded in mystery and haunted by his past.

His green eyes stared into hers and she nearly forgot he had asked her a question. "Great," she said and gestured towards the rogue. "He's the one being a princess. I never knew anyone who could complain so much over a few sticks and a bit of dirt."

Darius was grumbling and picking twigs from his wild brown hair. He turned and gave them a sour look. She couldn't help but laugh, and Gray chuckled as well. The rogue shook his fist. "What are you two laughing at? You'd be annoyed too if you just took a bath in these cursed things," he said shaking a shirt full of prickly burrs.

"Put your shirt on Darius," Gray said. "We've waited here too long."

Tying her cloak tighter against the morning chill, Ayva hefted her pack, "If you don't hurry, we'll be travelling at nightfall, and we don't know what's out there."

"We do know what's out there is the problem," Gray answered.

Darius stretched his arms with a loud yawn, passing them as he said loudly, "Welp! What are you two waiting for?" He slapped Gray on the shoulder, "Let's get going laggards!" Ayva looked to Gray who shook his head with another chuckle and together they headed down the wooded rise. They crossed into the desert and a wave of heat blasted her. With Death's Gate as a landmark in the distance, they traversed the shifting sands.

As they walked, Darius sang in a confident tenor,

Never have I met a man,
Who knows his merit in the sands,
Where blowing winds pick up the land,
And cast it far away.

The Ronin have traversed it once,
That ancient time so long ago,
Those warriors were made to pay.

The Sobeku Desert and its arid way
Two steps short of those stone Gates
Where blowing winds pick up the land,
And cast it far away.

By the time they made camp that evening, the sun was an orange ball, shimmering just above the horizon. Exhausted, Ayva collapsed where she stood, sitting cross-legged. "I can't move another step," she slipped off her boots and rubbed her tired feet.

The rogue kicked off his boots, examining his soles and cursed, "Dicing blisters." Meanwhile, Gray unpacked a set of sticks from his bag, and set up a small pile for a fire.

Ayva eyed the burning sun. "A fire? But it's still bright outside."

Gray shrugged. "I have a memory of the desert being a cold dark place," he said, breaking sticks. Ayva read his eyes—they seemed lost in the memory.

"You've been here?" Darius questioned.

He gripped his chest and answered, "It feels like a dream, but I'm certain of it." He scraped the flint against stone, but to no avail and he grumbled.

"What's wrong?" Ayva asked.

"I can't get it to spark," Gray said.

"You're doing it wrong!" Darius replied and snatched the flint and stone from Gray's hands. With flamboyant swipes, he bashed the two together. After a good while of grunting and frustration and no flames, the rogue threw the flint and rock to the ground, "Gah! It's useless!"

Ayva slowly picked up the rock and flint.

"It won't work," said Darius, "Damned thing is broken."

Rather than argue the notion of a rock being "broken", Ayva lifted the two, preparing to rub them when a golden spark flashed at her fingertips and a stray ember scuttled into the wood fluff.

"You did it," Gray marveled. "Nicely done."

Darius grumbled, "Beginner's luck."

Ayva, however, only looked to the rock and flint in confusion. She hadn't even touched the two. Had she? What felt like moments later, she watched as darkness enveloped the desert around them. She could scarcely see beyond the light of the copper flames.

Darius rubbed his hands eagerly. "What's for dinner?"

Ayva opened her bag. Her mouth went dry. There was a dry hunk of cheese, a bowl of white rice, and several rice-flour dumplings. She bit her lower lip and handed it out. The two dug in ravenously, hungry from a long day's journey. She remained silent, nibbling on a bit of cheese.

"What's wrong?" Gray asked, noticing her silence.

"This is the last of the food."

Darius swallowed. "Wait, this is it? What about the fruit we found?"

Ayva shook out the bag. Several moldy eggs and a few spongy fruits rolled out onto the desert sand. "I was afraid it wouldn't last."

"It won't matter," Gray said. "By the end of tomorrow, we'll reach the Gate."

A shiver traced Ayva's spine. "One more day until we're at Death's Gate," she repeated, her voice soft. "I can hardly believe it." She warmed her hands over the fire. She had never imagined the desert could be so cold. There was a stretch of silence. "Are you afraid, Gray?"

Gray sat cross-legged on the sand. He was huddled inside his threadbare cloak. He looked every bit the wanderer as he stared at the moon. It had been red every night since Tir Re' Dol. "To be honest, I've been afraid this whole time," he said with a chuckle. Then, as he often did, he scrubbed a hand through the back of his head in contemplation. "But now for once, I'm not."

"What happens when we get to the Gates?" she asked.

"Isn't it obvious? We head to Farhaven," Darius said. She noticed Gray. He picked up a stick and broke it in half roughly, as if the mythical land struck a chord. The rogue continued. "Back in Lakewood, I used to hear men and women talked about the magic beyond the Gates. They said the very air was filled with magic," he said, eyes wide.

"Farhaven is magic," Ayva added. "Imagine the elves and the city of Eldas. It is said the Kingdom of Leaf is full of glowing lights that hang amid the woods. And the Spire, a great tree that reaches endlessly high, or the forests of Drymaus, home of the mythical dryads. Not to mention Farbs, which is a city full of magic. They say the fires of the Reavers light the night sky for miles. I've even heard of creatures called sprites that have no form." Her thoughts towards Farhaven ran wild. She wanted desperately to believe it all. Ayva realized she was rambling and grew quiet. Stick your fool tongue back in your mouth, Ayva, she berated.

Darius threw a rock into the dark and it landed silently in the empty desert. "We all know the stories," the rogue said dryly.

Ayva shrugged, "Well, maybe Gray didn't know."

"I didn't know that, about the sprites or the city of Drymaus," he said.

"Really? Well, anyway, Drymaus, Farbs and Eldas are only three places I know. It's really nothing to brag over."

"Still more than I know," Gray said and stood. "But we should get some sleep."

Something rattled in the darkness. At the border of the fire's light, there was a quick flicker of a shadow and Ayva leapt. With a glinting flash, the shadow was pinned to the hard-packed earth. It happened in a matter of seconds. Gray was still reaching for his sword.

Ayva drew nearer, inspecting the shadow. In the light of the fire, lay a dead snake the length of her arm. Darius' pointed dagger protruded from the back of its leathery hide. The creature's mouth was agape with two glistening-wet fangs.

Darius walked over and with a small flourish withdrew his dagger, cleaned it with a flick and slipped it in his belt behind his back. "Well then, shall we get some sleep?"

Gray nodded slowly, still eyeing the dead creature. "We should," he said. He looked up, his face attentive again. "Tomorrow, we'll see the Gates. I'm not tired, so I'll take first watch tonight."

They all agreed. Darius offered to take middle watch and promptly set up his pack as a pillow on the hard desert ground. "Farhaven…" and "One thousand years…" she heard the rogue mutter again.

Ayva watched Gray as she made her bed. His faraway eyes reflected the dancing orange flames. She lay down, tired, but thinking she would never fall asleep with the excitement and fear pumping in her veins. But after a while, her eyelids grew heavy. Her eyes opened and closed one last time to the image of Gray's face, and she began to dream.

First Light

They headed out at first light. The desert stretched before Ayva, seemingly endless when she saw it—Death's Gate—the raw sight of towering stone. When it came into view she slowed to a halt. "Dear spirits..." she whispered.

"Dice," Darius murmured at her side. "It's huge."

"That's where we're headed. Death's Gate. Did you ever in your life imagine being here right now, Gray?" she asked. A sudden wind swirled at their feet and there was a sound like the press of air.

Darius' dagger was at his side, the flat of the blade pressed tight to his forearm. "Something's wrong," he said. The dirt at her sides began to spread, little pebbles tumbling away. Gray and Darius backed up slowly as the sound became louder.

"Ayva!" Gray called.

The ground at Ayva's feet darkened. Time slowed. Her eyes turned upward. A shadow blotted out the sun and the earth shuddered. Ayva was thrown to the ground—through her tangled hair, she saw it, and uttered a strangled word, "Dragon…"

A mere ten paces away, the giant creature moved sinuously. From its massive head to its scaled limbs the dragon's entire body, bigger than a house, was armored in glimmering gray scales like tiny pieces of overlapping plate mail. Its leathery wings folded out slowly, spanning three times the size of its own body. An ominous pattern branched across its scales like forked lightning or red veins. Its massive body eclipsed the light.

She heard her name again cutting through the wind. "Ayva!"

The dragon's huge, diamond-shaped eyes fixed on her. In a burst of movement, too quick for her to follow and impossibly quick for its size, it attacked. Ayva dove, but she was too slow. A cruel claw snagged her dress. She fell when a strange sensation of wind coursed at her sides. She was rolling. She came up, breathless and dazed. Gray held her with one arm at his side. Wordlessly, he ushered her back and gripped his sword with both hands.

* * *

The dragon swiveled its massive head, snorting steam. It took Gray in with one burning eye. Then with a deafening roar, it charged. He was ready. He channeled his power into a dive again, but this time he waited. The beast lashed. A scimitar-like claw dug for his open right side. Gray sucked in a breath, and the claw scraped along his ribcage.

He dove and his sword reached, aiming for the creature's underbelly. Morrowil scraped, sounding like steel against chainmail. The dragon bellowed. The wind brushed at all sides of his body and he completed his roll, skidding along the sand. He looked back. The beast barreled towards him. Gray dove again, narrowly scraping the creature's claws. The creature twisted. It dug its claws into the ground, using it as a pivot and swung its massive weight, creating huge burrow-like trenches in the earth as it flew towards him again.

Gray had no time to dive. He planted his feet in the sand, and called forth his power. Darkness clenched his heart and tendrils of black snaked along the sword and across his arms. No! He cursed. The darkness seethed, raging with uncontrollable power, begging to be used.

The beast hurtled towards him. He raised his hand, sending the dark wrath from his fingertips. The darkness obeyed and black lightning streaked across the air. It collided with the dragon. The beast howled in pain. More power flooded through him, gushing in his veins, growing ever greater. His eyes fogged with rage. The dragon's shrieks pitched. In the corner of his vision, he saw Ayva and Darius.

They covered their ears from the deafening roar, convulsing with the power that crackled in the air. Distantly, his mind shouted, you're killing them! He faltered and the dark lightning vanished. The dragon opened its mouth and a bolt of fire erupted, racing towards him. He delved inward, and light filled his frame, blinding his sight.

Suddenly, he was eyeing the back of the dragon. It was as if he had moved forward thirty paces in the blink of an eye. Despite his confusion, he grinned as the beast's head swiveled, searching. "I'm over here," he called confidently, pressing back the darkness, and gripping the nexus that pulsed within his mind.

The dragon turned. Hatred burned in the beast's eyes. It raked its claws, tearing large tracks in the sand, then charged. But this time, not at him. The creature snaked across the desert towards Ayva and Darius.

Darius jumped in front of Ayva. With one swipe of its giant wing, the beast flung the rogue aside. He summoned his power, and the nexus pulsed. As if he had leapt the divide, suddenly he was before the beast, falling from midair and swinging Morrowil with a cry. With one claw, the beast parried his strike and flung him to the side. Dazed, he looked up as the dragon reared upon its heavy hind legs. It beat its wings and a tornado of sand and wind buffeted him. He threw out his hand and golden wind coursed around him, deflecting the torrent, and spreading it to all sides in a fine spray. The sound of air hollowing through a tunnel was loud in his ears. The creature grabbed Ayva in its talons, and lifted her from the ground. The fury of sand and wind rooted him and he cried out.

"Gray!" She rose into the air.

As the beast rose higher, the wind that rooted him fell. Gray dashed after them, but he was too late. He watched as the creature flew north with its prize in its talons. "Coward!" he roared, falling to his knees, and thrust the blade deep into the sand. Staggering to his feet he found Darius. The rogue lay motionless. He froze when sand skittered before the rogue's parted lips. Gray sighed in relief, shaking Darius' shoulder.

The rogue jolted awake with a sputtering cough. "What's going on?" he said, rubbing sand from his eyes. "Ayva! Where is she?"

"The dragon took her," he said, catching his breath. He answered the rogue's unasked fear. "She's alive, for now."

Color returned to Darius' face. "Where is it taking her?"

Gray looked into the distance, towards the looming stone gates, "Death's Gate."

"Why Ayva? What does it want with her?" Darius asked.

Gray grit his teeth, rising to his feet. "The dragon is merely a pet of the Kage. It flies to meet its master."

"The Kage…" Darius said. "Then the dark army will be waiting there. How can we fight a legion of nightmares? We'll be killed before Ayva even knows we're there to save her! And what if that's the Kage's plan? What if they wanted us to follow and it's a trap?"

Gray gave a steady breath. "I thought of that too," he said and offered his hand. "Are you with me?"

With a sigh, Darius gripped his arm, "Dice! This is a fool's journey if I ever saw one! Well, of course I'm with you, but I said it before and I'll say it again, you better know what you're doing!"

Me too, Gray thought silently, looking towards the gate that scraped the clouds.

The Endless Tunnels

The ground shook with the cries of war.

Karil stood outside the door of the Dipping Tsugi when a heavy ballista rumbled past her. The white-paved streets of the city were alive with terror. A shadow larger than the inn raced over her head. A flicker of something lashed out and she grabbed Mura, pushing him to the side of the inn and ducking. A crash shook the street. She covered her ears as wood and stone rained down upon her.

Karil looked up. She saw a massive chunk missing from the inn. The winged creature vanished back into the dark sky as streaking arrows from archers followed it. She grabbed her uncle. "Are you all right?" she shouted, though her voice sounded muted as if underwater.

Mura was covered in a film of stone. He brushed himself off and nodded.

"Let's go," she yelled, pulling her uncle up, and together they ran. Before she knew it, she saw the stone archway of the Noble's District. The same quiet entry they had entered only a day before. The place was now teeming with guards. Soldiers ran along the walkways above the entry, while even more scrambled to close the wooden gate. They were already closing off the Noble's District, she realized, running faster. "We have to stop them! Rydel is still out there!"

As they neared, a dull clang reverberated through the streets. A massive timber thudded into place, locking the doors. She grabbed the nearest soldier, "Open that door!" she commanded over the tumult of noise.

The soldier shrugged off her grip, "Go back to your home!"

"Where is your commander?" she questioned.

The young man pointed with an elbow to a soldier crowded by others on the walkway above. Karil saw it was Mashiro. A herald was close at his side, carrying a dark blue banner. Mura at her side, Karil pushed through the throng. Mashiro saw her over the heads of his men, and made his way towards them. "What are you two doing here?"

"There's no time to explain, you must open that door!" she said.

"Why should I?"

"There are men, women, and children headed this way! They will be expecting that door to be open!"

"The Common's District is gone," Mashiro said flatly, "How can you be sure they are not already dead?"

Karil swallowed, but she held her ground. "They are not. Rydel is not so easy to kill."

Mashiro ground his jaw. "Still, I would not open this door and unleash the underworld that is threatening to fall down upon us. Not unless I was sure." There was an abrupt howl overhead and a winged shadow whooshed over the stone ramparts. Soldiers fell to their knees as the beast's tail thrashed, knocking one of the stone crenulations into dust. Karil heard another sound. Voices. Suddenly fists pounded on the gate below.

"Please…" Karil pleaded, clutching Mashiro's plated arm. He looked at her, wavered, and finally shouted orders for the gates to be opened. The villagers, Rydel in the lead, flooded through the gate. When the last man came through, the door was closed and the heavy wood padlock slammed into place.

Karil embraced Rydel, pressing her face to his hando cloak. Quickly she pulled away with tears in her eyes. "I was so worried."

Rydel smiled. "I would never leave you, my queen."

Mura clasped the elf on his shoulder. "Your face is a welcome sight."

"As is yours," he replied.

Meanwhile, Karil looked to the many men, women, and children. There were hundreds—far more than the villagers they had brought to the city.

Rydel followed her gaze and spoke, "Our numbers have swelled. I gathered as many as I could before the city was overrun. Most were wise enough to follow." Karil opened her mouth when a thundering clap shook the streets, sending townsfolk and soldiers to the ground with a chorus of cries. An eerie silence hung in the air until the hammering came again, pounding against the timbered door.

"Brace the doors!" the captain bellowed. At his command, men rushed to reinforce the door from another thundering slam. "Karil, you all must leave now!" Mashiro said as the door was battered once again. She watched as the wood bulged beneath the pressure while men cried out to hold the line.

"We can help!" she replied.

"There is nothing you can do. This is my duty, now you must do yours." He looked to the men, women and children. "Get them to safety. Go north, find the Sodden Tunnels. They are the only way out of the city now. We will hold them off for as long as we can."

Karil tried to keep her voice steady, "You are a good man."

"In the end, I suppose so," he said, and then urged her on, pushing her towards Rydel, "Take her. Go," he ordered. Mashiro returned to his post, shouting orders and urging the men to hold position as the door shuddered once again.

"Time to go," Mura said at her side, pulling her away with Rydel's aid.

The feeling in Karil's gut was all too familiar, as if she were abandoning the Lando and her people all over again. With the others at her side, she ran along the main road. They headed up the tiered rises of the city and towards the palace. Turning a bend, Karil nearly collided with Mistress Hitomi.

Everything about the iron-willed proprietor was completely unruffled, from her perfect bun of dark hair to her starched blue dress. Yet Hitomi wasn't alone. At her heels were nobles dressed in disheveled rich silks. Their postures were huddled in fear, and their faces stained with panic.

"Hitomi, you're alive. I'm so glad," Karil said.

Mistress Hitomi bowed curtly. "And you. I see you have quite the following. I have my own. I gathered all those who have the wits to know this city is lost, and the sense to leave."

Behind her, the men and women were laden down with stacks of books—the Dipping Tsugi's library.

"You are a crafty woman," Mura said in admiration.

"Do you know of the Sodden Tunnels?" Karil asked abruptly.

Mistress Hitomi faltered. "How did you—"

"It doesn't matter. Do the tunnels lead out of the city?"

Hitomi shook her head, "It has been a long time since I've read of the ancient tunnels. I'm not certain. It was used by the kings of old. They are supposed to lead to Death's Gate, however, they are long and dark, and filled with endless paths. One is as likely to get lost and die in there, as out here."

Another thundering slam rocked the streets, sending many to their knees.

The world swayed beneath Karil as she replied, "Our death is certain if we stay. We will risk the tunnels," she commanded, loud enough for all to hear. "Can you lead the way?"

"I will do my best," the innkeeper said and hiked her skirts, "Follow me and quick." She gave swift orders, gathering the fraught nobles, and together they headed up the sloping hill towards the palace.

As they ran, men and women joined the crowds, running out from the shadowed alleys. Karil's mind churned. She feared Hitomi's words. She thought she'd heard legends of the tunnels, often called the Endless Tunnels and with that recollection came a sense of foreboding. Just before the palace, Mistress Hitomi slowed. Broken stone littered the streets from the dragon's destruction and several bodies lay, unmoving. Karil saw a familiar face. Councilor Tervasian lay beside several dead guards. His robes of blue, and white stole were stained in blood and his face had been crushed by a huge, nearby stone. Karil was neither glad nor disheartened. Neither was their room in her heart for pity.

Inns and villas surrounded them just like the rest of the Noble's District. The only difference to Karil's eyes was a stone wall covered in thick vines and several torches to the right of the winding road. On the wall's center was a stone door.

With the aid of several men, they slid open the heavy door. Mistress Hitomi ushered the others into the dark tunnels until only she and Rydel were left.

“Go ahead,” Karil offered, and Mistress Hitomi ducked inside.

Just then there was a splintering crack, louder than all the others. It sounded from where they had come from. She knew what it was. It was the breaking of thick wood gates. She closed her eyes and gave a silent prayer for Mashiro.

“The spirits will find a place for him,” said Rydel.

Karil nodded, teary eyed. How many had died for her to live? She looked out over the city. Dragons circled in the air, while fires burned. She saw tall stone towers crumble in the distance.

“Come. We must go,” Rydel said, touching her arm.

At last, she averted her eyes and ducked inside the stone doorway, and into the Endless Tunnels.

The Cliff's Edge

"This damn forest never ends!" Darius griped once again. "No, no, now I'm sure I've seen that bush a hundred times! We're going in circles, Gray! I'd wager all my coin on it, that's the same dicing bush!"

For the hundredth time Gray sighed under his breath. He was striding ahead of Darius, his thoughts drifting. His feet ached from days of travel while his mind swirled with questions about the Ronin. How long were they able to distract the Kage from their trail and where were they now? His thoughts turned to Mura, Karil, Rydel and the villagers. He feared for them—the safety they had sought was abolished, the saerok's words confirming the destruction of the Shining City. But he still had hope. Ayva and Darius had said Mistress Hitomi knew of the tunnels. With luck, the innkeeper was still with the others. Gray's fist tightened at his side as he thought of the hermit. No. Mura would see them all to safety. They will make it out, he vowed. And in the end, his thoughts inevitably shifted back to Ayva, and the last time he saw her, hanging from the claws of the dragon.

"Don't ignore me, Gray," Darius said from behind him. "This is the same road and we both know it! I don't see how we're saving Ayva if all we're doing is sightseeing!"

Gray had been ignoring him until now, but at last, the rogue's quips hit a soft spot, and he clenched his jaw, preparing a sharp retort when his attention switched to the path ahead. His eyes narrowed.

Beyond, through the tangle of trees, he glimpsed a bright light. Gray burst into a run. He heard the rogue yell in confusion. He tore through branch and vine, when he breached a set of trees. He came to an abrupt halt, stones skittering in front of him.

Directly before him was a cliff. It dropped a thousand feet, and in the distance was a monolith of stone, soaring towards the sky. Death's Gate. But before Death's Gate where the White Plains should be was a menacing blackness.

"What in the light was that, Gray?" Darius shouted, catching up at last, "We both know I'm faster than you, so I'm not sure what you were thinking but—" The rogue's tirade cut short with a strangled sound as he took in the sight before them. "What in the seven hells..."

Gray remembered seeing the Gate from the Lost Woods. That seemed like ages ago now. "It seems so different up close." Then he looked back to the precipice at his feet, despair filling him.

Darius whispered, "Death's Gate and the White Plains... But why are they black?"

"It must be the taint we saw at Koru Village," Gray explained, unnerved by his own words.

Darius shivered. "A foul notion. But more importantly and since you seem to have all the answers, where did this cliff come from? Where are we?"

"I don't think this cliff is supposed to be here," he replied warily.

"What's that mean?"

Gray eyed the Gate. "It's just like the forest. I think Daerval is shifting under the effects of the Return." The idea terrified him—that the Kage had that much influence over Daerval made him feel as if they had already won.

"You mean this cliff just popped up out of nowhere because of the Kage?" Darius said in disbelief. "How is that possible?"

"I don't know, but let's find a way down." Even as the words left his mouth, however, he saw only the sheer drop, and to the east and west, more of the same.

Darius shook his head. "What do we do? We can't stop. What

about Ayva?" Gray was silent, wracking his brain for an answer, but Darius continued furiously, "No, I won't believe it! Why did we come all this way just to be stopped here? For light's sake, I can see the Gate!"

Gray paused. He had nearly forgotten he could sense the lay of the land. He pulled upon his power, envisioning the nexus. Air swirled at his feet, catching dirt and pebbles as it spun faster around him. Darius backpedaled. The wind grew in intensity and with a breath he released it, jettisoning outward. He flew over the land, gliding over rock and root, searching the terrain with his second vision. He glimpsed more trees and rock east and west, but no way down the sheer precipice. Still he pressed, further and faster, and the wind raced as images flooded his vision. At last he opened his eyes. Despair in the pit of his stomach, his legs collapsed as he looked out over the deep crevasse.

"Well, can't you just make another bridge?" Darius asked.

"It's too far," he replied, shaking his head. "I was barely able to survive the making of the last bridge and this is a hundred times farther. There is no way down." In the corner of his vision, he saw Darius throw his pack over his shoulder. "What do you think you're doing?"

"I'm going to save Ayva, like we swore."

He picked up a pebble, rolling it between his thumb and forefinger. "You don't get it. We're stuck. This is the end of the road." He threw the pebble, watching it plummet until the cliff obscured its sight.

"Well, forgive me for not lying down and dying."

Gray rose to his feet. "I'm lying down and dying? Who do you think has gotten us this far?" His anger surprised him.

"And what were Ayva and I?"

The darkness whispered to him and he gripped the blade at his side. "I was always alone."

"I see. I'm glad you think so highly of us," Darius said. The rogue laughed, "See that's the problem with you Gray, it's not that you never let anyone close enough to help, it's that if they are close enough, you're too much of a stubborn, blind fool to see that they've been by your side the whole damned way! I hope you trip on your own damned face!" he said and kicked the dirt before him, showering Gray.

Gray rose. Fury coursing through his blood, he strode forward. Suddenly, he tripped, falling on his hands and knees. He looked back. A thick root protruded from the hard earth. Was that there before?

Darius looked confused.

Gray rose to his feet again, brushing himself off. "You're ignoring the fact that this is an obstacle that none of your smug arrogance can fix," he said. As he said the words, he regretted them, but his anger and despair had the best of him.

"I'm smug?" Darius retorted, bristling. "Listen to yourself! You act so high and mighty the air around you reeks of it! Dice, I nearly choke on it every time I get close to you! Sure, you play a great game of humility, but admit it, we both know you're twice as arrogant as me deep down."

Gray turned away, "None of this matters. Ayva is going to die, and there's nothing we can do."

Darius laughed, "That's great! Ayva is going to die, and Mura and the others are all doomed," he said throwing up his hands. Gray narrowed his gaze. "Fantastic!" the rogue continued, "Now that we have that settled, let's throw ourselves off the dicing cliff!"

Gray froze. That was it... "You're right," he said.

"I'm what?" Darius' laughter cut short.

"You're right," he replied. His blood pulsed with purpose as he turned and moved closer towards the edge.

"Whoa! Wait!" Darius called out, but Gray was elsewhere.

He delved, touching the nexus in the back of his mind, feeling it. With desperation spiraling through him, the nexus pulsed powerfully. He felt as if he could lift mountains, and yet... a thread of doubt wormed its way through him. He stared out over the edge, a breeze tousling his tattered cloak. He could do it, he thought obstinately, gripping the nexus. But what if it doesn't work? His mind retorted, but the answer to that was clear... It's the only way. Gray paused, feeling the rogue's presence at his back. The rogue was saying something. He glanced over his shoulder. Darius will still follow me, he realized. Gray let the nexus sit, pulsing eagerly in his mind as he turned his attention to the rogue.

"Look, I was just joking all right?" Darius laughed awkwardly.

"I'm more arrogant, I swear. See? Listen to me, I can't stop talking. Just come back from the ledge Gray…" The rogue's face was etched with worry.

Gray glared at Darius. "Why did you two follow me anyway?"

"What do you mean?" Darius said. "When?"

"Back then, at the Shining City, when I left, why did you and Ayva follow me?"

Darius answered slowly, "Because we wanted to help you. I thought that was obvious enough," he replied. "We both saw the pain that you kept to yourself and well, I guess I kinda' understood that. When I saw you that first day back then, I knew you were different. I never told you this, but when I saw you it was like when I'm about to gamble it all. Dice! I don't know how to explain it. All I know is before you entered Lakewood, things just seemed boring." He chuckled, "Maybe that's why I gamble, to try to risk something, to find something worth meaning. And when I saw that look in your eye, I knew you were searching for that same thing. Don't you see? I knew we could help each other. And when you left the Shining City, even though we'd been nearly killed a hundred times, I realized

I had found it. I knew that regardless of my past, or even the future, for once, even in this chaos, things seemed somehow right. I don't care about adventure or gold, but I care about you, and Ayva. So I guess what I was missing all along were true friends."

"Touching story," he said coldly, looking away.

"What?"

"Did you ever think in all that, that perhaps I didn't need or want your help, or Ayva's?"

Darius looked at him in disbelief. "Do you really think that?"

"Maybe this will be more clear for you Darius—you wanted to be at my side, but I? I never wanted to be by yours." The rogue's brows knit together in confusion as the sincerity in his voice finally sunk in. "Ah, there we go! Now you're getting it. Go away." Darius looked stricken. "I'm not kidding, turn around right now and leave me be. If you're smart, you'll find a hole, hide there, and live. It might be the only thing you are good at."

Darius stepped back, his normally cocky expression twisted into one of pain and confusion.

Gray focused on the task at hand, knowing he would need it all and more. He heard Darius' footsteps, moving into the woods and away from him. He narrowed his focus on the Gate ahead. It sat shoulder to shoulder with the giant Burai Mountains. He looked to the White Plains below the Gate that were now blackened by the taint. With a deep breath, he summoned the nexus.

His power came, flowing through him. Like each time before, it filled him with life. Gray pulled even more into himself until he was filled to the point of pain. His gaze fell to the cavernous drop. Closing his eyes, he imagined the fall in the woods.

A dark green canopy raced towards him, as far as the eye could see… the wind lashed him as he plummeted… the rush of air sounded in his ears… terror flowed in his veins… The chaotic vision was halted and broken, but he held onto it, searching deeper. The wind howled as his eyes watered, vision fading, turning black... but he pushed beyond. In his mind he heard a quiet murmuring, a stirring in his veins as an ancient power was awoken. Then he saw it, the spell he had created, woven like a mesh of golden cords.

He pulled each thread, as if extracting the movements from a dream, and where he forgot, he filled in the gap with what the wind insinuated. The wind wove thicker and thicker strands, overlapping one another, but he made them loose, pliable. He wove those threads like a coat of armor, surrounding himself in a cocoon of wind that was alive. Placing his feet to the cliff's edge he closed his eyes with a breath and fell forward.

Through the lashing of the wind, a voice sounded, "Gray, don't!"

He twisted. Darius ran towards him. Surprise lanced through him. The nexus shattered. The wind that coursed around him vanished in a rush. With every fiber in his body, he lunged for the cliff's edge when Darius smashed into him.

The roar of the wind raged in his ears and his eyes watered, blinding his sight. His cloak filled his vision and he threw it aside. Darius clawed at him and they tumbled end over end. He tried to restrain the rogue's thrashing limbs, only to spin and lose contact. Colors blurred in a dizzying haze. More thoughts materialized, frenzied and incoherent, until he could barely think. Darkness began to creep, taking over his vision. No! His eyes fanned wide. The thought was like a lance, shrill but fleeting, and he plunged back into the dark abyss of his mind, searching frantically for the nexus. Below, the ground was spiraling closer. Something gripped him, choking him. It was Darius. Terror filled the rogue's wide eyes. But he didn't try to fight him. Instead, he shut his eyes, loosing a single breath.

Silence.

It was only a flicker, but he let it fill him. In that moment the nexus flickered. Gray gripped it like a drowning man who gasped for air. Suddenly, all the flows that he had conjured moments before came back in a rush that made his body jerk. Through his closed eyes he saw the ground, approaching too quickly. They were almost there. He wove the spell faster. Threads like spindly roots wove around them. He opened his eyes. A hairsbreadth from the ground, they were surrounded by a flame of wind. In his mind, he plied the spell, letting it take its course. Thick threads twisted and twined. Gently, the cradle of air lowered them the rest of the way, setting them down like a feather.

White mist fell. Snow, his mind registered. Around them, the snow had been blown back. Darius knelt, eyes still tightly clenched. Gray touched his shoulder.

"What just happened?" he whispered, looking as if he expected to be dead. How are we alive?"

Gray eyed his trembling hands. He was sapped of energy. Darius cursed and Gray turned. A tide of darkness sat before them. Huge vergs and lanky saeroks roiled. The dark army. What he thought was the taint of darkness from up high on the cliff's edge was in fact the dark army itself. A stone's throw away, a wave of grunts and snarls fouled the cold air as the army faced the other direction.

Gray panicked. He grabbed Darius, throwing a hand over the rogue's mouth and crouched. No creatures had noticed them yet. He eyed their surroundings for a place to hide, when suddenly a nightmare misted out of thin air, materializing behind the armies. A Nameless.

"Move, you worthlesss sacks of meat!" It shouted as it strode up and down the lines, taller than Gray remembered. Its black armor, overlapping plates of sinuous metal, undulated like snake scales. It roared and lashed the beasts with a dark whip. The dark army pressed forward.

Another Nameless materialized. It was even taller than its brother. "Onward you filth! The Kagehass will have your hidesss! Into the Gate!" it bellowed, urging the dark mass forward. Like a surging tide, the throng grunted and snarled.

In the distance, over the heads of the army Gray saw their destination. The huge stone face of the Gate now seemed impossibly far. Suddenly, a slim fissure ran down their center and a strange crimson light spread. Dread filled Gray's heart. The Gate has been breached.

Gray rose, searching for a place to hide when cold steel touched his skin above the collar. "Darius," he whispered thinly. The dagger pressed deeper and he choked, stifling his breath. Darius turned and his eyes flared. The rogue's hand shot for the hidden dagger in his clothes.

"I wouldn't do that," his assailant replied in a hard voice.

Gray didn't dare to look around. "Who are you?"

"Silence!" the man commanded in a low hiss. "I would not speak again, unless you wish to die. It is said a saerok can hear a mouse's scurry." Gray struggled against his grip. "Now I'm going to let you go. Don't make a sound or I will regret my decision," he said in a menacing whisper, then pushed him away.

He looked up, rubbing his neck and taking in his attacker. The man wore a ragged gray cloak. Its heavy hood was pushed far forward to hide his face. Other than that he was tall and wore the nondescript clothes of a wanderer. But his voice and demeanor was all too familiar.

"Kail," he whispered.

The man drew back his hood, revealing bright scarlet eyes. Kail's strong jaw was dappled with unshaven growth, peppered black and gray, while his long gray braid hung down, nearly reaching his shoulder. At Gray's side, Darius' jaw dropped. The rogue gained his senses and lunged for his weapon. But Gray was quicker. He grabbed the rogue's wrist.

"Gray, what are you doing? Dice, that's Kail!" Darius voice was full of panic.

"He won't hurt us," he replied. Then he looked to Kail who gave a wolf-like smile. "What do you want with us?"

"I see you decided not to part from your friends," the Ronin said.

"I tried, but I realize now that I'm not like you. I'm not alone."

"Perhaps not. But they will die, and you will pay the price," the legend shrugged. "Nevertheless, that is not why I am here. In light of your precious friendship, I've come to deliver a message."

"What message?" Darius asked warily.

"Your friend is in danger."

"Ayva. Where is she?" Gray asked, striding forward.

"She is being held captive upon the gates. The Kage are coming for her. They know that you possess the blade and they will use her to get to you."

"What do we do?" Darius asked.

Gray looked to the legend. "Take us to her. Take us to Ayva," he told the Ronin.

"So be it," Kail said with a crazed grin and the Ronin closed his eyes. He raised his hands and coils of air swirled upon the ground. They grew, surrounding them like a blanket of snow. The wind raged and the beasts turned with a roar. Gray saw saeroks and vergs racing towards them—but still the wind grew until it was a thick maelstrom of white, encasing them. Gray was suddenly weightless, his limbs frozen. The last sound he heard was Kail's maniacal laughter, rising above the wind.

Blue Skies

The dragon flew away, joining the others that circled like carrion birds waiting for the kill.

Ayva tried to slow her frantic breaths. Beneath her was a shelf of stone, not much bigger than a narrow plank. On hands and knees, she crawled to the edge. Her fingers gripped the lip of stone. She peered over. Fathoms fell beneath her, a dizzying abyss that made her head swim. The plains below were a roiling sea of black that obscured the White Plains.

"The enemy," she whispered.

Suddenly, the ground beneath her lurched. She pressed her back to the gate as the world beneath her rumbled. Her toes reached the edge and her nails scraped on the stone as she waited for the shaking to end. Finally, it did and Ayva opened her eyes. She saw a different part of the Burai Mountains, and the plains below had shifted. The Gates had moved. They are opening, she realized with rising dread. Hardening herself, she continued to search, trying not to think about the drop. She noticed a dark metal door behind her, but saw no handle. She searched for anything she could put her hands on. There was nothing.

She cried for help, but there was no answer, only the sound of wind. In the distance, she saw more ledges, but there was no way to reach them. Even if I could, where would I go?

Ayva slid down against the wall and held her knees with both arms. She thought of Gray and Darius. She imagined the two still far from Death's Gate. "At least they are safe," she whispered, cradling her head in the haven of her arms as the wind picked up and the cries of dragons assailed her. To her left, she saw the black door budge. At first she thought it was her imagination, but the door slowly opened outwards.

Her heart hammered in her chest. A head poked out from behind the black door and she saw a flame of white hair and a cloak with a symbol of a leaf. "Maris!" she cried, rising to her feet. "You have no idea how glad I am to see you."

He turned and a darkness grasped Ayva's heart, stealing her breath and all hope with it. Pitiless eyes of frozen blue fixed her. Patches of flesh were missing from its pale, corpse-like skin and writhing maggots crawled inside those dark holes. It was a face of nightmares.

"Kage," she said in a hoarse whisper.

The nightmare lunged, grabbing her throat. She gasped, and gripped its sinewy hand as it pulled her higher until she dangled a foot from the ground and she choked, trying to draw a sip of air. Boney fingers constricted and her eyes welled with tears. The false Maris twisted its head, soulless blue eyes stared into hers. The creature's lips peeled and rows of sharp fangs flashed. "Where is the boy?"

Gate's Edge

Gray was lost in a sea of white.

Abruptly, the shroud fell. His vision returned as his feet touched solid ground. Volleys of air and screams rained in from all sides. He looked down. Several leagues below them, the dark army writhed like an ocean of black. Beneath his feet, he saw he stood upon a small ledge of stone protruding from the Gate's face.

As the whirlwind fell, Darius flung himself to the wall. "Dicing, dice, dice!" the rogue cursed eyes fixed to the endless fall.

Gray knelt beside his friend. "Are you all right?" he asked.

Darius' hair danced wildly and he laughed nervously, "I'm not one for heights," he said, "I'll be fine." Gray gripped his shoulder as he looked behind the rogue and saw a tall black door.

"Embrace the nexus and let go, Gray," Kail shouted, his voice carried over the wind like a blade slicing through water. Gray turned and saw the Ronin. The legend stood at the very lip of the stone shelf, unaffected by the raging wind.

Darius shook his head, "Don't trust him," he whispered and gripped the wall even tighter. Gray gave him a reassuring look and let Darius go. He took a deep breath and pictured the nexus, letting the wind fill him. The raging zephyrs buffeted him, and now he felt them, down to their infinitesimal particles. With his eyes closed, the

Ronin's frame glowed golden, as if the wind around the legend was alive. Gray tried to match the threads and abruptly the wind shifted, sifting through his frame as if he were insubstantial.

He opened his eyes and teetered. His feet now scraped the edge. Gray's heart hammered, the heady sensation rushing through him—he was one with the wind. Still, the feeling was diluted by the terrifying shrieks of dragons.

"What in the seven hells of Remwar are we doing out here?" Darius shouted. "Why did you take us here, Ronin?"

Kail was silent, his gray cloak with its dual swords whipped in the wind.

Gray spoke, his voice also matching the wind's currents, "You know how to stop the Kage, don't you? You may not care who lives or dies, but I still do."

Kail turned his back and suddenly his shoulders began to shake. Gray realized he was laughing. The Ronin's cackles rose over the lashing wind. He's truly mad… The stories were true.

"Why are you laughing?" Darius raged from upon the ledge. "People are dying!"

Kail disappeared and reappeared in a flash of white, gripping the rogue's tunic. "You don't get it! It's always a matter of life or death! And it doesn't matter what you do, it always ends up the same." His hard eyes glazed. "I can try to save them, but each time they die again." Darius swallowed, and Kail's grip loosened as he turned away.

Gray's ire rose and he grabbed the Ronin. "It's too late for those you loved, but there's still good in you. I see it! Please, help me save them." He saw a gamut of emotions flash in Kail's features.

In a soft whisper, the man spoke, "I remember a time of green… When all was lush and full of life… Times before the land was stained… Before it was red and littered with bodies… Before the world was torn asunder."

He realized Kail was singing, and he shouted over the wind, shaking him. "Tell me!"

"It's no use, Gray! He's gone!" Darius said. "We should leave!"

But he ignored the rogue as he searched for sanity in the man's eyes. At last a faint light shone out from the dark abyss and the man spoke, "There is only one way to stop the Kage."

"How?" he pleaded.

"You must embrace the sword and conquer the blade's soul with the light."

"What's that supposed to mean?" Darius said, "Gray, this is a waste of time."

"Be silent!" Kail hissed, "Every word you say puts your friends' lives closer to the grave." Darius shut his mouth. The Ronin signaled to the black door behind them. "That door will take you to the halls. From there, find your way to the chambers. There you must use the sword, but listen closely for you must only change the sword in dawn's light—if not, it may cast a fate worse than death for us all."

"The dawn's light?" he questioned.

"I cannot answer that. You must figure that out for yourself."

Though not fully understanding, he nodded and turned to Darius. The rogue still gripped the wall. He tried to rise, but the buffeting wind took his cloak. "I'll come with you," Darius called.

"No," he shouted, "We can't forget about Ayva. She needs you."

Kail strode forward, "The rogue and I will save the girl. You must get to the chambers and save the others. Besides, the Kage are after the sword, they are expecting you. It would be safer for him and I to go alone." Darius' brows bunched in uncertainty.

"Can I trust you?" Gray asked.

"I swear upon the soul of Morrowil we will save your friend," the traitor replied. Gray knew that oath was more binding than his life or any other. "Go now, Gray, or see your world fall to ruin." Just as mine was, he knew, reading the man's sorrowful eyes.

Darius stood unsteadily. "Are you sure about this?"

He gripped his friend's forearm. "Save Ayva."

Darius shook him off and smiled. "Do me a favor. Don't play the fool hero and get yourself killed, all right?"

"I'll try," he said, and turned to Kail.

The Ronin smirked, "May the winds be with you, Gray. Go now."

With that, he touched the nexus and moved towards the door. He let the wind seep inside the door's frame. There was a handle on the other side. He pulled the threads of wind down and the heavy knob twisted. The door swung open and Gray stepped inside, silencing the howling wind and awful cries.

* * *

The door slammed behind Gray. He now stood in an empty stone hall. To his left and right, narrow archer's slits ran along the long corridor. The slits looked out over the armies below. Even in here, he could hear the muted cries of the dark army.

Kail's words swirled in his mind.

Get to the chambers. To stop the Kage, you must embrace the sword, conquering the blade's soul with the light of dawn. Gray unsheathed his blade and gripped it tightly. He didn't know what embracing the sword meant, but he needed to get to the center of the chambers—that much was certain. Ahead, the corridor continued without end. He looked behind. He saw the same endless hallway lit by moonlight. One is as good as another, he thought and began to trot, running through the hall ahead with sword in hand.

As he flew down the hall, he came upon a fork. Ahead was a maze of stone corridors. Rows of burning torches mounted in iron brackets stretched into the distance. His mind raced, eyeing the fork. The chambers must be deeper, but the hallways were a maze. What if I lose my way? The gates seem endless, taking a random path is a fool's odds. Still, he had no choice. In the end, he had to try.

Shrugging aside his doubts, he took to the fork, heading straight. As he ran, images of the imagined chaos beneath him flashed through his mind. He blocked the images and ran even quicker, legs burning as each second passed like an hour. The air stirred and he froze. There was someone coming. He clenched Morrowil tighter as he watched the long hallway. His heart beat against his ribcage, when suddenly a figure appeared.

The light of the torches lit her flawless face. "Vera," he said in surprise.

She saw him and before he could say another word she crossed the distance and buried her face in his cloak. Her slender frame pressed against his body. "Thank the gods I found you, Kirin," she said clutching him tightly.

Gray pushed away. "Vera, what in the seven hells of Remwar are you doing here, and how?"

"There's no time to explain, you have to follow me, quick!"

She pulled him back towards where he had come, but Gray pulled away. "I can't. I have to save the others," he replied, concealing the fact that he was lost. He looked to the path ahead. "Vera, those paths, they lead to the chambers don't they?"

"The chambers? Have you lost your mind? You must not go to the chambers."

"There is no other way, Kail said—"

"You spoke with the Traitor?"

"I don't have time for this," he said, "I'll find the chambers myself."

Vera grabbed his wrist tight enough to hurt. Her violet-flecked eyes fixed his with a burning stare, "Listen to me, Kirin! You will not get there in time. The Gate was constructed by the elves. It is a labyrinth of stone made with the sole intention of confusing enemy attackers, and granting time to those who defend…" He pulled away, but Vera grabbed him again and her voice gained force. "And that is the least of your worries, as hundreds of creatures roam the corridors ahead in search of you, and the blade you carry, the Kage among them. Even if you pass them, the chambers are overrun!"

"I have to help them, let go!" he said and ripped free of her grip.

Vera threw him against the stone wall with impossible strength, holding him by the collar. "Listen you blind fool! You will die!" Her fists glowed with a red light. "There is another way to stop the Kage! There is a hidden place, just like the chambers, and I know what you must do. You can still save your friends, Kirin, but we must go now."

Gray was torn. He wanted to listen to Kail, trusting the man more than Vera, but her words made sense. "Where is this place?"

"Follow me, I'll show you," she said.

"I have a better way," he announced, "Describe it and I will get us there." He remembered what Kail had done, transporting them to the Gate's ledge, and he thought he could mimic the threads.

Vera did as he said and described the stone landing. Then, closing his eyes, he painted the scene in his mind's eye, picturing the seamless stone and round platform. He carved the threads from the air as Kail had done. He looked down and saw thin swirls of air dancing, just like when he had fallen from the cliff.

"Hold tight," he commanded.

Vera encircled his waist and pressed her body close.

The wind gained speed. The torches sputtered at their side, and the stone walls began to blur. White filled Gray's vision and still he held onto the threads of wind, focusing, weaving them together in his mind in a vast web of wind and light. The nexus spun, faster and faster until the halls and the world itself blurred, then disappeared in a white, soundless rush and the two fell.

Power of Truth

Air swirled and lashed at Gray until his feet touched solid ground and he opened his eyes at last. White wisps dissipated as the teardrop shroud of wind fell. The view took his breath away. He and Vera stood on a flat stone landing overlooking Daerval. Far below was the black plague of the dark army, and the swarm of dragons, and beyond he saw the forest and the cliff they had fallen from, and even farther still were the rolling green hills. The world seemed to stretch forever. He couldn't believe it. They were on top of the gates. The pendant burned against his chest. He wondered if it was alive with the same exhilaration.

Words filled him, a forgotten memory. "The power of the arbiter flows in your veins—it is not the power of strength but of truth." Gray looked ahead.

Rising from the center of the stone was a large altar. Runes were emblazoned upon the stone's surface. Each one swirled and glowed azure as if beckoning him. At its center was a keyhole that blazed like a golden sun.

Vera fell to her knees before the altar. "It's really here," she said, her fingers crawling over the glowing runes. In the light, her flawless face flushed blue, almost translucent.

Gray unsheathed Morrowil. He held it in both hands, feeling its weight. It shone a more brilliant silver than he had ever seen, and the closer he got to the altar, the brighter it burned.

"This is it," Vera said, rising. "Finally, after two thousand years, it is you Kirin that will stop the Kage's reign of terror, just as the prophecy demands. Once you thrust the blade into the stone, the gate will shut and the Kage will die by the sword's powers."

He saw the light in Vera's eyes was no longer the same—where it once was alluring and full of promise, now it was lustful and dark. He peered at the altar beneath his feet. It didn't matter. He was here, finally.

"What are you waiting for? Use the blade and end it now!" She ordered.

He looked up slowly. "Why did you tell me Kail is evil?"

Emotions flashed across the woman's face, as always, too quick and hard to decipher. "What do you mean? Kail is evil, Kirin. Do you not listen? He's only after the sword."

"He's not," he countered before she could continue her lies. "Everything you told me about him was a lie. Kail is not evil, and neither are the Ronin." The loud screeches of beasts filled the air.

"How much of what you told me is a lie, Vera?" Vera's expression was emotionless. With the wind tousling his cloak, he lifted the blade and then pressed its tip to the hollow of her slender throat. "Tell me the prophecy again word for word, and this time, leave nothing out."

"Kirin," she whispered, eyeing the sword, "you would harm me?"

"Now," he ordered. Emotions raged inside him as the hurt on her beautiful face made his stomach twist in knots.

Vera's voice rose over the cries of the dragons—in that slim moment, Gray grasped the nexus and wove threads of wind and light, a spell that would decipher the truth in her cadence:

"The Arbiter seeks the final gate,
Where lies the golden grate—
Yet if walls of stone fall, all will crumble,
To death and misery.

Unless he who is destined,
Conquers the soul of the sword
And turns the blade its rightful hue,

Only then are legends slew."

He listened to the air's vibrations. Her words were true. Vera brushed aside the blade and strode closer to stand face to face. Suddenly she gripped his hands that held the blade. Tremors of black forked across her face, crawling beneath her skin like slithering worms. He tried to pull away, but her grip was like steel. "Only you can do this, Kirin. I am here for you. I swear it." Her legs buckled as she fell to her hands and knees. He released the threads of wind and light. Every word she spoke was the truth; he confirmed listening to the strands as they faded in the air.

He knelt and touched her shoulder. "I'm sorry, but I needed to know." He rose to his feet, knowing what he had to do, though he needed to hear one more thing. "If I do this, the Ronin will die... that is what the prophecy means, doesn't it?"

Vera rose to her feet, gathering herself, "Yes. The Ronin will die when you thrust the blade into the stone, but so will the Kage, Kirin, along with all the evil that they possess. You know what is at stake. You must finish this."

Gray approached the keyhole. His arms like lead weights, he lifted the blade. Morrowil's edge gleamed as its tip hovered. His heart pounded so loud it thudded in his ears while the wind of the heights lashed him.

Vera cried over the shrieks of dragons, "Do it now, Kirin!"

When he opened his eyes, wind swirled around him. Upon the sword, black veins streaked and coated his arms. No, he whispered. The darkness.

A vision filled him.

A king sat in a vast throne with a dark crown upon his head. In his hand, he gripped the pommel of a familiar-looking blade. Morrowil. Darkness coursed over the king's limbs and coiled around the sword. At his side, stood a woman with black hair and violet eyes. Vera. Upon the throne, the dark king raised his head. Gray gasped, staring at his own reflection. He opened his eyes. Cold gripped his heart. He saw his limbs wreathed in black. He fought it, railing against the dark power growing inside him when he realized... This is who I am. There is no use fighting it anymore. As if letting go of the branch before a fall, he breathed the darkness in, struggling no more. Power and euphoria flowed through his veins.

He lost himself.

Distantly, he felt warmth upon his skin. The sun. He heard Kail's voice, 'You must only change the blade in the light…' He tried to glimpse the sun, but the darkness pressed in from all sides, suffocating. A fleck of gold glinted in his vision amid a field of black. He clenched his eyes and he reached out for it. The sun's light warmed his hand. He gripped it. Light poured through him and he cried out. The nexus burst free. The darkness in the sword shrieked and recoiled. A golden blaze transformed Morrowil, absorbing the inky black. Still, the blade descended towards the keyhole of stone.

Then all of it was lost as pain filled him. His nails scraped something cold and hard. Stone. A metallic taste ran across his tongue. Slowly, he opened his eyes. He lay on the stone altar. He turned and saw the sword. Relief flooded him. It was paces away, still gold and glowing as bright as a hundred suns. He tried to get up, but more pain wracked his limbs.

Her voice sounded in his ear, falsely sweet, "Oh, Kirin, you disappoint me. You saw the image of what you could have been, did you not? How could you possibly deny it?"

He shook his head, dark spots floating before his eyes. "I saw only darkness and death," he said in a harsh tone.

"Power," Vera corrected. "Imagine, Kirin, more power than the Kage and the Ronin combined! Can you not see it? It's the power to rival all of the Lost Kingdoms, and bring the world to its knees!" Gray slowly rose to his feet as he wiped the blood from his mouth. "Join me, Kirin. Join me and all will kneel before us. Together, nothing can stand in our way!" And Vera offered her hand.

"You're mad," he whispered. Vera's once beautiful features were now a sick perversion. Patches of flayed skin marred her face, exposing bone and sinew. Still her violet eyes glowed. "It is a tainted power," he said, voice rising in fury, "You wish to control it, but it will only control you, Vera. You will be a puppet, just like you were a puppet for the Kage."

Vera gave a wrathful cry. "Only a fool would deny such power!" she screamed, thrusting a hand and red lightning shot forth from her fingers. He dove but he was too slow. Pain lanced through him. When his vision cleared, he gripped the stone, breathing heavily. He saw the hem of Vera's dress as her voice filled his head, seething with fury, "The prophecy promised you all that you could ever want, Kirin! Instead, you had to walk the Knife's Edge. A pity too, I thought you were more clever than most. Seems I was wrong."

He knew he had only a slim moment, but if he could catch her off guard… I have to try. In a flash, he grabbed for the nexus, leapt to his feet and lashed out, all in one fluid motion. Just as he reached his feet, pain filled his mind, sharp and blinding. His cry changed to a bloody scream. He clenched his eyes and gripped his head in both hands, trying to stop the pain. A hand clutched a rough fistful of his hair, pulling him up.

"Open your eyes!" Vera shouted and the pain spiked. He gasped, looking into her eyes as he tried to catch his breath through the agony. "I know you can still hear me, Kirin, so listen closely. Your power is now mine. I have burned it from your body and replaced it with a dark spell that will continue to burn inside you. Eventually it will consume you, and you will die."

His skull burned with every word. He tried to form words, but nothing came out. He held a single thought—Vera's throat. Through the torrent of pain, his eyes narrowed. He thrust out his hand and gripped her slender neck. But as he squeezed, pain burst in his mind, cutting like a jagged saw and his fingers slipped from her cold skin.

Vera smiled grotesquely. "I can see your thoughts, Kirin. I always could. The same reason I knew you would want to uncover your past. You've always wanted to understand everything." Then she laughed, it was loud and mocking. "And the bitter irony, my love, is that you've never really changed."

"Let me go," he said through clenched teeth. The pain was too much. He thought his mind would break as his vision turned black. "Please…" The pain stopped at last and he gasped. Before him, the wind raged. His vision spun as he looked down upon the cavernous drop, gripping the stone's edge.

"See? That was all you had to say." She spoke over the rising wind, "Now watch closely Kirin, for you are about to witness the birth of my true power." Reaching for the blade, she gripped it and gasped loudly. A blast of air flew over him and when he looked back, darkness shrouded the landing. The air crackled as Vera's body shuddered, lifting into the air. Suddenly, blood and flesh knit together over her exposed bone, as if her arm had never been harmed. The flayed skin on her face turned smooth once more. Dread filled Gray as an ethereal darkness took form, enveloping her limbs. Black tendrils unfurled from her back, extending high into the air like dark wings.

At the far end of the stone landing, he saw a flicker of movement. Hope bloomed, but Vera's screams drew his attention back. The sun was eclipsed by her hellish form, but his eyes were riveted on the sword in her hands. Morrowil burned black. Gray rose and with each step the wind grew stronger, buffeting him and threatening to lift him from the ground. At last, he stopped paces away.

Vera opened her eyes that were now orbs of black. "Why hello, Kirin." Her voice was altered, darker and throatier.

He fought his desire to run. "So it was all a lie?" he yelled over the wind, "Even those memories you showed me?"

Vera laughed coldly, "You always believed what you wanted to, Kirin."

"So then none of it was true," he confirmed, holding his ground, watching the tendrils upon her back, twist and turn, brushing past his shoulder as if playing with him. He twitched but didn't move, dreading their touch.

"No," she replied. "The memories were quite real, I merely twisted them to get what I wanted, and apparently what you wanted as well," she smiled seductively. The dark tendril brushed his cheek, burning.

"Tell me the truth!" He shouted. "If I'm to die, there's no harm in that. What were we?"

"You truly don't remember any of it, do you? A shame and our parents loved you so. You could do no wrong in their eyes." She neared, tendrils writhing in the air, as she whispered into his ear, "Brother…"

"No, I don't believe you," he said, stepping back.

"Oh, but it's true, dear brother," Vera said with a sinister light in her eyes. "Morrowil listens to only you and I. How is that possible? There is only one answer. The same blood flows through our veins."

He shook his head, "You're lying!"

"Then look and see the truth for yourself," she said and raised her hand, eyes flashing and images scoured his mind. Light flickered from the small candle. It sat on the corner of the straw bed, dimly lighting the small room around Kirin. There was no furniture—only four barren walls of clay. Kirin's stomach gnawed in hunger. He lay in the crook of Vera's arm. He was tired, but a thought shot through his consciousness. "When I get bigger, I will protect you," he vowed, eyes opening and closing. "I know you will. Now sleep, dear brother," Vera said, brushing his hair from his eyes and Kirin found sleep.

He opened his eyes slowly, eyeing Vera.

A predatory smile creased her lips. "A pleasant vision, is it not?"

"If I believed it."

Vera approached, dark tendrils writhing in the air, "Then let me enlighten you, for I still remember clearly. The Citadel adopted us, but the Kingdom of Fire, and home of the Reavers, is not an orphanage and outsiders are forbidden, so why would they take in two wayward children?

His eyes narrowed, "Tell me."

"It was because of our parents."

Fists tightening in anger, he strode forward, snatching her collar. Darkness seethed around his fists. "What do you know of them?" he asked roughly.

Vera didn't react. "They were robbed from us, Kirin… just as this world has stolen all else. We have only each other, now." He retreated and fell to his knees, gripping his head in his hands, and railing against her words. Vera continued, "We do not belong of this world. We owe it nothing! Join me, brother."

Gray raised his head. He watched the tendrils that floated in the air, moving around her wraithlike form. He held her burning stare. His jaw clenched. He knew what would happen if he denied her. But to join her would be a fate worse than death. With a steady breath he stood, "I am nothing like you, Vera. And no matter what you are to me, I would never join your cause of death and mayhem."

She sneered, "You always were the favored child. How predictable that you would choose the righteous path and die because of it."

In the corner of his sight there was a flash of a gray cloak, just enough for him to see, but out of Vera's vision. He had only to stall her. "If we are truly brother and sister, then why kill me?" he asked as he circled Vera.

"It's simple. What you see now is but a taste of my true power," she said and the thought made his blood run cold. "In the forgotten tomes of the Citadel, I discovered a passage in the Book of Prophecy. It told of a power to merge Morrowil and its wielder into one force—one infinite power. I tried once, long ago in the Citadel, and failed. It nearly cost me everything. Only later did I realize that I had to destroy all parts of my humanity to attain the sword. As you are my brother, you are the one thing that stands in my way. The last part of a human past." She grinned wickedly as dark tendrils grazed him.

The gray cloak flashed again in his vision. "Then what are you waiting for?"

"So eager to die?" she said and approached the altar. "Before I watch the life fade from your eyes, I want you to witness as I bring Farhaven to its knees!" She cried out and thrust Morrowil down, into the stone, when there was a sound like roaring wind. A sword whipped through the air slicing Vera's arm at the elbow. Morrowil and her arm dropped to the ground with a thud. The flying blade suddenly vanished as if it were made of air.

Kail stood at the end of the platform, motionless. His gray cloak wavered in the wind and Gray's heart hammered in triumph.

Vera faced the Ronin and seethed, "You…" With Morrowil severed from her grip, he expected the darkness to wither and fade. Instead, the fury in her eyes intensified. The black tendrils lifted into the air as if feeding off her rage.

Fear shot through him. "Kail!" he shouted.

Vera screamed as forks of black lightning shot from her fingertips, racing towards the Ronin. The lightning struck, sending shards of stone and dust into the air, and Gray shielded his eyes from the blast. When the sound ended, he peered through a haze of gold. Where Kail once stood was a billowing cloud of dust and stone. "A short lived victory," she sneered.

Gray's blood boiled with rage when he realized what was before him. A golden barrier. The nexus swirled. His power was back. Vera's spell must have fallen when the sword cut. Vera hadn't noticed. Her eyes were still fixed to the billowing dust. As she turned, he dropped the barrier.

"It seems I should dispatch of you and assume my true form before any others try to ruin my plans. Sorry, my love." Vera raised her unscathed arm. Gray gripped the nexus so tight it hurt, and her eyes widened. "You hold your power again? Interesting, but it will be of no use against my pet." Beneath her hand, a mist appeared, taking the form of the wolf.

The creature quickly took in its surroundings and bowed its head. "Mistress," it growled. Gray noticed the wolf looked different. A red tint coated its thick fur, and its eyes were a roiling black, just like Vera's.

"Drefah, I have something for you," she said coolly, and waved in Gray's direction. The wolf's massive head swiveled. It eyed Gray and its lips peeled back, revealing gruesome fangs. His wrist throbbed with the memory of his last encounter. Gray readied threads of air when Vera spoke, "Drefah is made of my magic now. Which means, dear brother, he cannot be harmed by your power," she said and turned to the wolf. "Make it quick."

The wolf snarled, stalking forward. "You were taken from me last time..." it growled, eyes glinting, "I had only a taste before that fool verg interrupted, but not this time!" Drefah leapt, and Gray thrust out a glowing shield. The wolf crashed through, its wide jaws snapping. Instinctively, he dove. Teeth clamped upon his boot and he drove his heel into the wolf's muzzle. The beast held on, snarling. He gave another sharp kick and the beast released its grip. He searched for something to defend himself, but saw only stone and the cavernous drop behind him.

The wolf growled, "Time to die!" And it leapt again.

Clutching the sputtering nexus, he formed rapid orbs of air, flinging them out—each ricocheted off the beast as if the creature's red fur were stone. Its huge paws pinned him to the ground, knocking the air from his lungs. The jaws lanced out, snapping in his ear, and he gripped the wolf's fur, holding it back. He tried to throw the beast, but the wolf was too heavy. Gray ducked his head as the fangs grazed his cheek. Through the torrent of snapping teeth and fur, he felt the cliff's sharp edge against his back. As the wolf's jaws raced towards his neck, he fused his limbs with the wind. Teeth gripped his throat at the same time as he shoved his knees into the beast's torso and pressed with a fierce cry. With the power of the wind, he threw the wolf. Its dark eyes widened as it dropped over the cliff's ledge and beyond.

A red mist formed and the air hissed. "Die!" Vera screamed. The air suddenly burned, and agony filled him. A voice cried his name, barely heard through the rush of pain. A blast of green collided against Vera's dark aura. She threw up her arm and the green blast dissipated like a stale wind. She twisted.

Maris stood at the other end of the platform, his clothes tattered and breath ragged. "Seems I got here just in time," the Ronin shouted. "Where's that fool Kail? He said he would be here by now."

As the words left his mouth, Kail appeared slashing at Vera's head with a fierce cry. Vera's black limbs caught the blade and raced for Kail. The Ronin leapt back, skidding across the stone.

Unfazed, Kail rose, brushing dust from his clothes, "I'm here you blind moron."

"Where have you been?" Maris growled, "You left before me!"

"While you were frolicking around, I was saving the boy's girlfriend on the edge of the Gates," Kail answered coldly.

"And? What took you so long?" Maris questioned.

Kail's voice darkened, "An unfortunate surprise. The Kage were there," he called in return. "We barely made it." Maris nodded somberly, the wind whipping at him. Kail turned to Gray, "Don't worry boy, the rogue and the girl are safe with your friends. But not for long. The dark army is swarming in quick from all sides."

Gray watched the whole exchange. The two men were talking to one another as if they were discussing the weather! Not as if they were fighting a nightmare, one that had cast aside their powers as a mere trifle. But as the two Ronin's cloaks wavered in the wind, they looked the very image of legends.

"Fools!" Vera raged. Her form and voice shook the ground and trembled the air. "Watch the boy you love die before your eyes!" She turned and four tendrils of darkness flew towards Gray before he could react. Both men disappeared in a flash. An arm wrapped around his waist, and Gray blinked. He opened his eyes and he now stood behind Vera. Her back and wraithlike limbs, seethed in darkness.

"Thanks," he said shakily, eyeing the Ronin.

"Don't mention it," Maris replied. All three watched as Vera slowly twisted. The living darkness that surrounded her swelling until the tendrils now eclipsed the sun and sky. A green blaze roared and engulfed Maris' sword. "Be ready to move," the Ronin said.

Gray saw Kail. The man's gray hair fell to the sides of his face, and the remainder was pulled back into a thick braid. His exposed forearms coiled as he held his sword in a white-knuckled grip. "Leave her to us."

Vera turned to face them, cackling manically. Judging by her size, her power was growing by the second. How is that possible? Dread churned his stomach when he realized he knew the power she possessed better than anyone. Or at least Kirin did. He pulled at the memories. Black tendrils impossibly quick… Forgha's bloody cries… Then at last…Ren's wide-eyes of surprise. Pain and guilt swept through him again, but he pushed it aside and spoke, "Watch for the black limbs. They are quicker than the eye and cannot be cut by your swords. If your weapon is touched, toss it aside or else it will consume your blade and then turn to your flesh."

"You've faced this before?" Maris shouted over the wind.

"Once."

"Why didn't you say so until now?"

"I had forgotten."

Maris seemed to read what was unsaid, but there was no time to say more. As Vera's cackle ended, all eight tendrils shuddered, ready to strike.

"Move now!" Gray bellowed.

The limbs raced towards them and they dove. He ducked and rolled, dodging the limbs as Kail and Maris blinked in and out of existence, slipping between the lightning-quick tendrils. Suddenly, a dark tether gripped his boot. He cried out and wind swirled at his left. Maris was at his side, ducking beneath a black limb. Two more tendrils reached for Maris and he thrust out an arm. "Watch out!" The Ronin, with no time to dodge, cut the tendrils with his sword, and the darkness latched onto Maris' blade.

The darkness dragged him along the ground, while slithering up his foot. He lunged for his boot, untying it quickly. Two more limbs flew towards him. He rolled to his left and right, and they smashed into the ground, sending chunks of stone flying. In the corner of his eye, he glimpsed Kail. The man flashed in and out, evading some of the tendrils with his speed and sending the rest veering with blasts of wind.

From the corner of his vision he saw Maris cut the last tendril with his sword, then immediately drop the blade to the ground before the darkness reached his flesh. Gray panicked as the tendrils touched his calf. With a blast of green from Maris, the darkness shirked and he yanked the boot free, throwing it away.

The air parted again, and he cried out, "Maris!" Two more limbs flew, too fast. Gray flung his arms out and shields of flowing golden light materialized. The tendrils crashed against them shattering.

Vera screamed in fury and another six tendrils exploded Gray's shield and rammed into Maris.

He cried out as the Ronin was blown back and over the edge.

Kail suddenly vanished.

Vera retracted her tendrils, absorbing them back into her form. "Like flies, hard to swat but easy to kill it seems."

Gray rose, filled with rage.

"Come at me Kirin, if you dare," she beckoned.

He let the rage consume him as he delved into his mind. Suddenly there was peace. Just as he had conquered the sword, and taken it in, he channeled his anger, funneling it all into the nexus. He didn't need Morrowil. It was already part of him. He charged. The tendrils waited for him, rising into the air. At the peak of his cry, threads appeared before his mind's eye. They curled through his fingers and summoned to life a blade of light—it filled his hands, not white like Kail's, but golden and bright.

Vera's eyes flashed wide in surprise.

The black tendrils raced towards him, and he raised his sword of light, the tendrils ricocheting and crashing to the stone. Vera screamed with rage and another four shot out in their place, twice as quick. The sword blazed in his hands, and the darkness shriveled.

Vera's scream heightened, and more tendrils and lightning shot forth. The darkness vanished but the lightning arced around the sword and collided and agony sent him to his knees. As he fell, he unleashed a final cry throwing the blade of light. It crashed into Vera and slammed her to the ground. Morrowil, thrown from Vera's grip, clattered across the stone, and he watched its dark glow swiftly fade. Vera writhed upon the stone pinned beneath the blade of light.

Gray stood, knees threatening to buckle, but he pushed forward. Vera's cries grew louder as he drew close. He reached her, and she turned to face him.

Her eyes fixed him, filled with fury. "How?" she seethed. "How did you? I was the most powerful! I traded everything for it, and still…" she struggled to free herself, grasping at the blade that protruded from her shoulder. "I should have killed you when I had the chance. It seems I am still too human."

Gray watched as the power fled from her, the tendrils shriveling. What remained was her slender form, no longer perfectly beautiful—now just a woman, broken and pinned. "You were the arrogant one in the end, Vera." He summoned another blade of light with the last vestiges of his power.

Vera's eyes went wide. "Kirin, you wouldn't slay the one you loved, would you? Your own sister?"

Slowly, he dropped his arm. "No. You already killed the person I cared for a long time ago," he said. He released the nexus, knowing he wouldn't be able to gather it again. As the golden blade dimmed from his hands, a sneer flashed across Vera's face. A tendril of darkness, hidden behind her back flew towards him. Every muscle in his body tensed as he tried to summon the nexus. It failed him. Drained of all energy, he could only watch.

In the last moment, white eddies of air swirled and a sword appeared.

Kail stood above Vera's head. Her eyes flashed. Before the tendrils struck, the sword lashed through the air and pierced her heart. She gasped and the tendril of darkness froze, inches from his face. The evil light in Vera's eyes dimmed, and then was gone altogether. Her eyes glazed and the darkness dissolved.

"Maris…" he followed Kail's gaze. Paces away, the Ronin lay on his back, motionless. His clothes and cloak were now burnt in the areas where the black tendrils had touched him, exposing raw red skin. Breathlessly, he fell in at the man's side, and looked back to Kail.

"I caught him just as he hit the ground. He seemed to survive the fall but the darkness still had him. Only when you threw your sword of light did it vanish from him. We were too late."

Gray looked back down to Maris. His breath came fast and hard, and he tried to slow it. He clenched his eyes to stop the tears from flowing.

Kail knelt. "Mourn for the dead later. Now we must save the living."

"How?" he whispered hoarsely.

"Now you must do what you were meant to do," Kail looked into his eyes, and then glanced to the stone altar. Morrowil was paces away from the altar beside Vera's corpse.

"No," he pleaded, looking up. "If I do that, you will all die."

"No matter the consequence, you must."

"I can't!"

Kail grabbed Gray's collar and faced him, eye to eye. "Listen closely, Gray. Long ago, before you were born, Morrowil turned on me." His gaze hardened with each word, the past swirling in his eyes, "When I realized the darkness inside me, I fled. For that I was called Traitor, but there was no time to explain to the others. The blade burning, I crossed the Gates. I left Morrowil in the desert city of Farbs for it to fall in the hands of the one foretold." Kail's grip tightened on his collar. "Gray, you are the prophesied true wielder of Morrowil, and the next leader of the Ronin."

The words overwhelmed him. "And as their prophesized leader, I am to kill the Ronin?"

"We are tied to the blades, just as the Kage are. For them to die, so must we," Kail answered.

Gray pulled away, emotions churning. "Is there no other way?"

"You must finish this. If you do not, those you love, and all others will perish. The Kage will not be stopped by any force now but the blade." In that moment he realized the Ronin was not giving his life—Kail had already done that long ago. Instead, he was merely seeing that act to completion. If he did not do what Kail requested, all that the Ronin had already given was a waste.

Slowly, he picked up the sword and approached the altar—its runes glowed fiercely in the dawning light. The sounds of the dragon's screeches were muted as the wind tangled his hair and clothes. Heart pounding, he looked to Kail and lifted the blade high into the sky. Light filled him just like before, and Morrowil flared a blinding gold. In the corner of his vision he saw Kail's eyes close, peacefully.

He thrust the blade down, and it pierced the keyhole of stone.

Suddenly he found himself inside a cavernous black room.

The dark army charged towards him from all angles, vergs lumbered and saeroks loped, raising claw and blade. Mist formed in the air around him, Nameless materialized. Nearby, Mura gripped his sword. Blood coated his arms as he charged towards the gnashing army. Karil, hair soaked in blood, ran with raised sword, Rydel at her side. Gray saw Ayva. She lay motionless. Before her, Darius gripped his dagger ready to charge into the waiting horde. In the distance, the gates parted in a blaze of light and the endless army flowed into the chambers.

Fear gripped his heart and then he saw them.

The Kage.

The nightmares stood upon a ramp that led to the chamber's floor. They watched the chaos coldly, corpses littered at their feet. They were the only ones that seemed to notice him. The leader raised his sword.

Gray looked down.

A stone altar sat beneath him, just like the false one from above. Runes glowed upon the surface and there in its middle was the true keyhole. Light and pain filled him, and two forks opened in his mind. Gray stood in a room of hazy white. Beneath his feet there was no ground, and above, no sky, simply a blur, except for two wooden doors. One to his left and the other to his right. "What is this?" he whispered.

"This is the final test," a deep, familiar voice replied, sounding from far away.

He turned in a circle, seeing only white. "Where am I?" And his voice echoed.

"You are in a time between worlds; a moment afforded by the pendant you hold, but it will not last long. You must make a choice now, my boy. Choose a door. Quickly."

"What are they?" he asked.

"They are your fates."

He eyed the door on his left. "What happens if I choose this one?"

"Simply put? It is the path where you do not place the blade into the keyhole. Through this door, you will remember who you once were. In so doing, however, the sword will lose its hue, and you will not be able to defeat the Kage."

He swallowed. "And the other?"

"You will have fulfilled the Knife's Edge. You will return to the moment, and end it, finishing the Kage by placing the blade into the stone, as you were meant to do, but you will remember nothing.

Your memories of your past will be forgotten forever. There is one last thing. Down this path, you will die in your world before the Kage." The voice faded. "Choose quickly, my boy…"

Gray took a step, reaching out. The world returned to its normal speed and life flooded him.

In the corner of his vision, he saw the Kage's blade twirl end over end, spiraling towards him. He had only to move, and the blade would miss. Yet before him, the dark army pushed. Saeroks and vergs bridged the last few paces. Gray thrust the sword down. With a cry, he buried Morrowil into the stone until the hilt shattered.

A burst of air flew over the hordes. Saeroks and vergs crumbled, rattling the earth beneath. The black mist shrieked and phantom swords evaporated, hissing like water scorched.

He gasped as blinding pain lanced through him, piercing his stomach. He glanced down and saw the Kage's blade, embedded to the hilt in his gut. He heard a cry and saw Mura running towards him. Upon the rampart, the nightmare Kage grinned. Its brothers gave spine-chilling shrieks, their forms bending and crumbling. From within the altar, Morrowil blazed and he shielded his eyes. The nightmarish leader shrieked as well. Air rushed towards the creature from all sides, and its body disintegrated into ash, leaving only a black pauldron that clattered over the ramparts.

"Gray!" Mura called, his voice found its way through Gray's dark world. Gray opened his eyes, his senses slowly returning, but even as they did, he felt them fading. He saw the others rush towards him, but the hermit was the first. "How?" the man whispered, as if he still couldn't believe what he was seeing.

"Mura…" Suddenly, he was sorry for everything he had said and done to the man, for abandoning him, and for never telling him how true a friend he was, and he opened his mouth to say as much.

"Don't speak!" the hermit cried.

"Light!" Darius cried at his side. "How did he get here? Dice!"

"He saved us…" Rydel said.

He saw Karil—she was doing something, touching his abdomen. Gray saw Ayva. Still motionless. He tried to speak, to ask if she was all right, but nothing came.

"Stop it!" Darius cried. "Stop trying to talk!"

There was a strange hum and he realized Karil was chanting. Her flawless features made him think of Vera. His sister… now dead because of him. He groaned in pain. Karil said something but the words made no sense. He was having trouble keeping his eyes open. The Kage's wicked sword that pierced his stomach suddenly vanished, crumbling into dust.

"I…" he said as the cold embraced him.

Karil's chants grew louder.

As he closed his eyes, he saw the faces of those around him. And through his fear was a single name. Kail. He remembered the final image on the man's face, as if the legend knew a secret. Surrounded, by warmth and light, Gray's vision faded.

Ezrah

Soft white light diffused the room and Gray squinted.

Before him was a round oak table. Upon the table, sat a board with intricately carved pieces. Though he didn't recognize the game, he could tell it was in progress. He picked up a wooden piece. It was smooth between his fingers, as if held by many hands. A door he had not seen opened on silent hinges, and a man entered, wearing long brown robes. His white brows hung over his hooded eyes like moss upon a low hanging roof, and his eyes held him like a hawk. Gray knew this man was dangerous. His face was wizened, but not old. Without a word, the man approached and sat at the table before him.

The man calmly folded his hands before him, "Long time no see." His voice was deep and resonated with authority.

Gray shrugged his shoulders, feeling for the bundled sword upon his back. Morrowil was gone. He leaned forward, looking deep into the man's eyes. He blinked as something clicked. "You're the voice within the chambers, the one that offered two choices."

The man's keen eyes crinkled as he bowed his head. "I was there."

"Ezrah," he whispered and then shook his head, "How do I know your name?"

Ezrah pulled back his robed sleeves, resting his elbows on the table, intent upon the board. "In a dream, you often know many things you can't remember when awake. In this case, my name. That is why I brought you here. Here you can walk through barriers that have been long standing, and see things you've forgotten."

A dream… his thoughts repeated, understanding why the room seemed so strange now. "I am simply asleep then?"

"More or less. This," he said, motioning to the dark stone walls and rows of shelves, "is a place between worlds, much like a dream." Ezrah moved a small piece upon the board. "Your turn."

He looked to the checkered board. "I don't know how to play."

"Yes, you do."

Seeing no harm in playing along, he grabbed a piece. It was a figure of a woman holding a scepter. He moved it to a black square, adjacent to a colored red pillar, one of the last two on the board. Ezrah made a sound of approval, scrubbing his chin. Gray took the moment to look around the room. There must have been hundreds of books and all appeared ancient. He rubbed his hands across the smooth table. It was familiar and real, as if he'd touched it before. He could scarcely believe it was a dream. "I've been here before."

Ezrah put a finger to the side of his broad nose in thought. He moved a piece that resembled a droplet of water while he answered, "You have. I brought you here because it is familiar to you. Long ago, you and I used to come here. You loved playing Elements," he said, motioning towards the board, "And you were quite good at it as well. In fact, this was the last game we played. The one we never finished."

"The game we never finished…" It all made sense. The pieces, the board, even the chair Ezrah sat in it—all of it was the same, as if frozen in time until now. "I touched these," he whispered, seeing the pieces before him in a different light.

Ezrah looked up, nodding encouragingly, "You remember, then?"

He closed his eyes as he held a wooden piece in his fist. His grip tightened and he tried to stoke the frozen memory to life. At last, he set the wooden figurine aside and shook his head. "I can almost see it—it feels so close, as if it were a dream I had just woken from, but have forgotten upon waking." Then he looked up, "Upon the gates, you said I would forget it all. But you know who I am, don't you?"

Ezrah didn't look up from the board. "I cannot answer that."

His jaw clenched. "Why? At last tell me why I went beyond the Gates. You seem to care for me, or did at one time, so I can only assume that leaving the world in which I was born had to be for a good reason."

Slowly, the man looked up. His eyes were tight, as if remembering a painful memory. "Were it anything but the gravest of circumstances you would still be here, by my side." He bowed his head. "However, I was too slow. Perhaps age slowed my wits, but more likely I was simply too confident in my power to halt the tide of events—too foolish to realize what was unfolding beneath my very nose." Ezrah looked away. "Once I did realize, it was too late…"

"You make it sound like a tragedy," he replied, prying for more.

Ezrah's features twisted, as if pained by the memory. "You do not remember because I took your memories away from you."

"You stole my memory?" Anger and confusion rose inside him.

"You asked me to," Ezrah stated. "In truth, you begged me to."

"Why?"

"I will tell you all one day, but we are out of time. Alas, we both must return to the world." Ezrah rose to his full height, placing his hands in either loose sleeve.

"No, you can't go!" He said, gripping the man's robed arm.

Ezrah looked down at him sadly. "If we stay, we may both die."

Fear and uncertainty flashed through him, but a part of him didn't care, even with the threat of death. He had to know. "I want to know. Tell me what happened."

Ezrah raised one hand into the air. As he did, the pendant grew warm on Gray's chest. Then, as if held by invisible strings, it lifted out of his shirt. The man spoke, "Long ago, I gave that to you. Because of its magic, it has the ability to bring the wielder, and the one who summons it to a place between realities. However, the power of the pendant is limited. It cannot sustain this dimension much longer. It may shatter at any moment. If it does, I do not know what will happen. It is possible we may be killed, or even be trapped for all eternity within this world."

His grip tightened on the man's sleeve, "Please."

Ezrah released a heavy breath, "Speak quickly then."

"Who am I? And who are you to me?" he asked.

The man touched his hand that gripped him, and his touch was warm, even in the dream. "To the first question, only you can answer who you are, my boy. There is no past or future but the present—and that is who you are. And to the second, you were born within Farhaven just beyond these walls, and then placed in your mother's arms. And I was the one that put you there. I am your grandfather."

"Grandfather…" he breathed as the room seemed to shimmer and fade.

"You play well for not remembering. Well won," Ezrah said, and Gray saw that both red towers were gone, and three of his flames surrounded the wooden house on Ezrah's side of the board. When did I move? He wondered, and then realized he must have been playing the whole while. Ezrah's face and form distorted. "Till next we meet, dear boy." The room and all else blurred, glowing a blinding white. Gray reached out, trying desperately to hold onto the image but it was lost as a voice sounded distantly, "I will continue to be with you..."

Motes of Gold

The lilting sound of a flute floated into his awareness. Gray opened his eyes. He saw clean white canvas above his head. Where am I? He glimpsed walls on either side of what appeared to be a tent, and through a crack he saw others passing. A ray of light warmed his arm. Midday. “I’m alive…” He sat up quickly, but fell back groaning in pain. White gauze bandages were wrapped thickly around his middle. Where the Kage’s sword had been, he remembered.

Gray took in the rest of his surroundings. He lay on a cot. Blue tufted chairs and a round wooden table crowded the small tent. Vivid green vines crawled up one side of the wall. On a nearby table was a white platter filled to the brim with food.

The pendant lay beside the platter, now shattered.

Gathering the pieces, he stared at them wondering how and when it had broken. Perhaps it saved me. But something about the pendant being shattered seemed ominous. He put the pieces back upon the table. It had served its purpose. So much had changed, and he was Gray, not Kirin. He realized he no longer yearned for a different life, content with who he was.

Careful of his wounds, he brought the platter of food onto his lap. The bowl was piled high with steaming rice that smelled of nuts, and strips of roasted yarro root. He wolfed down the meal, finishing with an odd looking purple fruit that had a tart sweetness. With his belly full, and the light warming him, curiosity overwhelmed him. With the help of the nearby furniture, he gained his feet, and stumbled to the tent's flap.

Outside the world was dazzlingly bright. He blinked as his eyes adjusted to take in the scene. Upon the lush green grass, villagers danced to a trio of musicians that strolled amongst them. Suddenly, from the crowd, a small girl with brown plaited braids ran up to him. She handed him a fistful of wild flowers and he recognized her. It was the little girl from the golden walkway, the one he had saved. Relief flooded him, and an invisible weight fell from his shoulders. The villagers are safe at last. He bent accepting the flowers with a smile, and the little girl ran off giggling.

Suddenly, a familiar voice called out.

Gray turned to see Mistress Hitomi approaching. She wore a long white dress under a turquoise sheath belted with braided gold, and her shiny black hair was elaborately piled on top of her head. He raised a hand in greeting, but without warning she embraced him. Gray struggled to keep his balance, trying not to grimace with pain as she squeezed him with more strength than he anticipated. "So happy to see that the elvin air agrees with you!"

He laughed and rubbed his side. "I'm glad to see you too!" He looked to the villagers. "Did you have anything to do with that?"

She nodded, "Indirectly. One of my books from my library mentioned a secret pathway to the Gates. The same tunnels you took I believe. However, ours was a more dangerous path I believe, but it was necessary. It got us to the Gates swiftly, but the way was not without peril."

He was curious. What unnamed danger had they encountered on their path that could make a woman like Mistress Hitomi afraid?

She smiled warmly. "On a lighter note, since arriving here in Farhaven I've been able to peddle a few of my tomes. I plan to use the coin for a new establishment. There are always visitors who need a place to sleep and a pint of ale."

"And I've no doubt you will build a wonderful inn for them," he said. "By the way, how long was I out?" he asked, eyeing the many tents. It was as if a makeshift town had sprung up overnight.

"Six nights. The elves did everything they could for you. Your wound, however, was beyond the Queen's abilities," Mistress Hitomi motioned to his stomach, "Fortunately, a higher elvin healer from Eldas arrived just in time. Though even with his aid, we were worried for you. There have been some who have sat by your bed and fretted the whole while."

"Who?" he asked.

"Who do you think? The young man got so underfoot that the Queen finally sent him on an errand."

Gray imagined the sight and it made him laugh. He looked up as a group of boys and girls ran by, chasing one another. He handed Hitomi the bunch of flowers the little girl had given him. "For you," he said, "Thank you for everything you've done."

"Thank you, Gray. Now, if you don't mind, I'm off to make arrangements for the new inn. And I imagine you have a lot of people to see. I am sure I will be seeing you soon," she said with a wink, and walked off.

Still dazed and feeling as if he were dreaming, he looked around. There were more people than he remembered. Their ranks had

swelled by leaps and bounds, and he recognized many of the people as inhabitants of the Shining City. Gray wove through the villagers who danced around a large bonfire that burned in the bright midday sun. They moved to the sound of flutes, a pounding dulcimer, and a peculiar horned-instrument. Above the music a familiar voice boomed. Balder stood there upon a box, gesturing wildly with his hands. A captive audience gathered around him listening with wide-eyes. His voice carried over their heads. "You should have seen 'em run …an explosion to scare the most hideous verg!" Gray grinned at seeing the man who was no doubt glorifying his escapades. He wanted to thank him for his diversion at the Sodden Tunnels, but he veered away. He had more important matters to attend to first. With luck, there would be time for revelry later.

As he went deeper into the camp, he was surprised by the numerous tents, poled lines for tethered horses, well-constructed troughs, and the sounds of blacksmiths' hammers. He sensed a weight in the air. Something was brewing.

As he entered a stand of low-lying tents of forest hues, he slowed to a halt. Here, elves moved with purpose, with little to no humans in their midst. Each nearby tent bore the mark of a leaf. He thought of Maris and his throat tightened. A tall elf glided past. He took in the elf's green-plated armor that appeared molded to his skin, while a shiny gold fragment was pinned on his chest. His long yellow hair fell around his face, highlighting his strange golden eyes and pale skin. Gray reached out and grabbed the elf's arm. The elf threw a hand to one of the slim blades that swung at his hips. But as he looked to Gray, the elf immediately dropped his hand from his sword.

"Excuse me, I need to find..." he said and then paused. She was no longer simply Karil, he remembered. "Can you tell me where the Queen's tent is located?"

"It's you," the elf whispered and fell to one knee, placing a fist upon the grass as he bowed his head.

Before Gray could speak, he looked up and saw the eyes staring at him. The sudden silence thundered in his ears. Recognition spread across the elves faces, and one by one, they dropped to one knee, their armor rustling.

"Eminas al servius," they said as one.

Gray worked his mouth, but nothing came out. "Rise," he said at last. None moved. He knelt before the golden-haired elf pulling him to his feet. "Please rise. You do not need to bow to me." The elf rose. Gray had a thousand and one questions, and he didn't know where to begin. First, he needed to find Karil. "Where is the Queen's tent? Please, it's urgent."

The elf's pale lips curved. "Of course. She is waiting for you," he announced. "I will take you there."

They moved away from the kneeling elves, and Gray felt his damp brow. Behind he heard the ring of hammers resume. As they wove deeper into the thicket of tents, more elves moved about, striding with urgency. They carried maps, baskets of food, and bundles of supplies, and they all wielded weapons, curved bows, and silvery swords. Gray looked at the elf beside him, "You said the queen was waiting. How did she know?"

"Ah, the queen is young but wise," the elf said, "just like her father, a great leader, one who I served for many years. She knows the Eminas will play a part in the coming battle. It is prophecy."

"Prophecy…" he cursed under his breath. Of course, and yet it was the very reason he sought Karil. The elf raised a curious brow.

Gray had forgotten about their heightened senses. He changed the subject. "What's your name?"

"Temian."

"I am—"

"Gray," Temian interrupted. "A strange custom you humans have, that of exchanging names. It is not done with my people. We believe that individuals should be able to communicate who they are without a name, but for the Eminas, I would tell my birth name."

He frowned, "Then why have names at all?" He pretended not to hear the elf's title for him and it seemed a contradiction.

The elf shrugged, "At birth, truthfully, we all look alike. We feel names should be like secrets, a precious thing, like a polished stone held deep inside that only those deserving should know."

It was a beautiful concept, Gray thought, and all the more intriguing in light of his struggle with his own identity. "Then, is it still all right if I call you Temian?"

The elf raised a brow as they walked, "Yes, Eminas, you may."

Again, he refused to ask what this Eminas business meant. And as they moved through the tents, closer to his goal, he could not help but feel as if he was willingly trudging deeper into the lion's den. All the more reason, he thought resolutely. No longer will I be controlled, not by the prophecy, not by anyone. "Temian, you mentioned that you served the queen's father. What happened to him?"

The elf tensed with anger in his normally placid features. "King Gias was murdered over one month ago, in the middle of a great meeting. Before his death he called a meeting with the nations to discuss the brewing strife. When during the Exchanging of Cups, he choked and fell dead before all. The High Councilor, Dryan, assumed the throne as the false king." Temian took a deep breath. "What is more, the king's death was only two weeks after our beloved queen, his wife, was taken from us in the final moment of prophecy. It was almost too much to bear for our people. From there things only worsened. After Dryan seized control he found no need for the rest of the High Council's advice and swiftly disposed of them. He even killed those who had nominated him, as well as any and all who whispered dissent. Thousands died." Temian's voice was hollow.

"I'm so sorry," he whispered. All this time Karil had borne this pain.

"It was a tragic thing, but in that moment the princess, forgive me, the Queen, stepped forth when we most needed her, courageous and strong just like her father, the true king. With little support, she challenged the High Councilor, and swayed those loyal to her side. This only aggravated Dryan. He bears more likeness to monsters than elves. In the wake of the chaos, he sent assassins, the Terma." Then Temian's face changed to one of pride. "I and the other Lando, or brethren in your tongue, came to the Queen's aid and helped her escape from our woods. She sought refuge beyond the Gates while we laid our plans for Eldas' survival—to return our beautiful land to peace and prosperity."

Gray was bolstered by the elf's words, and he appreciated Karil's resolve all the more. "I apologize for your loss, and while it seems you may have lost a king, you have gained a fine queen in return."

"You speak truth, Eminas."

"Forgive me for asking another question. You were at the Gates to help us, and I am thankful for that, but what led you there? Your timing was perfect."

Temian laughed, "I didn't believe it at first, but we were informed by a hawk of all things. Elves can tell much from a bird's flight, and this was no ordinary bird."

It couldn't be… How did the hawk know? All this time I thought the creature had disappeared. Gray laughed to himself and his guide looked to him strangely. "I suppose, in a way, I was a part of that," he replied.

Abruptly, his guide stopped. "We're here."

They stood before a tent—twice the height of the others. Its colorful canvas bore a large insignia on one flap that he could not decipher, and on the other a leaf just like Maris' cloak.

Two guards stood stone-faced before the tent's large entrance. Their tall pole arms planted to the ground while heavy steel blades gleamed in the light of the sun. A strange tension sat in the air, like the dawn before an imminent battle. He sensed Karil and Rydel within and he embraced the nexus. He marveled as currents of air moved differently around his elvin friend. The elf bowed. "I shall see you soon, Eminas."

They clasped forearms. "Good luck to you, Temian, and thank you."

"With the Eminas, luck is already on our side," Temian replied, "Until next I see you, my friend." With that, the elf blended back into the bustle of warriors.

Standing before the tent, Gray let the threads of the flow sift through his hands as if he had done it a hundred times before. It was becoming a familiar thread. He slipped the threads beneath the tent and suddenly, voices filled his ears.

"What news of the realm?" Karil, Gray knew immediately.

"Dire news, my Queen," said another. "The world is in an uproar. The peaceful tribes of the north have banded together, and turned savage. They raid the northern provinces, the peaceful towns and villages all along the Frizzian coast. The southern kingdoms fair no better. Ester and Menalas have erupted into civil war. They fight for a throne that's been lost for more than two thousand years. The reports of bloodshed span all across the Aster Plains, almost to the foothills of the Farbian desert."

There was a small silence until Karil replied, "The tribes together is ominous enough, but Menalas and Ester? Are you certain of this? I spare no love for the Menalas Council—in fact I will be the first to admit they are great fools, but the High Elder Fari? She alone would know that the great Kingdoms would never allow their union. Their vast power in the Lieon as a result of their iron mines was far too difficult to overturn."

"It is only rumors, my queen, but all reports whisper the same."

He heard Karil sigh. "And what of the Great Kingdoms? Where are the peacekeepers in all of this?" she questioned angrily.

The messenger's voice darkened, "Treachery. The Kingdoms see insidious acts from the inside out, just like Eldas all over again. What's more, the Citadel is even more quiet than usual."

"And at a time like this…" the elvin queen whispered, as if to herself. "And what of the armies of Farhaven?"

Gray could almost feel the messenger's gaze sink at Karil's penetrating voice. "The Covai Riders and Median's Warfleet are still intact, and King Garian is holding his kingdom together with an iron fist and still has a standing army, but that is not the issue. According to all reports, they know not who or what to fight—it is like an invisible demon is sowing strife in all the four corners of the world. Farbs seems to be the only kingdom that has not suffered too much damage."

"Farbs, Eldas, Median, and Covai are the Great Kingdoms," a voice seethed. Gray knew it was Rydel. "At all costs, they cannot fall or the whole world will tremble on the brink of ruin."

"I know this," Karil said quietly. Though not unkind, it was full of gravity. "King Garian holds strong, that is news to bolster the heart at least. He, and the Kingdom of Water, have always been a force to be reckoned with. We must send word to him at once of Eldas and Dryan's treachery, if he does not know. He has always been loyal to my family and loved my father dearly. Tell him, I am ready to fight for what is mine. And say it like that exactly."

Gray was lifted by Karil's words. "Yes my queen," the messenger vowed. "And what of the other Great Kingdoms, should I inform them of your return, as well?"

"Not yet," Karil said slowly, as if weighing her words. "I must wait until we know more. The treachery may run deeper than we expect. What other reports? How fare the elementals?"

"Not good, m'lady. My scouts cannot speak for the dryads or creatures of the wild, but reports say the sprites are all but gone," stated the messenger.

"Perhaps they do not want to be found?" She questioned.

"No," replied another abruptly, a strange and different voice full of power. "I can feel it in my blood. Their presence leaves a mark on the threads of magic. They are all dying. It portends ominous evil when magical beings fade from this world."

Karil spoke again, "Thank you. You may leave," she ordered. "Remember my words for King Garian, and keep sending your sentinels out. I want to be aware of all that happens here and beyond. Knowledge will be the key to our victory, even if it is bleak. Now go."

The messenger opened the tent's flap and bustled past Gray, his scent a mixture of fear and duty. Gray held onto the flows, listening.

"I wish Mura were here," Karil whispered, softer now.

"Your uncle is with the boy I believe, my queen," Rydel said.

"The boy is outside, listening to our conversation," said the deep voice. Gray tensed and loosed the threads.

"Come in, Gray," Karil called and he entered.

Inside, the tent was even more spacious than it appeared on the outside. He took in the shelves filled with books, with chairs and sitting areas to read. Nearly a dozen elves in green-armor with the same golden trinket as Temian above their hearts leaned over the tables, talking heatedly. But it was not the elves that drew his attention. Beyond the center floor covered in rich purple rugs was a throne, appearing carved from a single tree. There sat Karil, the true image of an elvin queen.

Her brow was drawn down as her silver eyes observed him. Her golden hair was no longer pulled back. Now it flowed down her white gown, while the dress shimmered as if dipped in liquid silver, gracing her slender form like silken water. Rydel had changed as well. He wore a fitted tunic of midnight black with gold trim—flashier than Gray would have expected from him. His silver and black hair fell around his sharp jaw, and his eyes were set upon Gray.

Yet another drew his attention the most and he shifted his gaze from Rydel's scrutiny. The elf with the deep voice stood behind Karil's throne. His face was wise with years. He wore a simple moss green robe that matched the color of his hair, and cinched with a belt that appeared woven from vines. Even from this distance, the elf seemed to emanate power.

Gray reminded himself why he was here and strode to the center of the tent. "I apologize for my intrusion. I meant no offense. My curiosity simply got the better of me," he confessed.

Karil laughed and startled him. He was surprised she could laugh after such dark news. "Don't be sorry," the elvin queen said. "I can relate well. My father always told me a curious nature is a good trait if well-tempered. Though Rydel claims mine is not so well-tempered."

"I have given up on that long ago, my queen," the elf said.

"And a good thing too, my friend," Karil replied. "Besides, there was nothing your ears shouldn't have heard. In fact, perhaps it is better that you did as it should save us time, and allow what I have to say to carry its full weight."

"May I speak first?"

The queen signaled to the others whose conversation had died, watching the exchange—they took her cue and left the tent, carrying their maps underarm. She motioned for him to speak

"I must leave," he blurted. Karil's brows drew down and he continued, "I have a feeling whatever you were about to say was contrary to my decision, but I know now that I must go to Farbs to uncover my past."

"How do you know what I have to say is contrary?" She asked.

He swallowed, but held fast in his reply, "I don't, and I'm sorry if I was presumptuous. An elf named Temian mentioned you were waiting for me, and that you needed me. But my decision stands regardless."

"And this decision of yours, you've given it much thought?"

Gray laughed slightly, "For the first time in my life I haven't… and yet, I know this is what I must do. I feel it in my heart, more strongly than I've felt anything before."

Karil nodded slowly. "I see. I learned from my father that one can always tell a person's truth not by listening to the words they speak, but by hearing the conviction of their heart." She smiled, "Yours speaks clearly."

"Your father was wise."

"You knew my father?"

"On my way here, the same elf told me about him," he explained. "He also spoke with the conviction of his heart."

"You've been awake for only a short while and it seems like you've heard everything there is to know. Can you tell me something though, your decision to leave, is it only to discover who you are?"

"No," he answered.

Karil's eyes widened, then they searched his. "You don't believe the Knife's Edge is over do you?"

He was taken aback. "You know of the Knife's Edge?"

"Bits and pieces."

"I must find it and I believe I know where to start. Where it all began."

"Farbs," she replied. Her silver eyes glowed, and he watched her thoughts churn. "I have only ever heard of prophecy spoken, that its written word cannot be held to page as it vanishes beneath the pen. A book of prophecy is a powerful and dangerous thing. To hold the future in one's hand could spell disaster or salvation."

He heard commotion behind him, and Ayva and Darius charged in.

"What's going on?" Ayva exclaimed.

"Where did you two come from?" Rydel asked crossly.

"We're going too," Ayva said. Then she hesitated. "Wherever that may be. We are joining you, Gray."

Darius joined Gray's side. "No offense, but it's getting a tad stale here," he said as he elbowed Gray's ribs with a smirk. "Miss me much?" The rogue had changed. His dark blue tunic and fitted black pants looked new. Even his stubble was shaved and his always disheveled hair was slightly more ordered.

Ayva gave Gray's hand a squeeze, and his mouth worked soundlessly. He didn't know what to say. At last, he smiled. At another time, he might have fought them, convinced them of the danger,or left under the cover of night. Now, in the end, he was only glad for their company.

Karil took in all three. "Then this is where our paths diverge. Perhaps when you discover what you seek, Gray, our causes will unite again. The Great Kingdoms are the lifeblood of this land, and they must not fall. We will need you all before the end."

"We will be there," he replied. "I cannot abandon a friend."

"I nearly forgot. Ayva, I have something for you." Karil reached behind her throne.

Ayva looked startled. Slant rays of light found their way through the tent's roof and lit her shiny auburn hair. He looked away, noticing the quiet elf watching him.

"Yes, my queen?" Ayva asked.

Karil bestowed the covered bundle in Ayva's open hands. "In a journey filled with darkness, you were a beacon of light. This item has been passed down to my mother, a prophet, whose simple smile and constant wisdom was always a guiding light. Go ahead, open it," the queen ushered.

Ayva threw back the wrapping to unveil a silver dagger, the blade the length of her hand. Eyeing Karil as if she would snatch it back, Ayva lifted it to the light. It gleamed as if it held the brightness of a white sun. "Thank you," she said, breathless. "It is a king's gift."

"A queen's," Karil teased and turned to Darius. Gray saw the rogue step back, his expression suddenly innocent. "And you Darius, come forth," she commanded.

The rogue stepped forward.

"For you, Darius, the most loyal of friends, I have saved a trinket of my father's crown. It is a mark of great prestige. It would please me greatly for you to have it. It may serve you in your journeys to come, especially amongst those who are loyal to me." She placed it in his hand.

"It will not leave my sight. Thank you," he said, holding the trinket tightly in his fist.

"For you Gray, I have only words. You travel in a world unlike anything you have seen before. I must ask—do you know the way?"

"I... do not," he admitted.

"Rydel will give you a map and directions, but be careful. You may have been born here, but since you have forgotten your past, this world is wholly new to you, and it is a world full of surprises to even the wisest. Farhaven is both beautiful and unpredictable, and you must always be vigilant.

"Furthermore, Farbs does not welcome outsiders. You may enter with your mark," she said, looking to his wrist, "But Ayva and Darius will be treated as outsiders, and by law, they will be forbidden to enter Farbs. Beware, for the penalty of trespassing is death. And lastly, trust each other. Till next we meet, dear Gray."

Gray bowed his head low. "Until then, my queen." And with Ayva and Darius at his side he moved to leave.

Darius leaned in, whispering beneath his breath, "What in the light did I just get myself into, and is it too late to back out?"

"Hush you fool," Ayva whispered back, her hands fawning her silver dagger. Gray laughed as he pulled back the tent's flap and entered the midday sun.

* * *

Karil watched the tent flap close behind them.

"You just let them go?" Rydel broke rank, striding to stand where only the King was allowed. Absent of a true King, she thought the implacable elf seemed a fine substitute—and truthfully, sharing the heavy weight of rule was a welcome notion. "What was I supposed to do?" she asked.

"All this time we've waited for him. What if he dies?"

"He is beyond our control now, Rydel."

"Still, I don't think you should have let him go." There was odd mixture of anger and frustration in Rydel's voice.

Karil knew where he was coming from, but she remained calm

and replied, “My dear friend, you heard his heart as well as I did, I could not change his mind. Even if I could, would that be the ally we want? A young man in chains at our beck and call? I hardly imagine that is how the prophecy intended his role.”

Rydel growled and crossed his arms, “This war is about more than just him.”

“You are right. Events now are far grander than any one person, yet he is not just anyone.”

His brows narrowed, “What are you not telling me?”

Karil looked away. “There was a part of the prophecy I did not tell him or you either.”

“The Queen has secrets?” Jiryn, the tall elf behind her said in his confident tone, “It seems you really are assuming the mantle of a queen and quickly. Your mother always held more than enough secrets from me.”

“What does a healer know about this?” Rydel snapped at Jiryn. He touched Karil’s shoulder and bent to her, “I was there when your mother passed away, what could she have told you that I did not hear?”

Karil couldn’t explain it—she had awoken with the prophecy in her head this morning. From everything she knew that wasn’t the way prophecy worked. Prophets were born once a millennium and instilled with the power at birth. Why now? Still, there they had been, words of prophecy. She spoke softly into the vast tent, and her words melded with the magic in the air,

“The Arbiter will ride upon desert winds,
To hidden truths within black walls,
To bring the false king down,
And dance upon the Edge.”

Her eyes looked beyond the canvas walls to where she knew Gray would be receiving his new gift, and riding off to his destiny with his friends at his side, “This is our battle, and Gray has his. I predict this is only the beginning for all of us.”

Made for a King

Gray entered the light of day and there stood Mura. He leaned against a tree with his arms crossed. Without pause, Gray vaulted towards the man, lifting him from the ground. "Mura! Light, am I glad to see you."

The hermit laughed, and then grumbled. "Settle down boy, you're going to open your wound."

Gray felt a sharp twinge in his belly as he put him down.

Mura clapped him on the shoulder. "Fool boy. I didn't carry you all the way here for nothing! And you were heavy I might add," he said as he knuckled the small of his back.

"You carried me all the way here?"

"Well, I had some help," Mura said and looked in Darius' direction. "I thought you'd at least want to stick around and try to part some elves of their coin," he said to Darius. "I hear they have gold and gems, not tin like the Shining City."

Darius shrugged. "Gambling isn't everything," he said, though he looked pained by the admission. "Besides, it'll calm down here soon, and where this party seems to be going is towards war, and that's not my sort of party. Not to mention, these two wouldn't get very far without me."

Ayva bristled, "Only because we can't lose you, even though we try."

Darius grumbled.

Mura spoke with a laugh, "You three will serve each other well. Watch over one another—there is nothing more treasured than the bond of friendship. However, if you don't mind, I must speak with Gray alone." Ayva embraced Gray wordlessly, then grabbed Darius and pulled him a short distance away.

"They care for you," Mura said.

"And I for them," he admitted.

"Well, maybe you're not the stubborn fool I once knew."

In that moment he wanted to tell his friend a hundred different things. Now that they were parting ways he didn't want to lose Mura.

"Things will be hard on the journey to Farbs," Mura said, cutting to the chase.

"I know. I'm ready for it."

"Almost," said Mura and he grabbed an object that had been resting behind the tree. "I believe you'll be needing this." In the man's palms rested the most elegant scabbard Gray had ever seen worked with silver leaves. "Take it," Mura said.

Gray ran his hands across the intricate silver work. "Where did you get this?"

"One of the elves discovered it in a chest at Death's Gate. Once you used the blade at the altar, the chest unlocked, as if it was triggered to do so at that very moment."

"It seems there are still mysteries to be solved," he whispered, and twisted the scabbard in his hands. "What blade is this?" he asked.

"See for yourself," Mura said.

With a sharp pull, he unsheathed it. Morrowil blazed pure gold in the light of the sun. Thoughts of Vera flashed through him, but he silenced them. "The handle, I thought it shattered?"

"It did. The elves remade it," Mura said.

Gray marveled at the blade and its new hilt, his fingers gripped the bone-white handle. It was smooth as polished marble, but its grip was surprising. "A scabbard befitting the grandeur of the blade," he said at last. He slung Morrowil over his shoulder on top of his faded cloak. Mura handed him his satchel as well and he put it on over the blade. "Mura, on the gate…" he paused. "There was a darkness inside me. I wanted it more than air. I know, even now, a part of me was connected to her."

"Her?" Mura questioned.

"Vera," he replied. "She was the one I met in the woods on the border of Lakewood." He swallowed the added truth.

Mura's eyes tightened. "Then I guess she was the one we found on the top of the gates," he said sorrowfully.

Gray looked away. He didn't need to say what had happened. "She turned out to be more than she said she was," he answered.

"How did you know her?" Mura asked.

"We held something in common," he said. How could he tell the hermit that the woman he had killed was his sister? Kail may have dealt the final blow, he admitted, but in his heart, he knew it was he that had put an end to her. And while he had made the right decision, he had still nearly betrayed the world. He couldn't deny that a part of him wanted to stand at his sister's malevolent side, and loose the limits of his power. He shivered in disgust at the memory, wanting to accuse the sword for that dark moment. But he couldn't. For after turning the blade golden upon the Gates, he now realized a truth about the sword… Morrowil was not evil. Though it was not entirely good either. Instead, the blade pulled upon tendencies within the owner, manifesting them into life. Thus, even the smallest shred of darkness could spell disaster. However, if the sword could manifest evil, he believed, or perhaps hoped, it could also manifest good. For how else could Kail fight the evil of the Kage for so long? Either way, he would have to be aware of his intentions, good or evil, from now on and be careful of that fact. Though if the sword was merely an extension of its owner, then Morrowil was not at fault. In the end, he had nearly fallen from the knife's edge, dooming the world, and he had only himself to blame.

"Lad," Mura said, breaking him from his thoughts. "You look pale as the grave—are you all right? What is on your mind?"

"Vera had a darkness, Mura, and I'm afraid I have it too. I know it lurks inside me."

"A darker side is within us all, my boy. I, myself, felt the darkness call my name within the Sodden Tunnels." A shadow passed across Mura's face, but then the hermit shook his head, "But here I am. The very fact that we do fear it is what makes you and me different than Vera. You made a choice upon the Gate. Though you may have desired ill, your actions and your true heart spoke clearly."

"I suppose you're right."

Mura touched his shoulder. "You must live in the present now, lad. You have much to live for." He tried to find words as he stared into the hermit's eyes and his throat tightened. Mura's eyes glazed with the same sentiment. "We will meet again soon." The way Mura said it told him there was no doubt.

"Until then," he said. "Watch over yourself, all right?"

Mura laughed, "It's you I worry for. Who's going to feed you while I'm gone? I think I should have brought a loaf of bread instead of a sword," he said. "Take care, my boy. I trust you'll find the answers you seek. But remember, finding peace with the answer is often the greatest challenge."

Gray embraced the hermit and after a long moment, Mura released him. With a final nod, they parted. Ayva and Darius waited for him. They seemed to be bickering good-naturedly. As he approached they turned to him. Darius whistled through his teeth, "Nice scabbard."

He almost forgot about the blade. It was a part of him now, the sword and his future. He took it off and showed it to them. Ayva's eyes went wide, and her hand ran across its silver inlaid surface. "It looks as if it were made for a king."

"Did you steal it?" Darius asked.

Ayva smacked his shoulder and the rogue winced.

"An elf found it," he answered. "After the sword was entered into the gate, apparently a chest was unlocked."

"A sword of stories could use a sheath of legends," Ayva answered. "It seems it was meant for you then."

He liked that thought.

"At least it's better than that ragged bundle of cloth. And if we can't afford our way, I'm sure that'd fetch a shiny coin or two," said the rogue.

Gray laughed as he looked out over the bustling camp. The elves moved about in the bright sun, flowing like the rush of water. With purpose, he thought, knowing it was about time they did the same.

"Eminas," a voice said abruptly and he twisted.

Gray saw Temian approaching with the reins of three cormacs.

"Temian," he said in greeting, surprised and delighted to see the elf, though unable to take his eyes from the mysterious and beautiful creatures at his side. The cormacs resembled a horse, but their proportions were distinctive. They were huge with long legs and their broad, powerful chests flaunted them as formidable sprinters. As for the rest, they had shorter muzzles and backs that slopped steeply into a silken tail, which brushed the ground.

"A final gift from the queen," Temian said. "The elvin kingdom wishes you well on your journey. It may be a difficult one, but at least you shall tread it swiftly. The queen bids you safe travels with the words, 'watch the east' for she fears something other than the Gate has been unlocked."

Gray noted the words, while the majestic beasts dipped their graceful white necks and pawed the ground. "The gift is too much. We have nothing in return."

"It is not necessary Eminas. To an elf, a gift is a thing of joy, for both parties. Besides, a cormac is not an easy thing to ride. You may not thank me yet," he said. Gray laughed and Temian motioned them towards the beasts. "Choose your steed."

Gray looked at Ayva and Darius—their eyes were as big as Farbian coins.

"Well, if you insist," the rogue replied, wasting no time, leaping astride the second tallest of the beasts, the most restless of the three. Ayva followed suit, choosing the smallest one, and Temian gave her a leg up. She glowed with excitement as she took the reins. Gray watched a breeze ruffle her newly cropped hair. Her dress was light-blue linen, embroidered and split for riding. It was strange, but pleasant to see her in something other than her boyish riding outfit.

"This is like riding on wind!" Darius cried as he cut the cormac in a wide circle.

Gray swung up onto the largest Cormac. He gripped a handful of its fiery red mane and settled into the deep saddle. "Are you with me?" He asked Ayva.

Darius fell in at his side, "Of course, how would you manage without me?"

"Us," Ayva corrected.

Gray laughed and coaxed the cormac forward. Darius was right. The creature moved as if its hooves barely touched the ground. He glanced over his shoulder. Temian and the other elves were bent on one knee, fists to chest.

The three wove through the last stand of tents. With the sword solidly on his back, he led them into the land of Farhaven. He knew where they had to go. Back to an impenetrable keep of black stone, full of Reavers and magic, where he had first gained the sword and fled in fear. His home.

As he rode, Gray rolled his shoulders, his pack feeling strangely heavy. Curious, he unslung the satchel. Inside, he saw a brown package.

"What is that?" Darius asked at his side.

He unfolded it and there lie the book… the same one Mura had given him in the Lost Woods. It felt like a lifetime ago. The tome opened as if on its own to the symbol of wind. There, in the center of the page, lay a scrap of cloak emblazoned with the twin-swords.

"Kail…" he whispered.

"Red stains the ground and orange lights the heavens under the fires of war, until the world will break in two."

- Prophet Everias, Queen to King Termias the Wise
Her last, 'Dying Prophesy' for the war of the Lieon,
600 of the Final Age

Lovers, killers, cutthroats and thieves,
Mothers, fathers, and all those that breed,
All will know the day legends Return.

For men will lay dead, their bodies bloated and red,
Women will weep, their soulful tears to keep,
And the heavens will watch the world beneath,
As the Ronin leave the world a ruined heath

- Unknown Author

Acknowledgements

This is always somehow the toughest part to write… After eight and a half years, people have come and gone. I imagine it like a tavern, and I'm the bard spinning a (seemingly endless) tale, and all the while customers come and go, some listening longer than others, pitching a coin, handing me a drink to wet my parched lips, but rallying me on. There have been bumps, naysayers and hecklers—more than one would like, but less than one fears. But at last, the tale is done. And in the end, I appreciate every individual who has listened. Whether you've gone with me to print the book out for the first time, sent me an uplifting text, or just simply nodded your head as I ranted about Kail's 'epicness'—either way, you have affected me and as a result, the book. So in no small way, you are to thank for the book's completion. However, this moment is also to say thanks specifically to my diehard fans, and true believers.

To my Mother: (Yes, she was in the beginning, but my greatest fan and friend deserves one last accolade.) Thank you mom, for being with me every step of the way. From day one, when I sent you the first chapter with a one-dimensional hero slaying goblins, to day 2,920; from the lowest pit, and darkest moment, to the highest mountain, from hundreds of rejections and acceptances, and every frustration and elation in the book –you've been there. Each time, you've rallied behind me, encouraging me to follow my dreams so wholeheartedly that you've made me not only a better writer, but a better man. Honestly, there are no words for how grateful I am for you and your support. So really, this book is for both of us, and I can't wait to begin the next step in the journey and do it all over again.

To my Sifu: Thank you… for listening to me rant, ah! Taking precious training time because I just had to tell you about "The Golden Walkway" and dragons raining down from all sides; for believing in my tale, in its depth, intelligence and creativity (before really even seeing the hard evidence). Perhaps you knew (and hoped) that it had to be good since I couldn't shut up about it, but most likely you knew because of my conviction. But ultimately, thank you for saying simply (when you read the book): "You deserve it," with utter conviction. It has only made me work harder, and I hope that the integrity that you have and seem to see within me, matches the integrity of the book.

To Doug: Thanks, bro. Whether it's relationship advice or book advice, you've always been there and believed in me. When you said, "You can easily feel confident that your book stands side-by-side with Jordan and the others"—it was a defining moment and one of the few that I've allowed to really hit me. I know I don't say it enough, but your support has always meant a lot.

To my Dad: I love you. Thank you for being the man you are, and I appreciate your support. Sharing the book with you has meant the world to me.

Also, thank you to Jason Daniel Kobylarz for your very generous support on Kickstarter!

And to all others: friends, family, acquaintances, people who've grabbed me by the scruff and lifted me up when I'm down, or simply listened to my tale, you all are amazing. So while it may be easier to say "I've done it"; the truth is "We've done it."

Thank you.

Matthew Wolf
March 24, 2013

Glossary

A Link – A bond between magic users that wields even greater power. It is said hundreds of Reavers were used in ancient times to forge epic creations, including the transporters.

Age of Passage – A rite of passage for those in Moonville and nearby towns (those called Milians).

Arbiter – A supreme wielder of magic, born of the Citadel. There are only three and some say ever were. Their power is equivalent to their rank.

Aurelious – A Ronin, also known as the Confessor. His element is that of flesh and his home the Kingdom of Covai. He is brother to Aundevoriä and known for having a small temper, but a fierce love for his brother, and loyalty for his Ronin brothers.

Aundevoriä – A Ronin, also known as the Protector. He wields Durendil, the stone blade and his home is the Great Kingdom of Lander within the impenetrable crags, a fortress of stone; it's walls thicker than most cities. He is known for his willingness to sacrifice all for the sake of humanity.

Ayva – Ayva is the tomboyish friend of Gray and Darius. She and her father run The Golden Horn in Lakewood. Ayva is an avid reader of the world that lies outside Lakewood.

Balder (Jiro) – A man who claims to be the leader of the Stonemason Guild (a well reputed guild), and he lives in the Shining City. Gray befriends him just outside the Dipping Tsugi.

Baro – A Ronin. His element is that of Metal, and his home is the Great Kingdom of Darmin—a city that is a mass of steel and steam. Its grand forges are lit with undying fires. He wields the blade Iridal, a giant sword made of unbreakable steel. In all the stories, he is larger than any man known, described as having a waist like an oak trunk, and shoulders as broad as an ox. He is also called the Bull and Slayer of Giants, often known as the one who led the vanguard of the Ronin into battle.

Book of Prophecy – The book Vera mentions which foretells of the power to merge Morrowil and its wielder "into one force—one infinite power."

Bueler – A gambler and rebel rouser who incites trouble in the Great Hall.

Burai Mountains – Endlessly tall mountains that reach towards the heavens, and are often called the spine, or back of the world. Death's Gate is nestled between these impassible peaks.

Calad – One of Hiron's famous twin swords.

Citadel – A great keep of black stone within the Kingdom of Fire, and home to both Devari and Reavers.

Common's District of Farbs – The main hub of commerce and trade for the city of Farbs.

Cormacs – Cormacs are elvin steeds. They have long legs and broad, powerful chests which makes them formidable sprinters. They have shorter muzzles than a horse, long silken tails, and slopping backs. Karil also mentions they are attuned to the spark.

Councilor Tervasian – High councilor of the Shining City, and trusted advisor to King Katsu.

Covai – Kingdom of Flesh, the city of men, women and beast, land of the mortals, and the largest spiritual sect of all the lands.

Covai Riders – A vast horse tribe from the Kingdom of Flesh that control much of the plains of Farhaven.

Curtana – Dared's twin daggers, thin with broken tips.

Cyn – (pronounced 'kin') A game played with small carved figurines, consisting of followers and a mark.

Daerval – A land without magic, on the other side of Death's Gate.

Dared – A Ronin, also known as the Shadow. His element is that of moon and his home is the Great Kingdom of Narim—a vast subterranean gem located in the dark hills, half above the land, half below. The least is known about Dared. He is said to never have spoken. Rumors of his powers include the ability to turn completely invisible in the night even under the brightest moon.

Darius – Darius is a wiry young man of seventeen who is from Lakewood, and we learn very little of his parentage; he appears to be an orphan. Darius is perhaps most well-known for his love of gambling, a skill he holds no modesty about.

Das reh vo menihas – Good-bye in Yorin

Death's Gate – The infamous gates that divide the two lands. The origin of the name is said to come from all those that died during the Great War which divided the lands, specifically during the final battle that stained the White Plains red.

Desiccating – To remove one forever from their innate spark. It is a dreaded occurrence that is often worse than death to any wielder of the spark.

Devari – An elite group of warriors who live within the Citadel, and they are masters of the blade. Using "Ki" they hold certain powers, including inhabiting another's body and feeling their sensations.

Dipping Tsugi – Mistress Hitomi's inn in the Shining City.

Direbears – Creatures of the Lost Woods.

Dorbin – Hulking body guard who works for Mistress Hitomi.

Drefah – Vera's wolf.

Dryads – Fabled magical creatures of the forest of Drymaus, a great mythical forest to the north of Eldas.

Dryan – High Councilor and elf who assumes the throne when Karil's father, the old king, is murdered.

Drymaus – Home of the mythical dryads.

Dun Varis – An offshoot and fragment of Lander, the Great Kingdom of Stone, rumored to exist again within Daerval, and Aundevoriä's homeland.

Durendil – Aundevoriä's famed sword. It has a wire-wrapped handle, and turns to stone.

Eldas – Home of the Elves, one of the nine Great Kingdoms, also the Kingdom of Leaf.

Elders of Eldas – Also known as the sages or High Council of the Kingdom of Eldas. They are the ruling council of the Great Kingdom of Leaf.

Eldorath – The old territory where Lakewood stands.

Elementals – Magical beings of Farhaven.

Elements – A game of Farhaven that Ezrah and Kirin play.

Eminas – The name for Gray used by the elves, and literally means eminent one, but its variant meaning is harbinger.

Erebos – A member of the Kin that Gray runs into.

Ester – A city once bound together with Menalas in what was called a "false kingdom".

Ethelwin – A powerful Reaver and lecturer who is only a few below in rank and prestige of the female Arbiter.

Evalyn – She is a powerful neophyte who vies for Kirin's affection and attention.

Exchanging of Cups – The process of peace accords, the event where King Gias was poisoned, murdered by a mysterious party and allows Dryan to seize control.

Ezrah – Arbiter of the second rank and lives in the Citadel. He is connected to Kirin.

Fael'wyn – Harrowing Wind in Elvish, which harasses them in the Lost Woods. It is also the name Gray gives his horse.

Farbs – The sprawling desert city wherein the Citadel resides.

Farhaven – A land full of magic, on the opposite side of Death's Gate.

Fendary – Also called the Storm-breaker, or the Sentinel. He is Fendary Aquius, a high general during the Lieon who supposedly fought the Ronin. The legend says he had a hundred men to the Ronin's nine.

Fisher in the Shallows – An advanced technique where one flows through Low Moon stances, and makes several sweeping horizontal slashes directed at the attacker's legs.

Fisher in the Shallows to Dipping Moon – A snaking thrust to an upward strike, from which its power is derived from the bending and swift upward lift of the legs

Flow – What is often called the source of all magic, or the "essence." It is what the Ronin wield.

Forgha – Devari, a "brother" to Kirin.

Frizzian Coast – Located in Farhaven, full of peaceful towns and villages along the coast and in the Northern provinces.

Heartgard – The name for Seth's famed sword; meaning brave, enclosed.

Full Moon – A defensive stance where one's blade is above the head and their knees are heavily bent in order to absorb and redirect coming blows. It mimics the pattern of the arcing moon in the sky or a sphere, where water flows off the perfectly round surface, unable to find solid contact.

Golden Horn – Ayva's father's inn, and where she works and grew up.

Great Falls – The falls where Gray and Mura fight on the edge of the Lost Woods. Maidens Mane is one of the Great Falls.

Great Hall – A grand hall within the keep, upon the hill of Lakewood.

Great Tree – The tree that is at the center of Eldas, and bears the spire; the great buildings where all nobility reside. It is where Karil lives until she is forced to flee her home.

Hall of Wind – Where the Vaults are located, and where Mura claims Kail stashed his most precious of weapons.

Hando Cloak – A black and forest green cloak Rydel wears. It signifies that he is one of the Hidden.

Haori – Colored vests, each matches the powers the Ronin hold, and the color of the Kingdom they represent.

Heartwood – Harder than most human metals, most of Eldas is constructed out of it.

Hel – A house of nobles from Eldas.

Heron in the Reeds – A powerful and agile strike from above—most often where one baits with the front leg, then pulls it into a "Heron" (a stance upon one leg), and strikes down at the now lunging and exposed attacker.

Herbwort – An herb that aids with shivers and insomnia.

High Council – The council of elves in Eldas that oversee affairs; they are also known as the Elders of Eldas.

High Elder Fari – The leader of the council of Menalas.

High Moon – A Devari stance where the back leg is heavily bent, and holding the majority of the weight, while the other foot rests lightly upon the ground. The fighter's shoulders are angled, just enough to minimize a target, but enough to engage their upper-body, turning for powerful strikes if need be. It is a stance few ever master.

Hitomi – Often called "Mistress" Hitomi. Hitomi is the proprietor of the Dipping Tsugi in the Shining City. When the others stumble upon several rare books in her packed library, they discover her obsession for books.

House of Nava – Stanch supporters of Karil's father.

Hoalin – Old name for the Shining City, one of the Great King-

doms.

Hiron – A Ronin, also known as the Kingslayer. His element is that of water, and the Great Kingdom of Seria. He is known as the peacekeeper, and the Ronin of wisdom and serenity.

Hrofi – An ancient city that was famous for its culinary skills. It has not been around in centuries. Mura recognizes when they are served a Hrofi dish within the library at the Dipping Tsugi.

Iridal – Baro's famed sword, rumored to be impossible to shatter.

Jiryn – A high elf healer from Eldas.

Kage – The nine nameless evils who pose as the Ronin and hold equal powers.

Kagehass – The saeroks and verg's name for what others refer to as the Nameless (the Shadow's Hand).

Kail – The once leader of the fabled Ronin. He is known by many names, from many eras including the blight seeker, betrayer of men, and the wanderer. He is rumored to have survived the Lieon, and still exists, told in fearful tales for the past two thousand years.

Karil – Karil is the queen of Eldas, home and kingdom of the Elves. She is half-human and half-elf. Karil is tall and beautiful, with silver eyes, and white-blonde hair. Her beauty is only equaled by her intelligence.

Ki – The source and power of a Devari.

Kin – Dark men and women who are agents of the "shadow", specifically the Kage. Gray runs into one in Lakewood when trying to retrieve the sword.

King Endar – A betrayer king that Maris reflects on when Gray enters the Sodden Tunnels. He remembers chasing down and kill-

ing the man for an act of treachery against the nine kingdoms.

King Gias – Karil's father and the King of Eldas.

King Garian – Powerful leader of Median.

King Katsu – King of the Shining City.

Komai tail – The braided hairstyle of the Devari; the longer the braid, the higher the rank.

Koru Village – The town Gray and the others run across. It is just north of Lakewood.

Kri Hook – A device with two metal bars that is used to hook and pull oneself up.

Laidir – The second of Hiron's famous twin swords.

Lakewood – A peaceful town, but resides close to the ill-famed Lost Woods. It is the home of Ayva and Darius.

Lander – Another of the lost three Great Kingdoms. Lander was the Great Kingdom of Stone. It was a city that had walls purported to be thicker than small cities.

Landerian Seal – A very tight masonry seal which Balder refers to.

Lando – Translates as "redeemers" or "liberators" in the common tongue. They are the group that saves Karil in the woods of Eldas.

Lieon –The Great War during the Final Age that lasted over a thousand years.

Lifeblood – Dark blood used to extract memories.

Lokai – The god Darius evokes; the god of "luck".

Lopping the Branch – A slashing strike, twisting the torso and attacking the opponents head.

Lost Woods – The infamous dark forest where Gray and Mura live, and said to be full of direbears and other nefarious beasts. Villagers say the woods come alive at night, and travelers who venture in are rarely ever seen again.

Low Moon – a Devari stance where one leg is heavily slanted for a low center of gravity for balance and stability, and the other is heavily bent and holds the majority of the swordsman's weight.

Maldon – A land within Farhaven.

Malik – Leader of the Kage. He has a spiked pauldron and is bigger than his brethren. He speaks to Vera and is the voice of the dark army.

Maris – A Ronin. He is also called the Trickster, a Ronin of many names and faces. He wields Masamune, the leaf blade—its powers unknown. His element is that of Leaf, and his homeland is the Great Kingdom of Eldas.

Marmon – Mura calls them a "safe haven for the wayward traveler." It has a hollow trunk and awning-like branches. Gray makes camp in the shelter of the tree when he gets lost in the Lost Woods before the two paths.

Masamune – Maris' famed sword.

Mashiro – Guard captain of the Shining City.

Mearus – Devari, a "brother" to Kirin.

Median's Warfleet – A powerful fleet of warships from Median.

Menalas – A southern city of Farhaven that was once part of Ester, together they were deemed a false kingdom denied the position of power as one of the nine Great Kingdoms. They were forced to split and divide up their power. Many of their inhabitants, however, still lust for a crown and throne that no longer exists. Moreover, they share an iron mine with Ester that was too difficult to upend in the Lieon, and was needed to fuel the fires of Darmin, the Great Kingdom of Metal.

Menalas Council – The council of Menalas, a powerful city.

Menithas – Famed war leader of the Shining City, who betrayed the Ronin and kingdoms of good, and did not come to their help in the battle for the survival of Eldas, where thousands of elves died.

Merai's – Servants of Elvin royalty, not elves but humans of a small, but ancient lineage when wars were fought and slaves were taken as servants.

Merhass – A curse of the Kin, an ancient dialect of Yorin.

Merian – A powerful Reaver who is desiccated by Vera.

Merilian Silver – Fine silverwork from the city of Meril.

Merkal Desert – White plains, lands of the east and north within Daerval, also called the salt flats.

Meruu sauce – Tsugi's famed sweet sauce that is used as a glaze for meats.

Mesia – An ancient city that held the Green Tavern. It's described as filled with lush gardens enclosed by white stone, and possessing a different breed of people too—their hearts too big for their small frames.

Milian – A person of the land of Milia.

Mishif – The town crier of Lakewood.

Mistress Sophi – She owns an inn in Lakewood, and taught Darius how to dance.

Moonville – A town on the way to the Shining City.

Mor 'in dunindas. Forgah 'l sendria tu va varius – Yorin and it means, "My lord, greetings and honor to you and your house."

Morrow – A city upon the windy high cliffs of Ren Nar that oversaw the world. It is the last banished element, the Great Kingdom of Wind. It is the last of the three lost Great Kingdoms and the most famous. It is Kail's homeland. It contains the Hall of Wind, as well—the famous meeting place for the great kings, queens, and generals who fought for the armies of Sanctity and against the Alliance of Righteous in the Great War of the Lieon.

Morrowil – The infamous sword that Gray inherits from Kail.

Motri – Gray's hawk and companion, who also seems to have a mysterious alliance with Karil.

Mura – Mura is a charming, but irascible hermit of unknown age. He lives in a cabin in the middle of Lost Woods where Gray stumbles upon him. Mura is wiry with thick gray brows and an often stern, heavily-lined face, and black and gray peppered hair. He is Karil's uncle.

Nameless – Created from Reavers, a horrible evil that mists from thin air, and is rumored to be invincible to "mortal blades." Their armor is made from overlapping dark plates. Gray and Darius fight them in the back alleys of Lakewood, behind the Golden Horn.

Narim – The Kingdom of Moon in the dark hills, half above, half beneath the land, and is a vast subterranean gem.

Neophyte – A wielder of the spark, a rank below a Reaver. They reside in the Neophyte Palace and wear gray robes.

Nexus – The source of Gray's power. It is a swirling ball of air that he focuses on to tap into his power.

Niux – A unit of twelve, that consists of vergs and saeroks that can cut whole swaths of armies to shreds.

Noble's District – The upper district of the Shining City where the nobles reside.

Omni – A Ronin, also known as the Deceiver. Omni's element is that of Sun, and from the Great Kingdom of Vaster. Omni leads the Ronin in Kail's absence.

Onne – "Come" in Yorin. It is what Mistress Hitomi says as she escorts the waitress out of the room.

Oval Hall – Where the Seven Trials takes place in the Citadel. It is beautiful and ancient.

Rai – A house of nobles of Eldas, who support Karil

Reaver – A powerful wielder of magic born of the Citadel.

Redsmead – A fine beer.

Rehn – A small flightless bird, typically found in the northern parts of Farhaven.

Reik flies – Pesky flies seen in the summertime in many areas of Farhaven.

Rekdala Forhas – "Honor and duty" in the Yorin tongue.

Reliahs Desert – The desert surrounding Farbs, sometimes called the Farbian desert.

Relnas Forest – The forest of Eldas, home of the elves. No humans are permitted to enter beyond its borders.

Ren – Close friend of Kirin's and leader of the Devari. He wears a graying Komai tail, a long braid, and is described as ageless. Most characteristically, he is a man hardened from years of training and battle, both mentally and physically.

Renald Trinaden – Warden and Keeper of the Silver, and author of The Lost Covenant.

Rensha – Karil's horse.

Rimdel – Trader's paradise or jewel of the Eastern Kingdoms – capital with no central rule, inhabited by only thieves, ruffians and traders as hard as stone.

Ro-ma-ro – A dance traditional to Lakewood.

Ronin – The legends of the Lieon, nine warriors who each holds a supreme power. According to the stories, they are dreaded and the bane of mankind.

Runile – a city in the Kingdom of Ice.

Rydel – An elf of the rank of Hidden, the most elite of guards that protect the royal family of Eldas, the Great Kingdom and home of the elves. He is Karil's ever-present companion and guard. He has shoulder-length dark hair and piercing eyes.

Sa Hira – "I see", in Yorin.

Saerian Vases – Rare and famous porcelain from the great city of Saeria.

Saerian bond – A staggered way of laying bricks, and a bad bond that Balder ridicules.

Saeroks – Creatures in the Kage's dark army. They are tall beasts with thin, patchy fur, sinewy muscled frames, and long gangly arms and legs with long claws. They walk on two legs, but can run on all fours for greater speed.

Seria vs Median – The Kingdom of Water, often called City of Tranquility. It is renowned for the Great Falls, waterfalls that seem to reach the heavens, as if spewing from the very clouds. It was thought to have been destroyed sometime during the Great War of the Lieon, just as the Kingdom of Wind and Stone were lost. Yet the Shining City and Median still exist and are both offshoots of Seria. The Shining City is a city of ice. Median is a great city built upon the Kalvas Ocean. It is renowned for its vast war fleet.

Seth – A Ronin, also called the Firebrand. Seth's element is fire, and his home is the Great Kingdom of the Citadel, a dark keep whose fires light the night sky. Seth is known for his fiery temper, and proud spirit.

Sevian Wine – A famous dark wine from the city of Sevia.

Shifting – A Ronin's rumored ability to transport great lengths of space in a short amount of time.

Shining City – The great city in the mountains. It is a part of a massive kingdom, and the last remnant of the Kingdom of Ice.

Shiroku Palace – The palace of the Shining City, and home of King Katsu.

Silveroot – A tree of both Farhaven and Daerval. Within Farhaven it is described as having veins of glowing silver that flow visibly beneath its bark, and bark that glows like fish's scaled bellies. Within Daerval, where there is no magic, it is simply a large evergreen, producing nut-sized fruits.

Silvias River – A magnificent river that flows south and divides much of Daerval.

Spark – The magic that all but the Ronin wield, including Reavers, Neophytes and Arbiters, and the majority of Farhaven's magical beings. It is said to be derived from the Flow.

Speech of Acceptance – A speech a young man gives to a girl's father to ask for her hand in marriage.

Spire – The highest building of Eldas where the council, king, queen and their family reside.

Sprites – Magical beings that have no form.

Star of Magha – A famous insignia that symbolizes the eight recognized kingdoms.

Stice – Aurelious' famed sword.

Taer – a land within Farhaven.

Tales of the Great Schism – Stories about the end of the Lieon and the Devari's split from old alliances to new ones, including their origin in the Citadel.

Tales of the Ronin – One of most famous books about the infamous deeds of the Ronin.

Tanglevine – A thorny root of the Lost Woods.

Temian – An elf with long golden hair, and strange golden eyes. Gray befriends the elf in the encampment beyond the Gates at the border of the woods.

The Battle of Gal, Letters of a General – Several reports from the famous general Fendary who allegedly fought against the Ronin.

The Great Kingdoms – The legendary cities. There were nine. Stone, Water, Leaf, Fire, Flesh, Moon, Sun, Metal, and Wind. Each kingdom was the home of one of the Ronin, and coincides with their powers.

The Green Tavern – The tavern Maris' reminisces about that used to thrive in Lakewood.

The Last Reliquaries of Tremwar – An account of the stories of the last King of Devari.

The Lost Covenant – A book that Ayva reads. In it, she uncovers truths about the Ronin and the Keeper of the Silver.

The Lost Road – The road to the forgotten kingdom of the Shining City.

The Red Moon – A mythical event that is said to coincide with "The Return" of the Ronin.

The Return – The fated return of the Ronin; an event the world fears. It is said they will finish the destruction of the lands they were rumored to nearly destroy during the Lieon.

The Rift – A rumored chasm where the world split thousands of years ago, before the Lieon and the Ronin even existed.

The Seven Trials – The trials that a Neophyte must pass to become a Reaver.

The Sodden Tunnels – The tunnels that lead out of the Shining City; a dark and dismal place with no light, full of thousands of misleading paths. At one point, Mura says darkness called his name within the Tunnels. Karil also refers to them as the "Endless Tunnels".

The Terma – Elite elvin warriors, the second highest in rank and skill in the armies of Eldas.

The Wasteland – A vile land where vergs and saeroks are rumored to be born. It is east of the Lost Woods.

Tir Re' Dol – Often called The First City. Appropriately named *as it was the first city to rise from the ashes of the Lieon, and soon became the capital of Daerval for millennia.*

It was said to hold the most magnificent of libraries called the First Library, which held books since before the First Age. The Library was made purely of glass shining like a prism so when the rising sun hit its zenith, the inside shone a thousand colors.

Transporter – A device that transports its wielder to a specific place by use of magic. They are hidden around the Citadel. Ren says they were created by a hundred Reavers working as one through the use of a "link."

Trimming the Stalks – A move that uses the rotation of the upper body and shoulders to lash at lower extremities, arms and sword moving in a figure-eight fashion.

Vaster – The Great Kingdom of the rising Sun, named for the shining keeps that gleam like alabaster jewels, always in the dawn's light. Omni's homeland.

Vera – A woman, originally from the Citadel and connected to Kirin. She is beautiful, but equally dark and would gladly use her looks as a tool to gain even more power.

Vergs – Brutish, behemoth like creatures born from the taint that are said to be intelligent.

Yen Tree – A tree with thin, willowy branches.

Yimar Plains – The flat plains beyond Koru Village on the way to the Shining City.

Yorin – The old human tongue for all of Farhaven.

Yronia – Great Kingdom of Metal backed against the deep mines, a land of steam and molten metal, and known for their gleaming steel and unbreakable walls of iron. Baro's homeland, and contains the Great Forge.

Author Biography

Matthew Wolf was born on March 14, 1986 in San Diego, California. He graduated from UC Santa Barbara as a literature major with a specialization in medieval studies and Japanese. Throughout college, he studied Old English and Japanese extensively, both of which are strongly tied to the languages of the book. He has also traveled considerably, from Switzerland and Scotland to Bonaire, and these sights inspire much of the land of Daerval.

Aside from the book (which is his main passion), he is also a Kung Fu instructor. His hobbies include woodcraft, archery, and of course, writing. He has several works of poetry published with Leafnotes in June 2010, a UCSB publication. And as of Spring 2013, The Knife's Edge is available to readers worldwide. Matt Wolf is currently building the brand of the Ronin Saga, giving rousing speeches, and encouraging others on the exciting path of writing.

The Abyss
FARHAVEN
Death's Gates
Burai Mounta
The White Plains
DE'GRAEL
Sobeku Plains
The Green Valley
Moonshire
Koru
Lakewo
The Silvas River
Burmen's Bank
THE LE

DAERVAL
Rimdel
Werkal Desert
The Gold Road
EASTERN KINGDOMS
The Crags
The Wastelands

CPSIA information can be obtained
at www.ICGtesting.com
Printed in the USA
LVHW02*0027190318
570290LV00002B/7/P

Brookings Institution Press

4/13/01

Dear Terry,

Many Thanks!
It looks good!

—Susan

P.S. Should I send a
copy to Donya?

1775 Massachusetts Avenue, N.W., Washington, D.C. 20036-2188-2188